THE
GRAY
FORTRESS

Book #2 of the Nordri Series

Jo Visuri

Pohjola Press

Pohjola Press
Solana Beach, CA
For information on bulk orders, contact info@pohjolapress.com.

ISBN 978-1-7377639-5-6 [paperback]
ISBN 978-1-7377639-4-9 [hardback]
ISBN 978-1-7377639-6-3 [ebook]

First edition 2022 printed in the United States

Cover design by Lena Yang
Illustrations by P. J. Visuri

Also by Jo Visuri

The Nordri Series:

The Undiscovered Descendants

The Gray Fortress

*For my nieces and sister,
your enthusiasm and
love keep me inspired every day.*

Contents

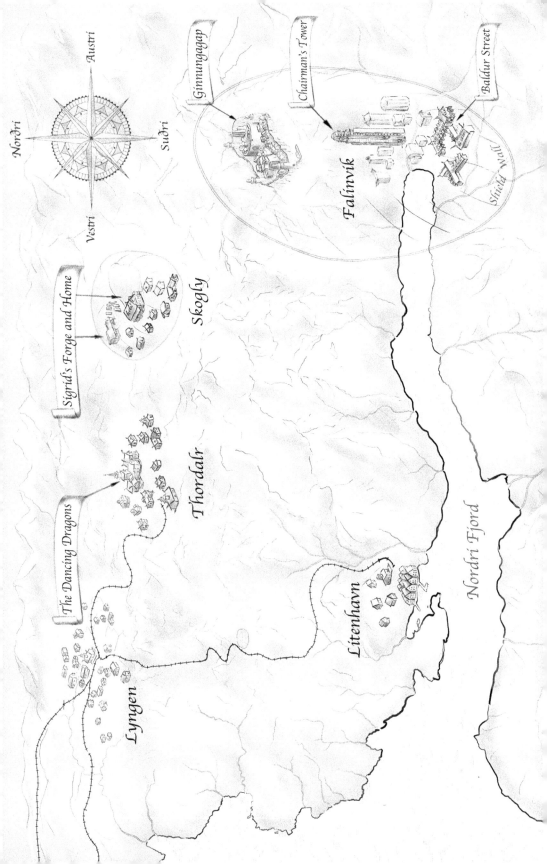

Recap

ELIN

N ever could I have foreseen how meeting Aedan Grady and Tristan Rees would so drastically alter my life. But it had. The past few months had changed everything.

Learning that there was a whole secret supernatural world that existed within our own would've been mind-boggling enough. But the fact that I belonged to it was just crazy.

Thanks to Aedan and Tristan, I now knew I was a rare "Dormant Descendant"—a person who could wake a latent supernatural gene.

Which probably would've been a lot cooler if I hadn't also landed in the middle of a long-brewing Clan conflict, pitting Nordri Clan members against each other—including Tristan and Aedan. The *Stór-menni* were on one side, blindly following the current Clan Chairman's opaque plans, and the Resistance was on the other, trying to save what remained of the true Nordri Clan.

I was still trying to wrap my head around the entire situation, especially the Dormant thing. And I probably wouldn't have believed any of it, if it wasn't for accidentally rousing my own *megin.* That's what the Clans called their supernatural gift, bestowed by their moon god long ago.

I guess I could thank Tristan for that whoopsie—not that I wanted to thank that jerk for anything. He'd betrayed me in so many ways it was hard to count. Faking a romantic interest, cheating on me, gaslighting me, lying to me about the Clan, using me for his own ambitions...the list could go on and on.

However, if he hadn't been chasing me through Ash Park in an effort to capture me and drag me to the *Stór-menni* like some trussed-up prize on that moonless night, I wouldn't have literally stumbled upon the ancient ash tree that grew in the forest. It was that mystical tree, with a little help from the Dormants' book of awakening, that woke the latent Clan gene in my body. I know—weird, right?

Helping me make some sense of everything over the last couple of months was Aedan. Despite being on the run from the *Stór-menni* Clan Hunters with his superhuman family, he'd devised a plan to get us into the Clan library, explained as much as he could about the Nordri Clan, been supportive about the Dormant thing, and even helped fend off the "mean girls" at school. He'd become a true friend—and perhaps even a little more during our search for answers.

What exactly that *more* was—I wasn't sure. Besides a hasty kiss for luck, our exploration of that subject had been cut short by his kidnapping...which was my fault.

He would never have been in Ash Park if it hadn't been for me. It was my need that had led us into the Clan library that night and straight into the arms of Tristan and his aunt.

We'd hoped the book of awakening would answer all my questions about Dormants. And while it had given some, the book had also left a lot unanswered. Now Aedan was gone, and I was grappling alone in the dark.

Given the dangers and craziness of the situation, I hadn't breathed a word about any of it to my family. Outside the Resistance and the Gradys, the only ones who knew were Joel and my best friend Mia. And that was because they'd been at boat landing on the night of Aedan's capture and witnessed some unexplainable things.

As a result of that ill-fated night, the only thing now keeping my family, the Gradys, and me safe was the assistance we'd received from the Resistance. To say it was a surprise to learn that Aedan's sister Claire was part of the organization would be an understatement. But it was only thanks to her resourcefulness that the rest of us weren't lounging in a *Stór-menni* cell next to Aedan.

I'd hoped that in his absence Aedan's family might be able to fill in some blanks left by the book of awakening. But as had come to light, especially with the Resistance's recent revelations, there was plenty even the Gradys didn't know—most astonishingly, that the *Stór-menni's* leader, Chairman Arild, had concealed that three of the original Clans who had been given powers were still very much alive. The fact that the truth had been successfully kept from the Nordri Clan members for years was a strong indication of the iron grip with which the Chairman ruled.

And if that wasn't shocking enough, the thing that had really sent my world topsy-turvy was that Chairman Arild was desperately searching for and kidnapping Dormants like me for some unknown reason. And now that Tristan had returned to Falinvik—the Nordri Clan's former home, now *Stór-menni* headquarters—with Aedan as a captive and information about my-Dormant-self, my life had suddenly become very complicated

Prologue

AEDAN

The onslaught began again. It felt like someone hammering against my skull. *Tap, tap, tap, tap.*

I knew what he wanted—but there was no way I was going to give it to him, at least not willingly. I now understood all the years of training my father had made us endure. And I was thankful.

I tried to concentrate on today's song lyrics. I'd chosen Jim Croce's "Don't Mess Around with Jim," hoping it might annoy him...although repeating the same song in my head for two hours was beginning to wear on me as well. Maybe I should try remembering the whole album?

His voice penetrated my thoughts. "Aedan, come now. What's the use of this? Just let me help you. You can fight for only so long. I'll show you everything. There is much we can offer you."

I pushed back harder, mentally increasing the volume of the song. *Tap, tap, tap, tap.* His voice faded back to the annoying but bearable knocking.

My father had taught me that the first rule of preventing mind intervention was to focus on something you loved—a book, a song, a poem, or even sports. Then, repeat it like a mantra, *ad nauseam.* The goal was to outlast your opponent. *Tap, tap, tap, tap.*

Oh, how I missed my family! It felt like months since I'd last seen them.

"Your family...yes...and your father did teach you well. But don't worry... soon we'll know who they are and have them back as productive members," his voice said, breaking through my momentary weakness.

Focus on the song—just the song. *Tap, tap, tap, tap.*

ONE

An Unusual Experience

ELIN

"Elin, why can't you just do as I ask and go get the broccoli from the vegetable aisle?" My mom was getting annoyed with me.

Her curly blond hair bounced around her cheerfully plump middle-aged face as she turned toward me. Her appearance drew a sharp contrast with my own gangly auburn-haired figure and amber eyes.

"Mom, it's just better if we go together," I replied, not having a straightforward explanation as to why I couldn't do the seemingly simple task. My mom stared at me with bewilderment in her hazel eyes.

"*Whaaat?* I'd just rather be with you," I said, returning her stare.

Giving up, she shook her head and carried on trying to find my brother Anders' favorite cereal box on the Nilsson's store shelf. I was hoping that perhaps she was finally getting used to my strange behavior over the last few weeks.

Ever since the night at the Clan library and Aedan's abduction by Tristan and his aunt Adis Haugen, I had heeded the advice from Aedan's mother Mrs. Grady about always being with a regular person when outside the invisible protective barrier, known as a Shield Wall, the Resistance had set up around our house.

The Resistance only had enough Shield Wall pucks to stretch bubbles over the Gradys' and my family's properties. The barriers kept the Clan hunters at bay since they weren't authorized to pass through them. But outside these safety zones, I had to be careful— really careful. Just one slipup could mean I'd be joining Aedan somewhere in Falinvik, and as much as I missed him, from what I'd seen in my scattered visions, it didn't look pleasant.

Given that my awakening had been only about three weeks earlier, I was still learning about my new abilities. Like the rest of the Clan, I was now stronger, faster, and had better night vision than regular humans—and, of course, I had my own unique talent. However, unlike other Clan members, I kept my powers even on moonless nights, and nobody seemed to know why.

My unique gift was what the Gradys called Temporal Vision. According to them, it was a rare and unpredictable ability, which allowed me to see events and people in the past, present, or future. Although, as of now, deciphering the three states was beyond my skill—let alone controlling anything else about my visions.

The only thing I had really managed to accomplish so far was to slow the frequency of the painful visions...and I mostly credited that to Aedan's cuff, a leather bracelet with his Clan medal, which Mrs. Grady had graciously lent me. She, on the other hand, had a more encouraging perspective on the achievement. She thought that it showed we were making real progress during our practice sessions.

During the past few weeks, it had also become clear that the *Stór-menni* Clan Council had been very busy. They'd wasted no time in sending Clan Hunters to Auor after Aedan's capture. Vacationers were highly unusual for the winter months, which made their lurking presence very noticeable. Plus, the Hunters had a different kind of dark, determined air about them. They were definitely not here to see the sites or relax in a vacation home.

So far, I'd experienced little trouble from the Clan Hunters— other than daily stalking incidents. The Hunters were very risk-averse to exposing their powers to Mannlegurs, which was what the Clan called regular humans—given the dire consequences any revelation of the Clan's existence to outsiders meant for them back home. So, Mrs. Grady's advice about keeping close to regular people seemed very wise.

To keep my family safe from the Hunters' attention, the Gradys and the Resistance had agreed that it was best for them to remain in the dark about the supernatural world I'd been thrust into. If there was a small benefit to the less-than-ideal situation, it was that my family had become my inadvertent bodyguards.

My mom's unknowing protection had already been on full display that morning as she and I walked into Nilsson's from the freezing parking lot. I'd noticed a strange-looking man and woman, pretending to be a couple, follow us inside the grocery store. They kept their distance, but every so often I caught them peering around a corner to check on our shopping progress. Clan Hunters.

"Elin...*Elin*," my mom repeated to gain my attention.

"What?" I asked as she interrupted my thoughts.

"Make yourself useful...help me find Andee's cereal. I can't seem to find it on the shelf," she said as she scrutinized the same rows again.

If Nilsson's had a method for shelving their cereal brands, it was beyond me. It seemed as if everything was just tossed on the shelves as it came in from the island dock. I peered at the names and designs on the boxes as I moved down the aisle, trying to find the oat-pillow cereal that Anders preferred. Bingo! I found it. As I turned to announce my prize to my mom, I realized she had already moved into the next row.

I was alone in the cereal aisle.

The little prickly hairs on the back of my neck rose. The female Hunter had just done an aisle check and saw that I was defenseless. She turned toward the passage, a sneer across her face. I glanced behind me. Her male companion was approaching from the opposite direction. I was trapped.

I stood with cereal box in hand, my mind racing to find a solution. If I surprised them with my speed, I'd be giving the *Stórmenni* information the Resistance and the Gradys had cautioned against. The Resistance wanted to keep my awakening a secret as long as possible. It gave us a small advantage, but even a small one could be useful when we rescued Aedan.

I eyed the woman in the chic black trench coat in front of me, trying to determine how I could get past her. I estimated that I had better odds against her than her male counterpart. But then again, I had no idea what her *megin* was, so I might be wrong in trying to get by her. I glanced behind me at the male Hunter. With his green field jacket and wool tweed flat cap, his style reminded me of my grandfather's wardrobe, but his eyes held a much more menacing expression. His cold stare caused me to involuntarily shudder.

I was about to flip a mental coin over which one to try tackling, when my mom appeared at the top of the cereal aisle.

"Oh, good! You found it, dear!" she exclaimed, seeing me clutching the box of cereal to my chest. "Well, don't dawdle, Elin. You know we have to get you to your session with Mrs. Grady. I think I've found everything else we need...plus what she requested."

A look of sour disappointment flashed across the female

Hunter's face as I walked by her. Her male partner joined her, and they followed close behind me until the end of the aisle, where my mom and her grocery cart awaited.

There was a slight awkward shuffle with the cart, as my mom had inadvertently wedged it between the shelves. It blocked the aisle and the Hunters' path. Finally, the male Hunter, growing frustrated with my mom's attempts to dislodge the cart, lifted the whole thing and brought it down with a bit too much force, rattling the wheels and cage.

"*Well,* I do *say!*" my mom declared in a slight huff. The female Hunter tugged at the male's arm, a nervous expression on her face, and they quickly moved forward, disappearing into the next aisle.

"These new visitors really are quite impatient, aren't they?" My mom shook her head disapprovingly as we turned toward the checkout line. "You'd think they'd be more relaxed while on vacation."

I drew a deep breath as the tension from a few moments earlier dissipated from my shoulders. That'd been close—too close. I would need to pay more attention going forward.

The skinny freckled-faced clerk behind the checkout stand greeted us and quickly rang up our items. Once the receipt was handed over, my mom and I zipped up our puff-coats bracing for the cold as we walked out the sliding glass door. A light flurry of early snowflakes greeted us as we headed to our VW station wagon with our groceries in tow.

Surveying the mostly empty parking lot, I easily spotted the same pair of Clan Hunters trying to look casual as they waited for us by their rented silver Honda CRV. Super subtle, guys, I thought. Clearly they were my escort for today.

I'd noticed that the Hunters seemed to be on some sort of daily rotational program over who was assigned to keep watch over me. I wondered if this had anything to do with the fact that the origin of the weekday names came directly from the old Norse gods. I chuckled to myself. I'd probably been reading *way* too much Viking history in the past few weeks.

Given the Nordri Clan's heritage, I'd been trying to learn anything I could about the old Norse world. A few surprising facts that struck me were just how far the Vikings had traveled in their two-bowed ships—from the western shores of Canada to the northern tip of Africa—and just how many gods abounded in their mythology—over sixty-six individual deities. It was enough to make your head spin, and I'd yet to tackle the origins of the other three Clans.

After the huge revelation by the Resistance that the Austri, Vestri, and Sudri Clans had not actually died but were alive and well, I wanted to learn everything I could about all of them. I had, after all, joined a whole new world that I knew very little about—especially where I, as a Dormant, fit in.

Even though the Gradys tried to be helpful, they didn't know much about Dormants. Plus, they were rightly busy with plans for Aedan's rescue and digesting the news of the other Clans' survival to have time to dig for answers. And I wasn't familiar enough with the Auor Resistance members to feel comfortable asking them—even though my curiosity was strong enough to burn a hole through my head.

The whole thing made me miss Aedan more than ever. He'd always been ready to help me discover more about Dormants and to share what he knew about the Clans. Before he was captured, he'd told me that the four Clans, like the points of a compass, originated from north, south, east, and west and had very distinctive cultures. Where Dormants fit within this structure was a lot less clear. They were the results of intermingling between humans and Clan members that could have happened ages ago with the Clan gene passing down through generations, but that was about all anyone seemed to know.

My mom's car hit a pothole in the dirt road, jostling me out of my thoughts. The drive to the Gradys was a familiar trip by now. I'd been going every other day after school, not only for my sessions with Mrs. Grady, but also to deliver any necessities they might need.

The Gradys were essentially in lockdown, living in the bubble created by the Shield Wall over their property. Since they'd decided to stay on Auor and work with the Resistance to rescue Aedan, they needed to maintain their anonymity. They hoped that preventing the Clan Council and the Chairman from discovering their true identities would keep Aedan safe as a lower-level captive. Apparently, Mr. Grady had at one point served in the Clan's Protective Services, or PS, which made him and his family high on the list of wanted fugitives.

At first, the Gradys were puzzled at how quickly the Hunters had located their home on the island. Aedan hadn't been the intended target for Tristan or Ms. Haugen but rather collateral damage from our Clan library intrusion. Thus, the assumption was that it might take a week or more for the Hunters to track down the Gradys' house. However, within a day of Aedan's capture, the first attempts to penetrate their Shield Wall had begun.

It wasn't until Aedan's best friend Joel made an offhand comment at one of our group meetings that the puzzle was solved. Apparently, Aedan and Joel had visited the town library, where Aedan had filled out a library card application. It wasn't until much later that Aedan discovered that the library was run by Ms. Haugen and that she was Tristan's aunt and an advisor to the Clan Council.

To make things worse, Joel and Aedan had a brief but unpleasant incident with her at the town library during the visit.

Undoubtedly, she'd recalled it and had accessed Aedan's application with his address within a few hours of his capture.

I glanced in the side mirror. The silver rented Honda temporarily pulled over at the intersection of the Grady driveway and the main road. I smiled. The Hunters were trying to figure out where to station themselves, since they couldn't pass through the Shield Wall.

There was a small shudder in the wall as my mom's station wagon passed through it. Neither the car nor my mom registered a thing.

Thanks to Aedan's cuff, I was now able to see *leynasked*, or hidden, items or people—even if to me they were blurry, shimmery objects. According to Mrs. Grady, the inability to clearly see the *leynasked* items was probably due to the medal not being my own. Since I'd never seen the alternative, it didn't bother me much. Besides, everything else in this strange *megin*-filled world seemed new and blurry to me.

"Okay, honey. We're here. Do you want to grab Mrs. Grady's groceries from the trunk on your way in?" my mom asked as she pulled the car to a stop in front of the Grady house.

To make sense of the Gradys' seclusion and Aedan's absence, we'd told my family and other Mannlegurs who needed to know that Mr. Grady was undergoing treatment for an autoimmune disorder that made him severely vulnerable to any disease. Thus, his family—including Aedan—was isolating from everyone except for a few select "helper" individuals. Meaning that, for the rest of the community outside of Aedan's family, the Resistance, Joel, Mia, and myself, Aedan was comfortably living at home, being homeschooled by his parents.

My frequent visits to the Gradys were explained as a combination of being a helper and having biofeedback sessions with Mrs. Grady to treat the sudden migraines that had begun plaguing me. The rationale was close enough to the truth that it made it easy for the Mannlegurs in my life to accept and assist where they could.

"Sure, Mom," I said as I opened the car door.

"Andee or I will be back to pick you up in a couple of hours," my mom said as she waved at Mrs. Grady, who'd come out to the wide front porch. "Say hello to everyone—especially Aedan!"

My mom's hazel eyes twinkled as she smiled, content in the suspicion of a budding romance between Aedan and myself. It was her unwitting contribution to the story of why the Gradys had chosen me as their helper, apart from the more rational version of the biofeedback sessions. Trying to correct her felt like a wasted effort, so I hadn't...although at that moment, with Mrs. Grady overhearing the comment and a flash of pain passing across her face, I wished I had.

"Okay, Mom. See you later!" I closed the car door to mute any further comments and walked across the gravel driveway to the car's trunk to grab the grocery bags.

As I closed the trunk and waved my mom off, Mrs. Grady came down to assist me. She was a slim forty-something woman who seemed to carry the weight-of-the-world on her shoulders. She smiled warmly at me. The corners of her sea-green eyes crinkled, displaying the worry lines that had etched themselves deeper over the past weeks.

"Hi, Elin. How are you today?" She bent down to pick up one of the bags, her wavy black hair falling over her shoulder.

"Fine, Mrs. Grady. How are you?" I replied.

"Oh, we're fine. Happy to see you and get some company. Any news?" she asked, trying to be nonchalant with the last inquiry.

I knew what she was really asking me. Had I had any visions of Aedan? Most of my visions of Aedan came at night when I was sleeping, and then I wasn't always entirely sure whether I was just dreaming or actually visiting him.

I'd noticed that when I had the medallion cuff on my wrist and a vision came, there was a faded blue light that lingered underneath the cuff after my vision was over. Despite it being another potential side-effect of having the wrong medal, the blue light had been helpful in practicing my *megin*. However, it didn't help answer Mrs. Grady's current question, as I didn't usually wear the cuff while I slept.

But because I knew that it comforted Mrs. Grady to have any news, no matter how small, I answered, "Not too much news. Aedan still seems to be in the same white cell as before and seems to sleep well."

For better or worse, that was what I saw during my nightly visions/dreams: Aedan, wearing a blue tunic and matching pants, curled up on a green mattress in a white cell. The tunic's chest had an embroidered insignia that looked like the letter Y with the bottom stem rounding into a large circle. According to the Gradys, this emblem represented the old fortress of Ginnungagap. It had led us to believe that was where Aedan had been taken.

"Good...good," Mrs. Grady said as she squeezed my arm and gave me a half-hearted smile. "Well, let's get these groceries inside."

She led the way as we climbed the wide porch steps into the Scandinavian modern house. My breath always caught as I entered the home. Even though I knew he wasn't there, I couldn't help expecting Aedan to appear from around the corner at any moment.

Instead, lounging on the beige L-shaped couch in the living room and intently reading some documents were Aedan's older sister Claire and brother Edvin. They called out their hellos as we passed them on the way to the kitchen.

Claire and Edvin were twins but not identical, not by any stretch of the imagination. They shared only three things: their age, the Gradys' signature wavy black hair, and a telepathic connection. Otherwise, Claire was a slender, graceful fashionista blessed with the gift of extraordinary speed, whereas Edvin was a robust muscular tank of a twenty-two-year-old, which meant that his unique talent of incredible strength came as no surprise.

They were surrounded on the couch by various documents and books that spilled onto the white rug and the nearby coffee table. It was pretty obvious that they were meticulously researching something. Probably a task that the Resistance had assigned to them but the purpose of which remained a mystery to me. For everyone's protection, many of the preparations for Aedan's rescue and other Resistance plans were compartmentalized and on a need-to-know basis. This was to avoid crucial information from getting into the wrong hands and ruining both missions. Everyone knew just enough to do their assignments. And whatever the twins were working on, I apparently did not need to know.

All of the secrecy left me with the impression that breaches had occurred in the past, which of course made me wild with curiosity. But all I'd managed to get out of Claire was that the Resistance included members from all four Clans—plus Mannlegurs—which made it an inherently complex organization. Divulging more, she'd said, would violate the aforementioned rules.

There was no sign of Mr. Grady in the downstairs living area, so I assumed that he was somewhere upstairs. My presence in their home was becoming routine, so no one stood on ceremony at my arrival.

After the groceries were securely tucked into the stainless-steel fridge and the cherry-wood cupboards, Mrs. Grady led the way to the back den, which had been converted into an office. It was a cozy room lined with bookshelves. By the window was a mahogany desk and chair, while a small green velvet couch and an armchair were in front of an unlit fireplace. She proceeded to pull out the now-familiar biofeedback equipment from its home in the corner bookshelf's cabinet.

In an odd coincidence, the biofeedback monitors that were used to help migraine sufferers were also the tools I needed to practice controlling my *megin*. The equipment sensed variations in skin temperature and muscle tension through small electrodes that Mrs. Grady placed on my body. They not only helped to bring my focus to achieving a meditative state but also signaled an impending vision as my body temperature dropped and my muscles contracted.

Mrs. Grady placed the electrodes on my body, and I laid down on the couch with the monitors in my eyesight. She began coaching me on the breathing technique for relaxation. The tones and light from the monitor's sensors indicated my progression into a meditative state.

Once I reached the ideal condition, Mrs. Grady said, "Okay, Elin. It's time to turn your attention to your third eye. Think of a person or place and let the vision slowly take over your natural sight."

I could feel Mrs. Grady tap into her own *megin* as the warm tendrils of her amplifying power began to support mine. Given our earlier conversation, my thoughts naturally shifted to Aedan. I wondered if he was okay. So far I'd only seen him sleeping, but that was probably because my visions of Aedan had been at night.

I thought of the last time I'd seen him—in Ash Park, while we were being chased by Ms. Haugen and Tristan through the forest. The memory of our hasty kiss for luck bubbled to the surface, warm and overwhelming.

Then, without warning, I was hovering above Aedan in a seafoam-green room. It reminded me of a hospital laboratory. Aedan was strapped down in what looked like a dentist's chair. Both his hands and feet were bound. In addition, there was a wide strap across his midsection locking him into place. He was blindfolded, so I couldn't see his eyes.

A side door opened and a man with slicked-back silvery hair entered. He was dressed in a long gray tunic with gold embroidery on the sleeves and neckline. Over it, he wore a loose black robe with a white velvet collar, much as you'd see on professors or judges in the regular world. He approached Aedan and stood next to him. For a moment nothing seemed to happen. Then I could see Aedan's face contort with effort. I didn't know exactly what was happening, but I could tell the older man was doing something to Aedan.

What could I do? I wanted to help Aedan, but I was just a wisp of air. I concentrated harder. Maybe if I could somehow let Aedan know I was there, tell him we were coming...I pushed harder, trying to call Aedan's name with my mind, since actual yelling never worked.

As I did, the most unexpected thing happened.

The silver-haired man whipped his face towards me as if he could tell I was there. His piercing gray eyes seemed to penetrate my soul. I scrambled, trying to find the ripcord for my vision. That was one of the first things Mrs. Grady had taught me—how to end an unwanted vision. However, now in the heated moment, I was struggling to find it.

My heart beat wildly in my chest as the silver-haired man's fierce gaze came closer to me. His gray eyes seemed to burrow into the edges of my thoughts. I felt like a deer in the headlights, wildly trying to find an escape. Then, not a moment too soon, I remembered. It was so simple. I had to think of the most mundane thing I could and focus on it. *Beach stone.*

The connection was severed.

I was back in the Grady's office, panting hard, with cold, clammy sweat making my shirt stick to my back. I was pretty sure the monitors would have been beeping wildly if Mrs. Grady hadn't turned them off to avoid disrupting my vision...although in this case, it might've been a welcome interruption.

"Elin, are you all right?" Mrs. Grady asked, standing up from the armchair to come kneel beside me.

I shook my head. I looked up at her, still recovering from the very unusual encounter. How did the silver-haired man know that I was there? I was about to tell her what I'd experienced and pepper her with a thousand questions when the office door burst open.

"Mrs. Grady! Oh, Elin...you're here as well. *Parfait!*" Monsieur Tibadeau's nephew Gabriel exclaimed in a slight French accent as he stood in the doorway. His ebony skin was in stark contrast to the white door frame.

He'd lately joined his uncle on Auor as a member of the Resistance to bolster their ranks, given the recent events. They were both connected to the Sudri Clan, as Gabriel's mother, Monsieur Tibadeau's sister-in-law, was a member.

"It has *finally* happened. The fjord is frozen! We'll be able to leave for Falinvik within a few days!"

TWO

An Old Phone

AEDAN

W hat had just happened? The visit with the Mind Interventionist had been abnormally short. He'd only just begun tapping on my skull with his mind when the session had stopped and the guards had been summoned to take me back to my cell. I'd become so used to the hours-long face-off that it almost felt like a letdown to be taken to my cell early. Plus, I'd really been looking forward to introducing my nemesis to Steve Miller's "The Joker."

I heard Reo's muffled voice calling me from the cell next door. I was sure he was just as surprised as I was by my quick return. I dropped to the floor next to my mattress to dig inside for the precious old tin cup.

While I'd never met Reo in person, our daily conversation, through a piece of string that had been passed through a tiny hole in the wall and then attached to tin cups on either end, was a true lifeline. The device would've been considered a child's toy in the regular world, but I was very grateful for the ingenuity of my cell's previous occupant. If not for the old string-phone and Reo's company, I'm not sure how I would have survived since my arrival at the gray fortress.

Looking back on the events from a few weeks ago, it all seemed like a whirlwind.

AFTER THE HARROWING CHASE THROUGH ASH PARK AND subsequent drugging by Ms. Haugen and her flying metal balls, I'd woken up inside some sort of transport aircraft. I'd been strapped down to a bed, unable to move.

I could hear Ms. Haugen and Tristan talking somewhere close by but couldn't see them. My view was restricted to the storage bins above me. Much to my relief, I gathered from their conversation that they hadn't succeeded in capturing Elin. I—an unregistered Clan member—was their sole prize. The two spent most of the flight bickering over who'd take credit for my seizure, leaving me to my own thoughts.

I prayed to the gods that Elin had made it to the emergency meeting point and had found my family. And that they all had been able to get away before more Clan Hunters had descended.

Elin had been amazing during our escape. She'd tried to lead the Hunters, Tristan, and Ms. Haugen away from me given my drugged-state. And it had worked for a while until the SASUs had been deployed. It was impossible to outsmart or outrun those automated devils.

I wondered where Tristan and Ms. Haugen were bringing me. I guessed Ginnungagap. My parents had, of course, told me all about the old gray fortress, which was now used as the *Stór-menni* reformation camp, but I'd never seen it for myself. I'd been just a toddler when my family had fled the Nordri Clan home of Falinvik, so many things about the city were still mysteries to me.

Ginnungagap stood high in the mountains above Falinvik,

which was nestled into a large cove at the tip of the fjord. From what my parents had taught me, the fortress had been built in the medieval ages as the Nordri Clan's original home. Back then, it had housed all of the Clan members, but eventually, the population had outgrown the citadel and its walled village.

When the transport finally arrived at our destination, what greeted me was both magnificent and terrifying—and confirmed my suspicions. There was no doubt that the gray fortress towering before me could be any other than Ginnungagap.

The transport had landed on a black modern-looking platform outside the tall exterior stone wall that encircled the fortress. I remembered my mother telling me how Ginnungagap had been built into the mountains above the fjord into a forgotten valley to give it the best defensive position. The chosen location was also how the fortress had earned its name, which literally meant 'abyss.'

From my flat position on the bed, I saw that the soaring, jagged cliffs that surrounded the fortress on three sides gave it a highly strategic advantage in any battle. In the middle of the stronghold, a wide cylindrical building seemed to take up most of the space. The central structure reminded me of the Castel Sant'Angelo in Rome...except this version was made of gray granite, much more foreboding than the warm orange travertine that makes up the Roman castle.

Upon deplaning, Tristan and Ms. Haugen, who was a small, wiry-framed woman, easily guided the hovering bed that I was strapped to over the cobblestone road, which snaked toward the looming gray fortress. All of it seemed unreal to me. My capture, the stealth aircraft, the massive citadel, and the gurney with no wheels. The bed simply hung in midair like a magician's table and moved in any direction at the slightest touch by the guider.

I might've thought the whole thing an unpleasant dream had it not been for the cold that bit into me as we exited the transport. Its icy claws easily penetrated the fabric of my pants and scraped against my flesh as a brisk wind blew the lightly falling snow into a frenzy.

As we got closer, an enormous wrought-iron gate with teeth-like spokes appeared above me. It had been raised into the overhead guard tower to allow entrance. From what I could tell, the gated entry was the sole access to the fortress. As we passed through the last interior gate, guarded by uniformed Clansmen, I noticed the buildings on either side of me looked like some sort of housing units.

We proceeded up the cobblestone passage, and before long I saw a mass of men and women dressed in blue wool tunics and matching pants. They marched in tight lines past my bed. I noticed that each of them wore on their wrist a metallic cuff with a blinking red light. They were being prodded by three or four men uniformed in black tunics girdled by a belt holding various remotes and a baton. The faces of the men and women in the blue tunics were drawn and gaunt. There wasn't a smile to be seen. A chill entered my chest—and it wasn't from the freezing weather.

Eventually, Tristan and Ms. Haugen guided my gurney through the doorway of the cylindrical building. Inside was a sort of check-in desk with another uniformed guard behind it. He greeted Ms. Haugen with reverence and Tristan with camaraderie.

"What do we have here?" he asked, stroking his brown beard.

Ms. Haugen proudly answered, "He is an unregistered Clan member. A real prize. The Chairman will be so pleased. He must be handled with kid gloves. Understand? I don't want him ruined before we can introduce him to Chairman Arild."

"Can you believe it? I...we caught him on my first solo mission," Tristan added, trying to seem relevant to the conversation. His normally tidy sandy-colored hair had become disheveled in the wind leaving him looking like an eager-to-please little boy.

"Did you now?" the guard answered with a wry grin. "And don't worry, Ma'am. We'll take good care of him."

He finished his sentence by my bedside, where he produced a wand-like item from his side pocket and loosened my strapped hand just enough so that he could move the blue light emitted by the wand over my palm and fingers.

"There. His imprint is now in the system." The guard looked at me. "Name, please," he requested.

I wasn't about to answer any question from anyone, so I simply closed my eyes in response.

"His name is Aedan Grady. Here are the rest of his particulars. The young fool filled out an Auor Town library card application," Ms. Haugen said, cackling.

Tristan and the guard laughed along with her. I grimaced internally, wishing I'd known who Ms. Haugen really was at the time instead of thinking she was just the island's librarian. I could only hope that my family had managed to escape along with Elin before the Hunters had shown up.

After my check-in was complete and a metallic cuff similar to the ones I'd seen on the people outside was strapped to my wrist, another guard appeared to transport me to my cell. After we traveled down multiple twisting stone hallways, he unlocked a cell in a small corridor and guided the hovering bed inside. In one swift move, he tilted the bed, opened the straps, and dumped me onto a green mattress. I was still too weak from the drugs to do anything but land with a thud on top of it.

As I was lying there pondering my circumstances, I heard a faint whispering sound. At first, it sounded like the noise wind makes when it finds a crack in the wall, but I estimated the cell to be much too fortified for that. As time passed, the noise grew louder and clearer. Someone was calling out the name "Gideon" over and over again.

As I regained motion in my limbs, I moved closer to the left-hand wall and noticed crumbles of dirt underneath one particular stone. The walls were whitewashed, but they were still made from the original stones of the fortress. I followed the seam between the stones and found the end of a string neatly tucked into the wall. I pulled it and heard a metallic rattle from the other side.

Then I heard a single word in response: "Mattress." I quickly moved to inspect the green mattress and found a slit on the side that was against the wall. Inside the opening, I located a small tin cup with a tiny hole in the bottom.

I immediately guessed what it was for. My siblings and I had played with a similar contraption when we were kids. I inserted the string from the wall into the bottom of the cup and tied a knot. With that, I gained a makeshift string phone and made the acquaintance of Reo Itō.

Initially, I was quite suspicious about whether Reo was a *Stór-menni* Clansman sent to elicit information from me. But slowly I started to trust Reo as I learned more about him and why he was in the adjacent cell.

Reo was an emissary from the Austri Clan. To say I was surprised would have been an understatement. From what my parents had told me, the three other Clans—Austri, Vestri, and Sudri—had long since perished. We believed the Nordri Clan was the sole survivor of the years of Clan infighting and wars.

Evidently, this was yet another lie that the Chairman had propagated when he'd maneuvered himself into the all-powerful position. To maintain the deception, he cut off all communications with the other Clans, jailed any emissaries as liars, and isolated the Nordri Clan, going so far as to change its identity to *Stór-menni*.

It had made Nordri Clan members completely reliant on him.

After all, there was no other Clan for them to seek out and join if they didn't like the Chairman's new society. It also simplified the Chairman's story. There were the super-powered *Stór-menni*, who were the lords of this earth, and the lowly *Smá-menn*, regular humans who could only hope to become like them.

The Chairman had quite literally created his own captive workforce who were trained to value productivity and efficiency beyond anything else in their lives. The main unanswered question plaguing me was: why? What was the Chairman's end game?

THREE

The Appointment

TRISTAN

My discovery of Elin and our successful apprehension of the unregistered Clansman was about to bear fruit. I could just feel it.

I had been summoned to the Chairman's office. It was a rare event for someone to have an in-person audience with the Chairman. So, this must be it. I was sure of it—I was going to be promoted to Captain. I would finally lead my own squad of Hunters. My body was buzzing with anticipation.

I confidently strode into the enormous high-rise in the center of Falinvik. The lobby was bustling with workers going about their business. It was the tallest structure in the whole metropolis and the headquarters for the Clan's main operational teams.

The building floors were divided by departmental function. The city logistics, such as energy production, waste management, transportation, and housing, were located on floors one through nine. The next three floors were dedicated to the Clan Identification offices. Along with issuing the authorization for *Stórmenni* medals, they handled work and mentorship assignments.

On floors 13 through 18 were the technology teams, who worked not only to research and develop innovations but also to implement them. The following six floors were restricted-access and available only to the members of Protective Services. Those were the floors I was used to frequenting. But today, I was going all the way to the 26th. The three top floors were dedicated to the Chairman's offices.

With a throng of uniformed employees, I approached the high-speed elevators, which were attached to the outside of the building next to the Autonomous Hover Vehicle, or AHV, landing platforms. Each floor, including the Chairman's, had its own platform. However, it was considered rude to fly directly to the Chairman's landing platforms unless explicitly invited to do so. I had not been offered such an option.

Instead, I boarded the express elevator for the 26th floor. After the time I'd spent in the *Smá-menn* world, the elevator reminded me of a vertical passenger-train car. I searched for a seat closest to the doors that led toward the building. I wanted to be able to exit as quickly as possible to retain my ten-minute-early status. This was one meeting I did not intend to be late for. No one made the Chairman wait.

Once all the passengers were seated, the elevator tilted into its vertical position and shot up the building side to the 19th floor. The trip lasted only a few seconds. Two more stops, I counted. The next one would be on the 24th floor, where fierce-looking Clan guards would board the elevator and request to see your medal and invitation to the Chairman's office.

I clutched my SRT—Self Reporting Tool—tightly in my clammy hands. The invitation from the Chairman's secretary was emblazoned on the locked screen of the device. One could hardly fail to see the non-dismissible red banner on the top, which read:

YOUR PRESENCE IS KINDLY REQUESTED IN **12 MINUTES AND 40 SECONDS** AT THE CHAIRMAN'S OFFICE ON THE 26TH FLOOR.

The designated time updated itself, leaving no doubt as to when you needed to be there.

Once clearing the guards, the last stop would be on the 26th floor. It was here where I would enter the lavish lobby of the Chairman's offices. I had only heard about it from prior visitors, but apparently there was no comparison.

The last passenger exited on the 19th floor. I was alone in the vehicle. As soon as the doors closed, they opened again. The elevator had reached the 24th floor.

Two guards dressed in black tunics with a Valknut symbol stitched in gold yarn on the left side of the chest entered. The Valknut had always been an intimidating sight, not only of its composition of three interlocking triangles and life-and-death significance, but because it was known as the center insignia of the Chairman's medal.

The guards approached me. I quickly pulled out my own Hunter medallion from underneath my tunic and held it up for the guards to scan. I also presented my SRT's locked screen with the red banner at the top.

"You're early," the guard stated upon seeing the banner. "No entry is permitted prior to ten minutes of the designated time."

"Yes, Sir. But as you can see, I'm a member of the PS, and ten minutes is two minutes away," I replied, holding my medallion higher and trying to reason with the uniformed man.

"No entry until ten minutes prior," the guard reiterated.

I was about to ask the stern guards what I was supposed to do for the two minutes when the elevator doors to the landing platform opened. I could see a single AHV parked behind the young woman who walked in.

Thyra Bjorndóttir. The constant thorn in my side. Her light-brown hair was braided into a tight bun, and she wore the dark-blue tunic of a PS Captain. Her jeweled seax dangled from the belt around her strong athletic figure. When had she been promoted?

The guards immediately saluted. She saluted back and approached my seat.

"Hello, Tristan. Here to see the Chairman?" she asked, her eyebrow raised.

"Thyra. How unexpected. Yes, I've been summoned by the Chairman," I said, straightening in my seat. "Do you have an appointment as well?"

"Frequently," she replied with annoying casualness. "Why aren't we moving?"

She had directed the last question to the guards, who glanced at each other, shifting uncomfortably in their shoes. It appeared that neither wanted to be the one to answer her.

"*Well?*" Thyra asked.

Finally, the guard who had addressed me earlier answered, "Captain, he is early for his designated time."

"Are you asking *me* to be late?" Thyra replied, staring intently at the guard.

"No, Ma'am—" the guard started to reply.

"Well, get on with it then. He's with me. I'll take responsibility for his early status," Thyra interrupted, waving her hand as if literally brushing aside the matter.

"Yes, Ma'am," the guards replied in unison, saluting Thyra and exiting the elevator.

Once the doors closed, Thyra had barely flopped into the seat next to me when the doors opened again. I quickly stood up, determined to be the first one into the Chairman's lobby.

With my fast reaction, I gained the advantage, and now I stood awestruck in the lobby. The inside of the room looked like a large Viking gathering hall. The walls and ceiling were made from wood and painted with golden runes in an intricate design. The ceiling was vaulted, with the exposed wooden beams painstakingly carved into full-length Norse dragons. The dragons' heads jutted out from the cornices that lined the room. Their eyes were made from jewels in a variety of colors and seemed to follow you as you moved.

Ancient shields, banners, and seaxes decorated the walls, reminding the gazer of long-ago clans. Three massive candlelit iron chandeliers hung from the rafters, secured by heavy black chains attached to the wall.

In the middle of the room was a large circular hearth with a blazing fire. On the other side was a wooden desk polished to a high sheen. Behind it sat an elderly woman in a yellow woolen dress. She peered at me through her spectacles disapprovingly.

"Young Sir, you are early—" she started to say before she spotted Thyra, who was walking to my side. "Oh, Thyra! How lovely to see you!" The elderly woman began to straighten from her chair.

"Mrs. Aland! How good to see you as well! No, no, please don't get up," Thyra replied as she rushed to warmly embrace the elderly woman.

I hadn't paid much attention to the guards' response to Thyra earlier since she was in a Captain's uniform, but this was strange. How did Thyra know the Chairman's secretary? And it was clearly not just an acquaintanceship, either.

I could hear the elderly woman asking Thyra if I was with her, at which Thyra nodded. After a bit more fuss, Mrs. Aland went back around her desk to announce our presence, speaking into a small device on her desk. This struck me as even more unusual, as it was still a good nine minutes before my designated time.

Before I could give it a second thought, the doors to the Chairman's office opened. Out strode a vibrant man with silver, slicked-back hair, dressed in a long gray tunic decorated with gold embroidery. He quickly glanced around the lobby. I immediately recognized him. Chairman Arild.

Upon seeing Thyra, he exclaimed with a wide smile, "Thyra! It's so good to see you. I want to hear all about your mission."

"Hello, Uncle Arild," Thyra replied with a grin.

I was dumbstruck. My nemesis from every competition growing up and my number-one tormentor was the niece of the Chairman? All the things I had done over the years to assure I was the victor and to get revenge for her inescapable teasing about my accent and formal speaking manner flashed through my mind. I was surprised she hadn't had me thrown into Ginnungagap long ago. My best tunic's collar was starting to feel oddly tight around my throat.

Why was she here at the same time as I? What if this was not a promotion but Thyra's final act of revenge? I felt a few beads of sweat travel down my back underneath my tunic.

Thyra's uncle greeted her with a strong hug. He put his arm around her to lead her back into his office. There had not even been an acknowledgement that I stood in the lobby. I shifted uncomfortably, wondering what I was supposed to do.

"Uncle, aren't you forgetting about something?" Thyra chided as she gestured in my direction. "I'll share all my stories with you after you keep your appointments."

The Chairman turned to look at me.

"Ahh, yes. Mr. Rees. You'll have to forgive my exuberance at seeing my niece," he said as he took in my appearance.

His gray eyes seemed to probe me. It felt as if it would be impossible to hide anything from their cold stare. Then he smiled.

"Yes, yes...do come into my office. We can better discuss your situation there." The Chairman swept his arm towards the open doors.

"Thank you, Chairman," I managed to squeak out in response.

The Chairman turned back to Thyra and proceeded to guide her into the office. I felt my shoulders tense. Was she going to be there for my appointment? I could understand that she would have significant privileges, but did that really include sitting in on other people's appointments? Maybe this *did* have to do with past resentments. I tried to steady my breath as I followed them.

The Chairman's office was a stark contrast to the lobby. Except for the wall that separated the office from the anteroom, all the rest were windows looking out onto the city below. The room itself was an ode to modern minimalism. It was a large, nearly empty space.

On the right side of the room was a wide gray desk with a luxurious, hovering chair behind it. I spotted a narrow slit embedded in the tabletop that projected the screens for the Chairman's version of the SRT. He, of course, would also have a handheld device, but this was his command center. It was where all the information from the floors below flowed to the Chairman's attention.

From our viewpoint, the screens were invisible. You couldn't even tell they were there. They displayed their content only towards the Chairman's chair. If I had not seen a similar setup at my aunt's Falinvik residence, I would have thought it was just an empty desk.

As we walked more fully into the room, the doors automatically closed behind us. I thought I heard the Chairman mutter something to himself. Immediately, two armchairs materialized, constructed from metallic beads that bubbled forth from the floor in front of his desk. Thyra casually walked over to one of them and sat down, completely at ease. She gestured for me to join her.

Not only was she going to be in the room for my appointment, but apparently she was going to be an active participant. I swallowed hard. My throat felt parched.

Hesitantly I closed the distance to the chair and sat down. The Chairman circled the desk and seated himself in the hovering chair behind it, crossing his fingers across his midsection as he leaned back.

"Well, Mr. Rees...Advisor Haugen has told me all about your adventures," he began as his gray eyes inspected me. I shifted uncomfortably. "She related how you together became aware of a potential Convert and nearly succeeded in her capture...what a *pity* that she got away. It seems the saving grace in your story is the acquisition of an unregistered Clansman." The Chairman leaned forward in his chair, resting his arms on the desk. His unnatural gaze intensified. "This, I suppose, earns some recognition, considering it was your first solo hunt...although as I understand it, he was not your intended target."

The Chairman paused, letting the weight of the last statement sink in. His cold eyes pierced me further. I sank a little lower in my chair. My mind raced.

As the silence became unbearable and I was about to interject with my rehearsed explanation, the Chairman leaned back in his chair again. "You should consider yourself very lucky that Thyra sees potential in you...despite your lack of discipline. She has indicated a willingness to take you on as her lieutenant...even with my reservations. She believes your initiative shows promise. What do you think, Mr. Rees? Is this an acceptable arrangement?"

Before I could answer, he proceeded. "Undoubtedly it is...and you should be profoundly grateful. After all, we would not want to waste your powerful ability without due cause. So, I'm willing to attribute these disciplinary...misjudgments...to your parents. My understanding is that their *megins* are passive...just in the trade-crafts...a talent in leatherwork or some such nonsense. What a blessing that we were able to place you with a great mentor like Henric. How could your parents have possibly brought up a warrior *megin* like yours? I'm sure with Henric's continued mentorship and Thyra's superb guidance, any residual family traits will be ironed out."

My mind was still stuck on the Chairman's statement regarding "not wanting to waste my ability" and what exactly he had meant by it, when he stood up. When I didn't immediately react, Thyra jarred me out of my stupor. *"Tristan!"*

I quickly jumped to my feet. "Thank you, Chairman. I accept," was all I could say as I tried to process the conversation.

"Very well, then. Given your history with this potential Convert and knowledge of the island, your new Hunter squad's mission will be to capture her and the family of the unregistered Clan member. I want them found and brought back to me unharmed. Thyra will lead the team. You will support her however you can and without question. This is an important assignment. I want no mistakes, understand? Thyra will fill you in on the particulars later. You're dismissed." The Chairman waved me off, already focusing on something much more interesting on his screen.

I glanced at Thyra, and she motioned for me to leave the office.

FOUR

A Change in Plans

ELIN

My weird vision of the silver-haired man had thrown a wrench into the rescue plans. The Gradys and the Resistance thought that the silver-haired man was most likely the Chairman. They couldn't be sure, since they hadn't seen what I'd seen, but Mr. Grady had provided the vital piece of evidence leading to that conclusion.

Evidently, only a select few individuals were privy to the true nature of the Chairman's *megin*, yet somehow Mr. Grady knew. Apparently, he'd been able to secure the information before the Gradys had escaped Falinvik. The details of just how he'd accomplished that feat were rather vague, but nonetheless, our team now had a valuable piece of knowledge: the Chairman was a Mind Interventionist.

Above the gasps and murmurs at our gathering, Mrs. Grady explained to me that Mind Interventionists were able to infringe on your thoughts. They could listen to your internal chatter and plant their own fresh ideas without your consent. A talented Mind Interventionist could ultimately even take over your mind entirely if they wished. The extent of the Chairman's ability—was nearly impossible to know.

A shiver ran up my spine as I thought about Aedan strapped to the chair in the seafoam-green room. Was his mind still his own?

None of those who attended our conclave had ever heard of a Mind Interventionist being able to intrude on a Visionary while they were in a vision. Up until that point, the understanding had been that a person had to be physically in the same room as the Mind Interventionist. Whispers and suspicious looks were thrown in my direction as I sat next to Mrs. Grady on the beige living room sofa.

A FEW HOURS EARLIER, WHEN I'D RELATED TO HER WHAT HAD happened, Mrs. Grady had hastily called the emergency meeting. There'd been a slight delay in sharing my strange experience, since Gabriel's proclamation regarding the frozen fjord had temporarily thrown the Grady household into an uproar. It was, after all, the day they'd been anxiously waiting for during the past three weeks.

Once the joyous shouts and hugs had subsided, I'd urgently sought Mrs. Grady's attention, hoping to get a reasonable explanation for the weird occurrence in my vision. What I hadn't expected was the commotion and confusion that followed.

"Elin, that's very disturbing indeed! You should've insisted on telling me right away. We could be in more danger than we know," Mrs. Grady said, anxiously reaching for her cell phone.

"But, Mrs. Grady...I don't understand. What does it mean? Surely he couldn't have seen me...could he?" I replied, taking a deep breath.

"I don't know, Elin. This is something I've never heard of before. To be safe, we've got to assume that he can," she answered as she typed something into her phone. "Which is why I've just sent a message for an emergency Resistance meeting."

She then tried to calmly settle me into the kitchen with a snack, after which she rushed out of the room in search of the rest of the Gradys. Before long, Aedan's family and I were gathered around the kitchen island, discussing the incident and stress-eating cheese, crackers, and apple slices.

As we waited for the rest of the Resistance members to arrive, Mr. Grady reluctantly shared his suspicion that the silver-haired man was the Chairman. He warned that anyone who learned about the Chairman's special ability was put in grave danger; since the Chairman was known to violently purge the minds of people who knew, especially without his consent.

After pausing for a moment to let the gravity of what we just learned sink in, Mr. Grady speculated that the vision had to be set in the present time. In his reasoning, it couldn't be a past or future event. The past had already happened, and the future was still malleable. Thus, a Mind Interventionist wouldn't be able to interfere in those realms.

"I suppose the silver lining...if there is one...is that we know Aedan is still alive. And we have further confirmation of where he's being held. Those seafoam labs are distinct and located only at Ginnungagap. They were remodeled in the 1950s as part of the hospital wing at the fortress," he said. After a short pause, he continued. "We can also surmise that the Chairman hasn't broken Aedan's mind yet...since they're still having sessions. Aedan always *was* rather good at clearing his mind with music during our training."

With the last statement, Mrs. Grady looked up at her husband, and they shared a proud but worried gaze. I silently sighed with relief—Aedan was still Aedan.

"Well, what are we waiting for? Can't we leave tonight?" Edvin broke in, impatient as ever.

"Edvin, we don't know how the incident in Elin's vision will impact our journey," Mrs. Grady snapped, uncharacteristically. "We've got to be prudent. This is one rescue where we can't afford to take any unnecessary risks."

Mr. Grady, standing next to his wife, gave her hand a short squeeze.

"Sorry...I'm still unclear as to how or why this impacts Aedan's rescue?" I said.

"Elin, while you've made great progress in exerting some control over your ability...you're still learning. With this development, you're now—quite literally—in the Chairman's sight. Without your own medal to assist you, it'll be more difficult to get to the level you'd need to be at to fend off an attack from the Chairman...or conceal your presence," Mrs. Grady explained sympathetically. "There's just so much we don't know about the Chairman's ability or what he can do with it. For example, since your connection with him, can he now read your thoughts or locate you whenever he wishes? Or do you have to use your power to be vulnerable? Does he need to be in the vision, etc.? And most worrisome of all, can he take over your mind and see what you see in your reality?"

The thought of those gray eyes probing me again made me shudder. Claire noticed my involuntary movement and wrapped her strong arm around my shoulders.

"So...what you're saying is that she needs her own medallion to have a fighting chance," Claire said. "Isn't our trip taking us right by Sigrid Malmr's home?"

Mr. and Mrs. Grady looked up at Claire's question.

"'Right by' might be a stretch...but we'll certainly pass the landing towards Thordalr," Mr. Grady confirmed.

Unfortunately, my questions about who exactly Sigrid Malmr was and why she was important were interrupted. The front doorbell had rung, announcing the arrival of the emergency-meeting members.

As the ten participants filed in, placing their cell phones in a soundproof box, I recognized a handful. There was Monsieur Tibadeau, his nephew Gabriel, Ms. Valistus, and Mr. McHaill.

I had been introduced to Ms. Valistus and Mr. McHaill shortly after the night at the Clan library. Ms. Valistus was responsible for the Resistance operations on Auor Island, while Mr. McHaill was a recent addition from the Resistance's central command. He was there to liaise—whatever that meant.

Ms. Valistus was a forty-something woman with bright-blond hair and steely blue eyes. Although shorter in stature than most of her male counterparts, she had a commanding air that left little doubt as to who was in charge. Mr. McHaill was an older gentleman with salt-and-pepper hair. The color was so pervasive that it reached all the way down to the whiskers that framed his wiry mouth. I'd only ever seen him in a dark-blue cloak that he wore around his thin frame like a protective shield.

I had yet to discover whether either of them had abilities or were Mannlegurs. The Resistance was composed of both types of people. I suspected the former but had seen nothing to confirm it. I kept my suspicions to myself, since Mrs. Grady had informed me that it was impolite to ask a Clan person about their abilities. She'd pointed out in no uncertain terms that "if a Clan person wanted to share the information with you, they would."

Had it been one of our scheduled meetings with the Resistance, Mia and Joel would've been invited as well. Ever since they had been at Arne Point on the night of Aedan's abduction, they'd been made aware of the strange supernatural world that existed on the periphery of their own. They had, of course, been so enamored by this new secret that they'd immediately volunteered to help the Resistance.

Despite my reservations about their hasty decision, I missed their presence tonight. Having Aedan's and my best friends to share the strange circumstances would've been a real comfort at the moment.

I glanced around the room. It was filled with unfamiliar faces... people who briefly met my eyes and then quickly turned away, betraying their curiosity and discomfort with a Dormant. I shifted in my seat on the couch, trying to find a more comfortable position in Mrs. Grady's shadow.

Once everyone was seated and had directed their attention to Ms. Valistus, she did something odd. Instead of launching into the agenda as she normally did, she stood up, stretched her arms out with her palms facing up, and closed her eyes.

Within seconds, a blue light began to emanate from the center of her hands. It grew and grew like a balloon stretching to encompass the entire room and the people within it.

I'd guessed correctly. Ms. Valistus *was* a Clan member.

Once the bubble's rim touched the room's walls, Ms. Valistus opened her blue eyes. "There...a little extra-precaution for *this* meeting given what we now know. The shield will keep any prying eyes or ears—including telepathic ones—out. For those not already informed, the Gradys called this emergency session as new information has come to light. Liam, would you like to proceed?"

Mr. Grady gave a curt nod "Thank you, Noora. Yes, we've had an interesting but serious development." Ms. Valistus sat down, and Mr. Grady went on to give a short summary of the events that led to the emergency meeting. At the end of his briefing, he shared his suspicion about the Chairman's involvement.

Gasps and murmurs erupted among the attendees. I could hear whispers asking "how is this possible" and "what does this latest odd revelation about the Dormant mean" sweep through the room.

Signaling with her hands to quiet the room, Ms. Valistus stood up again. "Remarkable and significant information, indeed. Thank you, Liam." Mr. Grady took a seat on the couch's arm and gave my shoulder a reassuring squeeze. "Well…given this latest incident, I think we can all agree that extra precautions are needed. I'll reach out to each team captain separately to discuss the measures we should take. Only McHaill and I will know the full details. We need to batten down the hatches." With those words, she dismissed the meeting and, with a wave of her hand, the shield bubble. "Family Grady and Elin…if I could have a moment?"

Mr. Grady nodded and led the way back to the kitchen. Once we were all gathered around the granite island, Ms. Valistus addressed me. "Elin, I'm so sorry…but given the situation, we're going to need to place further restrictions on what we can tell you regarding the rescue plans. In fact, we may need to re-evaluate whether you can be involved at all."

"What do you mean? I…I have to be involved…I have to go," I said, panicking. I had to go on the rescue mission. Aedan needed all the help we could muster—and I owed him. The whole situation was my fault, after all. "The team needs me…I…I can see things about where he is. Plus, I…I have my abilities even on a new moon." Desperation was starting to grow inside me. "I've already told my family about my trip to Paris with Monsieur Tibadeau. Won't it look strange if I'm suddenly held back?"

The trip to Paris was my cover story as to why I'd be gone. As far as my family was concerned, Monsieur Tibadeau was taking a select group of high-performing students to Paris on a language and culture trip during the last few weeks of the school term. The supposed students included me, Aedan, and a few others from schools on the mainland where Monsieur Tibadeau taught as well.

The cover story had solved numerous quandaries for our team —especially why a French teacher and a student were disappearing at the same time. Gabriel, who was a technical wiz, had already installed some sort of VPN thing on my phone that would disguise its location as Paris.

Of course, all of that might now be pointless. I looked around at the familiar faces in the kitchen, searching for someone to please intervene. But they all avoided my gaze. I couldn't believe this!

I was about to make a bigger fuss when Ms. Valistus interceded. "Elin, I understand your desire to help and what you offer the team. It will be a big loss...but we've got to consider the safety of everyone involved. Our priority has to be Aedan...and the team going to rescue him. We just don't know enough about your condition to rule out the risks." My heart sank. Ms. Valistus was about to sideline me. "I think it's best that you stay here. The Resistance will continue its protective measures around your home. Meanwhile, I think you need to inform your family that the Auor students are no longer going on the Paris trip." She paused for a moment and then softened her tone. "I'm sure, however, that we can think of a safe way for you to help the team from here."

There it was—the consolation prize. I'd been relegated to the B team. All my practice and plans gone to waste. Worst of all, what would Aedan think if I wasn't there to rescue him after everything he'd done for me? I couldn't let him down. But now, after what Ms. Valistus had just said, no one would take me. I hung my head as my eyes began to burn with hot tears of frustration.

Not wanting to cry in front of everyone, I rushed out of the room and house. I ran as fast as I could, inadvertently tapping into my *megin*. I just wanted to be home under the covers of my own bed.

Before I realized it, I'd reached the Shield Wall's boundary.

Not seeing clearly with the tears in my eyes, I ran directly into it. *Ow!* It was like hitting a stone wall.

I fell backward, landing with a thud on my backside. I grasped my head in pain. I'd forgotten that even authorized individuals could not pass through the wall while using their *megin*. It was a protection mechanism.

Having no one else to scream at, I hurled a few choice words at the barrier. How had I ever gotten into this mess in the first place? I threw some leaves and twigs at the wall, hoping those would have more effect than my words. But they gently floated to the other side as if nothing was there.

I'd only sat on the pile of brown autumn leaves for a few seconds, trying to stop my angry tears and nursing my head, when I heard a *whoosh* behind me. I turned my head to see Claire standing there. Aedan had always said she was fast. She sat down beside me and put her arm around me.

"I...I...I just...have to...be there," I blubbered through angry tears and hiccups.

"Hush now...I know...I know," Claire replied as she stroked my arm.

"I just can't stay here...and do nothing. It's my fault—Aedan wouldn't have been at the library or Ash Park if it wasn't for me." I looked up at Claire. "After everything he did for me, I have to help him. I owe him. And you know...Ms. Valistus won't let me near any of it...even here," I continued, sniffling.

Claire squeezed me tighter. "*Oh, Elin.* It's not your fault. Aedan wanted to go to the Clan library that night. And there's no stopping him when he sets his mind to something. Nobody could have foreseen everything that took place. The only ones to blame here are the *Stór-menni*. None of this would have happened if it wasn't for them. They're the seed that sprouted the weed." She paused for a moment studying me. "I miss my brother and want him back too. We'll figure something out. Don't give up quite yet, Elin."

Then in a hushed, contemplative tone, she added, "I might...I might just have a plan. Keep up with your practice sessions with my mom...and leave the status of your 'Paris trip' vague with your family for now, okay? This incident may actually be more of an opportunity than anyone realizes."

FIVE

An Early Visit

AEDAN

I'd nearly finished the morning bowl of something the guards called 'porridge' when they came for me. It was a lot earlier than usual. Their dedicated routine generally involved a midday Mind Interventionist session—not a first-thing-after-breakfast session. I wasn't used to going into mind battle on a full stomach. I hoped it wouldn't make me sick.

My face stretched into a mighty yawn as I watched the shuffling guards through the porthole in my cell door. My poor sleep the previous night had left me tired. My dreams had been filled with images of Elin. She'd been upset about something.

In the dream, she was trying to explain something to me in great detail, but I couldn't quite remember what. It often happened with my dreams—the more memorable bits were the images rather than specific spoken words. Elin's insistence that I understand her, however, kept me tossing and turning all night on the little green mattress.

The guards entered my cell, hassling me to get up. I slowly

complied. As they escorted me past Reo's cell, I could see his surprised older Asian face peering out from the circular window.

To help pass the time, Reo had recently started to explain to me in more detail about the various aspects of the four Clans— Nordri, Sudri, Austri, and Vestri.

I didn't know much about the other three latter Clans. While my parents had mentioned their existence, there'd always been a sense of sadness tinging the discussion that'd made me shy away from further questions. My parents, like the rest of the Nordri Clan, believed the falsehoods the Chairman had propagated about the three Clans' demise.

He'd succeeded in his lie by limiting the flow of information and movement. According to Reo, he'd begun by cutting off communication lines, blaming the Clan Wars. Then he'd forbidden Clan intermarriage with the justification that it divided loyalties, blocked unauthorized Nordri members from leaving Falinvik under the pretense of safety, secretly jailed the Clan emissaries, and turned away Clan pilgrims as liars at the outer Falinvik Shield Wall. Finally, when the Nordri Clan members hadn't seen or heard from any other Clans in decades, the Chairman proclaimed the lie that the other Clans had perished in the fighting.

When I asked Reo why the Chairman would do all this, he'd answered simply that he did not know.

"Aedan-kun, this is the question I have been trying to answer for years," Reo said in his slight Japanese accent. "Before I was jailed among countless others during the Night of Great Carnage twenty years ago, I was on the verge of some important revelations. I had managed to learn that many years ago, the Chairman's wife had been one of the four Goðar. A Goði was selected by each Clan as their representative in the Clan Assembly where interrelations and disputes were handled. It was a great honor to be selected for the position...but that is all I could learn of her. This Assembly, of course, no longer exists... nor does any further information regarding the Chairman's wife."

"What do you think it means?" I pondered, millions of thoughts racing through my head. Where was the Chairman's wife? Why was he hiding her? Why had the Assembly disintegrated?

"It could mean everything...or nothing," Reo replied thoughtfully.

A few moments passed with both of us lost in thought. I hesitated, then asked in amazement, "Reo, you've been here for twenty years?"

"Well...not inside this exact cell...but yes, I've been imprisoned for twenty years, three months, and seventeen days," he answered with a deep sigh.

"Aren't you an emissary? Why has no one come for you? Your Clan? Your family?" I inquired, awestruck.

"Aedan-kun, the only explanation that I have been able to accept is...they believe me dead. Otherwise, my daughter and wife would not have given up their search...nor the Austri leadership... I'm certain of this. It deeply pains me that they believe this to be true...someday I hope...I will see them again," he'd explained with a deliberateness that comes only from years of contemplation. Then abruptly he added, "I am tired, Aedan-kun. I wish you a good night and sleep." With that, Reo had "hung up" our string phone, his melancholy seeping into me through the thick, ancient wall between us.

As I had tossed and turned on my green mattress, I regretted asking the question. But at the moment, I'd been wondering where my own family was. My best guess was that it'd been nearly a month now since my capture. I knew I'd need to be patient—

because surely they wouldn't give up on me—but how on earth would they be able to extricate me from this literal fortress?

Now, as the guards dragged me by his window, I tried to give Reo a quick, encouraging smile. Once we reached the seafoam-green room, the guards as usual strapped me into the awkward chair. A few moments later, the Mind Interventionist, with his gray tunic and piercing eyes, strode in.

"Hello, Aedan. I hope you don't mind our early visit today. I have some pressing appointments later that are unavoidable," he greeted me.

Given his tone, and if I hadn't been strapped into the bizarre dentist chair, it could've been a friendly meeting among acquaintances. The other strange thing was that I was pretty sure he was speaking to me instead of trying to place thoughts inside my head.

"Yes, well...I see that you are ready for our meeting of minds, but I thought we could try something different today," he continued, not waiting for my response. "You see, I want the full pleasure of your attention as I have some very exciting news to share...and neither of us should be distracted by your incessant singing."

While relieved at the notion that he wouldn't be trying to bore into my thoughts, a slight disappointment nagged at me that once again his introduction to Steve Miller's "The Joker" would have to wait. At least my song for the next session was all picked out. More importantly, whatever his "exciting news" was, I knew it wouldn't be good.

He stopped pacing and turned to face me with a cruel smile.

"I wanted to let you know that you will soon be reunited with your family." Panic pulsed through my veins and into my stomach. Had they been caught? "You see, you've been instrumental in providing their location—we can't thank you enough for filling out that library card application. While the Resistance has thwarted our attempts at rescuing your family so far, a new moon is just around the corner...and they've been lulled into complacency by old technology. You see, there's a fatal flaw in their antiquated Shield Wall—but then again, I shouldn't give away too much. All you need to know is that soon the Resistance will no longer be a factor, and your parents—and whatever siblings you may have—will have a comfortable residence here. So, you see, Aedan...you no longer have to fight me."

My stomach twisted and turned at every word he uttered. I'd been concerned that the mind battle might make me sick, but this was far worse. My family was in danger—and there was nothing I could do.

"In fact, it will be far easier for your family if you simply provide their information now," he continued cheerfully. "That way, we can have the appropriate accommodations ready...and there'll be no added steps of information extraction for them." He paused for a moment, letting that sink in. I wasn't sure what he meant by "information extraction," but it didn't sound pleasant. "You can start by providing your true family surname. We know 'Grady' isn't real. It doesn't and never has existed in the Clan database."

What was he talking about? My family's last name wasn't real? While we did use aliases as we moved around, 'Grady' was our name. We only used it in the rare circumstance where we felt safe and most isolated from the rest of the world. Auor Island had seemed like such a place so many months ago. He was lying—but why would he lie about something like that?

"Come now, Aedan...this can't be news to you," the Mind Interventionist said as he noticed the astonished look on my face. "Surely your father would've trusted you with your true family name? Why wouldn't he tell you...his son?"

His voice and facial features were pulled into mock sincerity, but his cold eyes betrayed their enjoyment at my confusion. While I didn't believe him, I was positive there was a good reason if my parents hadn't divulged our real surname. But a tiny itch established itself in the back of my mind. Why hadn't my dad trusted me?

"Well...no matter; we can start with your siblings. How many and what ages can we expect?" the Mind Interventionist continued.

He looked expectantly at me. I closed my eyes and started to hum out loud.

"So, you prefer to inflict the hard way on your family...Fine," he said, sneering.

Given my lack of cooperation, I expected the mind assault to begin. Instead, he stormed out of the room, yelling above my humming, "Just remember, Aedan...I gave you a chance to help your family!"

The door to the room banged shut with such force that it knocked itself slightly open. I could hear the Mind Interventionist yelling at someone on the other side.

"YOU IDIOTS! What's so hard about tracing his DNA...even the *Smá-menn* can do *that* these days. I want to know who his father and mother are NOW!"

"But Sir...they are not in the *Stór-menni* database. We searched numerous times for a familial match," a whimpering voice pleaded.

"INCOMPETENT...THE LOT OF YOU! Useless fools... Run it against everyone in the Four Clans' database...from the beginnings of the Clans if necessary," the Mind Interventionist responded.

"Yes, Sir. But that will take some time," the whimpering voice replied.

"I DON'T CARE...JUST DO IT! Meanwhile, take him to his cell. Perhaps more time to consider his family's fate will change his mind!" The Mind Interventionist's voice faded as he moved away from the door.

The guards re-entered the seafoam room to undo the straps and haul me back to my cell. Once there, I paced up and down like a caged tiger, trying to make sense of everything I'd learned. There were two things I was certain of: my family was in danger, and our familial DNA was missing from the Clan database.

A deep, burning anger established itself in my chest. Thoughts of Clan Hunters with their seaxes drawn descending upon our home while my family slept wormed their way into my head. I slammed my fist against the wall. And what about Elin? What did this mean for her?

But what could I do? I was trapped in this cell with no way to warn them. This was exactly what we'd been running from for years—and now I'd provided the information that would lead to their capture. I leaned my hammering head against the cool stone wall. I could only hope there were additional safety nets in place to prevent their capture. At least I now knew that the Resistance was helping them. I wondered how Claire had managed to sort that out.

After drawing some deep breaths to calm my pulsing veins and soothe my aching fist, I tried to distract myself with the other valuable information I'd learned—the fact that our family genealogy seemed to be missing from the Clan database. How was that possible? My parents had still lived in Falinvik when the first registration requirements had been enacted by the Chairman. How had they managed to avoid it and not be imprisoned?

I hadn't shared much about my family with Reo. It was more a cautious habit than any real concern about him. Living as a fugitive for most of my life had made me tight-lipped—especially when it came to sharing personal information. However, in this case, I hoped that Reo might be able to shed some light on the latest mystery.

I knelt on my mattress and searched for the tin cup. I pulled on the little string and heard his metal cup thump against the wall. It was already connected. Reo must have been anxious to hear how the latest session with the Mind Interventionist had gone.

After I connected my cup and greeted him, I shared with Reo the unusual session and what I'd overheard. He made small grunts and sighs, indicating that he was listening. When I finished, he was silent for a long time.

"Reo...Reo...are you there?" I asked.

"Yes, Aedan-kun. I am here," he replied pensively.

"What do you think? Why would my family's DNA not be in the database?" I asked, eager for answers.

"Hmmm...there are not too many people who could access that kind of information. Only a small select group, in fact," he replied. "I am not sure...there is no clear answer here. But the fact that your Mind Interventionist has access to this knowledge is more interesting. Describe him to me, Aedan-kun."

"What...the Mind Interventionist?" I asked.

"Yes," Reo answered.

I closed my eyes to picture the silver-haired man. Gray tunic, sharp gray eyes, slicked-back hair, older, black robes with a white collar, definite air of authority...overall, a rather scary individual. I shared the description with Reo.

"Interesting...how very interesting," Reo mumbled in response.

"*What?*" I nearly yelled, remembering at the last second to keep my voice down.

"I believe, Aedan-kun, that you have been in the company of

the Chairman. Why he would take an interest in you, personally conducting your sessions, is an even bigger question," Reo replied.

I nearly dropped the tin cup at Reo's words.

For the past several weeks, the Chairman himself had been trying to break me.

SIX

The Night Raid

TRISTAN

The Outer Aerial Transport, or OAT, took longer to get to Auor Island than it had the last time. The PS had mandated new safeguards now that we knew there were Resistance forces on the island.

The PS was still not entirely sure how many Resistance members were on Auor since the resisters purposely blended in with the *Smá-menn*. The few individuals we had been able to identify came from the video footage that the two Security Aerial Surveillance Units—SASUs for short—had captured on the night of the library intrusion. It had taken some time to clean the footage, since it had been only partially sent and corrupted along the way. Apparently, someone had torn out the units' program chips before they could cleanly transmit the video.

The one image that the PS Surveillance Unit had been able to clean up showed a group of people standing in front of an old boat landing. There had been eight of them. And Elin was amongst the group. She was sitting on the ground, looking panicked.

Near her were three adults. Two of them had their backs

turned to the camera, so no facial identification could be made. The third adult had been kneeling on the ground with some sort of large canister weapon on his shoulder. The canister had partially blocked his face, but the Surveillance Unit was confident that with time they could recreate it for identification.

The four younger people crowded around Elin were two boys and two girls, none of whom were registered Clan members. I did not recognize three of them—the brown-skinned girl, the muscular boy, or the dark-haired girl. However, the boy with a skewed baseball cap, who looked to be in his mid-teens, seemed familiar to me, but I could not place him. My best guess was that I had seen him at Auor High School while I had been a student there. I relayed as much to Thyra as we studied the image together on the flight.

"Interesting. We'll definitely add that information to his profile," she replied, signaling to a nearby Hunter to do so. "We need to be able to track these resisters so we can eventually capture them all."

"Have all the individuals in the image been added as Resistance members in the Clan database?" I asked.

"Yes, of course. They've been caught not only in the company of known fugitives but also clearly with someone thwarting their capture by shooting down the SASUs. What could be more clear-cut than that?"

"How do we know whether they are Clansmen or *Smá-menn*?" I asked.

Thyra looked at me with surprise, as if it should have been obvious. "Does it matter? They are all trying to subvert the *Stór-menni* in one way or another and are now considered *Útlagar*. You know outlaws are not tolerated. They belong at Ginnungagap whether they have abilities or not."

"I guess not...I just didn't think the Clan Council would want to expose more of the Clan's existence to the *Smá-menn* than necessary," I said, trying to smooth over any discord.

Maybe I had spent too much time around the *Smá-menn* lately, but it was hard to see them as a true threat given their lack of supernatural abilities. And categorizing them as outlaws seemed severe. To be deemed an *Útlagi* meant that there was no room for reform and you would be spending the rest of your days at Ginnungagap. It was the worst punishment that the Clan could inflect—besides death.

"We are almost there," Thyra announced, changing the topic. "Listen up, everyone." She paused, waiting for the four other faces in the OAT's cabin to turn to hers. "PS Intelligence reports estimate that we should find three to four individuals at the unregistered Clan member's house. We'll be commencing the raid tonight on the new moon. There are two reasons for this timing. First, it's the only time the Resistance's outdated Shield Wall is vulnerable. Ivar and Arnis are here from the PS Technical team to exploit the flaw and bring the wall down." The men gave a short nod, acknowledging their mission. "The second reason is that we do not know who these fugitives are or what their abilities might be. We are tilting the playing field to our advantage by ensuring that no one has their *megin* available. Clan Hunters are skilled warriors with or without their powers. Fenja and Magnus plus the two Hunters already on the ground will join Tristan and me for the actual attack. We'll strike the Unregistered's house first, at moonset."

Magnus signaled his agreement by smiling and pulling out his seax and sharpening stone. His large muscles rippled under his black thermal shirt as he expertly guided the blade over the stone. His bulky frame took up most of the bench opposite mine. His brown, oily hair fell across his chiseled features as he looked down to test the sharpness of his blade. He was not someone I cared to meet in a Leikr tunnel anytime soon.

Near him sat Fenja. Her long black hair was pulled back from her face, revealing slightly Asian features. She had a fierce, intelligent air about her, yet she was quick to obey Thyra's commands. She gave a curt nod and pulled out her SRT to study the schematics of the Gradys' property.

Ivar and Arnis were a contrast in opposites. While light-haired Ivar was carrying a few extra pounds, Arnis with his straight black hair looked like he could use a good meal or two. They nodded to Thyra and then resumed huddling over the screen of a technical-looking device while having a hushed disagreement.

Everyone seemed to have a defined role on the team—except me. I glanced at Thyra, who had leaned back against the seat and closed her eyes. She had a slight smile on her face. Returning to the image on the SRT in my hands, I tried to make myself look busy.

I should have been the one running this team. Not her —*especially* not her. I still couldn't believe the outcome at the Chairman's office. How had things gone so wrong? It was supposed to be my day of triumph. I was finally going to receive a Captain's seax, but now instead, here I was answering to my longtime nemesis.

While I was grateful for having escaped the punishment the Chairman had alluded to, why did it have to be through Thyra? It was humiliating. Making it worse, I was now part of a team. Solo missions or commanding a team of Hunters were the only two options I had ever been trained for. So to my chagrin, I was once again on unfamiliar ground heading to Auor—and there was a lot riding on this mission— especially after what the Chairman had implied regarding my value.

The built-up tension in my shoulders was way beyond the

point of allowing me a quick catnap before landing. I stretched my neck side to side, trying to relieve the stiffness. So much had happened in the last couple of days since the meeting with the Chairman.

Moments after I had left his office, my SRT had pinged with a new notification, informing me that I was to report to the 24th floor the following day and to be prepared for mission deployment. The message was like salt in a fresh wound. I had still been trying to wrap my head around the fact that I was now Thyra's lieutenant —and she was *my* captain.

I could not quite believe that she and I had actually been placed together on the same Hunter Squad. We had been fierce competitors for so long that I had lost count of the numerous Leikr we had battled against each other.

The Leikr was the ultimate test of a Clan member's ability and productivity potential. It was a game of strategy where the object was to get all of your team members safely through a series of challenges before the other team did. In the final rounds, opposing team members encountered each other in a tunneled obstacle field. Their object was to get by their opponent while also trying to slow them down. Thyra and I had met several times in the tunnels with varying results over who could claim victory. Had I at the time known she was the Chairman's niece, the confrontations' outcomes would have been clearer.

The OAT's descent alert interrupted my thoughts. The pilot announced our arrival on Auor Island. We had chosen to land next to the lighthouse where I had shown Elin my *megin* some months ago. It was an isolated location on the island with a large meadow next to a parking lot, perfect for landing the transport. In addition, the ruins of the keeper's cottage would provide a sheltered venue to wait until it was time.

The back door of the OAT lowered, revealing a dark and

bitterly cold evening on the island. Our small team gathered our equipment and descended the ramp. Thyra led the way, stopping a good distance away from the transport and waiting for the rest of us to join her. Once we had all cleared the OAT's circumference, the rush of wind and kicked-up snow indicated its rapid departure.

Our breath came out in puffs as we surveyed the silent white landscape with our headlamps. Given the new moon, all of our abilities, including our enhanced night vision, were dormant. The distant, dark sea was sporadically illuminated by the still-working lighthouse beacon. I shuddered as an icy wind blew off the rolling water. I pulled the zipper of my black inferior *Smá-menn* parka all the way up to seal in whatever warmth was left. Before we left, we had been required to don *Smá-menn* clothing in case we ran into any of them during our mission.

"Okay. Let's move," Thyra commanded. "The cottage wall should provide some shelter. We have about an hour before moonset. That means a thirty-minute wait. Dreng and Bera should be here soon with our transportation."

Ivar and Arnis hoisted their black bags over their shoulders and started to make their way across the untouched snow. Luckily, it was only a few inches thick and mostly frozen by the sea mist. Fenja and Magnus followed, adjusting their seaxes to the outside of their parkas for easy reach.

"After you," I said, sweeping my hand in the direction of the others. Thyra gave a curt nod and followed in their footsteps.

With our black clothing, the only indication of movement ahead was the crunching of snow and the bobbing of headlamps as we moved across the field. Eventually, the first two lights stopped moving and congregated together. Ivar and Arnis must have reached the cottage wall.

Before long, the rest of us reached the low wooden fence between the main trail and the cottage wall. It reminded me of the last time I was here with Elin and how I had assisted her over the fence. Even then I had been helping her—without any returned gratitude. Well, things were certainly going to change tonight.

Ivar and Arnis had found the fire emulator in their bags, and its blue light danced towards the sky, emanating heat and casting a discreet circle of light. Fenja held her gloved hands toward the warmth, and Magnus rotated himself like a rotisserie chicken in front of the flames. Arnis dug further in his bag and his hands emerged with six small black pouches.

"Here. Catch. Half-shells," he said, tossing one to each of us.

Ivar was already opening his sack—his fingers the nimblest, having spent the most time by the fire. He pulled the black fabric out of the pouch and shook it in the air. Slowly, the fabric stiffened into a low half-dome structure that allowed one person to sit inside its cavern protected from the elements. Forming a tight circle around the fire, the rest of us opened our half-shells, which helped to conceal our presence and provided insulated seats.

After twenty minutes of occasional small talk about the team's previous missions, Magnus was starting to get visibly impatient. I glanced over at Thyra, whose passive face was illuminated by the fire's blue flames. She seemed to be ignoring Magnus's impatient foot-tapping and restless shifting in his Half-shell.

"Where are they? They should've been here by now," Magnus grumbled, checking the Communicator on his wrist.

In the dim light, I could see the digital time flashing on his Communicator's band: 7:14pm. Dreng and Bera had three minutes to arrive before causing fractures in our plans.

Ivar had made each of us strap on a Communicator before we landed. In addition to providing the time, the devices tracked the wearer and used the bones in their bodies to vibrate sound up to their ears, allowing users to discreetly talk to each other over great distances. You tapped once to talk. They were invaluable for raid coordination, especially on a new moon.

Magnus swiftly stood up, tipping his half-shell over and breaking the cocoon of the circle. The rest of the team immediately protested with groans and shouts as the cold air swooped in.

"Magnus, sit down," Thyra commanded, not bothering to look up from her SRT.

"*Odin's beard!* Where are those two? We should start walking or will miss our window entirely," Magnus said, reaching for his half-shell and stuffing it back into its pouch. He tossed it to Arnis and started walking toward the wooden fence.

His movement was quickly brought to a stop as a shuriken shrieked by him, lodging itself in the wooden post in front of him.

"I said, *sit down,*" Thyra ordered, having also risen. Her hands were toying with another shuriken, nimbly spinning the four-bladed weapon between her fingers.

Magnus slowly turned around to face Thyra. He bowed his head demurely.

"Patience, Magnus. We all need a little patience. They'll be here."

And as if to prove her point, bouncing headlights appeared in the parking lot. The rest of the team quickly rose to their feet, stuffing their half-shells into their pouches while Arnis extinguished the flame emanator and packed the items into his bag.

As I passed the shuriken embedded in the post, I couldn't help but be impressed by Thyra's throwing skill, especially in the dark and without any *megin*. She was definitely not one to cross—whether you were on her team or not. She expertly pulled the shuriken out of the post as she passed, ignoring my stare.

Once we reached the idling black vehicle, we could see a large dent in its side with a few pine needles protruding from the car-door cracks. Fortunately, we could still open the back door, and the six of us climbed inside what Dreng informed us was a Suburban.

"Apologies, Thyra, for our delay. We experienced a small road incident with black ice," Dreng said with clear resentment in his voice. "These *Smá-menn* have yet to learn how to efficiently remove such road hazards."

"Understood. How long to the house?" Thyra asked.

"Approximately twenty minutes...it should leave us somewhere between seven and ten minutes to prepare. Moonset is at 7:47pm," Dreng answered.

"Well, let's get going then," Thyra commanded.

Already having turned the large vehicle around, Bera put the car in gear and started to drive through their earlier tracks in the snow.

I watched the dark passing landscape from the window, looking for familiar landmarks. There was not much else I could do as I had been unlucky in my seat selection. Magnus's bulky frame, which took up his seat entirely and at least half of mine, had me pinned against the door. Every time he took a breath, I could feel his muscles expand and contract. But with Thyra on his other side, I held my tongue.

The trees and ground were covered by a layer of snow and icicles, making it difficult to distinguish anything. After a good fifteen minutes, I finally recognized the driveway to Elin's house as we passed it. We were getting close.

Another five minutes and Bera turned onto an old dirt road. It had clearly seen a lot of use recently, as the snow and dirt had mucked together into brown slush. We bounced around in the back seat for another minute until she finally brought the vehicle to a stop.

"We're here. The Shield Wall begins just beyond that boulder there," Dreng said as he pointed toward the left of the vehicle and slipped on a black wool flat cap. "The puck is about twenty feet to the right of the boulder."

"Okay, Ivar and Arnis. You know what to do. We have eight minutes to make this work," Thyra said as she opened the car door and got out.

Leaving the door open, I quickly stepped down into the slush. Glancing back, I could see that Magnus's seax was caught between the driver's seat and center console. He was struggling to slide out, since his seax was strapped to him. Trapped in the third row of the Suburban, Ivar and Arnis were clearly growing impatient for Magnus to exit the vehicle.

"Come, Magnus! We don't have all day," Ivar complained.

"By the ravens, I'm trying," Magnus responded as he pulled this way and that on his seax.

Arnis groaned loudly in frustration. Ivar pushed against the seat in front of him to see if it would fold over despite Magnus's bulk being in the way.

"Oh, for Freya's sake," Fenja murmured as she reached over the seat in front of her and undid the strap on Magnus's seax.

Now released, Magnus was able to slide down the seat and out of the car, muttering, "Of all the *small* vehicles to hire for this occasion."

Bera, overhearing, replied, "I'll have you know this is the largest vehicle we could get and still blend in with the locals."

Magnus snorted in response. He was about to reach back into the vehicle for his seax when Thyra intervened. "*Leave it!*" Magnus turned to her with a horrified look on his face, to which Thyra responded, "Just let them get out first."

Finally freed from their imprisonment, Ivar and Arnis hurried to the back of the car, slipping and sliding in the icy slush like a pair of puppets. This was the team of skilled hunters who was going to capture four fugitives of unknown abilities plus a Dormant Descendant?

I would have laughed if my own neck was not on the line. Trying to refocus on my preparedness, I adjusted my seax to the outside of my jacket and tightened the laces on my boots.

Armed with their black bags from the vehicle's trunk, Ivar and Arnis headed towards the boulder that Dreng had pointed out. Thyra instructed Dreng and Bera to follow them. She then turned to Fenja and me.

"You two go scout around the front of the house and report back...be quick about it. And stay hidden. We don't want to give away our surprise."

Fenja and I nodded.

"Come on, Magnus. We're going to do a little scouting ourselves," Thyra said as she motioned Magnus to move further down the road. Magnus grinned and gripped the top of his seax, which was once again secured to his waist.

After a short battle through the forest's undergrowth, Fenja and I came upon the driveway to the house. We followed it towards the building, careful to stay in the woods. Fenja had a small device in her hand that she used to scan the area in front of us so we didn't accidentally run into the Shield Wall. Without our powers, we could not see *leynasked* items or people.

"Here it is. About ten feet in front of us," she said as she stopped walking.

I moved to her side. We were about fifty yards from the house. We both stepped sideways out of the woods to survey it.

"What in the *Niflheim!*" Fenja gasped.

Numerous vehicles were parked outside the house. I exchanged an uneasy glance with Fenja. This was definitely not part of the plan. I tapped once on my Communicator.

"Thyra, we have a problem," I said, trying to keep my voice even.

"What?" Thyra replied.

"Looks like they have company. We count at least six vehicles in front of the house."

"There weren't any cars when we checked earlier," Dreng interjected.

"Well, there are now," Fenja answered.

Ivar's voice cut in from the background. "Not that wire... you don't *want* that one."

"I know what I'm doing. Just let me do it," Arnis replied.

"Thyra?" I asked.

"We still go...this is our only opportunity for a month," she responded with a tinge of hesitation in her voice. "None of them will have their powers, so we're better armed than them...and we have the element of surprise. We keep going. Just stick with your partners. We'll take them all!"

Fenja and I shared another look.

"Okay. Will the wall be down in time?" Fenja asked.

"Yes, if these two will stop bickering like a couple of schoolgirls," Dreng answered.

"No...I don't need *that* anymore... don't you *dare* connect that to my SRT." Arnis's voice could be heard cutting in again. "What? Yes...yes, almost done."

A moment later, Ivar started the countdown. "Counting down... in ten, nine, eight..."

Fenja and I quickly moved onto the road for easier sprinting. I drew in a couple of deep breaths and rolled my shoulders to warm up my muscles. This was going to be a bigger fight than we had bargained for. We had come for three or four fugitives and now we were trying to capture at least a half-dozen Resistance members.

"...Six, five, four," Ivar's voice continued. My heart was

pounding in my chest. "Three, two, one... now. It's *down*. Go, go, go!"

Fenja glanced at her device and nodded. We sprinted towards the house

When we were still a good twenty-five yards from the house, something entirely unexpected happened. The lights went out and metal shutters slid down over all the windows and doors. It was now a stronghold—with no easy entry. Something had spoiled our surprise.

Fenja and I slowed to a walk, breathing hard from our excursion. I tapped my Communicator.

"Thyra... we have...another...problem," I said between breaths.

"What?" she replied, breathing hard as well.

"The house... is... in some... sort of...lockdown."

"What...do you...mean?"

"There...are metal...barriers on all...the entry points."

"Ivar...Arnis...bring your...bags," Thyra commanded. "Tristan...we're...almost at the house. We'll meet...everyone at...the front."

"Yes, Ma'am. We are on our way," Ivar replied.

"We are here," I answered.

Fenja and I had made it to the steps of the wide front porch during the discussion. As we sat down to wait for the others, we distinctly heard something metallic rotating. Glancing up toward the sound, we saw a small gray ball with some sort of eye. It was attached to the roof overhang. Fenja got up and knocked it down with her seax.

"*Smá-menn* camera," she said as she inspected the rest of the overhang.

After a minute or two, we could see headlights bouncing down the road. When the vehicle got close, we could see the overly excited faces of Ivar and Arnis in the front seats. They got out of the Suburban and immediately went to the back of the vehicle. A few moments later they emerged with a small black case.

"Good, you have it," Thyra said as she rounded the corner of the building with Magnus. "Don't wait on ceremony. Launch the Spiders."

Ivar opened the case. Arnis reached inside and, one by one, took out small discs that he tossed into the air a few feet above the ground. The discs immediately extended eight wiry legs, landing gracefully upon them. Several red lights lit up on their bodies as they waited for instructions.

Once all ten Spiders were out, Arnis took out a slender black stick similar to a pen and carefully traced the outline of the front door. When he finished, the Spiders ran towards the door, attaching themselves equidistantly on the metallic surface. Then a red light sprang forth from each of the Spiders' bellies, easily carving through the metal. Lasers.

Thyra sat down on the edge of the porch with a satisfied smile. "We should be entering shortly. Take a moment to relax."

Before the rest of us had the opportunity to sit down, the Spiders suddenly fell, one by one, from their posts until all ten were down. Arnis, looking horrified, rushed to aid his little friends.

"*WHAT?* I...I don't understand. How is this possible?" he said.

He examined one of the Spiders. As he held it up to the car headlights, a distinct hole could be seen where the laser had been before. Arnis took his headlamp and shined the light into one of the holes in the metal surface. The light reflected back.

"Ahh, yes...mirrors...cheap but effective," he said with reluctant admiration. "We won't be able to laser through these barriers. We'll have to revert to old technology...which will take more time. Ivar, get the Dragon!"

"Why do I always have to get the Dragon? You have two good feet and hands as well—" Ivar began.

"ODIN'S BEARD! Will somebody... *just* get the Dragon!" Thyra yelled.

This was going to be a long night. At least our targets were stuck inside the house. So eventually, victory would be ours.

SEVEN

The Root Cellar

ELIN

The stars were so bright. With no moon, even the Milky Way was easy to see. If the air temperature hadn't been so icy, it would've been a perfect stargazing evening. I pulled the corners of my puff coat closer to my neck, trying to shut out the cold.

The first snows had come over the last few days, building a couple of inches of crunchy white across our lawn. The beautiful picture it created tugged at the back of my mind, reminding me of something that I couldn't quite put my finger on.

After dinner, Anders had set up his telescope outside to cheer me up. He'd studied astrophysics in college, but exploring the planets and galaxies above our island had always been our thing. Somehow it put our worries into perspective and reminded us of what a tiny part of the universe we were.

I felt bad about having lied to him, but Anders hadn't let up on me until I'd given him a reason why I was moping around the house over the past couple of days. I couldn't tell him about the Clan, the Resistance, or Aedan's rescue without putting him in danger. So, flailing for an answer, I'd blurted out that my school trip to Paris might be canceled. Now standing in the cold, I was figuratively on thin ice, as Anders pried deeper.

"So why is the school canceling the trip?" he asked as he adjusted the telescope's zoom.

"Um...I'm not sure...it might not even get canceled. They weren't really clear on the reasons," I replied, looking down at my boots instead of at the stars.

"What do you mean? I thought you said you weren't going." Anders turned his head from the telescope's lens to look at me.

"Well...it's complicated...um...a little in flux, I guess."

"Weren't you supposed to leave in a few days?" he pressed.

I shrugged. "Yup, we were... or are...I don't really know."

"Huh...vacillating on the trip so late in the game doesn't sound very responsible of the school," Anders said, his brow furrowing. "Maybe Mom or Dad should give them a call."

Despite the cold, I was starting to sweat a little under my jacket. I needed to change the topic. "Uh...maybe. See anything *interesting* yet?"

"Yeah, just lining up Bode's Galaxy," Anders replied, turning back to the telescope.

I glanced at my watch. It read 7:34pm. On top of everything else, I was missing the Resistance's all-hands meeting tonight.

Given the Gradys' efforts to stay anonymous and the protection offered by their Shield Wall, the Resistance had decided to hold their regular meetings at the Gradys' house. And tonight, Joel and Mia would be there. But Ms. Valistus's new restrictions had excluded me from the session.

Mia had come back to Auor from her boarding school, Breckhaven, for the weekend specifically so she could attend the meeting and learn what she could about the rescue plans. We'd planned to get together after the meeting so that I could fill her and Joel in on my strange vision and they could share what they learned from the night's conclave.

"Do you want to look? It's pretty spectacular. The Galaxy's spirals are super vibrant tonight," Anders said, straightening from his bent position.

"Cool! Yeah, definitely," I said as I stepped up to the telescope.

As I bent down to peer into the eyepiece, I thought I noticed a faint blue light emanating from the metal cuff strapped to my wrist. Disregarding it as a fluke, I gazed at the celestial view.

Slowly, my field of vision started to blur and fill with white light. At first, I assumed the telescope was having a problem...until the pain started to twirl behind my eyes.

No, no, no! Not now... not in front of Anders. What if the Chairman *was* there again! But there was nothing I could do. I had to let the vision start before I could pull the ripcord. My heart was pounding rapidly in my chest as I braced for the worst.

Suddenly, I was floating above the Gradys' house. I exhaled in relief. No Chairman in sight. I looked around the property. There were several cars at the front of the house but everything else looked normal. Why was I here?

I recognized Joel's truck and Mia's parents' car. Was this tonight's meeting? There were no clocks or watches or anything to indicate the date or time. But it was dark outside—very dark. The only light was from the house, and it refracted off the Shield Wall, causing it to shimmer below me. I turned my head to look at the sky. There was no moon in sight. It seemed like too many coincidences not to be tonight.

As I was wondering why the vision had brought me there, the Shield Wall's blurry shimmer started to disintegrate in front of me. What *was* happening? That shouldn't be possible. My heart started to race. I frantically scanned the area below, looking for an answer.

When the wall completely disappeared, I heard before I saw two figures running down the driveway at top speed. Both were dressed completely in black. I squinted to see their faces more clearly. I could have sworn one of them was Tristan. My heart was hammering in my chest. Clan Hunters!

This was really bad! How had they gotten through the Shield Wall? I had to warn the others. I just hoped I'd be in time. I thought of the most mundane thing I could—mud.

I was back at my home's front yard, gasping for breath and doubled over as Anders held me upright.

"Elin! Are you all right?"

"I'm...fine," I replied, coughing. I didn't have a second to lose—I had to run as fast as I could to warn the Gradys and my friends. "I'm sorry, Andee, but I have to go."

"What are you talking about? You're in no shape to go anywhere. Elin... Elin... what the hel—" But I was already at the tree line of our property, and Anders' voice was fading behind me.

I could tell Anders was in shock. He had just witnessed his baby sister running at an inhuman speed. But I had no choice. I had to use my *megin*. Running through the woods would be shorter and faster than taking a car. Never mind trying to explain to Anders why I suddenly and desperately needed to go to the Gradys'.

Obviously, the fastest way to communicate the danger would've been to call and warn the people at the Gradys', but the Resistance was super cautious about eavesdroppers. They made everyone place their phones and other communication devices in a soundproof box at the beginning of the meeting. The members could only retrieve their devices after the meeting was over—so any warning messages or calls would've been in vain.

I momentarily paused when I saw the blur of my home's Shield Wall. *Thank you, thank you, thank you!* It was still up. I slowed down and passed through it at a normal pace, remembering my encounter from a few days earlier.

A shiver ran up my spine as I thought of the unsuspecting meeting participants. I was fairly positive that since the Clan Hunters had planned an attack on a Resistance meeting, there'd be more than two of them. The Resistance would be completely caught off guard and without anything to defend themselves, given the new moon. I ran as fast as I could despite the burning in my lungs and the taste of blood in my mouth.

I could see lights up ahead. It had to be the Gradys' house. As I got closer, I could see the haze of the Gradys' Shield Wall. It was still up! Relief flooded through me.

Remembering that Tristan and the other Clan Hunter had approached from the front, I ran to the back of the building and up the back-deck steps. I pounded on the back door, breathing heavily.

"Elin, what are you doing here? You know you can't—" Edvin started to say as he opened the door.

"Hunters...here...get...out...now," I interrupted him, gulping for air.

He looked stunned, so I pushed past him into the house. I ran into the living room before anyone else could stop me. At least thirty faces turned to look at me as I stopped in front of the couches.

"Hunters...coming," I gasped.

A heavy murmur ran through the crowd.

"Elin, what do you mean?" Ms. Valistus said as she emerged from the entryway, along with Mr. and Mrs. Grady.

"They...bring... the Shield...Wall...down tonight. I... don't know...how...but they're coming." I managed to say between breaths.

People in the room started to stand, looking anxiously around them for an exit. The murmur became a loud chorus of agitated voices until Mr. Grady emitted a long, piercing whistle.

"No need to panic," he said, projecting his voice above the noise. "We have an escape plan. Everyone will get out. Edvin, please initiate."

Edvin, who had followed me into the living room, nodded and beelined to the dining-room china cabinet. He pulled a laptop from underneath the lowest drawer. He quickly opened it, typed something into the screen, and pressed Enter. There was a low rumbling noise as metal screens covered the windows and doors.

Mr. Grady pressed a few buttons on the TV remote and the entire screen was filled with various camera screens displaying the outside of the house. In the one facing the driveway, we could see two figures dressed in black with seaxes at their waists slowing down to a walk—Tristan and the other Hunter. Loud gasps escaped from a few individuals.

Mia and Joel were trying to make their way to where I was standing. Claire beat them, bringing me a glass of water and a packet of honey. Her light green eyes inspected me as she handed them to me.

"Here, drink and eat," she commanded. "The honey will help replace some of the energy you lost running here. And from what I see, you are going to need all of it tonight."

"Thanks." I took a deep drink of the water and ripped the honey packet open with my teeth.

"You've locked us in!" a panicked voice shouted from the crowd.

"Yeah, now we're sitting ducks for them," another closer, angry voice said.

Somebody else moaned, "We're trapped!"

"Now, now, settle down," Ms. Valistus replied, gesturing soothingly. "I'm sure Liam's plan doesn't end there."

"You're right, Noora. If everyone could please make their way to the basement. Edvin, please show them. You will all find an exit there," Mr. Grady said, motioning for people to move towards the entryway.

Edvin helped usher some of the older members to the door below the second-floor staircase. As I watched them line up in front of the basement stairs, it struck me what a wide age range the Resistance members had. Each had a specific role and made a valuable contribution, but it was taking all of them working together to fight the *Stór-menni*.

"Now, Elin, what else did you see?" Ms. Valistus had sidled up to me. Mr. McHaill wasn't far behind her.

"Not much, really. I pulled out of the vision pretty quickly because I didn't know the exact time of the attack and wanted to get here to warn you."

Mr. McHaill cleared his throat and smoothed the ends of his salt-and-pepper mustache. "Well, very good thing you did...yes, a very good thing indeed. This should not have happened...very curious thing...very curious."

He gave me an absentminded pat on the back and raised a thick eyebrow toward Ms. Valistus. He then headed toward the soundproof lockbox that Mr. Grady had opened and placed on the dining-room table.

"Yes, we do indeed owe you a debt of gratitude. Thank you, Elin. You have saved the Auor Resistance this evening." Ms. Valistus leaned a little closer and whispered, "You didn't encounter anyone else in your vision, did you?"

She gave me a meaningful look. I shook my head in response. Some color rose to my cheeks as she continued to stare at me.

"Are you okay?" Mia finally made it to my side, giving me a big hug. Letting go, she brushed her long black hair out of her caramel-colored face as she scrutinized me.

"Yeah, fine. Just a little tired from running," I replied, giving her a grateful smile.

The hum of the room's conversation was interrupted for a moment as the female Clan Hunter with Tristan smashed a camera at the front of the house.

"No matter. I have another," Mr. Grady said to no one in particular as he punched a few more keys on his remote. Another angle of the front porch popped up on the TV, showing Tristan and the female Hunter now sitting on the porch steps.

"Claire, what's in the basement?" asked Joel, who'd also joined us. His baseball cap was in its familiar skewed position, mostly covering his unruly brown hair, and his brown eyes brimmed with adoration as he looked at Claire.

I glanced toward the entryway, where a line of people had now grown.

"Edvin and Dad spent some time expanding the root cellar," she answered with a wry smile. "It now goes all the way from the edge of the forest to the basement."

"You mean there's a tunnel all the way to the trees from the house?" Joel's eyes were wide as he stared at the basement door with new appreciation.

"Yup, it's our way out in a tight spot...although I don't think we ever imagined this many people using it."

"Claire, you should grab your bags and anything else of importance," Mrs. Grady commanded as she passed us like a whirlwind.

Claire saluted as she hurried off after her mother to gather their essentials. Luckily, the Gradys were already fairly organized, given the weeks of preparations for Aedan's rescue. Since his capture, I'd witnessed a growing pile of go-bags in the laundry room. It made me wonder if anything had been packed for Aedan.

"I'll be right back," I said to Mia.

She gave me a concerned look, but I didn't wait for her response. I pushed past the people in the entryway and hurried up the stairs towards Aedan's bedroom. I knew his room was the farthest down the hall. He'd shared stories with me about the rotational program he and his siblings had on choosing their bedrooms in new homes and how he'd been the lucky one this time.

I opened the closed door into a tidy and sparse bedroom. It was a far cry from the cluttered, keepsake-ridden bedroom that had my name, or my siblings' for that matter. I guessed that Aedan hadn't been able to keep all the childhood and school mementos I was sure he'd garnered along the way. The Gradys' fugitive lifestyle wouldn't have allowed that.

The austere bedroom fanned a growing flame inside me. I knew the damage done by the Chairman's lies was much more significant and far-reaching than just Aedan's keepsakes, but somehow his bedroom captured it in the moment.

On top of his bed sat a medium-sized duffle bag that I assumed was his emergency go-bag. As I went to lift it off the bed, two things on his nightstand caught my eye. One was his iPod, charging on the charger, and the other was a tiny key.

The sight of his iPod made my heart squeeze. There had rarely been an instance where Aedan didn't have it on him—and now he was without it. He'd told me how music was the one constant thing in his life. I'd often teased him about his retro taste, but he'd just vowed to eventually make me a believer. Now I ached to hear some Beatles or Rolling Stones from his collection.

Eyeing the small key, I puzzled for a moment until I remembered Aedan and my conversation from the night of the dance. He had told me how he'd snagged a tiny key that had dropped from Ms. Haugen's keyring. At the time we'd ruled it out as the possible key to the Clan library, but now I wondered what it did open.

I grabbed both Aedan's iPod and the tiny key, stuffing them into my coat pocket as I swung his go-bag over my shoulder.

I hurried back down the stairs in time to witness Mr. Grady and Edvin cheering at the TV, which displayed tiny spider-like robots falling from the metal barrier covering the front door.

"That'll show 'em! Coming to my house," Mr. Grady said with satisfaction as he slapped Edvin on the back.

"Edvin! Liam! I *need* your help getting these bags to the basement." Waving an insistent hand, Mrs. Grady tried to get Edvin's and Mr. Grady's rapt attention away from the TV. "Liam, they're *right* outside. We need to go. I'm sure you're recording this."

Reluctantly, Mr. Grady looked away for a moment. "Yes, dear. Coming! Edvin, go help your mother."

Mrs. Grady shook her head and motioned for Claire to grab a bag. I couldn't believe how calm they were. My stomach was doing backflips at every sound from the front of the door. But then, looking down at five identical black duffle bags waiting on the living-room floor, it dawned on me that this was not their first escape.

"We can help, Mrs. Grady," Mia offered, motioning for Joel to pick up a bag as well.

"Yeah, sure...absolutely," Joel said as he leaned down to grab a handle.

At that moment, the sound of metal shredding and the odor of burning steel began to seep into the entryway.

"Time to go," Mr. Grady said, quickly turning off the TV, grabbing the remaining bag near Edvin, and ushering us towards the basement door. "Can't compete with a Dragon. We should still have about five to ten minutes for our escape. Turn on your headlamps and carefully hurry down now."

Nervous looks were exchanged among our small group as Mr. Grady handed each of us a headlamp. I kept mine off since with my enhanced night vision I didn't really need it. We started down the basement stairs single file. Bringing up the rear, Mr. Grady closed the basement door and slid a sizable bolt into place. A small bit of light leaked down the stairs from underneath the door.

Our small posse collected in the basement at the tunnel entrance. We were the last ones there. I noticed Mr. Grady reach behind a utility shelf and flip something that extinguished the remaining light in the basement and from the door crack above it.

"No need to make it easy for them." He smiled as our eyes briefly met. "Okay, on our way, everyone."

Edvin entered the tunnel first, followed by Mrs. Grady, Mia, Joel, Claire, and me. Now that Mr. Grady had turned off the electricity to the house, the tunnel was pitch black except for the bobbing of headlamps. I turned back to see Mr. Grady pulling another utility shelf in front of the tunnel entrance and then tightly closing the door, which blended in perfectly with the rest of the basement walls. I adjusted Aedan's bag on my shoulder and hurried to catch up with the others.

The tunnel had been dug through the earth but was braced with wooden planks and posts to strengthen it. It was tall enough so that Edvin and Mr. Grady could walk with a slight hunch. But it was also fairly narrow, causing the bag on my shoulder to occasionally bump into the wall and dirt to sprinkle on top of me.

After a few minutes, I could see the others heading up an incline. Before long we were all standing in the root cellar with our breath coming out in puffs in the cold night air.

"Where to?" Mrs. Grady asked as Mr. Grady entered the root cellar.

"Well, we should eventually head to the marina, but the Resistance won't be ready for a good couple of hours yet. Ms. Valistus is bringing up the departure for our trip tonight, but they need time to prepare. And I don't really like the idea of standing around defenseless while we wait," he replied, shaking the loose dirt from his jacket.

"We can go to my house. The Shield Wall is still up there," I interjected. "Plus, only Anders is at home and he'll be happy to help...once he understands. And I already kinda owe him an explanation."

"What do you mean, Elin?" Claire asked.

"Well...I sorta had to leave in a hurry after having my vision... and Anders was with me," I said, looking down at my boots.

"Oh...I see," Claire responded.

There was a moment of silence as knowing looks were exchanged in the headlamp light.

"What about us?" Mia said, motioning toward herself and Joel.

"I don't think we have a choice right now. We have to stick together. We don't know how much the Hunters know about each of us, so it's too risky to send you kids home right now. Our best plan is to head to the safety of the Shield Wall at Elin's. We can then make a better plan," Mr. Grady directed. "One of us should go out first to scout the route to Elin's and make sure it's clear. The path will initially bring us back by our house before we can head away."

"I'll go," I volunteered.

"No, I don't think—" Mrs. Grady started.

"I'm the only one with *megin*. I won't be using my vision...just my speed and strength. And I'll have the Hunters outmatched there...at least right now. It just makes the most sense," I interrupted.

Mrs. Grady and Mia were still making sounds of protest when

Mr. Grady said, "She's right. As much as I don't like it, it does make the most sense…but Elin…Edvin and I will be right behind you. You are the ultimate prize for these Hunters, and not even with your speed and strength can you take on all six at the same time."

I involuntarily gulped. I hadn't really thought about that when I offered to scout. But looking at the faces around me, I knew I didn't have a choice. I was the only one with any kind of advantage over the Hunters.

"I'm good. I'll go." I handed Aedan's bag to Joel and zipped up my pockets, securing Aedan's iPod and tiny key inside.

Everyone turned off their headlamps on Mr. Grady's instructions as he and Edvin helped lift the root-cellar door open. I scrambled out into the icy night air. We were on the south side of the house, which meant that I needed to head north through the woods. There was a big, wide stream just to the east on the Gradys' property that was difficult to cross, especially in the snow and ice. And we just didn't have that kind of time with Hunters lurking.

"Okay, Elin. We're ready. We won't be able to keep up with your *megin* speed, so scout a little and then come back so we can keep tabs," Mr. Grady whispered.

I nodded as I tightened the laces on my boots. Then without further discussion, I ran to the edge of the house, staying in the woods. I stopped behind a tree for a moment and listened. All was quiet, except for a few shouts and curses echoing from the house. I turned around and ran back to find Mr. Grady and Edvin.

They had progressed through the snow and trees to about a third of the distance I had covered—which was fairly admirable, considering the conditions. Mr. Grady waved to me and then tapped something into his cell phone. I guessed it was to let the others know the coast was clear. I gave them a quick thumbs-up before I turned to head back.

This time I ran all the way past the house to the edge of the road. I again stopped, hiding behind another tree as I listened.

Nothing.

Just the occasional creak of a tree branch bending under the weight of snow. It seemed like even the animals found it too cold to be out tonight.

I turned back and ran to the northern edge of the house, pausing to listen. I could hear my heart rhythmically beating against my chest. I saw some flashes of light from inside the Gradys' house. The front door was wide open, with its metal cover discarded on the front-porch steps. I was just about to start running again when I heard a branch snap somewhere close by.

I froze.

"It is nice to see you again, Elin."

Tristan. I recognized the voice immediately. My stomach dropped. I turned. Tristan was directly in my path towards the others.

"What are you doing here?" I managed to spit out.

"Well, I told you I would be back for you. So, here I am." Tristan started to walk toward me.

"This isn't even my house." I backpedaled away from him. "Why are you here?" If I could just keep him distracted and moving north, the others might have a chance to sneak by.

"Don't worry. You were next on our list. But we had to start somewhere. And turns out there's something unusual about the unregistered Clan member you helped us capture," Tristan replied, sneering a little. He was clearly enjoying needling me—especially about Aedan.

"I don't understand. What do you mean?" I took faster steps backward. Tristan was matching my pace. Good.

"Oh, so you don't know. Well, his family isn't at all what they seem...apparently, their name isn't Grady at all." Tristan smiled with satisfaction.

"You're lying. I don't believe you... I mean, just look at who you work for. The Chairman is the biggest liar of them all!"

"The Chairman is the most respected Clan member there is. Just ask anyone. It is the Resistance who are the terrorists." Tristan's smile vanished as he defended his leader.

We were almost to the bend in the stream. If I could draw Tristan some distance past that point, the others would have a clear path to my house.

"I did ask, Tristan. And the members of the other three Clans resent being designated as dead."

Tristan shook his head. "Now *you* are the one lying! The Chairman kept us safe while the other Clans battled and died off."

"Hate to break it to you, Tristan...but your Chairman *lied*. The other Clans are alive and well."

In his anger, Tristan started to gain ground on me. I didn't want to use my *megin* until absolutely necessary. I looked around for anything else to put between us.

Suddenly, as Tristan was about to launch himself at me, Edvin came flying out of the forest, tackled Tristan, and knocked him out with one punch.

I let out my breath. I hadn't even realized I was holding it. My head spun with everything that had just happened—my conversation with Tristan, seeing him again, and Edvin's sudden appearance.

Stunned, I stared at Tristan's still body. Somehow he looked so innocent lying there in the white snow.

"Come on, Elin! He's fine. Time to go," Edvin said as he grabbed my hand, pulling me back into the safety of the forest.

The rest of the group was anxiously waiting among the evergreens.

"Are you okay?" Mia asked, her worried brown eyes inspecting me.

"Are there others, Elin?" Mr. Grady grabbed my hand to help me over a rotting log. I shook my head. I wasn't sure who I was responding to—Mia or Mr. Grady.

Mrs. Grady came over to give me a quick hug. "That was too close, Elin. You really shouldn't have taken the risk."

"Come on, guys. We've got to go!" Edvin said, encouraging everyone to keep moving towards the road a few paces north.

Just then, we heard a commotion behind us. Voices from the house shouted Tristan's name—and they were getting closer.

We began to hurry through the frozen trees, each of us scrambling over icy rocks and fallen logs. We tried to be quiet, but there was no shushing our racket. Snow crunched and branches broke as we pushed toward the road.

The voices behind us were getting closer. I could hear one of them shout, "Over there! They're over there."

"Catch them," a female voice ordered. "Don't let them get away!"

Strong beams from their flashlights bounced around us. I glanced over my shoulder and saw Mia trailing the group. The duffle bag she clutched was dragging through the snow. I turned and ran back to her.

"What are you doing?" She panted. "You're the one they—"

I reached for the bag she was carrying. "Here. Give it to me!"

Using my *megin*, I easily slung it over my shoulder. I grabbed her hand and pulled her along, silencing any further argument.

I could hear swift steps behind us. The Clan Hunters were gaining ground.

Then without warning, something hurtled past us, striking a

nearby tree. With a glance, I saw a small dagger embedded in the middle of the trunk.

I tugged on Mia's hand pulling her faster. "Hurry, Mia—we've got to hurry!"

Another *whoosh* sounded close by. And then another. Somewhere behind us, I heard a female voice shout, "DRENG, STOP THAT! We need them alive! ARNIS—Arnis, send in the runners!"

I raced through the trees, following the bobbing shapes of Claire and Mrs. Grady as they weaved through the evergreens. Then, out of the corner of my eye, I saw Joel swinging at something with the duffle bag he carried.

There, sprinting next to him, was a mechanical thing that looked like a black mushroom top with two wiry, elongated legs. It must be one of the "runners", I thought. The machine easily matched Joel's pace with its red light bouncing wildly as it tried to find its target.

I was about to go to Joel's aid when a similar runner appeared behind Mia. It bounded like a gazelle unhindered by the snow as its thin legs stretched and compressed with unnatural grace. I pulled on Mia's hand, urging her forward.

My heart hammered in my chest. There was no way we could outrun these creatures.

I heard Joel cry out in frustration as the mechanical beast avoided his blows. Suddenly, Mr. Grady was next to him. He grabbed Joel's arm and pushed him through two tightly growing evergreens. Mr. Grady quickly followed—but he held on to a single thick branch.

Whack! Mr. Grady had let go of the branch as the runner came between the two trees. The machine flew into a large tree trunk and fell to the ground motionless.

Tugging Mia forward, I noticed a red beam bouncing on her

coat. The second runner had caught up with us. Wildly, I scanned around us for a similar set of low-branched trees that Mr. Grady had used. But there was none.

The only weapon-like thing I saw was a thick, broken branch sticking out of the snow. I grabbed it as we ran past. Then, a few paces in front of us, I saw a large evergreen that would have made a perfect Christmas tree. It had dense green branches that stretched out evenly. I rushed Mia behind it away from the runner. Then, I abruptly stopped, motioning to Mia not to move and to stay silent. I clutched the branch like a baseball bat.

I held my breath as I listened.

I could hear a mechanical clicking as the runner searched for us. Then, I heard rapid movement as its beam located us.

As it came around the tree, I let out my breath and swung hard like Anders had taught me with an actual bat.

Thwack! The branch made contact with the mushroom top's underside. The runner hurtled out of the snow and landed several feet away. Its red light fluttered a few times and then disappeared.

"*Wow*, next time we play—remind me to pick you for my team," Mia said, her eyes wide.

I grinned. "Come on! We better move. There might be more, and I'm sure the Hunters aren't far behind."

Mia and I began running again, pushing against dead branches that still clung to their trees. A few moments later, we heard frustrated shouts behind us as the Hunters found the disabled runners. While their bellows warmed my belly, they also revealed just how close the Hunters were to us.

Just when I thought we would never make the road in time, we broke through the trees and onto the road's embankment. For a moment, I felt relieved until I realized we were fully exposed. We no longer had the evergreens to hide us. What had seemed like a sound plan moments earlier was now a mistake.

Glancing around, Mr. Grady must've had the same thought. "Quick! Everyone into the forest on the other side."

We scrambled up the steep snowy embankment, our feet slipping and sliding. When we reached the gravel road, I heard the rumble of a car approaching.

I turned and saw headlights coming our way. Was it the Clan Hunters? Had they sent a car after us?

My heart pounded as we stood frozen in our tracks.

There was no way we could get to the other side before the car reached us. Mr. Grady turned his head left to right, seeming to weigh which was the better of the two bad options.

Behind us, I could see the flickering of the Hunters' flashlights between the trees. They were almost upon us. Mr. Grady quickly started for the other side of the road motioning for us to follow him.

We didn't make it.

We were in the middle of the road when the approaching vehicle's headlights ensnared us. I could hear the Hunters' jubilant cries as they emerged from the forest and saw us.

Mr. Grady shouted, "Keep going! Make for the trees."

He waved us forward while he remained fixed to his spot. It was clear he intended to stay to slow the Hunters down. Edvin joined him as the others moved toward the dark side of the road.

"No, Liam! I can't leave you two." Mrs. Grady had a desperate look on her face.

Mr. Grady kissed his wife. "You have to, Dara! Just think of Aedan."

A lump formed in my throat. I couldn't bear the thought of more separation and pain for the Gradys.

The vehicle rolled to a quick stop. Its bright headlights blinded me. Shielding my eyes, I peered at it. Something looked strangely familiar about it.

"Wait!" I exclaimed. "It's Anders!"

I recognized the odd-shaped headlights on his truck. He must have come looking for me. I heard the truck door creak open.

"Elli, what are you *doing* in the middle of the road? I've been looking everywhere for you."

"Oh, Andee! I'm *soooo* happy to see you!" I replied, running to hug him.

"Elli, what is goin—" The rest of the group rushed out of the darkness toward his truck. "What on earth?"

"Hurry! Everyone jump in." I turned to Anders. "It's a long story. I'll tell you all about it when we get home, but right now we need to get to our house as fast as we can."

"Um...okay...but you're *gonna* start talking in the car," Anders replied.

EIGHT

The Marina

TRISTAN

I sat on the living-room sofa in the unregistered member's house, nursing my right cheek with an ice pack that Thyra had found in the freezer. Someone had started a fire in the fireplace, and it lit the room with a yellow glow, warming my cold, achy muscles. The fire crackled and spat as it encountered sap in the logs, breaking the silence in the room.

The rest of the team was still busy searching the nearby forest for any Resistance stragglers. Given the close chase they had with Elin's group, they hoped to find one or two members so the night wouldn't be a complete loss. Somehow we had gone from certain victory to absolute defeat within a matter of minutes.

Earlier, when we entered the house and confirmed it was vacant, Thyra had immediately ordered Fenja and me to do a sweep of the exterior. For efficiency, I had gone east of the house and Fenja had gone west.

While I encountered Elin and was knocked out, Fenja had found and tracked several footprints in the snow in the southern section of the woods. She'd followed them until eventually she had stumbled upon me unconscious in the snow. Quickly realizing that the people responsible must still be nearby, she'd summoned the others with her Communicator. And the unsuccessful chase had commenced.

Meanwhile, Magnus, who was not much of a runner, had carried me back to the house to recover in its warmth, according to Fenja.

"There's no one else," Bera said as she flopped down on the couch next to me. "We searched everywhere. I just can't figure out how they got out of the house. I mean, we had them cornered for sure."

"Well, it doesn't really matter at this point," Thyra said, looking up from her SRT. She had sat down at the dining-room table with several devices in front of her. "Command isn't going to care how they escaped, just that they did."

Thyra ran her fingers through her loose brown hair, which hung framing her face. It was the first time I had seen Thyra look uneasy.

"I think it's best that we leave out from our reports any mention of the Resistance meeting at the house. There's no benefit to any of us in having lost more of an opportunity than just capturing a few fugitives."

Emerging from different directions in the house, the other team members collected in the living room as Thyra spoke. Each of them seemed to weigh her words.

Ivar and Arnis looked at each other and said in unison, "Agreed."

"Works for me," Magnus said as he took another bite of a rotisserie chicken leg that he must have found in the kitchen.

Dreng gave a curt nod as he sat down on a dining-room chair.

"Sure," Bera said with a dismissive hand wave.

"Fine," I said while rubbing my jaw, which still felt like a ton of bricks had hit it.

The only person who had not spoken was Fenja. She was leaning against the doorframe, looking slightly uncomfortable.

"Fenja? We all have to be on the same page about this," Thyra said as she eyed the Clan Hunter.

The rest of the team's eyes shifted to Fenja, waiting for her response. None of us wanted to add any more failures to our Clan file than was absolutely necessary. But we all knew the Hunter rules. If even one of us had a different version of the night's events, we would all be facing a harsh interrogation on our return to Falinvik. So it had to be a unanimous decision.

"What's the problem, Fenja?" Arnis asked, twirling a small gadget of unknown purpose in his hands. "There were no SASUs on this raid, so there's no video, nothing to prove what actually happened...just us."

Fenja's eyes flashed with anger. "This wasn't how I was trained. The truth is the truth...regardless of how we might wish it to be otherwise."

Magnus lowered the chicken leg from his mouth. *"What?* Are you suggesting we double up on the consequences for tonight?" He aggressively pointed the chicken leg at Fenja as he spoke. "Some of us have a lot more to lose here. There's no way I'm going back to the Ginnungagap guard towers. So you need to make the right decision here."

Ivar and Arnis murmured angry agreements. The number of infractions a Clan member had on their file determined the severity of the consequences they faced at their interrogation. Magnus's reaction reminded me of my own jeopardy if the mission was a failure. My body's current aches and pains seemed rather minor, all of sudden.

"Now, now...we need to give Fenja a moment to think this

through," Thyra said placatingly. "She may not have realized what's truly at stake here. As you know, *my uncle* gave this assignment specifically to our team because he holds *me* in high confidence...and he ultimately expects us to triumph no matter how many tries it takes. I'd hate to have to report that one team member's failings was the cause of tonight's mishap...but, as it is crucial for the rest of the mission to go on, all options are on the table."

Thyra kept a neutral expression as she spoke, but Magnus, Ivar, and Arnis could not help smiling with satisfaction as they took in what Thyra had said. The threat in her statement was clear —and another reminder not to cross her.

Fenja shifted uncomfortably. "All right...fine...there was no Resistance meeting."

"Great, we're all agreed then." Thyra rose. "Now for our next steps. We know that the Unregistered's family couldn't have gotten far. This is an island, after all. Any thoughts as to where they may have gone?"

"Shouldn't we go after the Dormant Descendant next and forget about the fugitives?" Bera asked as she leaned back on the sofa.

"It's too late," Arnis replied. "We've lost the moon window to bring down her Shield Wall. This was a tightly scheduled operation. Ivar and I were supposed to move to work on her Shield Wall right after we brought down the Unregistered's, but obviously plans changed."

The faces in the room seemed to sink even further. We had lost any hope of redemption by at least capturing Elin.

"Well, we can't go back and change things now. The only way is forward. So, what do we know of the current situation?" Thyra asked, leaning against a cabinet in the dining area. "We know from Tristan's encounter with the Dormant and our subsequent chase that she was with a group. Who they were, we can't be sure...but a good guess would be Resistance members. And if I were in their shoes, knowing that we brought one Shield Wall down, I'd be pretty anxious to move her to a safer location than where she currently resides."

"Yes, I see. Are you suggesting an ambush?" Fenja asked.

"What do you mean, 'ambush'? We can't attack if they're behind the Shield Wall," Magnus said, having been more focused on finishing his chicken leg than the actual conversation.

Bera rolled her eyes. "The whole point is that the Resistance is going to move the Dormant to another location, probably tonight."

"Why would they move her?"

"*Argh*...Magnus! Pay attention. Thyra *just* suggested that the Resistance thinks that we can bring the Dormant's Shield Wall down as well," Dreng said.

"But we can't," Magnus replied.

A collective groan escaped the rest of the team.

"*What*? What did I say?" Magnus looked baffled as he dropped the chicken bone on a nearby table and wiped his face with his sleeve.

Thyra closed her SRT. "Never mind that now. The point is that we *are* setting up an ambush. We watch the Dormant's home and wait for an opportunity. We know it'll most likely be a Resistance transport that picks her up tonight, so our *Smá-menn* exposure risk is minimal...plus, we might capture a bonus Resistance member or two in the bargain. But we've got to hurry—there's not a moment to lose. We don't know how quickly they'll act."

"Are you sure they will move her? The last ferry left already. Where would they take her tonight?" I asked as I rose from the couch.

"Nothing is certain, but there's a high likelihood...and I for one don't want to miss any opportunity to regain our footing on this mission. Plus, it doesn't really matter where they're taking her as long as we intercept them in the process," Thyra said, smiling slyly.

The team quickly gathered their equipment and loaded it into the Suburban. We then piled into the same seats as before except for Dreng and Thyra. Thyra now sat in the front passenger seat, and Dreng sat on the other side of Magnus. I could feel the seat move as Dreng restlessly shifted around, trying to find a tolerable position next to Magnus's bulk.

"I suggest that we pick up the other vehicle. I think having two might be useful in this situation," Dreng said.

I wasn't entirely sure which "situation" he was referring to—the ambush or his current seat next to Magnus. Either way, it sounded like a good idea.

"I agree. A second vehicle would be useful," I added.

"It's not far from here. It will take a total of ten minutes," Bera said.

Thyra thought for a moment. "Yes, fine. We'll drop off Tristan, Dreng, and Magnus to surveil the Dormant's house, and the rest of us will go pick up the other vehicle."

Once we were a few yards from Elin's driveway, the Suburban deposited Dreng, Magnus, and me on the side of the road. We quickly moved into the woods, not only to conceal ourselves but also hoping that the trees might shield us from the icy wind. Once settled, we watched the driveway for any signs of activity, but there was nothing.

After about five minutes of standing still in the snow, I stomped my feet on the ground, trying to drive some warm blood down to my toes. Magnus and Dreng were equally occupied with trying to keep warm when we heard a rumble of a vehicle coming down the driveway.

I glanced at Dreng and Magnus's drawn faces. It was clear they felt the same dread as I did. This might be our chance to capture Elin, but there was nothing the three of us could do without our powers or a vehicle.

I saw Dreng tap his Communicator. "Ummm...Thyra...we have movement."

"Now?"

"Yes, unclear as to the vehicle's occupants."

"We're four minutes out. Note the vehicle and direction. Bera, step on it!"

At that moment, Anders' truck rolled to a quick stop at the driveway's end. The three of us seemed to hold our breath in unison. His truck turned in our direction. We clambered to get the best vantage point while remaining concealed as he drove by us.

"Um...Thyra?"

"Yes?"

"We have one individual leaving the premises. According to Tristan, it's the *Smá-menn* brother."

I heard Thyra let out a deep breath. "Okay, good. We're two minutes out."

A few minutes later, the black Suburban and a silver car rolled to a stop in front of our hiding spot. We scrambled out of the woods, eager to get warm. My fingers and toes felt like icicles. We hurried to the vehicles.

Bera was still driving the Suburban, but Ivar was behind the wheel of the silver vehicle. Determined not to get stuck in the seat next to Magnus, both Dreng and I headed towards Ivar. Dreng immediately went to the driver's door and opened it.

"Out. I'll take over from here."

Ivar looked at Dreng for a moment, but quickly seeing that it was useless to argue, he switched to the back seat. I climbed into the front passenger seat and reached to turn the heat to high.

"Dreng?" Thyra's voice came through the Communicator.

"Yes?"

"You head in the direction behind you. Find somewhere discreet to wait where you can still see the driveway. We'll head in the other direction and do the same."

"Understood."

Slowly rolling down the road, we saw a small pullout on the other side. Dreng quickly pulled into it. We could still see the driveway, although at a distance.

To maintain some appearance of normalcy, whenever a vehicle passed us, Dreng would pick up his *Smá-menn* mobile phone and pretend to talk on it. It wasn't much of a cover but hopefully left plausible doubt in any inquiring mind. None of us relished, or even suggested, turning off the car motor and thereby the heat.

After what seemed like a long time, three large white Suburbans passed us and turned into Elin's driveway.

"Are you seeing this?" Dreng asked through his Communicator.

"Yup, be prepared and ready. We'll intercept them before they reach the main road. Use your vehicle to block the road if they come your direction."

"Yes, Ma'am."

A few moments later, we saw the first headlights emerge from the driveway. The first vehicle pulled out in our direction, quickly followed by a second vehicle, which headed in Thyra's direction. The last vehicle again pulled out in our direction.

"Thyra? Thyra, what do you want us to do?" Dreng asked, clutching the steering wheel.

"Follow them! We'll take the one that came our way."

The silver car spat gravel from the road as Dreng roared the motor to life. As we came closer to the intersection with the island's main road, we could see the white vehicles part ways again. One turned south and the other turned north. The Resistance had clearly come prepared.

"Which way? Which one should we follow?" Dreng yelled as we closed in on the intersection.

"Go south. The marina is that way," I instructed. "A boat is the only way off this island for *Smá-menn*."

Dreng complied. The car's tires skated a little as he violently turned the vehicle onto the main road heading south. We could see the taillights of the white Suburban ahead of us. They were still a good length in front of us. Dreng increased the vehicle's speed to keep up.

As we came into town, the Suburban instead of slowing down sped up, taking some sharp turns through different streets. It was clearly not heading toward the marina.

Dreng was doing an admirable job of staying with the vehicle until a large trash truck backed into the street right in front of us, separating us from our prey. The white Suburban sped away, leaving us in the trash truck's billowing steam.

"*Odin's beard!*" Dreng yelled as he slapped his hands against the steering wheel. "Now what?"

"Hmm...I'm pretty sure that was a decoy. It didn't even try for the marina," I said, still thinking through my theory. "I think they're going to try to get off this island tonight—there is too much at stake for them to stay—but like I said, the only way for them to do so is by boat. I think we should head to the town marina and wait for them to show."

"You're that sure, are you?" Ivar asked. "What if they aren't trying to get off? You're willing to risk the mission on your hunch?"

Ivar's tone was rubbing me the wrong way. I was the lieutenant. What was he besides a lowly tech?

"I am. Besides, what else are we going to do? We lost both

Resistance vehicles. They are long gone by now...trying to pick up their trail is a lost cause."

"Maybe we should check in with Thyra first," Dreng replied.

"Fine. Check in with Thyra. You can tell her how we lost the Resistance."

Dreng glanced at me, looking uncomfortable as he tapped his Communicator. "Um...Thyra? We...um... the Resistance vehicles got away."

"*WHAT?*"

"Well...you see...they split up...and we followed the one going south—"

"I see. I don't need the details now. Where are you?"

"We are in town," I answered. "I thought we could go watch the marina. The fugitives may try to leave the island tonight."

"Weren't you the one saying the last ferry left already? I doubt they'd risk going into the icy waters at night without a large boat. There's sure to be ice chunks in the waters by now. No, I don't think they'll go tonight...but by all means, drive by the town marina and see."

"Which way did they go?" I heard Magnus ask in the background. "I don't see them."

"*By Frieda!* We just lost them!" Bera yelled in the background. "These Resistance drivers are tricky devils!"

"Well, that's it then," Thyra said. She sounded deflated and tired. "We regroup at the Unregistered's house. We'll get some rest there and contact Command for leads in the morning. Tristan, if you want to carry out your hunch about the marina, be my guest... but unless you see signs of a large boat, I wouldn't bother contacting the rest of the team."

"There, you see? No point," Ivar said as Thyra signed off. "We should just go join the rest of the team...and get some sleep and food before it's all gone."

"Dreng, take us by the town marina," I said, ignoring Ivar's groans from the back seat.

We were only a couple of blocks away, so it didn't take long for Dreng to circle back to the marina. He drove to the end parking lot on the causeway and stopped as we looked at the boats in the harbor. The only movement was from the few fishing boats still in the marina, shifting with the current. There were no larger boats or people on any of the docks.

"Now can we go?" Ivar asked.

Ignoring him again, I instructed Dreng to drive along the road to the Old Boat Club. As I recalled from the Harvest Dance, it too had a marina, although a smaller one. Dreng did as I asked without comment as it was the general direction that we needed to go anyway.

The gates to the boat club parking lot were closed as we drove by, so a closer look at the marina was impossible. However, oddly, a few of the island's courtesy hiker-pickup vans were parked near the marina entrance. I remarked on it.

"They probably just use it as a storage facility for the extra vans during the off-season," Dreng answered.

"Yeah...you are probably right," I replied, although something about it still nagged at me.

Dreng continued driving past the boat club, back towards the Unregistered's home.

NINE

Ice Breakers

ELIN

The five-minute ride home was spent trying to explain to Anders...well, everything. But it only left him more confused and upset than ever. I *had* to admit that five minutes was hardly enough time to explain anything very well—let alone everything that had happened over the last few months or even that night.

Anders stared at me in bewilderment. "What the *hel*"—Mrs. Grady gave Anders a disapproving look—"*Haaalloween candy*, Elin! I can't believe you kept all of this from *me*."

"It was to keep you safe, Andee." I tried to explain.

Ignoring my feeble attempt, he continued, "So, let me get this straight: you all have abilities, but only Elli has abilities right now...because she is a Dormant Descendant...or because it's part of her unique ability—you're not really sure which. And Hunters are after you because they kidnapped Aedan about a month ago...and they've now invaded your home." Anders had a look of disbelief mixed with something more serious as he recounted back to us what he'd garnered from the conversation.

I was fairly certain that if it had been only me trying to explain the situation to Anders, he would've been ready to check me into a hospital. However, he couldn't ignore the six other people around the dining-room table staring at him earnestly.

"Yes...well...mostly...It'll suffice for a quick summary of the situation," Mr. Grady replied, taking a sip of the hot tea in front of him.

"So...um...what's to stop these Hunters from attacking our home next?" Anders asked, glancing out the window.

"Well...you see, there's this Shield Wall—it's invisible to you— that the Hunters can't pass through....and we've got one protecting our house," I explained.

"Why didn't the Gradys have one?"

"Uh...They did...but the Hunters managed to bring it down somehow." My plan to reassure Anders was failing.

"I see...so how *exactly* are we safer here?" Anders asked, cutting to the chase.

Mr. Grady cleared his throat. "An excellent point, Anders. First: your Shield Wall is still up. Second: the Hunters have lost the element of surprise. And third: you, Anders, should be perfectly safe. The Hunters can't assume that you know anything about our world...and as long as you pretend not to know, they'll leave you alone, as it would cause them serious problems back home to expose our world to a Mannlegur."

"Mannlegur?"

"Normal human," Joel piped up, trying to be helpful.

"Okay...what about the rest of you? And what about Elin? Didn't you say she's someone they particularly want?"

"All good questions. As you can see, everything's in a bit of flux at the moment...but rest assured that we're working on it. Most of us are leaving Auor in a few hours to rescue Aedan. For Elin, Mia, and Joel...we'll have to make arrangements with the

Resistance for some kind of added protection," Mr. Grady answered, stroking his chin as he pondered the predicament.

"We should come with you...to rescue Aedan, that is," I said. This might be my chance to turn things around, I thought.

"Absolutely *not!*" Anders interjected before I could continue. "You've already been in more danger over the last few months than I realized. The last thing you're going to do now is go traipsing into the lion's den."

"I totally agree with Anders. Besides, we still don't know how your visions and the Chairman's abilities are connected. The prior concerns are still valid...despite this kerfuffle with the Hunters," Mr. Grady said.

My frustration was quickly rising to the surface. "I'm not just going to sit here and let my family become more endangered as the Hunters become bolder and more desperate. It's not safe for them —or us—to stay here—"

"Hold on a minute," Claire interrupted. "I may have a solution. We already established earlier in the week that our journey to Falinvik will take us right by the path to Thordalr. We know Elin needs her own medal to gain full control over her power. And we know Sigrid Malmr lives near Thordalr. Going to the tiny village would be a safe trip for Elin, Mia, and Joel since we'd see them more than halfway there. And the *Stór-menni* would never suspect or find them at Sigrid's...especially considering the lengths she's gone to in order to conceal herself."

"Hmmm...that's a very interesting idea, Claire. We could hit multiple birds with one stone." Mr. Grady stopped speaking and looked at Mrs. Grady. "What do you think, dear?"

Mrs. Grady thought for a moment. "It would certainly take the kids out of harm's way until the Resistance can regroup and we're back with Aedan. Plus, Sigrid is one of the best Nordri medal Forgers I've ever known. How she was able to hide that fact from the *Stór-menni* is a mystery in itself. And Elin having her own medal would definitely strengthen her protection against the Chairman's abilities."

Mr. Grady turned to Anders. "What do you think?"

"You say this medal thing is something Elin needs, right?" All of us nodded. "And you can trust this Sigrid person?"

"Yes, a hundred percent. She has helped hundreds of Clan members escape from the *Stór-menni*...including us. She is a unique personality, but completely trustworthy," Mr. Grady responded.

"Well, then...I think it's up to Elin, Mia, and Joel." Anders looked at me. "Mom and Dad think that you're still going to Paris, which is a perfect excuse."

I cringed a little.

"What?"

"The Paris trip was the original cover story."

"Oh...so it's not real?"

"Um, no. But you're right...it does work perfectly." I hastily continued before Anders could really digest the fact that the original rescue plan had included me. "I'm good with going to Thordalr... Mia? Joel?" Anything that got me closer to where Aedan was a good thing in my book. It might give me a way to still help him somehow.

"I'll go, but what do I tell my parents? Don't we leave tonight?" Mia asked.

Joel nodded. "I'm with her on both counts: ready to go but need an excuse."

We all instinctively leaned back in our chairs. You could've heard a pin drop in the room with everyone lost in thought. Then, after a few moments, Anders suddenly straightened in his chair with a sly smile on his face.

"I've got it! We can tell your parents that a couple of students dropped out of the Paris trip and there are now two already-paid-for spots open. You and Joel have been invited, but you've gotta leave tonight because...um...there's an impending airport-worker strike."

We all turned to look at Anders. His story was good...perfect, in fact.

"What? I didn't go to college for nothing. Besides, someone is always striking in Paris." He grinned proudly, leaning back in his chair with his hands interlaced behind his head.

"Okay, good then." Mr. Grady looked at his watch. "We have about two more hours before the Resistance boats will be ready to go. Joel and Mia need to get to their homes to pack and explain their sudden trip to Paris. I think the safest option there is for Anders to take them and then bring them to the marina. Anders, you good with that?" Anders nodded. "Meanwhile, Elin can get her things ready here. I'll let Ms. Valistus know the new plan and that we need secure transport to the marina from this house."

As our plan to leave Auor was being arranged, the situation at the house quickly spiraled into a perilous high-wire act when my parents arrived home early from their evening out.

Luckily, Anders had just finished concealing Mia and Joel in the back seat of his truck and was somehow able to calmly greet my parents—and not spill the beans. But inside the house, it was a very different story.

Upon seeing my parents drive up our driveway, a mad scramble commenced to find a sufficiently large hiding place for the Gradys and their black duffle bags—given that the sight of them and their luggage in the middle of the living room might've seemed slightly odd to my parents.

Complicating things further was the fact that the hiding spot also needed to be somewhere from which they could discreetly exit once the time came, making the upstairs bedrooms impractical. Plus, we didn't know how long it would be until the Resistance's transports showed up, so outside was off the list as well. It was simply too cold for the Gradys to wait out there.

Finally, at the last minute, it dawned on me—the back porch. Even though it wasn't heated, it was a covered porch with double-paned windows and thick walls.

Whispering promises of a forthcoming space heater, I helped the Gradys stuff themselves and their duffle bags into the small space just as my parents turned the lock on the front door. With a quick pull of the backdoor's insulating curtain that blocked the draft and, more importantly, the view onto the back porch, I turned to greet my parents as they entered the kitchen.

"Hi, Mom, Dad. How was dinner?" I nervously fiddled with a teacup on the counter that hadn't quite made it into the dishwasher.

"Hi, sweetie. Dinner was fine. It was so good to see the Petersons. You know they just finished remodeling the kitchen, and you wouldn't believe that change. It looks so much bigger, Elin," my mom prattled as she finished peeling off another layer of clothing.

My dad headed for the stove, where the still-hot teakettle sat. "Freezing out there tonight. I'll put the kettle on. Dear, would you like a cup?"

"Careful, Dad, it's *still* hot!"

"Oh, did you just make some?" Using a hot mitt, my dad picked up the kettle to test the water level. "You know, Elin, it would boil a lot faster if you didn't put so much water in here."

I nodded, hoping the extra water wouldn't draw further scrutiny. "Yeah, uh-huh."

"Where was Anders going? He barely stopped to say hello," my mom said.

"Um...he...well, he...uh, wanted some ice cream. He went to make a run to the store. We're out."

"In this weather?" My mom shook her head in bewilderment.

I shrugged. "I guess when you have a craving for something, the temperature outside doesn't matter." My voice squeaked. I tried to draw a deep breath discreetly to calm myself.

"Well, I hope he hurries home. I don't like you kids driving on nights like these. It's bound to get colder tonight, with more ice building up on the roads," my dad said as he busied himself with finding his favorite herbal tea.

"Speaking of which," I said, trying to appear calm and sound casual. "I have some news. The Paris trip is leaving tonight. Apparently there is an impending airport strike or something...so the organizers are coming to pick me up soon."

"You're leaving tonight? Why didn't you call us?" My mom turned to look at me with a stunned expression. She glanced at the wall clock. "I don't understand. How are you going? The last ferry is just about to leave. I think you'd much better wait until morning."

"*Mommm*...it's not like it's my choice. We have to catch a flight tonight or risk not being able to go at all. Besides, I think they're chartering a boat to get us to the mainland or something."

"Well, this all sounds a bit sudden to me. Perhaps we should rethink the trip. Especially if there are strikes in Paris...is it really safe for you to be visiting right now?" my dad asked, cradling his fresh cup of tea.

"Dad...there's *always* strikes in Paris," I replied, relying on what Anders had said earlier. I had to convince them—everything depended on it. "And this might be my only opportunity to go. Besides, Mia and Joel are now coming and their parents are okay with it."

So maybe the last part was a bit of a stretch since I didn't exactly know how Mia's and Joel's conversations with their parents were going, but hey, these were desperate times. Plus, parental peer pressure could be very powerful.

My dad turned to my mom. "What do you think, dear?"

"Well...it *is* a wonderful opportunity for her, Leif. And if Mia's parents are okay with the arrangements...they're usually so careful about these things...then it's probably safe. It's a school trip, after all. And your teacher Mr. Tibadeau will be with you, right?"

"Yup, uh-huh. He'll definitely be there," I answered. It wasn't a lie. My French teacher, also a Resistance member, had been assigned to the rescue mission, so technically he'd be on the trip with us—at least some part of the way.

"Well...if you're sure, dear," my dad said, still clearly apprehensive. My mom nodded. "Then okay."

"'Then, 'okay I can go'?"

"Yes, Elin, you can go. Since your mom thinks it's fine, then it's fine by me. I'm not happy with the school over this fly-by-night departure...but I suppose that can't be helped."

My mom clapped her hands together, an excited smile on her face. "Well, Elin... you best go pack. Do you need any help?"

Given that I was packing for a very different kind of trip than my parents expected, I quickly assured my mom that I could handle it. Before they could second-guess their decision, I encouraged my parents to go enjoy the crackling fire in the living-room fireplace. The living room also just happened to be the farthest place inside the house from the back porch, making it the safest place for my parents—and the Gradys.

As my parents settled onto the couch, I rushed around the house packing the necessary items. I also managed to slip a space heater to the grateful Gradys huddling on the back porch.

The rest of the evening was relatively unflustered. A few close

calls with my parents and the Gradys, but nothing I didn't manage
to divert—until the transports arrived.

There was a bit of confusion when three white Suburbans
came and left without so much as a word. The Gradys had exited
the comfort of the back porch, ready to depart ,when the vehicles
had abruptly turned around in the driveway and left.

Adding to the chaos, the Gradys were left scrambling for a
hiding place in the front yard when my mom poked her head out
the front door, convinced that she had heard a car. She and my dad
had been in my parents' upstairs bedroom, which faced the back of
the house, so they had missed the actual parade of white
Suburbans—but apparently not the sounds.

Luckily, my mom didn't see the Gradys, and they didn't have
to wait too long in the cold. Shortly after the last Suburban left,
three courtesy hiking vans, which shuttled hikers to and fro from
the base of Mt. Aldinn and Mt. Hamar, pulled into the driveway.

My mom, who had barely closed the front door, flung it wide
open as she hurried down in her extra-fluffy green bathrobe and
snow boots to have a word with the drivers. Worried that the
Resistance drivers would be unprepared for the onslaught of my
mom's Paris-related questions, I tried to call her back into the
house—but she persisted.

Thankfully, the drivers were equal to the task. I heard them
calmly reassure my mom that all would be well but they really
were on a tight timeline. My mom, puzzled by the three empty
vans, was told that I was just the first stop on the drivers' pickup
route.

They were amazing. The drivers had believable and logical
answers for everything.

Finally satisfied by their explanations, my mom hurried back
into the house, complaining that her fingers and toes had gone
numb. I yelled to the drivers that I would be a few minutes,

hoping the Gradys heard me, after which I firmly shut the front door.

As I madly tried to come up with an excuse for why my parents didn't need to help me with my bags to the waiting vans, given that the Gradys were now hopefully ensconced in one, two things happened. Anders arrived home and my mom's iPad began to ring with the familiar tone of my sister's FaceTime call.

Maria was now in her third month of college and with the initial thrill having worn off, slightly homesick. Plus, having a surly roommate and being separated from her boyfriend Erik, who was at a different college, was adding to the toll.

There was a flurry of activity as my mom rushed around trying to find her iPad, making distressed noises at each unsuccessful attempt. Meanwhile, my dad was busy greeting Anders and reminding him of the dangers of black ice on the road. Anders was attempting to mollify my dad with reassurances of his driving skills while trying to catch my eye.

I was trying to take advantage of the chaotic moment to say goodbye and hurried after my mom. Finally, managing to stop her search for a moment, I gave her a tight squeeze.

"Love you, Mom. I'll see you when I get back," I said.

"Oh, honey...love you too! Don't you want to say a quick bye to your sister? I'm sure I'll find the iPad any minute," my mom replied, her eyes still darting here and there as she looked for the ringing device.

"They're waiting for me, Mom. You say hi and bye to Maria from me, okay? I hope things are going better for her."

"Okay, sweetie. Have the best time...but stay safe. You know you can call us if anything comes up. I'll be so excited to see all your pictures when you get back." My mom drew me into another tight hug, leaving me slightly breathless. "Leif, come say goodbye to Elin."

She resumed her search for the still-ringing device and suddenly announced, "Oh...oh, I found it!" My mom held her iPad jubilantly up in the air, having located it between the couch cushions. My dad joined us in the living room, wrapping his arms around me for a large bear hug.

"Have a great trip, Elin. Be sure to visit the Eiffel Tower. The view is spectacular."

He kissed me on the head and then let go. By now my mom had Maria on the iPad screen and was explaining to her that I was departing for my trip. I gave Maria a quick wave as I hoisted my duffle bag over my shoulder.

"Here, honey, I can carry that for you to the van," my dad said as he extended his hand toward my duffle bag.

I looked at Anders for help.

"Uh...don't worry, Dad...I got it. You talk to Maria with Mom."

"Thanks, son. Enjoy yourself, Elin, and don't forget to call or text to let us know how things are going."

"Okay. Bye, Dad...bye, Mom...bye, Maria!"

My parents and Maria replied with their farewells as my parents settled around the dining-room table to talk with Maria. Anders and I were left alone in the hallway.

"Elli, the Resistance encountered Hunters with their decoy vehicles, so you need to be extra careful. Luckily, I was able to get Joel and Mia safely to the Old Boat Club marina without any incident. They're waiting for you there along with some other Resistance members. By the way, did you know old fisherman Hans is one of them?"

"Um...no. I thought he'd lost his sight." Anders shrugged in response. "Good to know about the Hunters and other stuff. And thanks, Andee...for everything. I know it's a lot...in a very short amount of time." I gave him a lopsided smile. Then, adjusting the bag on my shoulder, I said, "You probably shouldn't walk me out either...especially if the Hunters are still lurking. It's probably better that we don't give them any reason to think you're 'in the know.'"

"You sure? That looks heavy. And don't worry, I can handle it. What's so special about finding out that there's a super-secret supernatural society living right under your nose...and that it's at war with itself...oh, and your sister is now one of them. Totally normal everyday stuff." Anders grinned as he pulled me into a tight hug. "Just be careful, Elli. Don't take any risks. There's so much we don't know or understand about their world...and I want you home safe sooner rather than later."

"Okay...okay," I responded, muffled by the layers of Anders' coat as he held me an extra second longer. "I'm sure I'll be home before you know it."

I smiled at Anders and pulled open the front door. I stepped outside onto the porch and swung it closed behind me. The light from the dining-room windows spilled onto the snow below, reminding me of the warmth and love inside. A lump formed at the back of my throat. I was filled with a strange sense of déjà-vu as I took a last look at my home.

I DROPPED ONTO THE CABIN'S BED, SLUMPING AGAINST THE boat's wall. We were finally safe—at least for now. I closed my eyes and breathed in deeply as I consciously let the tension in my body slowly ease. The last thing I needed right now was to trigger another vision. The evening had already been eventful enough.

I could hear the slight thumps against the small icebreaker's reinforced hull as it made its way through the coastal waters. It wasn't unusual for ice chunks to form in the archipelago over the winter months. I could even remember childhood winters where the water had frozen thick enough across the surface that my parents had taken Maria, Anders, and me skating on it.

With the thought of my family, unease wormed its way into my heart. I didn't like keeping my parents in the dark about where I was going, but there was hardly a better alternative. I really didn't have a choice. I was the catalyst for both the Hunters' and the Chairman's determination to capture us all, so I had to go. And keeping my parents ignorant of the Four Clans was their only protection from the Hunters—especially now that the *Stór-menni* could bring down the Resistance's Shield Walls.

Plus, perhaps most importantly, the only way to be sure the Chairman didn't learn their faces was to keep me away from my family. The Resistance had warned that should the Chairman control my thoughts, he would also be able to witness everything I saw.

At least Anders knew everything now. A small sense of relief blossomed inside me. I'd hated keeping secrets from him. We'd always been comrades-in-arms, facing life's big events together, and what could be bigger than suddenly converting into a supernatural human?

I frowned slightly as I wondered how Anders would manage pretending not to know. He wasn't the best at keeping secrets. And we'd thrown a lot of surreal information at him in one evening. The Resistance had promised to keep an eye on him...I just hoped their protection and guidance would be enough to keep Anders out of trouble.

I leaned my head back against the cool wall. I hadn't been able to shake the feeling that I'd previously experienced my departure, but that was impossible.

Unless...

My eyes flew open. Of course—it was my vision from months earlier. I'd seen my departure over and over. It was the one event that had consistently repeated and always been the same.

I shifted uncomfortably. I couldn't help it...it was still a little creepy when the things that I saw in my visions actually happened. Somehow it made everything feel preplanned—like we didn't have a true choice in anything. Mrs. Grady had assured me that wasn't the case. She said that the visions would change when different choices were made...but how could she possibly know?

I mean, yes, technically she was the one with the *megin* experience and she'd known a Clan member with Temporal Vision, but she hadn't known a Dormant with Temporal Vision— and she certainly wasn't seeing the things I was. Everything I'd seen so far had come true.

She tried to encourage me to see the situation in a more positive light, since it would help me manage my power. "You can't control something if you're rejecting it," she'd pointed out during one of our sessions.

Making an effort to take her advice to heart, I supposed there was a flip side to the preplanned thing, which was to see it as comforting that there actually *was* a plan. Or perhaps Mrs. Grady was right and things changed as people made different choices. The only thing I did know for sure was, the whole thing left me unsettled.

I looked at Mia on the bed on the opposite side of the cabin. Her arm was lying across her face, with the rest of her body snugly tucked under the covers. The only noise emanating from her was steady breathing. My revelation didn't seem worthy enough to wake her from her sleep.

A large uninvited yawn forced itself across my face. It'd taken me a bit longer to settle in than the others, since I'd been the last to board the boat. The courtesy hiker vans had left one at a time from my home, each taking a different route to the Old Boat Club. The drivers had insisted that I be in a separate van from the Gradys, so I'd arrived last at the marina.

Two small icebreakers had been waiting at the dock when I walked down to meet the rest of the group. Both boats were making the journey towards Falinvik. The Gradys, Mr. Tibadeau, Gabriel, Mia, Joel, a small Korean woman named Bae, and I were together on one of the boats along with the boat's captain and two-person crew. The other boat had a similar number of crew members plus a team of six Resistance fighters, including Mr. McHaill.

All Joel, Mia, and I knew of the Resistance team's mission was that it was separate from the Gradys'. We knew keeping us in the dark about the details wasn't a malicious effort. Nobody, except perhaps Ms. Valistus and McHaill, knew everything—which had us speculating that the mission had to be significant if McHaill was along for the trip.

The limited information sharing was to keep everyone—including the missions—safe and secure. Less people who knew all the particulars, the less likely it was that the operations would be compromised. But that didn't stop us from being curious.

The three of us had been able to chat for a few moments once on board the boat before Mrs. Grady had ushered us towards our beds. All the passengers on our boat had been asked to share a cabin with another person. Mia and I quickly paired up. Claire was with Bae. Mr. and Mrs. Grady were with each other, and Mr. Tibadeau was sharing with his nephew Gabriel. This left Joel, to his dismay, with Edvin.

He'd begrudgingly followed Edvin to their cabin as we said goodnight. Joel had heard about Edvin's epic snoring from Aedan, but he was much too intimidated by Edvin's super strength to actually protest the assignment.

It was close to midnight when Mia and I finally settled into our cabin. Mia efficiently unpacked her bags and was in her pajamas climbing under the covers before I'd even had a chance to find my toothbrush. She'd mumbled a few words that sounded like "goodnight" and "talk tomorrow." Then her eyes had shut. She always did have an amazing ability to fall asleep.

Another large yawn interrupted my thoughts. Time for bed. I quickly and quietly rushed through my bedtime routine. As I lay down on the bed and pulled up the covers, I thought of Aedan. His sea-blue eyes and smile flashed in my mind. I closed my eyes and sent a silent message into the darkness: "We're coming, Aedan!"

TEN

Fabrics and Legends

ELIN

Snow flurries danced before my eyes. They were all around me. I could see nothing but white. Then, slowly, sharp rocky peaks materialized below me. The swirling snow seemed to become lighter as I descended lower among the clouds. I could now clearly make out an ancient yet somehow modern-looking gray fortress in the valley between the jagged gray peaks. It stood high above the treetops. A snaking river fed from the waterfall on the left side of the fortress's outer wall, and then the water made its way into the dense forest below.

The back of the fortress melded into the gray peak behind it, making it impossible to tell where one began and the other finished. In the center of the fortress was a large cylindrical building made of the same granite that surrounded it.

Suddenly I was hurtling towards that very building. There was no stopping it. I was falling faster and faster. My heart raced. I covered my face with my arms, readying myself for impact. I dared only a quick peek through the crack made by my arms when the impact never came.

It was so strange. I passed right through the roof without feeling a thing. I kept descending but more slowly now. Nothing seemed to stop my fall—not the concrete floors or stone walls.

The first few floors I passed through seemed to be some sort of office space, but the lower I went, the creepier the rooms became. Some had just one person lying on a mattress while others had several people crammed into a tight space.

All the people had two things in common: drawn faces and a look of hopelessness in their eyes. It made me shudder. A coldness seemed to claw at my heart as I lost count of the number of floors, rooms, and people. I tried to ask them where I was. But none of them seemed to see or hear me. Who were they?

Finally, I slowed to a stop. I was clearly in an older part of the fortress. Even though the walls were whitewashed, you could still make out the large, ancient stones that made up the walls. This room had only one individual. I couldn't quite make out the person's features, since they were huddled against the wall holding something to their ear. My body refused to go lower, which was maddening considering I'd just fallen all the way there from the sky.

I squinted to see in the dark. Why wasn't my *megin* working? I should have been able to see fine in the dark. I could just make out black hair. No, wait...black *wavy* hair.

"AEDAN!" I yelled. "Aedan!"

Nothing. It was like he couldn't hear me. I tried again, forcing my voice to be loud.

"AEDAN!"

I could see his hand lower whatever he was holding from his ear. He was starting to turn his head.

"Yes! Aedan, it's me!"

. . .

"Elli...Elli...wake up!" It was Mia's voice. Everything faded to white. I opened my eyes. I was back in the boat cabin with an anxious-looking Mia holding a flashlight to my face.

"Elli, are you okay? You were yelling Aedan's name."

I shielded my eyes from the light. Mia immediately lowered it.

"Yeah, I'm...I'm okay. I think I just saw Aedan. It was so strange. I think he almost heard me in my dream this time." I sighed deeply. "I guess I just miss him, you know. It's probably why I was dreaming about him."

A few weeks earlier, I had told Mia about everything that had happened in Ash Park, including kissing Aedan. I'd also confessed that I didn't know what it meant or what he'd thought about it. She'd tried to reassure me that she was sure Aedan liked me, especially given everything she had seen. But I remained unconvinced—I mean, *I* had kissed him. Not the other way around. And Aedan and I had never had a chance to talk about it.

"Um, Elli. I don't think you were dreaming."

"*What*? What do you mean?"

"Aedan's medal on your wrist was glowing blue underneath... just like you told me happens when you get a vision."

"Are you sure?"

"Yeah, it was pretty obvious."

"*Great*." I frowned as I sat up, pulling the covers around me. "I'm supposed to avoid my visions or pull the ripcord immediately when they start. Mrs. Grady will be *sooo* thrilled. The Resistance doesn't want to take any chances with the Chairman. But the thing is...it's really hard to tell in your sleep what's real and what's not, let alone what's a vision."

"Hmmm, I bet." Mia paused for a minute as she thought. "Aren't there any common signs between your visions?"

"Not really. They're all so different...except for the ones that repeat. At least with those I know what's going on."

"Well, what did you see this time? Something about Aedan, right?"

"Yeah, it was super weird." I went on to relate to Mia what I'd seen in my vision—especially the part where I thought maybe Aedan had heard me.

"Interesting...I suppose it's possible that he heard *something*... but what we can't be sure. I mean, you said he didn't react the first couple of times you said his name, right? I don't want to burst any bubbles, but we probably shouldn't jump to any conclusions, either."

Mia and her infallible logic. She was right, of course. It could've been another noise Aedan reacted to—but I still had a nagging sensation that Aedan had heard *me*.

Mia continued, "I think what's more interesting and important is the location of his cell and, what was he doing huddled up against the wall? And what did he have against his ear?"

"I don't know. I could barely see him in the dark."

"Do you think we should tell the others?"

"Uh...I don't know. They're not going to like the fact that I had a vision right here on this boat."

"But it's not like you could help it."

"True...but I'm not sure that'll make it any better."

"Well, I think you should definitely consider it. That detail about Aedan's location in Ginnungagap could be helpful."

"It wasn't really that specific. I mean, I was falling through floors...and I definitely lost count on the way down. If I'd known it was an actual vision, I would've paid more attention."

"Just think about it. We only have one more night on the boat."

We'd already spent nearly three days making our way toward Falinvik.

"Okay...I'll think about it." I hugged my knees closer to my chest. "What time is it, anyway?"

Mia shone the flashlight on the clock on the cabin wall: 5:46am.

"We probably should try to get some more sleep," Mia said, moving towards her bunk.

"I don't think I can sleep after that. You should've seen those poor people, Mia. Their eyes…their eyes were just so empty. Like they'd lost their reason to exist."

"It sounds awful, Elli." Mia rubbed her arms, almost hugging herself. "I get why you wouldn't be able to sleep. Do you wanna get dressed and go find an early breakfast instead?"

"Yeah, sure."

Anything than risking another vision in my sleep. I swung my legs over the bunk's side. Mia located the lamp on the cabin's desk and flipped the switch. A warm yellow glow immediately cast an aura around the desk and lit the room enough for Mia to see her way around.

We both got dressed in layers, including putting on long underwear underneath our jeans. The first day on the boat's deck had quickly taught us how the open sea amplified cold weather. The final touch was pulling on our long puffy coats, hats, and gloves. We now resembled two large marshmallowy grapes, one green and one purple.

The fastest way from the boat's cabin side to the common-use area, where the kitchen was, was by crossing the open deck. Once satisfied that we were sufficiently layered, Mia and I opened our cabin door and waddled down the cream-colored hallway toward the deck door. We braced for the cold as I rolled the lever to unlock the door and pulled it open.

We were immediately greeted by a freezing sea-salt-y wind. I could feel my cheeks and nose turn pink as the icy breath caressed my face. I stepped over the doorframe onto the frozen deck illuminated solely by the yellow-orange glow of a floodlight above.

The further north we traveled, the longer the winter darkness remained during the day. We'd estimated that we currently saw daylight only somewhere between two and three hours a day. The rest of the time, as far as the outdoors were concerned, it could've been nighttime.

Mia joined me on the deck, and we linked arms to hold each other up as we started to cross the slippery surface. Our progress was slowed by the boat's motion as it encountered undulating waves, and we were forced to grab onto whatever happened to be close by. We'd gone only a few paces when we could make out a small figure behind some of the cargo containers.

"Who is that?" Mia asked. "It's a bit early to be out here, don't ya think?"

"Um, don't know who, but I hate to break it to you...we're out here."

Mia chuckled. "You're right. Just us crazies up at the crack of dawn...oh, wait, dawn hasn't even happened yet!"

Both of us erupted into loud laughter, easily amused in our sleep-deprived condition. The figure turned around.

"Hi, ladies. You're up early," Bae said.

Bae was a petite, pretty Korean woman with short, glossy black hair and a face devoid of wrinkles, making her actual age difficult to decipher. I guessed that she was in her mid-thirties mostly because of her mannerism and self-confidence. She was always ready with a warm laugh or joke, but there was also something beneath the smiling face that screamed, "Don't mess with me."

She was dressed in what looked to be a lightweight, fitted, dark-blue hooded coat and matching pants. She had the hood pulled up, framing her face in a light blue fuzzy rim. How she wasn't freezing her pants off was beyond me. Don't get me wrong, she looked amazing, but the outfit just didn't seem warm enough.

Mia returned the greeting. "Hi, Bae. Yeah, we couldn't sleep."

Then as if reading my mind, she continued, "How are you not an icicle out here in that outfit?"

Bae smiled. "It's the magic of Clan fabric. It regulates your body temperature with your environment so you're never too hot or too cold, while allowing you the ease of movement. Of course, in Falinvik, they tend to use the fabric in a more traditional tunic style, but the Resistance put their own spin on it...plus some upgrades, including camouflage and impact mitigation."

Mia and I looked at each other in our marshmallowy-grapeness.

"Two, please!" Mia said without hesitation.

Bae laughed. "I'm surprised McHaill didn't issue ones to you already. The entire team should be getting them...if they don't have them already."

"Great! I'm freezing just standing here. Can't even imagine how it will be even further north," I replied, shuddering in the cold breeze.

As if to add insult to injury, a large wave rocked the boat, sending a spritz of frosty water to mist down on us. In order to stay upright, Mia and I clutched at the cargo nets, which tied down equipment to the boat's deck.

"Why don't we get you girls inside," Bae said as she extended her hands towards us, somehow completely comfortable with the boat's unpredictable motion.

Hand in hand, the three of us started toward the common-area door.

"What were you doing out here anyway?" Mia asked Bae.

"*Mia...,*" I said, worried that she was prying into things Bae didn't want to share.

"What?" Mia looked at me with a confused expression.

"No, no...it's totally fine. I was out here practicing with my *megin,*" Bae answered.

"You can't do it inside?" Mia asked. "I mean, it's kinda cold and wet out here."

Mia was conveniently forgetting that it was impolite to ask about Clan members' abilities, but I stayed silent, given that I was equally curious.

"Believe me, I wish I could...but my ability...well...it requires some space," Bae responded. Mia and I stopped, turning to look at Bae and hoping she would elaborate. "It's just probably easier if I show you. Stand over there, well clear of me."

Bae pointed toward a set of cargo boxes about twenty feet in front of us. Mia and I, still hanging on to each other, moved as quickly as possible to the indicated spot. Neither of us dared to say a word in case Bae changed her mind.

To pass the time during the last few days, Joel, Mia, and I had been trying to guess whether the boats' passengers were Clan members and if so, what their ability might be. On our boat that meant Bae, Monsieur Tibadeau, and Gabriel were up for discussion. And now we might be able to knock one mystery off our list.

Bae glanced back at us, making sure we were at our safe location. Then slowly she began to move her arms. They swayed this way and that. Her hands drew strange figures in the space in front of her. The movements reminded me of tai chi. A few years back, when my mom had been on a health kick, she'd dragged me to a tai chi class at Auor's recreation center.

As Bae finished her final hand motion, her fingers seemed to be pulling the space in front of her open. To our astonishment, a bluish bright-white light appeared between them, growing wider as Bae literally seemed to be ripping open the space in front of her. When the opening was about as wide as the distance between Bae's outstretched hands, we could clearly see the inside of what looked to be a garage on the other side.

Mia's mouth had fallen open. I gave her a quick nudge.

"OMG! What is that?" Mia said.

Bae let her hands drop as she turned to face us. The rip immediately began to close, leaving only the dark ocean as the backdrop again.

"That was my garage back on Auor," Bae said, smiling.

"Wow, that's so cool. Can you open a...um...a...uh...rip to anywhere?" I asked, unsure of what to call what we'd just witnessed.

"A portal. Perhaps eventually...right now my garage is the best I can do. But that's a big improvement from my bedroom. It's taken me a while to be able to stretch it that far," Bae answered, somehow looking both proud and annoyed at the same time.

"Can you travel anywhere in the world from your garage, then?" Mia asked.

"Oh, no. My portal is only one-way...for the most part. I mean, I could go from my garage to my bedroom, but that's not very exciting...although it *can* be convenient at times."

I thought for a moment. "So basically, you can open a 'portal' to your garage *from* anywhere but not *to* anywhere."

"Yes, exactly."

Mia, Joel, and I had been wondering why the Resistance had chosen the members it had for this mission. Now I think I finally understood why Bae had been selected. What little I'd heard about the Resistance's plans, there'd been even less talk about how they planned to leave once Aedan had been rescued and the other members had completed whatever their missions were. And no one had seemed to be particularly concerned about it either. Not having an exit strategy seemed like a rather large omission —until now.

Mia smiled. "That's so cool...and handy. Thanks for sharing."

She shivered as another strong gust of wind brought a glacial drizzle of seawater down upon us.

"Time to get you girls inside and warm," Bae said, ushering us towards the common-area door.

Mia and I obeyed without argument, looking forward to the warmth inside. We somehow managed to maintain our balance long enough on the slippery deck to make it safely to the common-area door. We rolled the lever to the unlock position, opening the heavy watertight door. After the three of us stepped inside, Bae quickly closed the door and rolled the handle to seal it.

We were in a large room divided into two parts. On the left-hand side were four metallic tables with chairs to match. Double-paned windows with rounded corners were evenly spaced along the wall behind the tables. They brought natural light into the space when there actually was any. Currently, they showed only darkness and the splatter dots from the waves glimmering in the artificial light from inside.

On the right side of the room was a long rectangular opening that had been cut into a quarter-length of the wall and exposed a galley on the other side. Further towards the door we'd just come through were two navy-colored couches positioned in an L with a decent-sized coffee table in the middle. Bae started towards the galley door at the back of the room.

"You girls hungry? I think the boat crew usually has a slow cooker making porridge overnight. I'm sure it's ready by now."

"Sure, sounds great," I responded.

Mia frowned. She wasn't much for oatmeal. "Is there anything else *warm* to eat?"

"I'm sure there's something in the fridge you can put together. I'm not much of a cook," Bae answered as she disappeared to the other side of the swinging door.

"Porridge is fine then." Mia wasn't much of a cook either,

outside of helping her mom prepare their traditional Indian foods for celebrations.

"I can make you some eggs and toast, if you want," I offered.

"No, it's fine...as long as there's cinnamon and brown sugar."

Just then Bae appeared on the other side of the galley window, sliding a jar of brown sugar, a container labeled blueberry-raspberry sauce, and a jar of cinnamon along the wide ledge.

"As you wish," she said, smiling.

Before long, the three of us were crowded around one of the four tables, enjoying a hot cup of green tea and a bowlful of the slow-cooker porridge with an assortment of toppings. The tangy and sweet combination of wild blueberry-raspberry sauce, brown sugar, and hot oats was quickly disappearing from my bowl, making me wonder about the possibility of seconds. But Mia had other plans up her sleeve.

"So, Bae...are you from the Nordri Clan as well?" she asked without batting an eye as she leaned back in her chair.

"No, I'm from the Austri Clan." Bae scooped up another mouthful of porridge. She had a distant look on her face as if she was thinking something over. Then as if winning an internal struggle, she asked, "How much do you girls know about the Clans?"

"Not much, really. Everyone's been so busy preparing for the mission and shocked that the other Clans aren't dead that no one's had time to tell us much of anything. I mean...of course, it's understandable." I couldn't help the edge of frustration that crept into my voice. Logically, I understood the reasons why those conversations had been sidelined, but it'd left Mia, Joel, and I trying to navigate some very strange waters without a paddle.

"Well...where to start, then." Bae leaned back in her chair, contemplating our eager faces. "I suppose the very beginning—our origin—is the best. Of course, to be clear, my perspective is colored not only by my Korean heritage but also the Austri Clan's history."

She reached for her tea, cradling the cup in her hands as she spoke. Mia and I leaned forward in our seats, ready to hear whatever she'd tell us.

As Bae started speaking again, a commotion began outside the common-area door. The door lever rolled one way and then another, with some intense jerking between the rolls. Finally, the boat rocked strongly and the lever clicked into the correct unlocked position. Slowly the door opened, revealing a desperate Joel trying to remain upright on the slippery deck surface.

"Argh! Doggone...stupid...confounded door!" he berated, clinging to it as he stepped over the threshold. Wearing his beloved sneakers, his feet slipped mercilessly on the icy deck. After making it safely inside, he pushed back his hood, which had fallen over his eyes, to find the three of us staring at him trying not to snicker.

"Morning, Joel!" Bae was the first to regain her composure.

Joel's eyes lingered on the three of us. His cheeks grew beet red and his mouth worked this way and that until he apparently came to a decision.

"Morning, ladies," he said, his face dropping into his best lopsided grin. "So, what's up with these levered door-handles...I mean who exactly are they trying to keep out?" To emphasize his point, he jerked his thumb towards the door behind him.

"Morning, Joel," I responded. "You're up early. Come join us."

Joel approached our table, unzipping his at-least-one-size-too-large winter coat and pulling off his hat, making his unruly hair spring into a multitude of directions. "Yeah...well, when you've endured hours of eruptive freight-train snoring, the definition of 'normal waking hour' gets a little blurry."

Mia and I nodded sympathetically. Aedan had often joked about Edvin's loud slumber.

Bae looked confused. "Aren't you using the Clan-tech noise-canceling earplugs? They really do work."

"What earplugs? Nobody gave me any noise-canceling earplugs." Joel looked genuinely surprised.

"They should've been in your boat-pack... along with the Resistance-issued Clan-fabric coat and pants." At our puzzled faces, Bae continued, "I'm starting to get the impression that a significant oversight has been made. Fear not...I'll talk to the Captain later today and get this sorted."

"You mean this whole time I could've slept like a baby despite being—" Joel couldn't even finish his sentence. His crestfallen face more clearly expressed his feelings than anything else he could've said.

"Oh, cheer up, Joel. Sounds like you'll be able to get some sleep tonight. Plus, Bae was just going to tell us about the Clans' origins," Mia said, her eyes glimmering with interest.

"Grab a bowl of porridge and come sit down," I chimed in a bit more gently.

Joel crinkled his nose at the word "porridge" and glanced at the empty bowl in front of Mia.

"No, really. It's quite good...if you put enough blueberry-raspberry sauce on top," Mia said, witnessing his response. "Now what were you saying, Bae?"

I chuckled to myself. If it was possible, Mia was even more curious about the Clan and its legends than I was.

"Well...let's see...where was I." Bae leaned back in her chair again. "Oh, yes...I was just saying that every Clan has a slightly different spin on the origin story. What's common amongst all the Clans' legends, of course, is that long ago, the moon god or goddess —depending on the Clan—came to our ancestors, bestowing on each of them enhanced abilities in order to help fight the monsters and beasts during the end times…but that much you might already know."

Bae took a sip of her tea. "When looking at each Clan's pantheon of deities, the moon gods and goddesses are a bit mysterious, and little is known about them. Their oral legends have degraded as they've been passed down and traveled with descendants to new locations and then been influenced by surrounding folklore. That said, the Korean version of the Austri story is…that long ago at the height of the gods' reign, the moon goddess Dalnim learned that the same tiger…who'd chased her and her brother—the sun god—up a rope into the heavens at Earth's formation…was going to devour them during the end times."

A loud screech interrupted Bae. Grimacing, Joel slowly finished pulling out the noisy metallic chair next to Mia while delicately balancing his too-full bowl of porridge. The dish seemed like it contained more blueberry-raspberry sauce than actual porridge. Joel threw an apologetic look toward Bae and mouthed the word *sorry*.

Bae cleared her throat and continued, "Thus, to prevent her brother's and her demise—and of course, to ensure humanity's continuity—Dalnim decided to create a superhuman army to help fight the monsters and beasts that would eventually come to harm them. However, not knowing from which direction or when the beasts would come, she decided to bestow her gifts upon four clans near the Earth's cardinal points—North, South, East, and West—and ensured that their superpowers were passed down from generation to generation. But, being only a minor goddess of the pantheon, she could only enhance the humans' natural abilities and empower them while her moonlight shone upon them. Hence, once a month on the new moon, when her lit face was completely turned away, Dalnim, her brother, and humanity would be vulnerable. To prevent this knowledge from spreading to her enemies, she swore her newly created army to keep their powers and existence a secret from the regular humans."

Bae brought her teacup to her lips and drank the last of her tea. After a small pause, Mia piped up.

"So, that's why Clan members don't have any powers during a new moon...sorta like the tides that ebb and flow based on the moon's cycle."

"And why the *megin* only enhances our natural abilities and talents," I added.

"Yes...well, at least according to the legend," Bae answered.

"Don't you believe it then?" Joel asked, scraping the remaining bits from his bowl.

Bae leaned forward to pour herself some more tea from the pot on the table. "I do think there's truth to the tales, but I don't think they explain everything. I mean, Elin is a perfect—" She stopped herself.

"I'm 'a perfect example'...because I have my powers all the time," I finished for her.

"Well...yes. There's clearly a lot we still don't understand about ourselves or how our powers evolve, especially when mixing with Mannlegurs. I don't suppose the goddess ever foresaw *that*." Bae shifted around in her chair while unzipping her jacket, revealing her Clan medallion resting on her navy shirt.

"That's beautiful," Mia said, staring at the silver medal.

It was the same shape and size as the rest of the Clan medals I'd seen, but the etchings were very different. The symbol in the middle looked like an elaborate, skinny dragon. And where the runes typically lay on the four compass points, there were four Asian-looking symbols.

"Thank you," Bae responded, unconsciously fingering the chain from which the medal hung.

"It's so different from the Nordri ones. What does the symbol in the center mean?" I asked.

"Well, like I was saying earlier, each Clan has its own social structure and beliefs, which naturally led to distinct medals for their people. In the case of the Austri Clan, all members have the Azure Dragon in the center." When we looked like we didn't know what she meant, Bae continued, "The dragon is one of the four magical animals that guard the cardinal directions. When the goddess Dalnim gave powers to our Clan, the medals and national boundaries didn't exist yet. But now, in the complexities of modern-day, a powerful symbol was needed to unite the different nationalities in the Austri Clan and remind us that we all originate from one Eastern Clan. But of course, at the same time, we can't ignore our individuality...so we use our native languages to express our personal symbols. For Korean *bon-gwans*—family groups—in the Austri Clan, we use Hangul words in the same way the Nordri Clan uses their runes."

"That's so cool that you have unity and individuality both baked in," Mia said. Then after thinking for a moment, she asked, "What are the other three animals that guard the cardinal directions?"

"Well...let's see. There's the black tortoise to the North, the vermillion bird to the South...and oh, yes...the white tiger to the West. All the guardian animals appear in the same mythic capacity for the East Asian countries. And they even have meaning beyond their guardianship...including a season of the year, an emotion, a virtue, and the natural elements of wood, fire, metal, or water. They are very ancient and powerful symbols."

"So what guardian animal represents Elin, then?" Joel asked.

Mia gave Joel a "don't" stare.

"*Whaaat*? I mean, is she Nordri, Austri, Vestri, or Sudri?"

"*Jooeell*...not helping," Mia muttered.

"No, it's okay," I replied. "I've had the same thought. We might as well say it: where exactly do I fit in with the Clans?"

"Hmmm. It's a good question...and one I don't have an answer for." Bae's deep-brown eyes seemed to inspect me as she spoke. "I suppose it'd have to do with your lineage, who it was that introduced the gene into your family pool...but I'm no expert."

Joel and Mia turned to look at me as well. I shrugged in response. I genuinely had no idea. I'd gone over it a million times in my head and even talked it over with Anders in a small, stolen moment amid the chaos of the night I left. Neither he nor I had ever heard any whispers or insinuation about a family member having a superpower or being connected to a secret society. Perhaps my parents or grandparents knew, but I couldn't exactly ask them about it. So, it would remain a mystery—at least for now.

After a few moments of silence, Mia broke the awkwardness. "Sooo...on a different note. How are we getting to Thordalr?"

"Now, Mia, you know I couldn't answer that even if I knew," Bae chided good-naturedly. "The safeguards are in place for reason and especially important, given Elin's encounter with the Chairman. I'm sure as you get closer all will be revealed. Meanwhile, I'm happy to answer anything on Clan history and the like...but mission questions are out."

"*Okaaay*...you can't blame a girl for trying." Mia shrugged

At that moment, the door lever rolled to the unlocked position on the first try and the door easily swung open. Mia smirked at Joel and a little color rose to his cheeks. The boat's captain and one of the crew members walked in, ending our discussion of Clan history.

"The waves were more intense before," Joel grumbled, defending his earlier struggle with the door.

"Uh-huh," Mia teased.

"Oh, Captain...can I have a moment?" Bae asked, giving us a wink before approaching him.

As Bae walked away, Mia whispered to Joel, "Sooo...guess what we learned today."

"What?" Joel replied, inspecting his bowl to see if he had really finished the last of the porridge.

"We know what Bae's power is," Mia said, incapable of keeping the lilting self-satisfied tone from her voice.

Joel's head snapped up. He looked at me first and then at Mia to see if we were being serious. Unable to contain herself any longer, Mia went on to relate to Joel what we'd witnessed earlier that morning on the deck. After she finished, I shared my suspicion about how we might be getting home after the rescue and Resistance missions

"Well, that's handy...and sneaky of the Resistance. Can't wait!" Joel said.

"What can't you wait for?" Bae appeared behind Joel at that very moment.

"Oh...um...uh...well, you see—" Joel stammered.

Mia came to his rescue. "We were just talking about the Clan fabric. Joel's super excited about it." Bae raised one eyebrow as she inspected our faces. Mia hastily added, "So, any word from the Captain about our boat packs?"

If Bae didn't believe Mia's explanation, she didn't address it. Instead, she said, "Yeah, he's just sent one of the crew to go fetch them from 'storage'. He apologizes for the 'oversight'...if it was that."

"Don't you believe him?" I asked.

"Him, I believe...the crew not so much. We've had incidents in the past where Clan-tech items have gone missing. They're considered extremely valuable out here in the Mannlegur world, and as you can guess, a black market has sprung up." Bae frowned.

"Unfortunately, we can't always be very selective about who we deal with as part of the Resistance. The group, after all, started with smugglers and thieves helping Clan members escape."

Suddenly, the Resistance's strict "need to know" measures were starting to make more sense given its origins and the black market. Their secret information would probably fetched a far greater price than their Clan-tech in the wrong hands. The Captain approached our table, carrying three neat packages tied up in brown parchment.

"Apologies for the oversight," he said as he handed each of us a package with our name on it. "Should never have happened."

Joel looked like he was having Christmas morning as he tore into his package. Finding a small box labeled Earplugs, he heartily grinned, "Sleep at last. Tomorrow, don't expect to see me until noon!"

"Oh...I'm afraid that won't be possible. We'll arrive at our destination at 6:00am and will start to disembark immediately. I understand McHaill has a tight schedule to keep, so you may want to pack and have breakfast in advance," the Captain said, smiling apologetically.

Joel made a noise similar to a whimper. I felt genuinely sorry for him.

"There's always afternoon naptime today, Joel. And just think...this is your last night sharing with Edvin," I said, hoping to cheer him.

ELEVEN

Command's Decision

TRISTAN

The night had been an odd one. With no power at the Unregistered's home and the new moon still upon us, we were left with the few candles we could find, a Clan hovering lantern that hung in the air above the living-room couches, and a fire in the fireplace as our sole heat source. The other Clan equipment included in our provisions was intended for outdoor use—and no one even suggested sleeping outside.

We scavenged in the Unregistered's kitchen for food and picnicked in front of the fireplace with what we found. The conversation was sparse as we ate and mulled over the repercussions of the evening's double failures. I could not afford another failed mission—yet here I was. I racked my brain to come up with some solution to avoid the unpleasant consequences that awaited me in Falinvik. But the answer eluded me.

Slowly, the dark house became colder and our bellies fuller. Yawns started to appear on the team's faces. One by one, they slipped into their Clan-fabric sleeping bags, each lost in their own dismal thoughts. With nothing left to do, I joined them and soon drifted off into a fitful sleep.

I woke to the sound of Magnus's loud snoring and someone placing more logs in the fireplace. My breath formed small clouds in the frosty air of the room. Still in my sleeping bag, I rolled over to see who was tending the fire. Thyra. Of course. She was always the first up and last to sleep.

I glanced at the rest of the crew sprawled out in the living room. Magnus and Thyra had been the lucky recipients of the L-shaped couch for a bed. The rest of the team had opted for the living room floor as opposed to the house's freezing bedrooms.

By unanimous consent, Thyra, being the Captain, had been granted the right to a portion of the couch and a comfortable night's sleep. However, Magnus had gained the privilege by suggesting that we fight him for it, "out of fairness." There would have been nothing fair about the fight given that it would have been massively skewed in Magnus's favor, especially with the new moon's effect on our *megins*. So, no one had taken him up on the offer, and he had claimed victory through forfeiture.

Thyra started to rummage through the drawers by the fireplace. Her loose brown hair fell over her shoulders as she bent down to peer into one of them. I guessed that she was looking for matches as the logs were now neatly stacked on the grates but no flames were visible.

"Here. Let me," I said, wiggling an arm and hand out from the sleeping bag.

I was not helping Thyra to help *her*, I told myself. It was just efficiency and productivity. The faster the fire started, the warmer the room would become.

I closed my eyes and felt the small tendrils of *megin* waking in my body. A sense of intense heat coursed towards my palm and a small flame burst forth from it. I aimed at the logs in the fireplace and threw the scarlet ball. With a satisfying crackle, the paper Thyra had tucked between the logs ignited.

"Thanks," Thyra responded. She moved closer to the fireplace and held her fingers towards the warmth.

"What time is it?" I asked. It was still dark outside, so I guessed we were still in the early morning hours.

"It's about half-past seven."

"Any word from Command?"

"Nothing yet. But I'm expecting word any moment now."

"How did they take our fail—our report?"

"Well, they weren't pleased, if that's what you're asking." Thyra glanced at me. "There's a lot of pressure to get answers about this Unregistered's family. I've never seen the Command Operators so jumpy."

"Why is the Unregistered and his family so important?" asked Fenja, who had woken to our conversation. She unzipped her sleeping bag and swept her long black hair into a tight bun at her neck, fastening it with a clip.

"I'm not sure," Thyra replied, looking thoughtful.

"Could he and his family be from another Clan?" I asked.

I hadn't told any of the team about Elin's comment regarding the survival of the other Clans. It was a pot that did not need stirring. Plus, the likelihood that her statement had any truth was very slim. But just to be sure and given who Thyra was related to, I asked the question to see her reaction.

Fenja huffed. "That's impossible. They're dead, remember?"

I didn't bother responding to Fenja's remark. I was keenly aware of the fact, especially since the Sudri Clan had perished. My father's side was Sudri, after all.

I didn't have many memories of my childhood before the mentorship program, but the few memories I did have were of the visits from my paternal grandfather and my father's siblings. Their visits had filled my parents' orderly home with the chaos of a boisterous family. Their ancient Egyptian language, which was so different from Arabic spoken by *Smá-menn* Egyptians, had rippled through every corner of the house like an incessant waterfall.

I could recall my mother telling me that in my younger years I had gone through a period where I refused to speak anything but Egyptian—much to my grandfather's delight. Of course, that changed once their family visits stopped and I was sent to Henric's for the Clan mentorship program. But the one thing that had persisted was the formality with which I spoke.

The learning of new languages emphasized understanding and being understood rather than informal slang or colloquialisms. Thus, given the numerous dialects which had ebbed and flowed around me during my childhood, my speaking style had become formal. Clan adults loved it, seeing it as a sign of respect, but growing up, kids my own age had seen it as a target for teasing—especially Thyra. Her mocking still rang in my ears.

She interrupted my thoughts. "No...the RDS would've told us if he wasn't one of us, and no reports were issued saying that there was a problem with his detection scan. No...no, this is something else," Thyra replied, moving to the dining-room table to check her SRT.

If she knew something about the other Clans, she was hiding it well. I hadn't witnessed even a blink out of place. And her assertion of the RDS, or Registration and Detection Scanner, was true. I had been there when the guard had conducted the scan. But then again, her statement did not mean she did not know something. After all, Clan Hunters were trained in the art of deception.

With the exception of Magnus, the others were starting to stir in their sleeping bags. Arm stretches were combined with shivers as they emerged from the Clan-fabric cocoons in search of their clothes.

I started to dress, slipping on my black wool sweater, which I'd left neatly folded on top of my other clothes. I had kept my thermal undergarments on during the night for extra warmth.

Soon the room was filled with the sound of zippers, the rustling of fabric, and hushed talking. I was nearly fully dressed when Thyra rose from her seat at the dining-room table.

"We have word from Command. They want us—" Magnus's loud snore interrupted her. She looked up at the team. "Oh, for Freja's sake...will someone please wake Magnus?"

Dreng grabbed a pillow off the couch and expertly threw it, hitting Magnus square in the face. I had overheard talk of Dreng's enhanced knife-throwing abilities. Apparently, it extended to other objects as well.

"What...*what*?" Magnus lifted his head, looking confused.

"Rise and shine. Thyra has news from Command," Dreng said, cocking his head towards Thyra.

"Why didn't someone wake me? I hate being the last up," Magnus grumbled.

Bera and Fenja rolled their eyes as if this was a common occurrence.

"As I was saying...Command has determined the Dormant's destination. They want us to go to Paris." Thyra closed her SRT and started to gather her other remaining items from the table. "A transport is already on its way to pick us up."

"Why Paris?" I asked. It made no sense. The more I had thought about it overnight, the more convinced I was that they had left by boat the night before. And I very much doubted that their destination was Paris.

"Command relayed that all indications were that she left

under the pretext of a school trip to Paris early this morning," Thyra replied.

"That makes no sense. What about the Unregistered's family? Where did they go?" I pushed back.

"Command emphasized that our primary target now is the Dormant...especially, since they have no current information on the Unregistered's family's whereabouts."

"Doesn't that seem odd to you, that they have a clear indication for the Dormant but nothing on the Unregistered's family?"

Thyra was starting to look annoyed. "Are you questioning Command's decision?"

"Of course not," I said. "Just the information they are basing their decision on."

The rest of the team had stopped what they were doing and were intently following Thyra's and my discussion.

Thyra scoffed. "Well, I certainly think they have better sources of information than anything you have." Then, noticing the team's intense stares, she took a deep breath and let it out slowly. "Command has given us an order and we'd best—"

A loud pinging started to sound from Arnis's bag. He quickly dropped the other items in his hands and grabbed his SRT from the bag.

"Uh...Thyra, we have a problem. The SASUs I programmed for the top of the driveway just alerted me that a police car is turning into the driveway."

Without hesitation or panic, Thyra commanded, "Everybody grab your things! We have only a few minutes. Exit through the back and into the woods. We head for the vehicles."

The last thing a Hunter wanted to encounter was local police. They asked too many questions even under normal circumstances. And finding eight strangers in a local resident's home with a broken front door and the local resident not there would definitely count as extraordinary.

With amazing speed, equipment and sleeping bags were tossed into Clan backpacks. The bags emitted a whooshing sound as they compressed everything into a more manageable size. With an occasional trill from Arnis's SRT warning of the policeman's progress, we made efficient work of packing up.

Before long, we filed out the back door and into the morning darkness in a silent single line. The outdoor air was icy and the snow crackled under our feet. We hurried to the tree line just in time to see the policeman's flashlight approach the house.

Luckily, Bera had insisted we park the cars on the same logging road where we had commenced the Shield Wall operation the prior night. It now seemed like keen foresight under the circumstances.

I fell into step next to Thyra as we walked the worn snowy path towards the vehicles. She was quiet. An uncomfortable feeling started to twist inside my chest. Had I pushed her too far? She held all the reins to my future. Even a small insult or annoyance like questioning her in front of the others might have been too much.

"Listen, Thyra...sorry about before. You are right, of course. I should not question Command's decisions. If you and they say Paris, then that's where we will go."

"I appreciate that. You do have a point. I was surprised by their instruction as well, but we have little choice. If we don't do as Command says, it'll leave us wide open for interrogation when we get back. I can't put the team in that position without firm evidence to the contrary."

"What if we don't *all* go to Paris?"

"What do you mean?"

"Thyra, you brought me on your team despite knowing the

risks I had taken in my previous mission. The rewards should have been greater there, but...but my instincts were right. Why not let me follow those again? You and the rest of the team go to Paris. I will follow the leads here. If I hit a dead end, I will join you. Otherwise, I will send you periodic reports. It is a win-win. You are following Command's instructions but also covering your bases for something they might have overlooked. The reward potential is great and has very little risk for you or the others."

Thyra was silent as she kept walking. Then she stopped and turned to face me. "If you're willing to take the risk, then I don't see the harm of splitting up. However, you're on your own, at least until you find something solid. That means no Transport...no calling Command for help. We have to appear to *all* be going to Paris as far as they're concerned, at least for now. You understand?"

"Yes, fine. Just drop me off at the top of Sparrowhawk Lane. I can handle my own transport from there." I smiled, thinking about how much I had missed my motorcycle, which was still housed in my aunt's shed.

TWELVE

Just Ice
___

ELIN

I woke up to the sound of dinging bells coming from Mia's phone. It was the morning alarm she'd set. I stretched to full length before rolling over to look at the clock. It really was 5:00am already. Mia and I had packed all our items the night before but had estimated that we'd still need at least an hour to have breakfast and get ready to leave the boat.

I glanced over at the new Clan-fabric coats and pants folded neatly on top of our Clan backpacks. Below that sat two new pairs of retractable-cleat winter boots. The boots and backpacks were additional surprises in our boat packages.

Mia had figured out the boots' retractable-cleat part accidently while admiring them. She and I had only ever owned ice-grippers, which were worn on top of your footwear, never boots that combined both into one.

The Clan backpacks held their own secrets. They were like compression sacks but on steroids. It had taken us a moment to figure out how they worked, but when we did, it was like a miracle.

Everything that my large duffle bag had held was now safely packed into a backpack roughly the size of my school bag.

The backpacks' main compartment had about a zillion little pockets that held small pouches. Once you pulled out a pouch and opened it, it expanded into a larger sack. The reverse happened once the pouch was zipped back up. And yet, somehow nothing got squashed. Mia and I could hardly get over it, which is probably why we'd stayed up much later than we'd intended.

I couldn't hold back a large yawn as I swung my legs out of bed and straightened to stand in the complete darkness of the cabin. Mia was still in bed, but I knew she was awake, since she had pulled the covers over her head in a hopeless attempt to muffle the alarm. I moved to the desk and snapped the lamp on for her. Instantly, a warm glow lit the cabin.

Mia groaned as she folded back the covers, revealing her face.

"Morning," she said, rubbing her eyes. "Notice that I omitted the word 'good.' Is it seriously time to get up? I feel like we just went to bed."

"Yeah, I know. It was all that experimenting with the bags. We should've just stuffed everything in one and gone to bed."

I pushed aside the curtain on the window and looked out into the blackness. I expected to see some indication of land, but there was nothing besides thick ice and snow. The icebreaker had started to break ice yesterday afternoon as we'd finally traveled far enough north to where the ice formed sheets instead of chunks.

"You see anything out there?" Mia asked as she rose from her bed.

"Just ice and snow...I don't see any land. It must be on the other side of the boat."

"Well, I guess we'll soon find out exactly where we've landed... but not before some breakfast. I'm hungry this morning."

Everything about our boat trip had been kept under tight lock and key. As per usual, only the folks who needed to know knew the details.

Mia and I hurried to get dressed in our new Clan-fabric clothes and boots, ready to test whether Bae was right about their ability to hold off the cold. As we stepped onto the dark frigid deck heading for the common area for breakfast, Mia and I smiled at each other. For once I was perfectly warm and comfortable standing there—well, except for my face, which was being stung red by the sharp, salty wind. I pulled the fuzzy rim of my coat's hood as close as possible.

"They work," Mia said, smiling.

I nodded. "They sure do. But let's get inside...not sure how much more wind-lashing my face can take."

We crossed the remainder of the icy deck making it to the common-area door unscathed, thanks to our new boots. Mia rolled the lever while I pulled the door open, revealing the entire Grady family, Monsieur Tibadeau, Gabriel, and even Joel feasting upon scrambled eggs, turkey bacon, oranges, toast, and apricot jam. The aroma of salty bacon and buttery, warm toast made my mouth start to water.

We were greeted by numerous "Morning"s as we stepped inside. Looking at the table, I noticed that everyone seated there was dressed in their Clan-fabric coats and pants, but theirs were white instead of the navy Mia and I had on. It made me wonder about the difference.

The discussion at the table was already lively as Mr. Grady, Monsieur Tibadeau, and Gabriel were having an intense conversation at one end while the rest of the Grady family and Joel were talking at the other. We sat down in the two empty chairs by Mrs. Grady. Before we could protest, she was heaping eggs and turkey bacon onto our plates.

"Oh, thanks, Mrs. Grady, but that's really too much—" I began to say.

"Trust me. You're going to need all of it today. It's still a long journey for you to get to Sigrid's...and we're going to be spending a lot of time on the ice this morning," she replied.

Mia and I exchanged a puzzled look. "What do you mean, Mrs. Grady?"

"You'll find out soon," Edvin answered with a smirk while shoveling eggs into his mouth.

"Ice sailing," Claire said.

"Oh, come on, Claire! I wanted to see their faces when we disembarked," Edvin grumbled.

"I think they've got enough new experiences in front of them, so telling them a half-hour in advance is a kindness," Claire replied.

Joel looked at Mia and me and mouthed "ice sailing" with a baffled expression. Mia shrugged and looked at me. I shrugged back. I hadn't a clue what it meant.

Since the conversation had already moved on, Mia and I dug into the generous portion of food in front of us. One thing I'd come to learn since my awakening was that taking Mrs. Grady's advice was usually wise.

After a while, I noticed that Bae had yet to arrive. "Where's Bae?"

"She's helping with the equipment. She had her breakfast ages ago," Claire responded, rising from the table with her empty plate in hand and her dark wavy hair swinging around her face as she turned to walk toward the galley window.

She looked amazing in the white outfit, which seemed to shimmer in the light as she moved. Joel's fork was suspended halfway toward his mouth with some precariously balanced eggs on it. His eyes followed Claire's slim figure.

"Well, I'm off to pack my remaining items. See you all below!" Claire gave a wave as she headed for the exit. Joel lifted his other hand to wave back.

"*Joel! Hello*...you're dripping scrambled eggs," Mia said, as she dug into her own eggs with a little more ferocity than usual.

"Nice, man." Edvin snickered as he took in the scattered eggs around Joel's plate.

Still chuckling to himself, Edvin rose from the table. Somehow the white Clan-fabric coat and pants seemed to fit him just fine as well despite his bulky frame. He was about to leave his plate and mug behind when Mrs. Grady intervened.

"Edvin, I think you forgot something." She gave him a look while draining the last of the coffee from her cup.

"Yes, Ma'am," Edvin said, obediently reaching back down for the items.

"Hey, Mia...have you noticed we're the only two in blue?" I asked her.

"Of course." Mia took another bite of her toast.

"Well, don't you think that's strange?"

"I guess. I just tossed it up to a size thing."

"But even Joel's is white. And it kinda...shimmers."

"Hmmm, that *is* strange. I hadn't noticed before."

"Hadn't noticed what, dear?" Mrs. Grady asked, overhearing.

"We were just wondering why everyone's coat and pants are white while ours are blue," I responded.

"Oh. Well, that's simple, dear. You haven't activated the camouflage feature yet."

"The *what* feature?" Mia asked.

"Camouflage. The Resistance added a feature to the Clan-fabric where, based on certain environmental data points, it can determine the best color to help conceal you in your surroundings. Here—stand up and I'll show you how."

Mia, who was seated next to Mrs. Grady, stood up. Mrs. Grady reached under the bottom flap of her coat, clearly searching for something.

"See? Here it is, under this flap...a tiny toggle switch. You just push it towards the right...and *voila!*"

Mia's coat seemed to come to life. Scales were now visible in the fabric, and they flipped from navy to white all the way to the hood.

"Just don't get it confused with the auto-sizing feature—you don't want to turn that off. The pants have their own toggle on the front by the button."

"Oh, wow! That's *sooo* cool," Mia exclaimed, turning around with her head twisted, trying to see if it had worked on the coat's back.

"How'd you do that?" I pushed back my chair from the table, opening my coat.

We both inspected the bottom flap of my coat. Finding the tiny toggle, we pushed it to the right and watched the magic happen again, on my coat. She was right. It was cool!

By the time Mia and I finished our breakfast, everyone else had rushed off to gather their remaining items. We quickly cleared our dishes to the galley window and hurried to the deck door. I glanced at the clock on the wall before stepping out of the warmth and into the biting wind. It was 5:50am. We had ten minutes.

It was still dark outside, so the strange bluish light emanating from below the boat's starboard side was clearly visible. I nudged Mia and pointed toward the light.

"What is that?" Mia asked.

"Dunno."

"Let's go take a look."

We made our way to the boat's right side. With the icebreaker now surrounded by ice and at a standstill, there were no waves and hardly any rocking, making our traverse a lot easier. We peered over the railing.

Neither of us expected the sight that greeted us. There, on top of the ice, stood most of our team including Mr. McHaill and two others from the second boat's Resistance team. They were huddling around some sort of blue flame. Near them, the remaining Resistance members and Bae were securing the last sail to the back of a skinny bobsled-looking boat.

Mia and I looked at each other, smiling.

"Ice-sailing," we both said at the same time.

We hurried to grab our remaining items from our cabin.

WITH MY NEW BACKPACK SECURED TO MY BACK, I STEPPED onto the metal gangplank extending from the boat to the solid ice across a small gap of freezing water. Someone had hung a string of lights down the railing helping non-Clan team members see their way in the dark. The ice below was illuminated by two large blue flames that danced wildly in the wind. The flames were attached to some sort of metal contraptions and placed on either side of the cluster of ice sailboats.

I looked beyond the vessels into the darkness. We were nowhere near land. It was just ice as far as the eye could see.

A wind gust whipped my auburn hair into a frenzy. I tried unsuccessfully to tuck the strands back underneath my hood with one mittened hand while clutching the railing with the other. The strength of the wind was just too much. Finally giving up, I focused on following Mia down to the ice.

Once my feet hit the surface, my curiosity took over and I walked to the unusual sailboats. I was immediately thankful for the new cleated boots as there was no way I would've remained upright without them. Only a dusting of snow topped the ice, and the wind blew it every which way, exposing bare patches. The cleats dug into the ice with a crunch.

All eight ice sailboats looked the same. They were white and narrow-bodied. The only bulge in the streamline was the main cockpit. Otherwise, the boat's hull transformed into narrow blades towards the front and back. There was a large, sharp-looking skate in the front, and two skates, one on each side, in the back where they attached to outstretched wings. The outline of the boat looked like a tiny fighter jet with an enormous white mast jutting upward from behind the cockpit.

As I inspected the boat's traveling compartment, all our new clothing and equipment started to make sense. Besides being no match for the freezing temperature on the ice, my winter puff-coat's bulk would've been an unnecessary nuisance when squeezing into the boat's narrow seats.

The main cockpit had tight inline seating for two underneath a transparent roof that reminded me of the clear canopies I'd seen on fighter jets in the movies. There was a small storage space behind the last seat, which is where, I supposed, the Clan backpacks came in. It was laughable to even think that my duffle bag would've fit the space.

Moving on for a closer look at the main compartment, I realized that the front passenger must steer the boat and manage the sail. In the front footwell, there were foot pedals connected to wires, which seemed to run to the front blade. And the front sideboard had a winch with a rope wrapped around it. The rope, I assumed, controlled the sail.

To my surprise, besides its sleek design, nothing about the boat looked like advanced technology. There were no fancy gadgets, instruments, or screens inside the boat. In fact, all the mechanics reminded me of my Uncle Bertie's sailboat. It seemed odd considering all the high-tech equipment I'd come to expect from the Clan and Resistance.

I looked up and noticed a few team members hoisting the remaining sail on the last boat. One of them pushed down some sort of anchor on the front skate, securing the boat to its spot. Then he yelled over the flapping sails, "ALL GOOD TO GO!"

"Okay, team. GATHER AROUND, PLEASE!" McHaill called out.

I walked over to the blue flame. On the far side, I found Mia and Joel standing together, warming their hands in front of the fire. Before I could tell them about the boats, McHaill started to speak.

"As we all know, we're about to embark on dangerous missions. We've taken every precaution...but there are still a great many risks involved." He paused for a moment, smoothing his frozen whiskers and letting the gravity of his words sink in. "For the next several hours, we'll be ice sailing to Litenhavn. We'll disembark just before town—all the skippers know where. But before we commence, I ask that you all turn off any electronic devices you may have in your possession. We don't want to alert the *Stór-menni* of our arrival!" McHaill watched as we reached into a pocket or backpack to fish out our cell phones and other devices and turned them off. "And this really does mean *any* device...even the earplugs. Rest assured, the boat hulls have been soundproofed, so you'll not need them on the journey. The *Stór-menni*'s electronic sensors are quite sensitive and have a long reach, so please be sure everything is off."

Once the pocket and bag rummaging had died down, he continued, "To be clear...despite the above measures, we do expect *Stór-menni* SASUs to give us a once over as we enter the fjord. Some of you may be wondering how we will elude them. I can now share with all of you—and with their permission, of course— that Tanya, our Illusionist, and Boris, our Weather Manipulator, will provide us with the necessary cover." Two Resistance members on the other side of the blue fire gave a short nod acknowledging McHaill's statement. I took them to be Tanya and Boris.

"Once we are five miles from the coast—skippers—please remember to slow and congregate into our practiced tight formation. As you know, this is *crucial* so that Tanya's illusion can reach around all of us and Boris can effectively manage the snow squall to stop the SASUs from a closer inspection. Should anyone fall outside of the formation when we reach the fjord's entrance, it will send a red alert to the *Stór-menni*...placing our missions and us in grave peril. So please be prudent and follow the plan. Now... any final questions?"

McHaill looked around the circle with one eyebrow raised above the rim of his spectacles and his mouth stretched into a thin line below his mustache. His expression reminded me of the look teachers gave students right before they placed an exam in front of them.

After a moment's pause, McHaill continued, "Very good. Now skippers, please find your passengers...and good sailing!"

Mia, Joel, and I looked at each other.

"So, this is it...we're finally off!" Joel grinned.

"Joel, we've been traveling for *four* days already," Mia pointed out. She had a slight frown on her face and a thoughtful look in her eye.

"Yeah, but this is different. We're finally getting off that icebreaker and seeing some action. I can't wait to see how fast these boats go...and more importantly, how Tanya's and Boris's powers work. What you do gals think—are we in for a show?"

Ever since Mia and I told Joel about Bae's demonstration, he'd reminded us on a daily basis that he had been deprived of it. My guess was that he felt a bit left out or behind somehow on Clan knowledge, which now explained his eagerness to witness Tanya's and Boris's abilities.

"Um...not sure...maybe. I guess we'll see," I replied with a smile. The crowd around the fire was growing thinner as skipper-passenger pairs walked off into the darkness. "On the boats...they look pretty fast, from what I can tell—although they're fairly low-tech compared to the other Clan equipment. But I guess that makes sense given what McHaill said about the *Stór-menni* sensors." I paused, thinking for a second. "I didn't see any brakes, though...wonder how the boat actually stops?"

"What do you *mean,* there's no brakes?" Mia said, turning to me.

Joel put a comforting hand on Mia's back. "Don't worry. I'm sure it works the same as an actual sailboat. Those boats don't have brakes either—you just turn the boat into the wind."

"But we're on *ice*! What if there's a break in the ice or something? And there are no brakes? We can't even see where we're going in the pitch-black...and now we're going to be chased by SASUs—have they really thought this through?" Mia's outburst was interrupted by Bae's approach.

"Hey there, passengers," Bae said, smiling broadly as she walked up. "Not to worry, Mia—all the skippers are Clan—so we can see just fine in the dark given the moon's phase. And Boris and Tanya are pros. The SASUs won't even see us." She winked while grinning. "Joel, you're with me."

"Aye aye, Captain," Joel responded as he grabbed his Clan backpack off the ice.

"Have a great trip, ladies," Bae said as she motioned for Joel to follow her.

"Bye, gals. Everything will be fine, Mia. Enjoy the sail!" Joel said, giving Mia a fumbling side-hug and a mock salute to me before he and Bae started to walk away.

"How can he be so excited? I mean, we're essentially climbing into deathtraps!" Mia turned to me looking both anxious and annoyed.

"Don't worry. I'm sure the Resistance has thought this through. I mean, why would they risk the whole operation by coming this way if they hadn't?"

Mia still didn't look quite convinced. Meanwhile, Joel and Bae hadn't gone but a few steps before we could hear Joel peppering her with questions about Tanya and Boris. They gave a short wave in passing to Claire as she approached us.

"Hi, Mia. Hi, Elin. How are you girls holding up?"

"Fine...I think," Mia said. Her tone left me doubting the conviction of her statement.

"Good, thanks. Who's your lucky passenger?" I replied, giving Mia's arm a comforting squeeze.

"Oh, I've got Mia. And we'll be just fine—ice sailing can actually be quite fun," Claire said, smiling reassuringly at Mia. She must've guessed the cause of Mia's nervousness.

"Guess that means I'm with you, Edvin," I said as he joined our group.

"Yup, I'm your skipper. You ready to get this show on the road?"

"Ready as I'll ever be. See you on the other side, Mia!" I smiled and hugged her tightly before following Edvin.

"Yeah...see you, Elli," Mia replied with an unsure smile.

The boat I was sharing with Edvin was in the middle of the pack. After opening the clear canopy, Edvin instructed me to climb in. He then went to the front of the boat to release the anchor.

The seat wasn't as uncomfortable as it looked from the outside. I was able to stretch my legs most of the way out, and the seat was well-cushioned. I looked up to see that Edvin had remained outside of the boat instead of climbing inside as well.

"Edvin, is something wrong? What are you waiting for?" I asked.

"The signal."

And as if on cue, a loud whistle sounded. Edvin started running at top speed. There was the sound of cleats digging into ice, the boat's skates gliding, the untightened sail flapping, and the wind whooshing. Once the boat had reached a sufficient speed, Edvin jumped in.

I glanced behind me. I caught sight of Claire jumping into her boat and closing the canopy. The rest of the boats were left in the distance, impossible to make out. Edvin and I had taken the lead.

Edvin closed the canopy, shutting out noise other than the steady whir of the boat gliding over the ice. It reminded me of the hum inside an airplane. He put the crank in the winch and tightened the sail.

It was impossible to tell our speed, given that there were no landmarks to judge by. "Edvin, how fast will we go?" I asked.

"Well, once I get her going—and given the open runway here—I'd say we'll probably get to 100 to 120 mph for our fast-traveling speed."

"*Wow*...that's fast!" I'd never been inside anything that traveled that fast on land—or ice. "How long is our trip?"

"Are you really already asking me if 'we're there yet'?" Edvin chuckled at his own joke. "Our trip to Litenhavn is about one hour at our fast speed and then another hour at much slower speeds as we dodge the SASUs."

"What about after that?"

"After? Well...that's when we separate. You three—meaning you, Mia, and Joel—will be off to Sigrid's. The rest of us will start making our way to Ginnungagap."

"How are you going to get there? And how are Mia, Joel, and I getting to Sigrid's?"

"You're full of questions, aren't you?" Edvin glanced behind us, I assumed to see everyone else's progress. "You guys will be taking a nice, warm, comfy train...while the rest of us cross-country ski in the fjord's frozen, snowy woods."

"Isn't there a faster way for you to get to Ginnungagap?"

"Not unless we want the *Stór-menni* up our butts. Their electronic sensors are placed all the way to the Outer Shield Wall. And as you heard McHaill say, the sensors will pick up the tiniest device, so anything that has an engine is out for our trip. Besides, the roads around here are few and far between, and what few there are...well, they are snow-laden. So that rules out car travel."

"Why not ice-sail closer?"

"Well, the closer you get to the Outer Shield Wall, the more sophisticated surveillance equipment there is. Even with Tanya's and Boris's help, it would be like sending up a red emergency flare if we continued past Litenhavn."

"Huh. I see." I thought for a moment. "So how are you going to get past all the surveillance equipment on skis? And how are you getting through the Shield Wall?"

"Okay, *wow*, Miss Nosy." Edvin shifted in his seat. Then, in a surprisingly gentle tone, he added, "I'm sorry, Elin, but even if I wanted to, I wouldn't be able to share much more with you. First of all: you know the Resistance's rules. Second: you've got the whole Chairman thing to contend with. And third: there are things I don't even know. So these are the final two questions I'm answering...and with that, I've probably told you too much already.

Edvin cleared his throat and then continued, "The *Stór-menni* don't pay much attention to Mannlegurs. In their view, Mannlegurs aren't worth their effort. They're only really concerned with anything big, supernatural, and/or high-tech...like an aircraft or drones. Their surveillance units are programmed to ignore Mannlegur activities. Cross-country skiing is a common pastime around these parts, so our group will pretend to be on a Mannlegur ski trip. As for the Shield Wall, it can only be entered and exited at the guard stations. Even I don't know the details of how *exactly* we'll get through...but apparently, the Resistance has a way."

I was about to follow up with a few more questions when Edvin interrupted. "Nope, that's it. I told you...I'm not answering anything more."

With Edvin promptly ending our discussion, I gazed out into the vast darkness through the canopy. The ground was an endless sheet of white. I looked up. The sky still shimmered with flickering stars while the crescent moon hung in the distance, advertising its coming growth.

I pondered what Edvin had told me about the *Stór-menni* surveillance and Shield Wall. And what he had meant when he said Mia, Joel, and I would be taking a train.

I woke to Edvin's cursing. "*ODIN'S BEARD!* Where in the *Niflheim* did that *just* come from?"

Our boat veered to the left, tipping precariously on its skates. Then with a loud *thump*, it was back on all three blades. Edvin tightened the winch and the boat shot forward at remarkable speed.

"EDIN, WHAT? What the heck is going on?" I shouted, recovering from being slammed into the side of the boat.

"Oh, good, you're awake! We've got a SASU on our tail!"

"WHAT? Weren't we supposed to avoid them with the whole 'formation' and 'illusion' stuff?"

"Yeah, that *was* the plan—but then nobody expected there'd be *one* circling FIFTEEN miles from the coast! ELIN, QUICK, LEAN LEFT!" Edvin banked the boat to the right trying to shake the SASU. I braced my hands against the right side, pushing my body left to help balance the boat so the skates stayed on the ice. At least some of my Uncle Bertie's sailing lessons were coming in handy.

"*Where* are the others?"

"I'm not sure. We weren't supposed to form up until five miles from the coast. You and I took the lead when we left the icebreakers."

I glanced behind us. In the darkness, I spotted a metal object roughly the size of a basketball flying high and closing in fast. Its red light was steadily blinking. "Edvin! It's gaining on us."

"Yeah, thanks. I know!" Edvin cranked on the winch, tightening the rope, and the boat burst forward. "Elin, I have to be honest here. There's only a little more rope left to trim the sail, which means we'll reach our top speed soon. And I don't think that it'll be enough to lose the SASU...that thing is just *too* fast!"

"Um, *okay*...so what do we do?"

"Well, we can't risk turning on any electronics to communicate. The *Stór-menni* would track us in seconds—and it wouldn't help anyway since our team has theirs off. Neither of us has a power which can take that thing out...so our only choice is to try to stay ahead of it until we can reach the formation point with the others—and hope *they* can deal with it."

"But I thought you just *said* we're going to reach our top speed soon...and that thing is still gaining on us!"

"Yup...so things *aren't* looking too peachy for us right now."

"What's it going to do if it catches us?"

"Well...you'll have to smile pretty for the Chairman because that thing will send our image to *Stór-menni* headquarters and every nearby Hunter. Once they have it, they'll descend upon us within minutes—if not faster...and we can say '*hasta la vista*' to our mission, Aedan, and our freedom."

I swallowed hard and turned to look behind us. The SASU was still matching our speed.

Was this *really* it? Was this how it all was going to end? I couldn't help but think of Aedan and how his capture had been by two smaller versions of what now followed us.

A wave of burning anger ignited inside me. We couldn't let this happen. For the two of *us* to jeopardize the missions, especially Aedan's rescue, was unbearable. We had to find a way —some way to get out of this mess! We couldn't just leave Aedan to rot in some Clan prison cell thinking we never came for him.

Desperately, I searched my seat and footwell for anything we could use to stop the SASU. But there was nothing. Everything I had was in the storage bin—not that anything in there would have really helped.

Suddenly, an idea popped into my head. "Edvin, you said earlier that the *Stór-menni* wouldn't be interested in Mannlegurs... couldn't we just pretend to be normal people out for an ice sail?"

"That would work if we were closer to the mainland in daylight—but Mannlegurs would never come out this far in the dark. It's too dangerous for them...and the *Stór-menni* know that." Edvin tightened his grip on the winch again. "The only things we have going for us right now are our speed and kicking up snow so it can't get a good look at us. HANG ON! LEAN RIGHT!" Edvin veered the boat slightly to the left, twirling a cloud of snow in our wake.

I glanced back. The SASU was slowed momentarily by the

swirl. Its red light beamed like a laser through the haze as it searched for us.

Edvin made a small crank on the winch, and the boat sped forward. The landscape of ice and darkness gave no sense of the boat's speed, which I was honestly grateful for at that moment. The boat's intense vibration and groans were enough to convince me that the word 'fast' was an understatement.

Then out of nowhere, Edvin whooped, "THANK, FREYA!"

"WHAT? What now?"

"Look behind us!"

I turned in my seat. In the distance, I could just make out another sailboat.

"Who *is* that?"

"It's Claire...she *finally* got close enough to hear my calls."

I'd almost forgotten that Claire and Edvin shared a telepathic connection. "What's she saying?"

"She's going to try to ram the SASU with her mast. We just have to keep going straight so she can get close enough."

"Is that going to work? I mean, it's not exactly a large object." I turned to look at the basketball-sized object behind us.

"It's better than doing nothing."

"Fair point." I crossed my fingers and sent a little prayer into the universe.

"Just hold tight and lean left with everything you got when I say so. Claire isn't going to be able to slow down once she starts. We'll have to get out of her way after she hits the SASU. And we only get one try at this!" Edvin adjusted his seat, clearly preparing his steering leg for the boat's sudden turn. "

I braced my hands on the right side so I could push my body left on Edvin's command. I looked to the rear and saw Claire's boat racing towards us and the SASU. The metal ball was only a couple of yards from our boat. Claire was closing in fast. Thankfully, the SASU hadn't yet noticed the second boat.

I held my breath and watched.

With great speed, the mast on Claire's boat made impact with the SASU. The metal ball went tumbling into the boat's sail and bounced off. It spun wildly towards the ground. I could tell it was fighting to regain control and nearly had it when it struck the ice—hard. Pieces of metal went flying in every direction.

"NOW, ELIN!" Edvin ordered.

I pushed my full body weight to the left as Edvin swerved the boat right. The boat groaned loudly. I could feel it tilt perilously onto two skates.

I pushed harder to the left and silently prayed we wouldn't topple over. At our high speed, it would be a disaster. I saw Edvin slam his body hard into the left side of the boat.

Claire's boat zoomed by us. Its wings and the rear of our boat were close—really close. A matter of inches. We were near enough where I could see Mia's petrified face in the backseat.

With a great *thud*, our boat straightened from the turn, and the third skate returned to the ice. We shot forward.

"WOOHOO! *Yeah*! We did it!" Edvin whooped.

I let out my breath. "Um...let's *not* do *that* again!"

"Agreed!" Edvin relaxed the rope on the winch, and the boat slowed. He then more gently turned the boat in the direction Claire had gone. He turned his head and grinned at me "It worked, though! That SASU is a goner."

I smiled back. "Tell Claire a big thank you from me."

"Will do." Edvin was silent for a while. Then he said, "*Sooo,* we have a small problem."

"Oh, *lordy*! What now?" I moaned.

"Claire and I just confirmed that we are off-course for the formation point. The shenanigans with the SASU brought us too far South. There is no time to turn back, so we'll have to try to course correct but—" Edvin mumbled something.

" 'But' what, Edvin?"

"It's really nothing—so don't freak out...but there's a minor break in the ice that we'll have to cross."

"WHAT? How can there be a break in the ice?" I was stunned. I could only imagine Mia's face when Claire told her the news.

"Well, you see—we've gotten too close to shipping lanes that run on the southern edge—and so there's an icebreaker path that we're on the wrong side of."

I thought back to the churned-up ice wake left by the small icebreakers we'd been on. It had not been a small gap. The shipping lanes would have much larger icebreakers carving the path. "Edvin, how *minor* is the opening? And how are *we* going to cross it?"

"You'll see in about two minutes."

"WHAT? Edvin! I'm not ready—"

"Elin, how *exactly* are you going to prepare? Are you going to squeeze the armrest a little tighter? Or perhaps you need time to close your eyes?" The sarcasm was thick in his voice. "We have to do *this*—there are no choices here."

"*Emotionally* prepare," I mumbled begrudgingly. "But fine—what's the plan?"

"We are going to build up as much speed as possible. Then, when I say 'Now' you are going to push the lever next to your right leg to the floor."

The boat's vibration had already increased tenfold as Edvin and I spoke. I glanced down and, for the first time, noticed the lever on the right side of the footwell. "What's the lever do?"

"It's going to help us sail over the gap." Edvin grinned.

"I get that but how—"

"NOW, ELIN! Push it now!"

Without hesitation and purely on reflex, I did as Edvin commanded. A loud *screech* and *bang* rang out. The boat shook. Then, I felt it rise off the ice. I looked behind us. Half of the boat's mast had split into two horizontal pieces, with the sail making perfect wings. I was both terrified and awed as I took in the sight.

Glancing down, I saw that there was still ice left underneath us as we climbed higher, but a short distance ahead was a large opening with the gaping black sea. Ice chunks bobbed in the arctic water. The other side of the breach was nowhere to be seen.

"Edvin, how long can we stay in the air?"

Edvin turned his head and grinned reassuringly. "Long enough. Don't worry—we'll make it to the other side."

Next to us, I saw Claire and Mia do the same maneuver. Their boat lifted smoothly off the ice. Through its clear canopy, I could see Mia's horrified expression. I was pretty sure, as far as she was concerned, Joel and I would never be living this down—although, in our defense, no brakes had been needed.

THIRTEEN

All Aboard

ELIN

I probably would have been more excited by Tanya's and Boris's display at the formation point if we hadn't just been relentlessly chased by a SASU and made a death-defying jump over an ice gap in a sailboat. That isn't to say that it wasn't cool to witness Tanya and Boris yield their powers—because it was. But apparently, my adrenaline rush for the day had been met.

Tanya went first, creating a large, shimmering illusion bubble that enveloped us underneath its half-dome. Then, Boris brought in a snow squall that swirled energetically around the bubble, hiding us from prying eyes. It was a lot like being inside a snow globe that had been vigorously shaken.

I wasn't sure at what point I fell asleep, but I woke to bits of sunlight breaching the boat's canopy. It must have been close to eleven, given the amount of light. I rubbed the sleep from my eyes and looked around. Land! I could actually see land now.

There was a shore of dense trees that came right up to the edge of the ice. Beyond that, a snowy granite slope began to quickly climb towards the sky. If it hadn't been for the clear roof of the boat, I wouldn't have been able to see the top. The other side looked much the same. We must've entered the fjord.

I could tell that Edvin had slowed the boat, because the vibration wasn't as strong. I glanced behind me to see the seven other ice sailboats close by.

"Morning, sleepyhead," Edvin said as he sensed my movement. "Just in time, too. We are only a few minutes from the landing point."

"What happened to Boris's snow squall?"

"Oh, we don't need it anymore. We are way past the fjord's entrance and the SASUs guarding it. Tanya's illusion is enough to get us to the landing point."

Edvin loosened the rope on the winch, and the boat's speed lessened. Two of the Resistance team boats shot past us at remarkable speed.

"Where are they going?" I asked.

"To make sure the coast is clear—literally. McHaill doesn't want any surprises. The landing party will secure the area before the rest of us arrive."

"Got it, how are we getting from the landing point to the train?"

Edvin glanced at me. "I guess we're close enough that I can tell you. It's a fifteen-minute snowshoe into Litenhavn. The train starts from there and eventually gets you up the mountain to Thordalr. Claire will tell you the rest at the station."

"Okay. Good to know."

Watching the scenery whip by us, I realized that Mia, Joel, and I would soon be on our own—and there would be no one with the answers to what came next. It felt somehow freeing and terrifying at the same time.

Moments later, we arrived at the landing point. One of the

Resistance team members waved the all-clear from the shore near what looked like an old boathouse.

Edvin expertly steered the boat to a stop facing directly upwind next to the other two boats already parked. Joel had been right about how the boats stopped. Edvin loosened the remaining rope on the winch, letting the sail relax.

I could see that the landing team had stayed busy while waiting for us. Their boats were already nearly dismantled and the pieces stacked in a neat pile. I was wondering what they were going to do with them, when Bae's and Joel's boat pulled up next to us.

Of course! Bae's garage. She could just open a portal and the dismantled sailboats would be back in Auor in a flash. Talk about adhering to the "leave no trace behind" nature rules.

Edvin pushed open the boat's canopy and the salty, cold air greeted us with a flourish. I took a deep breath as I stretched my arms out. The sun felt amazing on my face. It was a rare occurrence to have a sunny day instead of the normal gray clouds that showed themselves during daylight. Without the brisk wind, the temperature felt warmer than on the open ice.

Edvin eased himself out of the boat and went to secure the anchor. I could see that Claire and Mia had parked their boat on the other side of Bae's and Joel's. I couldn't wait to share with Mia and Joel everything I'd been able to pry out of Edvin on the trip.

The three of us reunited a few steps away from the boats, excitedly talking about what each of us had experienced—and more importantly, learned—on the journey.

"Joel, you won't *believe* what we've just been through," Mia said. She launched into a dramatic description of the events with the SASU and about flying over the ice gap. "I'm starting to wonder if I don't have the gift of premonition."

"Or just a heightened sense of fear," Joel muttered.

"*What?*" Mia asked.

Joel gulped. "I said, high...sounds very high. Amazing you survived."

"*Joel Larson*, are you making fun of me?" Mia demanded.

Joel smirked. "I wouldn't dare." Mia swatted him on the arm. "Hey, now! *I said*, I wouldn't dare."

Joel smiled, feigning innocence. Mia rolled her eyes.

Starting to feel a bit 'third-wheelish', I said, "*Sooo*, did you guys learn anything else interesting during your boat rides with Bae and Claire?"

From what Mia and I could gather, Bae's and Joel's conversation was mostly about Tanya and Boris, the boats, and sailing. Mia and Claire had apparently talked more about Clan history. And as I finished sharing what I'd learned from Edvin, Mrs. Grady came to usher us off the ice and onto the shore. She shepherded us to a spot next to the boathouse.

"Wait here. I'm just going to grab our equipment and the rest of the Gradys, and then we'll be off to Litenhavn."

"But what about the rest of the team? Shouldn't we help with the boats?" I asked.

"We're going ahead of them. They'll stay to take care of things here. We've got to get you on your train and safely on your way, and we don't have much time. The trains run on schedule around here. Don't you worry...everything's been planned." Mrs. Grady patted me on the arm and bustled off to corral her family and equipment.

After everyone had been outfitted with snowshoes, the Gradys, Mia, Joel, and I were off, trudging through an evergreen forest. The dark-green trees bowed under the weight of snow that sat on their branches. An occasional ray of sunlight flickered through the growth, causing light to refract rainbow colors across the snow's surface. It would've been an amazing scene to stop and appreciate if we hadn't been in such a hurry.

Even with the fancier Clan snowshoes, our progress was slow. Mrs. Grady was starting to worry if we'd make our train. Claire volunteered to break trail using her *megin* speed. We all might've used our *megin* speed, but with Mia and Joel, it was pointless. They wouldn't have been able to keep up. However, thanks to Claire's efforts, our pace picked up.

After ten more minutes of plodding along, we saw the first signs that we were close to the port town. There was a wide lane that had been trodden down by snowmobiles and sleighs. We quickly adopted the path and within five minutes were in the center of Litenhavn.

The town turned out to be a small fishing harbor around which homes and shops painted from deep red to bright yellow colors were clustered. A train station was visible a few blocks up a snowy road from the cobblestoned plaza in which we stood. A sign reading LITENHAVN STATION danced in the cold sea breeze from the fjord.

As we removed our snowshoes by the frozen plaza fountain, Joel collapsed on to a nearby stone bench and grumbled something about why couldn't we have used snowmobiles to get to town.

An annoyed Edvin responded, "*Hmm*...why didn't we think of that. Oh, wait , 'cause did you see a path big enough in the woods we just came through? I sure didn't."

"Now, now, boys...settle down," Mr. Grady said. "There's a reason behind every decision. Let's just be glad we've made it in time."

"I think we might have some hungry troops on our hands," Mrs. Grady observed. Glancing down at her watch, she continued, "Too bad we don't have time for a proper meal all together. Liam, why don't you and Edvin go find the tavern where we're meeting...

um…everyone else." Mrs. Grady threw a furtive look around her. "Claire, I think you'd best take Mia, Joel, and Elin to the station and get their tickets sorted. Time is running short. I'll go hunt down something for them to eat on the train."

"Okay, Mom," Claire responded. "Come on, you three. Let's get you on your way!"

"So, I guess this is it," I said, looking at Edvin and Mr. Grady. "I…um…thanks…for everything, and…um…tell Aedan… well, I mean…good luck!" I lamely finished. There just wasn't enough time or words to express everything I wanted to say to them—particularly the things I would've wanted them to tell Aedan. A tinge of embarrassment struck me as I thought of not being there when Aedan was rescued. What would he think? Especially given that I was the reason he was there to begin with.

"Good luck to you as well, Elin," Mr. Grady said, interrupting my thoughts. He gave me an unexpected, hesitant hug. Then looking at all three of us, he added, "We'll look forward to a mighty reunion once we're all back together again. Take care of each other on the journey and be sure to listen to Claire's instructions carefully."

Edvin was less measured as he picked me up in a great big bear hug. "Stay out of trouble, Elin. Only so many times I can save you." He winked at me before turning to Mia and Joel. "See you two. Stay safe and together!"

"Off you go then!" Mrs. Grady said, motioning with her hands towards the station. "I'll see you in a few minutes."

Claire turned up the road towards the station with the three of us trailing behind. It was a short, frigid walk among the colorful buildings, and we were happy to enter the small station's waiting room, where a hot iron stove pumped out some much-appreciated heat. While Claire approached the ticket window, the three of us huddled around the stove, stretching our frozen fingers towards the heat.

At first, I thought I was just chilled from the cold outside. But when the goosebumps underneath my thermal shirt refused to go away and a strange, unsettled feeling started to grow inside me, I knew something else was up. The only time I'd felt something similar was on Auor when I'd first almost "met" Aedan at the beach. But after my awakening, the goosebumps hadn't appeared again—until now.

I glanced at Mia and Joel. They were quietly talking to each other. I didn't want to alarm them, especially since I didn't know what to tell them. "Hey, let's get outta here 'cause I've got goosebumps" didn't seem like a great reason. I let my gaze casually travel around the station room.

It was a paneled in pine wood room with a few wooden benches and chairs placed against the sides. On the walls hung various train maps, pictures of the fjord, and advertisements for cross-country skiing in black frames. It was a cozy environment that would've become stifling in a crowd.

There were a surprising number of people waiting for the train, given the remote area and size of the town. Seated on the wooden bench across from the door were three elderly people bundled up in some old-fashioned cloaks that didn't look nearly warm enough for the temperature outside. A family of four, dressed in parkas and snow pants, sat at another bench in the corner with their luggage stacked beside them. By the doors to the tracks, two men were leaning against the wall with their cross-country skis in hand, talking to each other. In a chair opposite, there was a single woman in a long woolen coat with her hood pulled up, reading a book. And there was a man—at least, I thought it was a man—walking towards the track doors in a navy parka with the hood pulled up and low over his face. He disappeared outside before I could get a clear look at him.

"Okay, then," Claire said, walking up to us. "The train should be arriving any minute. I have your tickets right here."

She handed one to each of us. Reaching for the ticket, I noticed that the goosebumps under my sleeves had simmered down. The flare up must just have been a strange effect of being in the cold for so long. I looked down at my ticket, expecting to see "Thordalr," but instead, next to the destination it read "Lyngen" with an asterisk at the end.

"Um...Claire, my ticket says Lyngen instead of Thordalr."

"Yes, that's right," Claire answered. Then she motioned for us to come closer together and in a quiet voice, she continued. "Now you need to listen very carefully. As far as the Mannlegur passengers are concerned, the last stop is Lyngen. But for those going to Thordalr...at Lyngen, you need to move to the very first two cars of the train. It's very important that you do—those are the only two carriages that will continue to Thordalr. The asterisk tells the conductor your actual destination."

"You mean Thordalr isn't a Mannlegur town?" Joel asked, looking somewhere between thrilled and apprehensive.

"Shhh...quietly...that's right. Now here, take these." Claire reached into her backpack and produced three tiny pouches.

"What are they?" Mia whispered.

"They're Clan cloaks. People still tend to dress in a more traditional style in Clan towns. You can keep your Clan-fabric coats underneath as they'll adjust to the additional warmth, but you need to wear the cloaks...especially Mia and Joel." Claire handed one to each of us. "No, Joel! Don't open it *here*."

Joel nearly dropped the pouch, startled by Claire's command. Fumbling, he somehow managed to regain control of the sack at the last second.

"Only put them on once the Mannlegurs clear the train at the last stop and you move to the first cars. You don't need to advertise your destination before then," Claire said, trying to retain her composure.

"What about once we get to Thordalr? How do we find Sigrid's?" I whispered.

"Yes...well, I was just getting to that," Claire said, still keeping a watchful eye on Joel. "Here."

She held out a slip of paper to me. I unfurled it and looked down. Written on the paper was a long number string.

Claire's hand slipped over mine, folding the paper back up. "Keep that safe and away from prying eyes."

I nodded.

"Once you get to Thordalr, at the station hire a sleigh and put that"—she pointed to the slip of paper—"into the destination screen."

"Hire a *what*, now? And put that into *where*, exactly?" Mia whispered.

"Hire a sleigh. It's sorta like a taxi...or car rental...you'll see. And it'll be clear where to enter it once you get in the sleigh." Claire smiled. "Simple enough, right?"

"Um...I guess...but one problem with the sleigh-hiring part," Mia said. "How are we supposed to pay for it? I only brought a credit card and my phone. Do they accept those in a 'Clan' town? And can we turn our phones back on?"

"Yes, you can turn your phones on. But just so you know...the rest of the team will be keeping ours off until we're back on Auor. Also, you don't have to worry about—paying or money, I mean. Nothing costs anything in Clan society." When the three of us looked even more confused, Claire elaborated. "Everyone's basic needs are taken care of. That includes food, lodging, and transportation. If you want something beyond that, then it's a token system where you use your abilities as a currency."

"What do you mean, a 'token system'? Is that like Clan money?" Joel asked.

"No. Think of it more like an 'IOU' card. You're basically giving someone the right to have you use your ability for their benefit," Claire explained. "Obviously, you want to be pretty careful about to whom you give your tokens, but you three shouldn't need to worry about that. Now, any more questions, or are you clear on the instructions?"

"Uh, I think we got it...best as we can at this point anyway. Take the train, switch cars, put on cloaks, hire sleigh, and enter this," I replied.

"Yup, you got it. Just follow those instructions and you'll be fine," Claire said, giving my arm a squeeze. "The train ride is only two hours, so you'll be there before you know it. I'd go with you but Aedan's rescue team is already small...and I think we can all agree that takes precedence." The three of us nodded. "It should be a simple train journey...and once you give Sigrid our name and explain the situation, I'm sure she'll welcome you."

"You mean she doesn't know we're coming?" I asked, surprised.

"There was no way to contact her. She doesn't have Mannlegur communication devices, and normal Clan methods would be too risky. But don't worry, she'll be very welcoming... once she knows who you are."

At that moment, we heard a train whistle nearing the station. All the people in the waiting room began to collect their belongings and shuffle towards the double doors to the tracks.

"Wait! Elin...Claire!" I turned my head to see Mrs. Grady rushing through the street-side station door. "Oh, I'm so glad I got here in time. Here...I found you some savory pastries at the bakery.

They should tide the three of you over until you reach...um...your destination. I believe the train has both cold and warm drinks on board, so you should be set on that front as well."

Slightly out of breath, she handed me a large, warm paper sack. I caught a delicious whiff of warm, buttery pastry as I accepted it.

"Thank you so much, Mrs. Grady. It smells amazing!" I replied.

The train whistle hooted again, announcing the train's arrival. Our posse turned for the track doors. Outside on the platform, I caught another glimpse of the man in the navy parka boarding the train. Something about him felt familiar, which was absurd. Who could I possibly know in this part of the world?

"Elli...Elli." Mia tried to gain my attention by waving her hand in front of my face.

"*Whaaat?*" I was still trying to see the man's face as he entered the fourth train car.

"Are you going to tell them?"

"Tell them what?" I focused on Mia.

"You know...about Aedan...your vision? This is your last chance."

Mia's eyes told me that she thought I should. I hadn't found the right moment before—or that's what I'd at least told myself. But what she said was—true. This was my last opportunity. And seeing as we were about to make a quick getaway, perhaps this was the right moment.

"You think I should, don't you?"

Mia nodded with vigor.

"Okay, fine...Here goes nothing." I turned to get Mrs. Grady's attention. "Uh...Mrs. Grady...can I talk to you for a minute?"

I went on to relate everything I'd seen in my vision from two nights earlier and how I had been uncertain about whether it was a dream or vision but for the blue light from Aedan's cuff that Mia had seen. Mrs. Grady stood grim-faced and silent, along with Claire, who'd turned to listen.

"All aboard!" The conductor called out. We were the last people on the platform.

Suddenly, Mrs. Grady pulled me into a warm hug and whispered, "Thank you, Elin. I'm sure that'll be helpful information. Just...just try to pull the plug on your visions until you have your medal. I'm glad the Chairman didn't make an appearance in this one...but it doesn't mean he won't in future ones." She gave me a good final squeeze. "Now mind what Claire told you and have a good journey!"

Claire gave me a quick hug while Mrs. Grady embraced Joel and Mia, giving them similar advice to follow Claire's instructions. Then, as the conductor yelled his final "All aboard!," Mia, Joel, and I climbed into the third passenger car.

FOURTEEN

Drugged Again

AEDAN

I tossed on the little green mattress for what seemed like the hundredth time. Sleep was elusive. I kept pondering why the Chairman hadn't called for me since telling me of the plan to capture my family. It'd been at least five or six days now. It was hard to keep track inside the windowless room. The only indication of time's passage was when the guards turned on the lights for twelve hours.

Did the Chairman's silence mean the Hunters had been successful at capturing my family? Or was it an unsuccessful attempt that kept him away? In any other situation, I would've been glad for the reprieve from the mind-probes, but any news, however small, giving indications one way or the other would have been welcome. The gnawing questions and worry were becoming unbearable.

Then there was the strange incident a few nights prior. I'd been on the "phone" with Reo when I could've sworn I'd heard Elin calling my name. Reo had assured me that it wasn't unusual to have some hallucinations after being locked up for a significant period. As if being stuck in this cell for the last several weeks wasn't enough, now I was going to have to contend with hearing things as well...*great*, just great!

Trying to make me feel better, he'd recounted his own incidents with seeing and hearing his family in his cell. He called them his "dark moments." But he also said how his family's images and voices had reminded him of what he still had to fight for, helping him out of his "deep, dark well."

Elin's voice had felt different from what Reo had described, but I hadn't pursued the subject further. The slight quiver in Reo's voice as he spoke had given away the pain he'd endured.

Elin had been near my thoughts ever since we parted ways in the Ash Park woods. I'd tried to avoid thinking about her in case the Chairman was able to pry something loose from my mind. At least then, she wouldn't be the first thought he'd capture.

But just the mention of Ash Park and Elin flooded me with memories of our harrowing effort to escape—and her unexpected kiss. Her lips had been so soft. Their touch on mine had sent a tingling sensation down my entire body. Had she felt the same thing?

My family's fugitive lifestyle hadn't exactly been conducive to starting romantic relationships, so it wasn't like I'd kissed a lot of girls. I wondered what our kiss meant—if anything. Had it just been for luck, like she'd said? Or were we something more now?

Argh! What was the point of wondering anyway? I was trapped in a cell with no signs of getting out anytime soon. I turned over again on the mattress, trying to shut down the thoughts. Hadn't I just said that I needed to protect Elin from the Chairman's mind probes? She was his ultimate prize, after all.

Although, now that I thought of it, the Chairman had never asked me about Elin—only my family. Why was that? From what everyone said, weren't the Dormants his obsession?

Keys jangling on the other side of my cell door brought me upright in the darkness. It was the middle of the night. Why would the guards be coming for me now? It was an odd time for a mind intervention.

Oh, crap! I'd left the tin cup out and attached to the string. My heart nearly jumped out of my chest. It was my only lifeline. I'd left it out in case Reo wanted to talk some more. I couldn't let the guards see it. I blindly scrambled to locate it on the floor in the darkness.

Ever since the check-in guard had placed a metallic cuff on my wrist, I'd lost all my *megin*. Reo had informed me the bracelet was a *Hepta Baugr*, an abilities dampener, which meant I was as powerful as any Mannlegur. The cuff was unremovable while powered on, as its blinking red light constantly reminded me. Thus, I had no night vision to aid me in my mad search.

I could hear the guard outside my cell door muttering frustrations about the key ring and the number of keys. My fingers worked the ground at furious speed. Finally, they landed upon the cup wedged between the mattress and wall.

There was a metallic click from the keyhole. The correct key had been inserted.

My blood pounded in my ears. I quickly separated the tin cup from the string. My fingers followed the thread to the hole in the wall. As fast as possible, I worked to re-insert it. Then I frantically searched for the small tear in the mattress. At last coming upon it, I stuffed the cup back into its secure location.

With my heart still thundering, the door to my cell opened. Two guards I didn't recognize entered.

"What's going on?" I asked, feigning like I'd woken at their entrance.

"On your feet," one of the guards commanded.

"Why? Where are we going?"

"Now! Don't make me force you." The second guard made a threatening move toward me.

"Okay, okay," I answered, raising my hands in surrender. I took my time getting up, in no hurry to do as they wished.

The second guard, growing impatient, approached me. He put a stern hand under my arm and with force "assisted" me to a stand.

"Quit your dawdling. We don't have time for this tonight," he said, yanking me towards the door.

The first guard grabbed my other arm as they hauled me out of the cell at a speed that I was unaccustomed to. I managed a quick backward glance at Reo's door.

In the porthole window, I could see his face lit by the eerie green-hued lights from the hallway. His grim expression gave me no comfort.

The guards sped me along the fortress's corridors until I lost all sense of direction. We went up some stairs and down others. We turned right and then left into different hallways. The only thing I was sure of was that our destination wasn't the seafoam-green interrogation room.

An unnerved heaviness was starting to grow in the pit of my stomach. Had the Chairman finally grown tired of my resistance? Was I now going to be tortured with the "extraction" method he'd alluded to with my family?

Finally, we came to a small room with benches lining both stone walls. At the far end of the room was an ancient, heavily fortified steel door with a large metal bar running across it. Above the benches, fastened to the wall was a row of coat hooks. Black cloaks, with the Chairman's three-triangle insignia stitched on the front, hung from a few of them.

"Here," the first guard said as he pulled a cloak off the hook and slid a pair of black winter boots from underneath the bench. "Put these on."

At my hesitation, the second guard shoved me toward the bench where the first guard had tossed the items. Rubbing my arm where his vise-like grip had dug in, I sat down and proceeded to put the winter boots on.

All indications were that they were taking me outdoors. I couldn't help but wonder what exactly lay beyond the door. Nothing good, I was sure.

The knot in my stomach tightened as I thought about my options. There was no way I could take on both of the guards without my powers. I tried to estimate if I'd have time to stand and smash the *Hepta Baugr* against the wall to disable it, even for a moment, before the guards could react. There was no guarantee that it'd work. I'd spent hours in my cell trying to pry the cuff open or off my wrist to no avail. But what choice did I have?

If I was successful, my options for escape were limited. The way to the room had been so convoluted that I knew I wouldn't be able to find a way out before I was recaptured. The only option was the back door. What awaited me outside it, I couldn't be sure —but it was my only potential path. I slid the cloak around my shoulders, hoping it might help to conceal my intent when I stood up.

As I was about to put my plan into action, the second guard approached me and, without a word, jabbed a needle into my neck. Immediately, my surroundings became woozy. I felt my muscles become loose and unresponsive. My eyelids became heavy.

The first guard pushed a hover-chair to my side. Then, ungraciously, the guards rolled me into it. Through drooping eyelids, I saw the second guard lift the steel bar from the back door and open it. A blast of frigid air entered the room, stalling the effects of the drug circulating in my body. I tried to open my eyes wider to see what was beyond the door in the cold darkness.

The room's yellow light poured out through the open door, highlighting whirling snowflakes as they danced above a small black landing pad. Upon it sat a large, well-kept black AHV with the Chairman's insignia emblazoned across the left door. I could hear the engine's whirr as the hover vehicle idled.

The chair and I seemed to glide towards the machine. I struggled to stop my eyes from closing and my head falling forward onto my chest. With one last effort, I managed a glance at the passenger in the vehicle. She was a girl close to my age with light brown hair braided into a tight bun. She wore a dark blue tunic that Reo, while describing a Hunter squad's hierarchy, had informed me was a Captain's uniform.

OH, MY HEAD! I TRIED TO SLIDE MY HAND UP TO RUB MY temple, relieving it from the pounding inside, but my hand refused to budge. With effort, I managed to open one eye and then the other.

I was lying on a big, comfortable bed with a soft white pillow under my head. The rest of the room was large, with two walls made entirely of windows. It was still dark outside, but I could see a multitude of lights near and far beyond the glass.

A bedside lamp lit the room with a warm glow and a cheerful fire danced in a fireplace directly in front of me. There were two large wingback armchairs angled towards it. The rest of the room's furnishings echoed that of the chairs, in a modern and expensive-looking style.

My tongue felt heavy and dry inside my mouth. Underneath the lamp on the bedside table sat a tall glass of what looked like water.

I tried wiggling my fingers. The movement reminded me of

the car ride in Ms. Haugen's electric vehicle back on Auor Island when Elin and I'd both been in a similar drugged state. Moving our tingling limbs had helped back then. And I was pretty sure that I'd just had another dose of the *Stór-menni*'s favorite immobilizing drug. The question was, why? Why had they brought me here? Wherever here was.

And on a different note, was the drugging *really* necessary? I mean, couldn't they just have told me that a nice comfy bed and warm fire waited for me?

I continued to work on getting the feeling back into my arms and legs. After a while, I managed to move my left arm and hand with some effort. I reached for the glass of water on the table, eager to quench the dryness in my desert-like mouth.

Just as I grasped the glass, a female voice said, "Oh, *good*. You're finally up."

The AHV's other passenger stood up from one of the wingback chairs, set a device that looked like a tablet on a nearby table, and approached the bed.

"I was starting to think you might sleep the entire day." Her voice was friendly. "Here, let me help you with that. The *hvíla* drug can really do a number on your coordination."

She slipped a hand behind my head, tilting it, while her other hand helped guide the glass towards my lips. I took a large gulp, grateful for the moisture as it washed the dry, acidic taste in my mouth away.

The question of whether drinking it was safe flashed through my head. But I figured they could've killed me a dozen ways already, so the likelihood that the glass contained a poisonous substance was low.

"There...that's better, isn't it?" She took the glass from my quivering hand, placing it back on the bedside table. "Oh, now where are my manners? I'm Thyra Bjorndóttir. And you are

Aedan Grady." She held out her hand towards me. I pretended that my right hand was still unresponsive. The last thing I wanted to do was shake my captor's hand. "I know, I know...you must have a lot of questions. Well, let me just inform the Chairman that you're awake...and hopefully, you and I both can get some answers. I know he's anxious to see you."

She dropped her hand and moved back over to where she'd lain the tablet. My stomach flip-flopped as she said the Chairman's name. I wasn't in any condition to resist a mind intervention at the moment. My head was still pounding and I was barely able to follow what Thyra was saying.

Plus, I could still feel the *Hepta Baugr* digging into my right wrist. Not that my *megin* would've been able to help me anyway. All I could do was lie there and wait for the Chairman's arrival. I watched as Thyra relaxed into the same wingback chair that she'd risen from and tapped on the tablet.

After what was about twenty minutes, according to the small antique clock on the fireplace mantle, the room's only door effortlessly slid open and the Chairman strode in, his familiar black robes swinging around him. Thyra immediately rose from her chair and warmly smiled at him. But instead of continuing toward her, he turned to my bedside.

"Good morning, Aedan. So good to see you again." His mouth stretched into a satisfied smile. His gray eyes probed my blue ones, but his mind stayed out of mine. "I see you've met Thyra. She'll be your guide for the time being."

Thyra couldn't hide the look of surprise that flashed across her face. She approached the bed as well. "But Uncle...don't you need me on the...um...other important matter we're pursuing?" Had she just called the Chairman "*uncle*"?

"No, I think we have that well in hand, from what you've reported. Aedan is now your priority. You and your team will be introducing him to the Leikr." The Chairman looked at Thyra and smiled. He put a hand on her shoulder in a fatherly way as he turned back to me. "In fact, all of you will be entering the games under my flag."

"*WHAT?*" Thyra's mouth fell open. "Uncle, are you unhappy with me? I know our...um...efforts weren't quite as we'd...hoped... on my recent mission...but I do think we're recovering nicely...just on the cusp of that major breakthrough. Besides, wouldn't one of the more-recent players and teams be a better choice to introduce Aedan to the Leikr and represent your flag? I'd hate to lose the momentum we've created on the mission."

"No, Thyra. I want you." The Chairman shifted his eyes back to her. "After all, it's a great honor to bear the Chairman's flag in the games, is it not? So we want the best players. And these games are...are special. I'll leave the choice of your teammates up to you. I assumed you'd want to use your current team. But if not, I'm sure you'll pick a winning one. Just be sure to save a spot for Aedan."

"Sure...um...absolutely, Uncle. As you wish." Thyra's voice firmly portrayed the enthusiasm that the Chairman expected but her eyes told a very different story.

"Excellent. I'm so glad that's settled, then. I want Aedan to experience all possible aspects of Clan life here in Falinvik. His parents and his recent stay at Ginnungagap may have given him the wrong impression about us. Our aim should be to correct that... and who better than you, Thyra. After all, family should stick together." The Chairman gave another squeeze to Thyra's shoulder before turning back to me. "Now Aedan, I'll leave you in Thyra's good care. You should have all that you need in this room —fresh clothes, food replicator, shower—but should you need anything else, don't hesitate to let Thyra know."

With a pat to Thyra's shoulder and a small head nod to me, he exited as a gracious host.

Thyra seemed to be at a loss for words. Her eyes had a distant, thoughtful expression as her fingers absently tapped the bedpost.

"Well...this was an unexpected yet intriguing turn of events," she said at last. Her brown eyes turned to me. "You should rest. The next few days will be grueling. Entering the Leikr under normal circumstances requires months of training. We have days... and playing under the Chairman's flag...well, that's no joke. It puts an immediate target on our backs. Hmmm...wonder what he's really up to?" Her last words were uttered more to herself than to me.

Thyra turned back towards the fireplace, collecting her tablet from the side table. Then she walked to the door and waved her hand in front of it. The door slid open.

"I'll be back tomorrow morning. If you need anything before then, there's an intercom by the door."

She pointed at the wall next to the door. Then she walked through the opening, and the door slid closed. And I was left to digest everything I'd just heard and witnessed.

FIFTEEN

The Dancing Dragons

ELIN

Making our way down the train's jostling corridor, Mia, Joel, and I found an empty compartment four doors down from where we'd entered. The cabin was small and narrow, with four facing seats. We piled our backpacks into the empty seat, hoping to discourage other passengers from encroaching on our privacy.

Joel sat down in the seat next to the bags while Mia and I took the other two seats. Snow-covered evergreens seemed to glide by the compartment's window, as the train was already moving at a steady pace. From what I could tell, we were heading north.

"I wonder why we couldn't have just taken the train to begin with. I mean, Lyngen isn't that far of a drive from the biggest city in the north. We could've flown there, taken the train, and avoided all the hassle of the boat trips...and the rest of the stuff," Joel grumbled.

"Jeez, grumpy much?" Being nearer to the cabin door, Mia leaned over and slid it closed. "According to what Claire told me on the ice boat, the train lines in this area are heavily patrolled by

Clan Hunters. Apparently, in the early days of the Chairman's rule, they were used as a main escape route for Clan members and a conduit for Resistance activity. *So*, if we had all traveled together in our large group using the routes, we would've attracted a lot of unwanted attention."

"Wow, I had no idea about the train patrols. No wonder Claire didn't want us to put on the cloaks until the last minute," I said, surprised. "I guess as long as the Hunters think we're Mannlegurs, we should be fine, right?"

"Um...we *are* Mannlegurs...well, most of us anyway," Joel grinned.

"*Oh*, is there *something* you want to tell us, Joel?" I innocently quipped.

Joel laughed. "Maybe someday, if I'm *really* lucky."

"Hmm, not sure about the lucky part...at least right now." I frowned. Coming into my powers in the middle of a supernatural crisis wasn't exactly what every new superhuman hopes for. Changing the topic, I added, "How about some food?"

I opened the paper bag Mrs. Grady had given me, and immediately the cabin air filled with the scent of warm buttery crust, melted cheese, and sautéed mushrooms. My stomach rumbled. I quickly unpacked the napkins and the savory pastries from the bag, placing them on the small side table.

Each of us grabbed a pie, our mouths watering, and bit into the flaky crust. My taste buds sang with delight. After an early morning of sailing and snowshoeing, the assortment of tartlets were just the thing to sate the gnawing gremlins in my stomach.

After filling ourselves on the baked goods, quenching the inevitable thirst became the next order of business. Through the cabin-door window, I'd seen a few passengers pass by our compartment carrying paper cups and recalled Mrs. Grady saying that there were drinks on the train.

As Joel and Mia had started a game of gin rummy, I volunteered to go find the drink stand. I opened the compartment's door and headed in the direction I'd witnessed the other passengers walking from.

When I drew near the end of a train car, I could see people milling around a tea dispenser and water cooler in the vestibule. Suddenly, goosebumps sprang to life on my arms. A familiar prickly electricity seemed to fill the air around me.

What was happening to me? Who was doing this? Was this a Hunter trap? I took a deep breath, trying to calm the nervous butterflies that had taken flight in my stomach. Panicking wasn't going to help.

I inspected the passengers in the vestibule, watching for a knowing look or a suspicious movement. But none of them were paying any attention to me. I glanced behind me. An elderly couple was making slow progress down the corridor towards the drink stand. They looked innocent enough.

All the passengers looked like normal Mannlegurs. But then, I was no expert on Hunter disguises. I waited for a moment, prepared for an attack—but nothing happened.

The elderly couple was getting closer. I'd soon be in their way. Trying to shake off my nerves, I approached the water cooler, reaching for the cups on the adjacent table. As I did, I happened to look up and caught a glimpse of a navy parka as it exited the vestibule into the next car.

I was certain that it was the same coat I'd seen on the man in the Litenhavn station. He'd been standing behind a corner in the vestibule out of my sight. Had he been watching me? Or was it just a coincidence? Was he causing my goosebumps? Could he feel them too?

Part of me wanted to follow him and get to the bottom of the mystery, but I knew I couldn't risk it—especially not with Mia and

Joel along. It was crucial that we reach Sigrid's safely. Once there, I planned to figure out how I could help Aedan—and that was the most important thing. I hadn't given up yet, even if I wasn't part of the official rescue team. And as long as the man in the navy parka wasn't interfering with that, then he could keep his secret.

I filled three cups with water and carefully balanced them between my hands for the trip back. I decided to keep the interaction with the man in the navy parka to myself for the time being.

THE REST OF THE TRAIN RIDE TO LYNGEN WAS UNEVENTFUL. I mostly stared out the window at the beautiful wintry scenery while Joel and Mia either played cards or read books. I did turn on my phone to check for any messages. A few delayed text messages from my mom and Anders pinged onto the screen. Both of them wondered how the trip was going—although my mom's notion of my trip was very different from Anders since he knew our actual destination.

I decided to text them back once we reached Sigrid's. Gabriel had cautioned against too much communication. He'd assured me that his VPN precautions were ironclad for disguising our location, but less was still more in this case.

We passed a large frozen lake where the blue-white ice glimmered in the sunlight as the thin top layer of snow melted. Then the train began to wind up the mountainside. At first, we were among the evergreen trees, but they quickly gave way to rocky granite cliffs as the train climbed into the higher elevations. Waterfalls seemed to be around every corner of the serpentine track. Some were frozen in place, waiting for the spring thaw, while others showed their strength by defying the arctic environment. The pacing of the short tunnels became more frequent as the train rebelled against gravity, reaching for the mountain top.

I couldn't help thinking to myself that some of the enormous granite faces would've made for amazing rock climbing...although perhaps beyond my skill set, particularly in the icy conditions. I mentioned as much to Mia, who glanced out the window, agreed with my assessment, and then refocused on her competitive card game with Joel.

Watching her and Joel play, it struck me how far their friendship had come from the midnight boat excursion to Tower Island a few months back. It seemed like genuine trust had formed, even if they were both quick to deny it. Being the only two teenage Mannlegurs in the Resistance probably had a lot to do with their forming bond. Plus, the Clan world in its current state wasn't exactly welcoming.

As the train exited a long tunnel, the conductor announced over the loudspeaker that we'd shortly be arriving in Lyngen. Looking back out the window, I noticed that we were now traveling between two mountain peaks, the tops of which seemed like a stone's throw away.

After about ten more minutes of snaking between a rushing river and a snowy hillside, the landscape opened up into a wide valley and buildings began to appear at regular intervals. They were easy to pick out, given their black A-line roofs and colorful walls.

The conductor came back on the speaker, giving a five-minute warning of our impending arrival.

"Oh, man! I was sure I was going to win this time," Joel said, looking more relieved than frustrated. "I guess we'll just have to postpone our game to later."

"I guess so," Mia replied with a knowing smile.

"We'd better get our cloaks ready and pack things up here," I said.

Mia and Joel both rose, ending up in each other's way given the smallness of the cabin.

"Oh...um...sorry," Joel muttered as he tried to move aside.

"No...that's alright...I'll sit back down," Mia replied.

I watched their awkward shuffle as Mia tried to sit and accidentally knocked into Joel's knees. He fell forward towards her. Their faces were now only inches apart. They remained like that, eye to eye, for a moment, neither quite sure what to do.

"I'll just...you know...um," Joel said, straightening himself back to a standing position and running his hand through his unruly hair.

"Yeah...aah...that's good." Mia looked down, breaking the gaze. But even Mia's darker complexion couldn't hide the color that had risen into her cheeks. I smiled to myself. I guess I wasn't the only one developing feelings for a boy.

The thought of Aedan was bittersweet as I wondered how he was. The Ginnungagap cell hadn't exactly looked comfortable, never mind the Chairman's efforts to break him. Those gray eyes from my vision still haunted me. Worry nestled further into my heart, and I silently prayed that the Gradys would get there in time, before the Chairman could inflict permanent damage on Aedan.

After a few quiet minutes of stuffing our unfurled items back into our backpacks, I pulled out the small pouch Claire had given us. "So, when do you think we should put these on?"

"Hmmm...I think maybe after most of the Mannlegurs leave the train. Then we can put them on and move into the second carriage. Claire said the first two cars, right?" Mia asked.

"Yeah, that's what she said," I replied.

"Sounds like a plan to me," Joel said.

A few moments later, the train pulled into the Lyngen station. We waited for the other passengers to leave. Once we were sure the majority had exited, we opened the pouches and found simple light-gray cloaks inside. We swung them around our shoulders. The cloaks fastened with a silver clasp in a modern off-center fashion.

The three of us looked at each other in our new garments. One would've thought we had either traveled back in time or into the future. It was anyone's guess as to which was the accurate depiction.

"Okay, then...you guys ready?" I asked.

Both Mia and Joel nodded. I opened the compartment door, carrying my backpack slung over one shoulder, and headed for the next train car.

The second carriage was an open model with four facing seats at each grouping. It currently held a total of seven people. A family of four sat in one of the center clusters, and the three cloaked elderly travelers from the Litenhavn station had ensconced themselves in another.

Mia chose seats midway in the carriage. She and Joel sat next to each other facing forward while I plopped into the window seat positioned towards the rear.

The train conductor came on over the loudspeaker, calling for an all-clear. We heard some commotion from the vestibule between cars two and three, after which the train lurched forward. My guess was that they had decoupled the carriages.

Just as I was breathing out a sigh of relief at having successfully completed phase one of our journey, a person in a navy cloak entered from the vestibule. Goosebumps blossomed on my arms and the feeling of electricity ignited in the air. My heartbeat quickened. It had to be the same man as the one in the navy parka.

The hood of his cloak was pulled over his face, concealing it. He stood at the back for a moment and then slowly lowered himself into one of the forward-facing seats. This was starting to feel like more than a coincidence.

Trying to look casual, I leaned toward Mia and Joel, placing my arms on the narrow table between us. "Don't look now, but I think we're being followed."

"*WHAT?*" Joel gasped.

"Shhh!" Both Mia and I replied. Whispering, I went on to tell them about my goosebumps and the earlier incidents with the man in the navy parka.

"Hmmm...that *is* strange. But maybe the goosebumps are just a fluke? Coming so close to Falinvik and more Clan members... perhaps it just woke your...um... 'radar'," Mia said.

"Sure...could be. Your guess is as good as mine...but it doesn't explain why the man is always there when goosebumps come and being so stealthy. If he was just a regular Clan member going home, why would he be hiding his face?" I asked.

"It's a good question...and I don't know," Mia said. "I think your plan of not bothering him if he doesn't bother us seems like the best solution at this point."

"Yeah, definitely." Joel nodded, looking nervous. "Let's not go poking any bears." Mia and I looked up at him. "*Whaaat?* I'm not one for trouble, okay? More of a lover, not a fighter."

Mia looked at Joel, cocking an eyebrow. "Seriously? 'Lover, not a fighter'?"

"It's a figure of speech," Joel huffed.

"Okay, then," I said, hiding my smirk. "We all agree: no bears are to be poked."

THE TRAIN TRIP TO THORDALR WAS A THIRTY-MINUTE zigzagging descent into a snowy valley. We passed large granite boulders that were sprinkled amongst the dense evergreen and deciduous trees. Everything was covered in white fluff, like someone had had too much fun with a can of whipped cream. In the distance, I could see dark wooden houses dotting the landscape, with a cluster of them where I assumed the village of Thordalr stood.

The sun was starting to set by the time the train pulled into the station, even though it was only 2pm. The man in the navy cloak quickly disembarked, and I didn't see any sign of him on the platform as we stepped down.

"So...um...where do we go from here?" Joel asked.

"Well...I guess we need to find the sleigh-hiring place," I said, looking around for any indication of where that might be. "Anybody see any sign?"

"No," Mia answered, looking left and right. "We'd better ask."

"Are you sure that's a good idea? Aren't we trying to blend in?" Joel pointed out.

"Um...yeah...but not sure how good our cover will be if we're just standing around looking lost."

"Okay, fair point. Who do we ask, then?"

"Him," Mia said, pointing to the train conductor, who was supervising the unloading of bags and supplies from the train.

"I think only one of us should go talk to him...help lessen the risk a little," I said, about to take on the role.

"I'll go," Joel said, surprising both Mia and me.

Mia looked at Joel. "You sure?"

"Yeah. I can handle this," he replied, cocking his head and shrugging nonchalantly.

We watched as Joel went to talk with the conductor. A minute later, he returned, smiling triumphantly.

"It's this way," Joel announced, motioning toward the right of the station.

We followed him as he led us around the small station, which looked as if it'd been plucked out of the 19th century with its wood construction, arched terrace, and lace cornices. As we rounded the building's corner, we were plunged into the village of Thordalr.

The architecture of the town was something I'd never seen before. I was used to seeing red- and yellow-painted buildings with A-line construction, but here all the buildings had exposed timber walls varnished in tar, resulting in dark-brown exteriors.

What was even more impressive was the number of large eaves on the houses. They jutted out in every direction from the steep roofs. The tops of the eaves were embellished with heads of dragons or serpents. Some structures had two or three layers of them built one on top of another. The whole town looked like something out of a fairytale.

Given the roofs' sharp angles, not a speck of white remained on them. However, piles of snow formed a uniform row on the ground below. A break existed only where the entrance to the store or home required it.

"Wow, this is amazing! I've never seen Dragestil construction on such a large scale before," Mia said.

"Draga-what?" Joel asked, turning to look at Mia in amazement.

"Dragestil...it's the building design. It was inspired by the Viking and medieval art and architecture of Scandinavia. My family and I saw a building last year on holiday." Mia's memory for trivia never ceased to impress me. She was so matter-of-fact about it that she never came off as arrogant. She was simply stating a fact.

"It's pretty spectacular—like nothing I've ever seen," I agreed.

At that moment, a sleigh carrying several bundled passengers in two rows but without a visible horse or harness passed right in front of us. It followed the tracks wedged into the snow on the road.

"Now, that's cool!" Joel gushed. "Come, gals...let's go find us a sleigh!"

He led the way diagonally across the road to a shop whose wooden sign, dangling above it, had an image of a sleigh. A bell jingled, announcing our entrance. Joel held the door, gesturing for Mia and me to enter.

A middle-aged man in a dark-gray wool tunic emerged from an alcove behind a large stone counter. The shop's inside was surprisingly modern compared to the outside. It was decorated in Scandinavian minimalist style, with two metallic chairs flanking a small, round glass table in the customer area and nothing else. The walls were sheet-rocked and painted a light yellow but nothing hung from them.

"Hello. May I help you?" the man asked.

"Um...yes. We'd like to hire a sleigh," I replied.

"For what length of time do you require its service?" The man pulled out a tablet from underneath the stone counter and donned a pair of spectacles.

I glanced at Mia and Joel. They shrugged.

"Ahh...just today...I think."

"And when do you need it by?"

"Immediately."

"I see. Well, we can certainly accommodate your request for a sleigh today. However, 'immediately' is not possible. Our last sleigh was just hired. And"—he glanced down at the tablet in front of him—"we don't expect another return for two hours."

"*Oh, man,*" I heard Joel sigh under his breath. "What are we supposed to do for two hours?"

I turned to Mia and Joel. We didn't really have another choice. We'd have to wait. I shrugged.

"We'll wait," I said, turning back toward the clerk.

He tapped something into the tablet. "As you wish. May I suggest trying the comforts of the Dancing Dragon Inn in the meanwhile? They offer superior food and hot Gløgg."

"Excellent suggestion. Where can we find it?" Joel asked, grinning.

The clerk gave him directions. Then he turned back to me. "And under what name may I enter your reservation?"

I was drawing a blank. I couldn't give my own name, as I was sure that would send alarm bells racing across the whole Clan region. I wasn't really ready to take a chance on using Joel's or Mia's names either.

Before my hesitation became suspicious, Mia piped up. "Dragestil. Please put it under Dragestil."

"Very good, miss," the clerk replied, tapping into his tablet.

We thanked him and exited before he could stump us with another question.

"Nice one, Mia," I said, once we were outside.

"It was the only thing I could think of on the spot."

"Well, it worked," Joel agreed. "Hey, did either of you notice the strong resemblance between the clerk and the train conductor? I mean, they could've been twins."

"Not really, but I didn't see the conductor's face close up," Mia said as she avoided walking into a large pile of snow. "Where is this inn, anyway? It's getting cold and dark out here now that the sun has set."

"Just up ahead and around the corner, according to the clerk," Joel replied. "They really did look the same. Wonder if they're related?"

"Could be. It's a small town," I said, hurrying to cross the road before another autonomous sleigh came shushing down the street.

"There it is," Joel said, pointing to a sign lit by a lantern swinging in the wind above it. Painted on the sign were two dragons, one gold and the other red. They were circling each other in what either was a dance or a fight.

The inn's entrance was an arched red door with a gold handle. The door's color contrasted starkly with the building's dark wood exterior. There was a large overhang held up by two posts on either side, keeping the snow clear of the steps leading to the door.

"Oh, good. Let's go in," Mia said, blowing warm air on her hands.

Joel led the way up the stairs and opened the red door. We were immediately greeted by laughter, strange music, and the sounds of dishes being knocked together. Mia entered first, eager for the warmth from the roaring fire in the round central fireplace. Joel and I followed.

The room was large, with a collection of varnished wooden tables in various sizes, including three long ones that ran its length. Benches or chairs accompanied each table, depending on its size. The walls were of the same dark wood as the exterior, lending a cozy yet mysterious feel to the space. It was lit by a few ancient-looking black lanterns that amazingly hovered unattached near the ceiling. A large, modern, steel bar counter was to the left of us. Behind it stood a man polishing glasses as he chatted with a customer seated on a wooden stool on the other side.

The room was an odd juxtaposition of modern and old. If you looked only to the right of us, you might've thought yourself transported back to the age of Vikings, given the ambiance and the people dressed in cloaks and tunics. If you turned toward the right, the modern bar and the several machines with blinking lights tucked into the wall behind it would've brought you into the future.

The three of us surveyed the scene, looking for an empty table where we might stay inconspicuous. Many of the tables were occupied by townsfolk enjoying a mug of hot Gløgg or a glass horn filled with what I assumed was dark beer. The unusual music was nearly drowned out by their merry, loud chatter.

Craning my neck, I finally spotted four empty places at one of the long tables. We claimed the seats just in time, as another party made a move for them.

"Well, this is a lively place. Kind of surprising for a town this size," Joel remarked as he settled onto the bench.

"Yeah, definitely. Maybe there's not much else to do around here. I mean, it's already dark outside, and brutally cold," Mia said.

"You're probably right," I agreed. "Do you think it's table service, or do we go to the bar?" I asked as I sat down next to an older Clansman with a long, graying beard, dressed in a dark-green tunic.

Overhearing me, the old man turned to me and smiled. "It's bar service only. You three new around here?"

"Thanks...yeah, we're just visiting," I replied, giving him a friendly smile but then turning away to avoid having to answer any more questions.

I sent Mia and Joel a pleading look. Talking to unknown Clan members wasn't part of any plan we had. Mia immediately engaged me in a hushed conversation about nothing important. Joel rose and said, "I'll go get us something to eat and drink."

As Joel disappeared into the crowd, a sudden hush fell over the room. Then, like a slow rumble from table to table, we could hear the word "Skraeling" being repeated over and over again. Some people rose from their tables, craning their necks towards the bar. Mia rose slightly to see what the commotion was.

"What is it?" I asked.

"I don't know. I can't see a thing. There are too many people standing up. Do you know that word they're saying?"

"No, I've never heard it."

The old bearded man next to me leaned over again. "Not too surprising for young'uns like you. It's an old word for the Vestri Clan's fiercest warriors. They successfully defended their lands from our ancestors many moons ago and earned a fearsome reputation. I certainly wouldn't want to meet one of them on a moonless night."

"So why are people saying it now?" I asked.

"They think there's one in this very room." His sharp blue eyes twinkled mischievously.

"Isn't that rather unlikely?"

"One would think...but they're whispering that there's a man with dark skin and a long black braid at the bar."

"But I have dark skin—" Mia started to say.

"Yes, yes...but you don't have a fierce Vestri look about you. Skraelings have a certain unsettled air about them. And I'd bet your genes fall more towards Austri anyway," the old Clansman interrupted, waving a dismissive hand.

Then across the low hum of awestruck voices in the room, we could hear Joel loudly and clearly say, "*WHAT?* You won't serve him just because he has *dark skin?* I think that's the stupidest thing I've ever heard...You think he is *what?* Oh, come on—I don't even know what that is."

"Mia, I think we'd better go up there. I think Joel might've poked a different bear," I said, getting up from the bench.

By the time Mia and I pushed our way through the crowd and got to the bar, the bartender was red in the face. Joel was shouting something about him being an uncanny triplet and a bigot. Then out of nowhere, the goosebumps on my arms blossomed and electricity sizzled around me.

Next to Joel stood a man in the navy cloak.

It was unmistakably him. The man from the train. My goosebumps confirmed it. His hood was askew, revealing high cheekbones and light-brown skin. A long black braid with a single feather attached rested on his chest. He had a hand on Joel's arm, and he was saying something to calm Joel down. Then as if sensing my presence, he whipped his head towards me.

More of the crowd was gathering close to the bar to witness Joel's tirade against the bartender. In a single swift motion, the man in the navy cloak grasped Joel's arm in one hand and mine in the other and ushered us out the door, over Mia's strong protests.

Once outside, I wrenched my arm free from his hold. Mia was hot on our heels. Thankfully, she had the presence of mind to shut the inn's door, muffling the angry shouts from within.

"Who are you?" I demanded.

"I'm a friend. Now let's go," he said, motioning for us to follow him. None of us moved. "Come on. Your choices are to stay and face that mob and all their questions after that stunt your companion pulled in there, or to come with me."

"I was trying to help—" Joel began to say, but at the same moment, the red door flew open, revealing the angry faces of several Clansmen, including the bartender. Without warning, an unusual gust of wind quickly slammed the door shut, stopping their exit.

"Choose!" The Skraeling's free hand was firmly pointed towards the door.

Joel stared at the door and gulped. "I say we go with him."

Mia nodded.

I relented. "Okay, fine." We'd definitely outstayed our welcome in Thordalr. I wasn't sure we could fully trust the Skraeling, but our choices were limited if we wanted to get away quickly.

The Skraeling twisted the hand that was pointing at the door, which sent a small whirlwind packed with snow racing to block the door and brought down the posts holding up the awning. "This way! That'll only hold them for so long...hurry now!"

He raced down the dark street, his navy cloak billowing behind him. We ran after him as fast as we could through the snow. At a small alley between two large houses, he ducked right into the lane.

As we followed, I heard Mia say to Joel, "What happened to being more of a 'lover than a fighter'?"

"I can't stand bigots," he replied. I glanced behind me and saw Joel smile at Mia while slipping a little on the alley floor.

The ground in the narrow corridor was icy. The snow had melted from the buildings' heat but frozen in the night air. After sliding along for a few minutes and falling behind the Skraeling, who seemed to manage without any issue, Mia remembered the retractable cleats. The three of us eagerly switched our respective toggles to expose the spikes.

We caught up to the Skraeling where the alley widened into another road. A sleigh was stopped on the side of the road and a man in a green cloak with the hood pulled up stood beside it. He turned at our approach.

Mia, Joel, and I held our breaths. It was the bartender.

He wore different clothes, which made me wonder how on earth he had time to change, but it was definitely him. A few steps ahead of us, the Skraeling continued towards him as if there wasn't any problem.

"What's he *doing*? Isn't that the bartender?" Mia asked.

"Finally! You're seeing it too...I was starting to think I was going crazy," Joel said. "That's the third man identical to the train conductor I've seen today."

"Seriously?" I asked.

"I swear on everything holy," Joel responded.

Mia peered more intently at the man. "You sure it's not the bartender?"

"No way! He couldn't have changed and gotten here so fast," Joel said, echoing my earlier thoughts.

"How strange," Mia pondered, looking once more at the man.

The Skraeling spoke to the man and handed him something. Then he turned to us and waved us over. The man in the green cloak walked away, melting into the dark street.

"Who was that? He looked exactly like the bartender," I asked as we drew closer.

"He would. They're called Replicants...or I should say, their ability is replication. The original person can split himself into several clones. The *Stór-menni* find them useful as spies and messengers, particularly in the more rural towns. They only have to deal with one person to know everything all their replicants know. However, luckily for us, Replicants are *not* beyond being bribed, especially when you have one of their tokens." The Skraeling winked and gave us a sly smile. "Okay, up you go...into the sleigh."

We climbed aboard, snuggling under the warm, thick wool blankets that were on the seat. The Skraeling gracefully hopped on last. The feeling of electricity grew thick as he sat down beside me.

"What is that?" I was positive that he must feel it too. It was just too strong to be one-sided.

"I'll explain later," he whispered to me. Then more loudly, he said, "So where to? I assume you've got a destination besides this little town."

I hesitated for a moment. Then, I dug for the piece of paper that Claire had handed me. At least at Sigrid's we'd have help getting rid of the Skraeling, if necessary.

There was a small screen embedded into the front of the

sleigh. I pressed it and immediately, it illuminated, displaying a number board. Covering the keypad as best I could, I entered the numbers from the slip. There was no need to share with the Skraeling any more than necessary.

I hit the Go button once finished and the sleigh began to move forward. I smiled. At least, something had gone smoothly.

"How about a little privacy...and warmth," the Skraeling said as he leaned toward the screen and tapped a few additional buttons.

A clear top began to emerge from the back of the sleigh while turning a black-tinted color. Before long, it had covered us in a bubble-like enclosure, blocking the wind and prying eyes. Then a steady stream of warm air began to fill the inside.

"Now...that's better," he said, pushing back his hood and exposing a handsome face that made him look to be about the same age as Anders. A narrow, still-healing scar ran from his left brow to his cheekbone. His black hair was pulled black into a low braid, but a few escaped strands hung loosely around his face.

He unclasped his navy cloak, revealing navy Clan-fabric clothes and a strong muscular body underneath. His jacket and pants were much more similar to the ones we wore underneath our cloaks than those of the Clan members in Thordalr.

Smiling, he turned to us. He looked even more attractive than before. I felt a little color rise to my cheeks. "So...I suppose it's time for some introductions. I'm Nodin Fayerweather of the Vestri Clan. And you three are—?"

I couldn't believe it. He'd just confirmed he was of the Vestri Clan. Why would he do that—especially in *Stór-menni* territory? Was he really from the Vestri, or a *Stór-menni* spy? Mia, Joel, and I hesitated. Could we trust him with our true names?

"Hmmm...I can understand your cautious nature in these parts. Perhaps it might help if I told you that I already know that you aren't quite what you pretend to be. In fact, two of you aren't even Clan, are you?" It wasn't a threatening statement but just a fact, in the way he spoke.

Mia and Joel glanced at each other. Still unsure of what to do, none of us could look at Nodin.

"Alright...how about we just start with first names? We might need to know them in case anything else happens."

It was a reasonable request, especially since he'd already given his full name and Clan affiliation to us. But I wasn't quite ready to trust him entirely. "I'm Elli."

"Mia."

"Joel."

"Nice to meet all of you." Nodin nodded to each of us. "Now for an even trickier subject...where exactly are we heading?"

Glancing out of the sleigh's bubble, I could see that we'd left town some time ago. The sleigh had automatically increased its speed on the outskirts.

"To a friend's. We'll be safe there."

"I see. That's good, then," Nodin said as he leaned back, settling more comfortably beside me.

Suddenly, my pocket began to vibrate. It was soon followed by a familiar ringtone. My mom. I hadn't talked with my parents in the past two days. Gabriel's VPN precautions made it seem as if all my texts and calls were coming from France so I could talk with my family when I wanted. He'd even given me a few Parisian backgrounds I could use for photos to send to my parents, if needed.

Nodin arched an eyebrow, listening to the commotion coming from my jacket. "Are you going to answer that?"

I could feel the redness surging into my cheeks as I hastily fumbled with my cloak and jacket. Finally locating my phone, I realized my mom was FaceTiming me. I groaned. Before I could stop him, Nodin reached over and slid the toggle to accept the call.

I quickly angled the phone so that only Mia, Joel, and I were in the image.

"Hi, honey!" my mom said. She was sitting at our dining-room table with half my dad's body hovering in the background.

"Hi, Mom. How are you?" I tried to sound casual and carefree.

"Oh...hi, Mia and Joel. Don't you three look cozy."

"We're in a cab, Mrs. Bodil," Mia replied. She always was quick on her feet.

"Isn't it late there? I thought you'd be at the hotel by now. Where's Mr. Tibadeau?"

"We're just heading to the hotel now, Mom. In fact, we'll be there any minute. Mr. Tibadeau is in another cab. There wasn't a big enough taxi that could fit us all coming from dinner."

"I see. Well, you three be careful. Paris is a big city, and you aren't used to all their ways."

"Ain't that the truth," Joel snorted.

Mia elbowed him in the side. "We sure will, Mrs. Bodil. Oh... looks like we are just turning into the hotel now."

"Oh, okay. Leif, is there anything you want to say to Elli?" My mom turned and looked up to where I assumed my dad's face was.

Suddenly, my dad's face loomed large on the phone's screen as he leaned over. "Hi, sweetie! You having a good time?"

"Yeah, Dad. We're having the best time." I smiled, trying to look happy. I didn't want my parents to worry.

"Good...good. Don't forget to visit the Eiffel Tower," he said before straightening again.

"Sure thing, Dad. Talk soon...we've arrived at the hotel. Love you," I replied, waving.

Mia and Joel waved as well while my parents responded with their farewells. I pressed the red button to end the call.

"Thanks for the assist, Mia."

"No problem."

I glanced at Nodin, who had his eyes closed and, much to my annoyance, had a small satisfied-looking smile on his lips. He'd learned more than I'd wanted from the call, but there wasn't much to be done about it now.

The motion of the sleigh turning onto a small, snowy country lane interrupted my thoughts. We were crossing a small meadow. It left the dark skies wide open to the millions of stars that twinkled back at us. It was awe-inspiring. I'd never seen so many. You could even see the haze of the Milky Way. Then, as if to really give us a show, green, purple, and pink lights began to stretch over the dark sky in various wave patterns. They were gorgeous.

"Hey, look. It's the Aurora Borealis," I said.

"Wow...that's so beautiful," Mia gushed.

"Awesome. I've never seen it before," Joel replied.

My announcement seemed to stir even Nodin, who looked up through the sleigh's clear canopy. "Or otherwise known as the Northern Lights. My Vestri Clan ancestors believed it was the great spirits playing ball in the sky, while the Nordri Clan forefathers thought them to be reflections off the Valkyries' armor. Either way, they were thought to be omens."

"Omens of what?" Mia asked.

"Whatever the current events of the time were and what the Seers could predict."

"Huh. Interesting," Mia said.

We spent the rest of the sleigh ride marveling at the sky and all its celestial magnificence. It wasn't too long after the meadow that the sleigh entered a forest and then stopped by a frozen stream. I looked around. There was nothing else there.

Nodin leaned over to press a button on the screen and the sleigh's top began to retract. He hopped out into the deep snow.

"I guess we're here," I said, looking at Mia and Joel. They shrugged, equally puzzled.

Then a small shimmer began to appear between two pine trees. A middle-aged woman dressed in long purple robes with a high collar appeared. Two floating lanterns followed her, illuminating us in a warm yellow glow.

"Nodin Fayerweather! How good to see you. But what brings you this far north?" The woman smiled warmly at Nodin and embraced him as he came closer. "And I see you've brought friends...who are these young ones?"

SIXTEEN

Hunting Skills

TRISTAN

As the snowy scenery whipped by the train window, I wondered what my mentor Henric would have thought about my journey over the last few days. My fate was his fate, so he probably would have been appalled at my decision to once again disobey Command's orders—especially considering all the ways it could have gone so very wrong.

Henric and I were forever intrinsically linked because of the way the Clan's mentorship program worked. My success and failures were his to share. Our entwined fates were "a motivational commitment for the mentors to do their best for their mentees," according to the Clan Council.

Henric had made sure that I was the perfect Clan Hunter for many years, strictly following every edict to the core. Yet in the past few months with the start of my first solo mission, everything had gone wrong.

I blamed Elin entirely. If it hadn't been for her, I would have captured my first mission's fugitives and would now be making slow but steady progress towards the rank of Captain. Instead, here I was again betting everything on her. At least this time, I was using my hunting skills rather than being at the whim of a simpering girl. And the results were already beginning to show.

A few days earlier after separating from Thyra and the team, I had picked up my motorcycle at Aunt Adis's, thankful she was still in Falinvik and not at her home on Sparrowhawk Lane. Given our previous hasty departure from Auor, my 1950 BSA Gold Star motorcycle had been left behind, carefully sheltered in her shed.

Excitement vibrated through my body as I removed the motorcycle's tarp. I quickly went through my mental checklist to evaluate its state before pausing for a more thorough inspection of its all-weather tires. There would be no skidding incidents to slow me down this time, I thought, recalling my initial encounter with Elin.

Once satisfied, I swung my leg over the saddle and roared the engine to life. A large grin replaced the frown I had worn for days. Having complete control over the machine made me feel a bit more like myself. After locking the shed back up, I sped out of the driveway towards town. I was on my own again—and it felt good.

I spent the rest of the day poking around Auor Harbor, looking for any leads on the Unregistered's family and Elin. When I stopped for lunch, I overheard some local ice fisherman talking about seeing two small icebreakers docking at the Old Boat Club House marina the prior evening and how strange that was. My stomach nearly dropped to my feet as the realization dawned at how close we had come to capturing the Unregistered's family and Elin. I had been right—they had left by boat. I was positive the icebreakers were their transport. It made perfect sense. If the others had only listened to me!

Later, on the mainland, I picked up the trail of the icebreakers as I listened to the radio chatter from other *Smá-menn* shipping boats. The icebreakers were heading north, which was the opposite direction from Paris. Vindication again swelled my chest as I typed a report to Thyra on my SRT.

```
Initial scouting concludes northerly
direction. Will follow and report back on
exact destination.
```

I kept it short and without detail, knowing full well that our communications would be monitored by Command. To them, it needed to be plausible that I was with the rest of the team in Paris.

Within moments, I received a short reply.

```
Understood. Very interested. Keep me
posted.
```

A FEW DAYS LATER, I WAS POSITIVE ABOUT MY HUNCH AS TO where they were headed. I followed the *Smá-menn* boat communications until the icebreaker sightings became sparse. The dangers of winter's frozen waters kept most boats from traveling farther north.

Pausing for a break at a roadside pullout, I surveyed the icy coast. The shoreline was frozen, with snow piled in windblown mounds around the edges. Further afield, I could see large ice chunks floating in the frigid waters.

I was still a day or so behind the boats, but I was now sure of their ultimate destination. There was only one reason they would have gone so far north, toward Falinvik.

I removed my thick leather motorcycle gloves and pulled out my SRT from my saddlebag. As I typed another report to Thyra, I couldn't help but smile at the futility of the other team members' search in Paris.

```
Expected destination in sight.
Ginnungagap. Possible extrication of
Unregistered.
```

It had taken but a moment for Thyra to reply.

```
Excellent news. Already on route to
Falinvik. Rest of team to follow. Will
send transport to Litenhavn.
```

THE TRAIN WHISTLED AND THE CARRIAGE SHOOK AS THE oncoming train toward Lyngen roared past on the parallel tracks, knocking me from my thoughts. I watched the whisking windows, wondering if the *Smá-menn* had any idea that the train's actual destination was Thordalr.

I had been to the proudly Norse village once with Henric on a tracking mission for some recently escaped fugitives. The village had left an impression on me, with its fierce commitment to maintaining the old, dramatic style of architecture with its steep eaves from a bygone age.

I pondered Thyra's message again. Why was she already on route to Falinvik when I sent the report? What could have brought her back early—and without the rest of the team?

A knock at my compartment's door interrupted my musing.

"Hello there, Tristan," the train's conductor, Birger, greeted me.

He was a Replicant and a patriotic spy for the *Stór-menni*. I had come to know Birger during my Hunter rotation on the train line. He always had some interesting bits of news to share or a report of Clan fugitives. I wasn't sure if he was the original or a clone, but it hardly mattered since they all knew what the others knew.

"Birger. How are things?"

"Fine, fine. The usual...you know how it is."

"Any unusual occurrences?"

He seemed to hesitate for a moment as if weighing his thoughts. "Nothing that panned out to be anything of significance to Command."

"Well, it sounds interesting anyway. We have a few minutes until Litenhavn...entertain me, even if it is of no importance."

Closing the compartment door, Birger sat down, eager to share his gossip. "Well, now...Command may receive some reports from my brother, the barkeeper, about a scuffle at his establishment."

"Really? Was it just a drunken row?" I leaned back on the seat, glancing out the window and a little less interested.

"Perhaps. A few fools mistook a dark-skinned fellow for a Skraeling. Can you believe it? You know how they can get, up there in Thordalr. Their stories grow bigger with every uttered phrase, and any stranger is an immediate threat. By now I'm sure the fellow was ten feet tall and had dozens of feathers in his hair and a battle-axe in his hand." He laughed, slapping his knee.

"Yes, I suppose they are rather isolated up there." I smiled.

"Indeed, indeed. My brother is just sore about the damage to his establishment's front door. The poor dark-skinned fellow had to make a hasty exit into the cold night...and brought down a barricade to block the fools trying to follow."

I looked down at my own dark olive hands. "But he escaped, then? No harm done, besides structural."

"Yes, yes...no harm to anyone. You see...something that really was nothing." Birger rose from the opposite seat. "Well, must go—we'll be pulling into Litenhavn any minute now. Good to see you, Tristan."

"Oh...yes...likewise."

As Birger exited, the train hooted its arrival at Litenhavn.

Stepping out onto the snowy street from the Litenhavn station, I glanced up and down the street. My breath came out in clouds in front of me. The cold was brisk. Only a few people hurried up and down the street, ducking into shops or colorful doorways. The sun was already starting even though it was only 2pm.

My stomach rumbled. I had to skip lunch in order to make the train in Lyngen. I craved a nice meal at the local Litenhavn pub, but I was sure my transport was already here. I walked briskly towards my favorite bakery, knowing their savory pastries would be just the thing to tide me over until the next real meal in Falinvik at the PS headquarters.

"Hellooo, Tristan," the baker, Agda, called out as I entered the shop.

The aroma of buttery pastry and freshly baked bread filled the air, making my mouth water. "Hello, Agda. How is business?"

"Good, especially today. Lots of tourists...ski season, you know."

"Glad to hear it. Any large groups stop by?"

"No groups, but we did have a large order come in. Why? Friends of yours?"

"Sort of. Just expecting some potential travelers through Litenhavn."

"Visiting your inn, are they?"

Agda was a *Smá-menn*, so she, like the rest of the Litenhavn *Smá-menn*, was under the impression that the *Stór-menni* ran an exclusive and high-security inn further down the fjord. The story helped to explain all the Hunter traffic through the little harbor town. We were the inn's employees.

"Yes, they are making their way there...although the timing of their arrival is unknown. You know how those VIPs can be."

"Yes, of course. I'll keep an eye out for them."

Henric had taught me the value of creating relationships with local people. They could be very useful as inadvertent spies, telling more in one casual conversation than in any interrogation.

"Perfect. Thank you."

"Now, what'll you have?"

I selected two large savory cheese pastries from the glass case, paid, and then said my goodbyes as I exited the shop. Once outside, I bit into the flaky pastry, savoring the taste of melted cheese as it burst in my mouth.

I continued to eat as I headed to the harbor's east side, where snowmobile tracks led away from the town center. There, by the edge of the evergreen forest, sat a lone hovercraft with a young Clan Hunter casually stretched across its seat, smoking a pipe. He was the only one there, which left little doubt that he was the transport Thyra had sent.

The Hunter was clearly an Illusionist, as the hovercraft appeared as a *Smá-menn* snowmobile instead of its true form. Given our training, Clan Hunters could easily recognize it for what it actually was. There was a certain obscure way the illusion's light refracted from the vehicle that betrayed the trick.

The Hunter rose to his feet as he spotted me. He nodded, and I responded in kind.

"Hello, Sir," he said as I drew nearer. "Ready to depart?"

"Yes. I'm eager to get back to Falinvik, so don't hold back the throttle."

The young Hunter looked confused. "Sir, I have orders to take you straight to Ginnungagap...not Falinvik."

"I see. Were you given any other message for me?"

"Oh, yes...almost forgot, Sir." Heat rose to his cheeks as he sprang towards the back of the hovercraft. He opened the storage compartment and then turned back to me with an envelope.

I grabbed it from his hand and tore it open, annoyed that the young Hunter had not immediately given it to me. The letter was from Thyra.

Tristan - Excuse the antiquated method, but given the circumstances, this was the best option for private communication.

First, excellent work tracking the Unregistered's family and the Dormant. You were clearly right that Paris was a diversion.

Second, I was unexpectedly called back to Falinvik on an urgent mission for the Chairman. The rest of the team will soon join me. Therefore, we cannot meet you at Ginnungagap, but the Chairman has been fully informed of your great progress.

With that in mind, he has instructed that you make the preparations for the uninvited guests' arrival. This is a great honor and a show of his trust in you. Don't let him down! You have leave to request anything you might need for a successful apprehension. The transport will take you directly to Ginnungagap.

Good luck and keep me posted on your progress.
Thyra

This was it! I clutched the paper in my hand. The Chairman was finally seeing my worth. Not even Thyra could deny it. All I had to do was lay a trap at Ginnungagap, and the Captain's rank would be as good as mine. I would finally capture not only Elin but the Unregistered's family as well. I could already see the honor guard at my celebration.

I climbed onto the back of the hovercraft. "Quickly, man. No time to waste. To Ginnungagap."

The young Hunter leaped onto the front seat. He roared the engine to life and sped the vehicle down the snowmobile tracks into the forest. After we cleared the town's perimeter, he would drop the illusion and let the hovercraft rise into the skies, hurrying us along to the gray fortress.

SEVENTEEN

Skogly

ELIN

O ur arrival at Sigrid's created quite a stir in the entire commune. Apparently they didn't receive many visitors, at least not like our party of travelers.

To our surprise, and I think even Nodin's, the protected enclave included not only Sigrid's house but also dozens of other Clan-refugee homes. According to Sigrid, the little forest shelter had grown over the years, eventually becoming a village.

I think the community's surprise may have been equaled only by Mia's, Joel's, and my shock at the warm greeting Nodin received from Sigrid when we first arrived. Our mouths must have hung open for a good minute as they embraced. Nodin ended up introducing us to Sigrid, since we sat frozen and flabbergasted in the sleigh.

"Sigrid, I would like to introduce you to my fellow travelers. Elli...Mia...and Joel." He indicated each of us. "We bring a rather unusual tale of acquaintanceship...and I suspect, very different reasons for our visits."

"A warm welcome to each of you. And I confess that I'm

intrigued by your introduction, Nodin. Perhaps we should enter our commune, as it's quite a bit nicer inside." Sigrid swooped her arm towards the space between the two trees from which she'd emerged. One of the two floating lanterns moved closer to the trees, lighting the indicated spot. "Oh, before I forget...Nodin, would you be so kind as to erase the sleigh's navigation information and send it back to where it came from? As you know, we like our privacy here."

Shaking ourselves out of a stupor, Mia, Joel, and I gathered our belongings from the sleigh. Mia and Joel stepped down first into the deep snow and trudged over to shake hands with Sigrid. As I proceeded to climb down, Nodin approached, offering his hand to help me descend. Goosebumps blossomed under my sleeves and down my legs. I looked into his hazel eyes and grinning, handsome face. Butterflies burst into flight in my stomach, but also a pang of guilt. Here I was inexplicably drawn to this attractive stranger while Aedan wallowed in some cold, dark cell.

I jumped into the snow, avoiding Nodin's hand. He laughed and climbed into the sleigh to fulfill Sigrid's request. Heat coursed into my cheeks as I realized that I was now stuck in the snowbank into which I'd leaped. The snow was up to my thighs, and I was finding it impossible to lift my feet out of it.

I looked up to see Nodin leaning on the sleigh's side and watching me with a slight smirk on his face. Then he lifted his hand and twisted it. A small wind funnel emerged, pushing the snow aside, freeing my legs, and clearing a way to the worn path Joel and Mia had traveled.

"Thanks," I said, holding my head high as I walked past him.

Sigrid warmly greeted me as I made it to her side. She was a middle-aged woman, tall and thin as a reed. Strong streaks of gray and white were mixed into her golden-brown hair, which was braided into one long braid and piled on top of her head like a crown. She had a regal, commanding air about her, and I could feel her strength and a small crackle of electricity as she shook my hand. What was that? First with Nodin and now with Sigrid. I'd thought my days of being zinged by an electric current were over.

"Welcome to Skogly, Elin," she said, smiling and glancing down at our locked hands. "I look forward to hearing your tale."

"Thank you. Oh, and Mr. and Mrs. Grady send their warmest hellos," I replied.

A look of surprise flitted across her face. "Oh, I see. Now I'm even more interested in hearing how you've ended up here...and with Nodin."

The sleigh's movement caught my eye as it left along the same path as it had come. Its lights flickered through the trees before disappearing into the darkness. With a carefully aimed wind current, Nodin erased any sign of its tracks or ours. Then he joined us, and Sigrid placed an affectionate hand on his shoulder.

"Shall we?" She motioned towards the two trees where Mia and Joel stood waiting.

"After you," Nodin said with a little bow to Sigrid.

Sigrid led the way, which left Nodin and me to follow with the goosebumps on my arms standing up in salute. When she reached the two trees, Sigrid seemed to touch an invisible barrier between the pines and push it aside as if it was a curtain. She held it open as we passed between the evergreens.

If I was amazed by the unusual Shield Wall that I later found out that none of us could see even with our *megin*, it was nothing to the astonishment that waited for me on the other side.

A warm spring-like breeze greeted us as we emerged inside the barrier. The light of a sunset flitted through the fresh green leaves of deciduous trees and pine branches as they swayed softly. To our left, a babbling brook flowed unhindered by ice or snow. It was as if we had entered a totally different world.

"This is amazing," Mia said, exchanging looks with Joel and me.

Joel's mouth gaped open for the second time in less than ten minutes.

"How's this possible?" I asked, looking at Sigrid.

She smiled, enjoying our surprise. "Well, we tend to prefer spring conditions to the harsh winter weather. It allows us to stay self-reliant all year long instead of risking trips to Thordalr or beyond...and nothing is more motivating than necessity when it comes to invention."

Sigrid later confessed that the Bubble Shield Wall, or BSW, as she called it, was a creation of the village Inventor. She marveled at the resourcefulness of the Inventor and Engineers who had constructed it from Clan-technology scraps.

Initially, the BSW had been created to camouflage and secure the refugees' homes from any intruders or passersby. But as the village had expanded, the climate-control element and artificial sunlight had been added so they could grow their own food and survive the harsh winters with less difficulty. Apparently, it was all powered by the geothermal energy that quietly flowed and brewed in deep dark recesses of the forest floor.

According to Sigrid, an uninvited person could walk right through the center of the village and never see a single home or person. The BSW would encase the passerby in a sphere, showing them only the same forest, streams, and large boulders that they'd seen outside the village, and guide them through the commune without their running into anything or anyone. It was rather ingenious. The passerby would never question whether they had taken a walk through the woods.

As an added layer of protection, there was only one entrance to the commune. And no Clan member or Mannlegur could enter through it without permission—no matter what your *megin* was.

The now-extinguished floating lanterns led the way through the forest until we reached a large meadow. In the heart of the swaying green grass was a crystalline mountain lake that fed a wide, gurgling stream.

On our side of the lake, dozens of log houses dotted the hillside. The homes were of various shapes and sizes. Some were newer and some older, but all were constructed from wood and had a moss-covered roof.

The entire village exuded warmth and safety as we walked through it. Carefree kids played outside their homes in the remaining sunlight while their parents relaxed on porch swings talking with neighbors. Dogs lazed on front steps, raising curious heads as we passed, while chickens roamed freely in yards.

Each villager greeted Sigrid with a wave and friendly smile. But their eyes always shifted to us with a curious look and an even more blatant stare at Nodin.

By the time we reached Sigrid's home on the lake's edge, we had attracted a following of children and dogs, each with their own agenda. One of the little boys finally plucked up his courage and tugged on Nodin's cloak.

"Sir...um...ah...um—" he sputtered.

"Yes?" Nodin smiled, crouching to bring himself to the boy's eye level.

"Are you...um...a Skraeling?" the little boy asked, straightening his back. The other children crowded closer to hear the answer.

"Well...what do you think?" Nodin replied seriously while suppressing a grin that threatened to emerge. "Do I look like one?"

"Uh...I don't—well, you see...I've never seen one before," the boy admitted. "But I heard old Lara say you are."

"I see. Well then, you're very brave to come so close. You never know what a Skraeling might do." Laughing, Nodin swept two children under his arms and pretended to chase the others down the path. The children squealed in delight while the dogs barked and chased after them.

A woman of about Sigrid's age appeared from the log home, standing on the covered porch holding a large red jar. She wore a blue ankle-length woolen dress with long sleeves and a white apron that stretched across both front and back. The simple style felt modern yet ancient at the same time.

"I see Nodin didn't waste any time getting back to his usual tricks...and that I'm once again late to the party with these oat cookies," she said, smiling. "Although I suppose these two little fur ones might like a treat or two." The two elderly dogs, who had resisted chasing after the children, eagerly wagged their tails at the woman. "Here you go." She gave each dog a cookie and a good pat on the head.

"Oh, Brigitta...you'll only encourage these mutts to come back," Sigrid said as she affectionately ruffled the ears of both dogs.

"Well, I do hope so. Now, Sigrid...who are these lovely young people?" Brigitta asked.

"Meet Elli, Joel, and Mia—our guests for the foreseeable future, I'm guessing, although I've yet to hear their tale."

"So pleased to meet you all, and welcome to our home. I'm Brigitta." She stepped down from the porch to give a warm handshake to each of us.

As I slipped my right arm from underneath my cloak and reached forward to clasp Brigitta's hand, Aedan's cuff slid forward on my wrist, exposing his medal. Sigrid grabbed my arm.

"This is not yours," she said, intently eyeing the cuff and me.

Taken aback by the sudden tone change, I responded, "You're right. It's not—it's on loan to me. And it's rather a lengthy story, which I fully intend to share with you." Honesty seemed like the best policy in the situation.

"I see. I think you and I'd best find a quiet corner and talk.

Nobody, you see, would willingly give this up." Sigrid, still clutching my wrist, lifted it to emphasize her point.

"Sigrid, give the child a moment to rest before—" Brigitta began to say.

"No! This cannot wait. I know the owner of that medal—I'm the one who forged it."

"Alright. Then take her to your study, and I'll bring some refreshments. Meanwhile, why don't you two follow me, and I'll get you settled in the house. There's no arguing with her when she gets that look." Brigitta addressed the last part to Joel and Mia.

"Uh...I think I...um...should stay with Elli," Mia replied, looking apprehensively at Sigrid.

"Yeah, me too," Joel said, stepping a little closer to me.

"Guys...I'll be fine. Go with Brigitta. Claire wanted me to share our story with Sigrid, remember? Plus, you must be hungry by now." I smiled at Mia and Joel, hoping to ease their jitters.

"Well, no point in discussing it out here any further...we're all going into the same house. Besides, we are starting to interest the neighbors a bit too much," Brigitta said, glancing toward the villagers seated on the porches of nearby homes, craning their necks.

"She's right—we should go inside," Sigrid agreed, ushering us up the steps of the large wooden home.

As I entered the house, I noticed that the floating lanterns had nestled against the wall on either side of the entrance. They now looked like ordinary porch lights.

The home's threshold led into a large living room with big frame windows and French doors showcasing the shimmering lake on the other side. The furniture was a mix of modern and antique pieces in a pale bluish-gray color. Sheer white curtains fluttered in the breeze from the open windows, and the smell of lilacs permeated the house. You couldn't help feeling like you had entered a tranquil spa.

"This way," Sigrid said, motioning for me to follow her.

I glanced at Mia and Joel. I smiled, hoping that it showed the confidence I was yet to feel myself.

With her purple robes swinging around her feet, Sigrid walked to a door on the right side of a large stone fireplace and opened it. I could hear Brigitta addressing Joel and Mia behind me and asking them to follow her up the stairs, which were on the other side of the living room.

The door that Sigrid had opened led to a cozy room with two large walnut bookcases lining the adjoining walls in front of me. They were filled with colorful books of various shapes and ages. On my left were French doors identical to the ones in the living room. They opened to a back terrace overlooking the lake. The wall to my right shared the large fireplace from the living room. There was a large, polished wood desk with a chair to match, and two plush, well-worn armchairs angled toward the hearth.

Sigrid cleared her throat. "Well...now that we have a little privacy, why don't you make yourself comfortable and tell me exactly how you've ended up with Aedan's cuff?"

I let my backpack slide to the floor beside the armchair and sat down. Sigrid eased herself into the other armchair. She patiently waited as I collected my thoughts.

"There's so much to tell...I'm not entirely sure where to begin," I said.

"Hmmm...when faced with a similar conundrum, I often find the beginning to be the best," Sigrid offered with an empathetic smile.

"Alright. It all began on a rather windy day at the beach with my sister..."

The story poured out of me. I told Sigrid about Aedan, Tristan, the Clan library, our capture, our escape, and our separation. At one point, Brigitta interrupted, bringing in some sandwiches and tea, knowing that we might be ensconced in the study for hours.

When I finally got to the part about getting my powers, I hesitated. I hadn't shared the exact details of the occurrence with anyone. Gnaritas from the Sopitam Hominibus book, or book of awakening as we'd called it, had been so adamant about protecting Dormants' knowledge that I'd always been vague about what had happened.

Sigrid raised a questioning eyebrow at my silence. "So how exactly did you awaken your power?"

I'd been honest thus far but still felt the need to protect the Dormants' secrets. "I didn't say...and I don't intend to."

"I see. Then the Dormants' secrets will continue to remain so." Sigrid smiled, taking a sip of her tea. "Good. It is as it should be. But you've yet to explain to me how you gained Aedan's cuff."

"Yes, I was just getting to that."

I launched into how Aedan had been kidnapped, how I'd seen it in my visions, and how Aedan had given his cuff to Mia so she could warn his family and they'd actually believe her. I then explained my uncontrolled visions and how Mrs. Grady had loaned Aedan's cuff to me in an effort to help. Finally, I recounted the Clan Hunters' attack, the Resistance and the Gradys' mission to rescue Aedan, and my vision with the Chairman.

Up until that point, Sigrid had remained cool and collected, mostly listening—even when I'd revealed that I was a Dormant, which usually astonished Clan members. Now, however, she set her teacup down, stared at me intently, and took my hands. The familiar current established itself between us.

"Elli...it's imperative that we forge you a medal immediately. First thing tomorrow. There's no time to waste." I nodded. She let go of my hands, leaned back in the armchair, and swept her hand over her face. "It's really miraculous that Aedan's medal has performed as well as it has for you. But...it was never intended for you, which leaves a rather large, gaping hole for the Chairman to take advantage of. We must correct that...for everyone's sake." Sigrid rose to her feet, stifling a yawn.

"Why does it leave a hole? How can the Chairman take advantage of that? How would he know?"

Raising a hand, Sigrid interrupted my stream of questions. "I realize you are filled with questions, some that I may be able to answer and some that I won't. However, both of those will remain the same even after a good night's sleep. It's already past midnight, and Brigitta will have my head if I keep you up any longer. Come, let's find your room and get you to bed."

Unable to suppress the yawn that followed Sigrid's words, I rose to my feet, ready to follow her.

"Perhaps just one simple question, then. How do you know Nodin?"

"*Ha!* That's not a simple answer. But—boiling it down—he came to us as a young boy in need of a very special medal, one which his Clan was unable to forge. And no, I will not answer anything more on that tonight. Now, how did you come to know him?"

"By accident, really. We were on the same train, and then he saved us from a tight spot in Thordalr."

"Hmmm. Doubt that—the accident part, I mean. But you'll have to ask him about that yourself."

Sigrid refused to elaborate further on what she meant. And I was left to contemplate how I was ever going to fall asleep with the numerous questions bouncing around my brain.

Leading me up the wooden stairs, Sigrid motioned for me to be quiet as she opened a door on the right-hand side of the long hallway. Inside the room and under a lavender-flowered comforter,

Mia slept on a twin bed close to the window. A similarly adorned comfy-looking bed was a bedside table away from hers. I stepped into the room, and Sigrid whispered goodnight as she closed the door behind me.

There was another door in the room, which I discovered led to a small bathroom. After brushing and washing, I crawled under the down comforter on the other bed and sank into the plush softness. Then I heard Mia whisper in a very sleepy voice, "Everything okay?"

"Everything's fine. Talk tomorrow...go back to sleep."

Mia replied with something that sounded like "okay" and "good."

I stared at Aedan's medal on my wrist. Tomorrow it would be gone. I was excited to get my own—but a nagging loneliness crept into my chest at the thought of having to give Aedan's up. With his cuff on my wrist, I felt connected to him. I hated to lose that.

As I pondered the rest of my discussion with Sigrid and what she had meant by Nodin needing a special medal, my eyelids became heavy, and sleep finally overtook me.

EIGHTEEN

The Herbarium

ELIN

I woke up to the sounds of birds singing in the trees outside, and bright sunlight pouring through the small crack between the purple curtains. I rolled over to see that Mia's comforter was thrown back, and she was no longer in her bed. I sat up, rubbed the sleep from my eyes, and found that she wasn't in the room either. The door to the small bathroom stood open, and it was empty as well. She must've woken up and gone downstairs in search of breakfast. She'd always been an early bird after a good night's rest.

I reached for my phone, which I'd left on the bedside table, remembering that I hadn't been able to find a wall outlet to plug it into the previous night. I hoped it still had enough juice to tell me the time. To my great surprise, the phone immediately lit up at my touch and displayed the "fully charged" symbol. How was that possible?

My next shock was to discover that it was nearly 10am. The others must've been up for hours while I slept the day away.

A new message pinged on my phone. It was from Anders.

ANDERS BODIL: HI ELLI - HEARD MOM & DAD SPOKE
WITH YOU LAST NIGHT. YOU WERE IN A TAXI?? 😳
EVERYTHING OK?

I quickly typed a reply to Anders.

ME: HI ANDEE - EVERYTHING'S FINE. 🙂 JUST BAD
TIMING ON M&D CALL. 🕯 WAS IN UNUSUAL
TRANSPORT TO GET WHERE WE NEEDED TO GO. BUT
HERE SAFELY NOW...SO DON'T WORRY. COULDN'T BE
MORE PROTECTED. 🏰 ALL WELL WITH YOU? 🐾

I was about to climb out of bed when Anders' reply popped up
on my phone's screen.

ANDERS BODIL: GOOD TO HEAR. CAN'T WAIT TO
EVENTUALLY GET DETAILS. ALL WELL HERE. NO SIGNS
OF 🐗🐗. KEEP ME POSTED.

I smiled at Anders' use of the supervillain emojis. I sent a
thumbs-up and a heart emoji back. I felt relief settle in my chest
now that I knew the Hunters were leaving my family in peace—at
least for now.

I swung my legs out of bed and walked over to my backpack. I
was looking forward to dressing in my normal clothes and avoiding
the additional winter layers. I dug through the backpack and
looked for the tiny pouch holding my favorite jeans, t-shirt, and
fleece-lined hoodie. Finding the sack and extracting my clothes, I
hurried through my morning ritual and was ready to exit the room
ten minutes later.

As I descended the last few steps of stairs into the living room,
goosebumps erupted on my arms. Nodin must be close. I rounded

the corner into the dining room to find him stretched out over two of the bluish-gray dining chairs with his bare feet dangling over the arm of the second. His hair was pulled back in the same braid as before, but he wore a simple white t-shirt and jeans—and it was annoying, how good he looked. The last thing I needed right now was a distraction. There were so many answers I needed, and I still had to plan how I could help Aedan.

He put down a tablet-looking device on the long rectangular table as I approached. "Morning, Elli. How'd you sleep?"

"Fine, thanks. Where is everyone?"

"Well, your two friends are enjoying some alone time on the terrace." Nodin tilted his head toward the French doors. Through the square windows, I could see Mia and Joel sitting together on the edge of the terrace, dangling their feet above the water. "And Sigrid and Brigitta are making preparations for the medal ceremony."

"There's a *ceremony?* I thought Sigrid just needed to forge the medal." I frowned. My distaste for being the center of attention remained firmly in place.

Nodin laughed. "No...no, there's quite a bit more to it than that. Your emblem and runes don't just get plucked from the sky."

"Oh. I had no idea...all of it's pretty new to me." I fiddled with a fork from the lone place setting at the table. Plucking up my courage just like the little boy from the day before, I dove into the question I really wanted to ask. "So...um...is...is that what happened for your medal forging...here?"

"Hmmm. I guess Sigrid has been sharing stories?"

"Oh, not much, really. Just that you came here for your medal because...because your Clan couldn't forge you one."

"That's true, but perhaps you should grab some breakfast first. This will be a longer conversation, and I wouldn't want you to get *hangry*." Nodin smirked as he straightened in his chair. I resisted the temptation of a snappy comeback, or worse, sticking out my tongue at him. He really was starting to remind me of Anders. "You can find a food replicator in the kitchen, or there are some eggs and toast on the warming plate over there." He pointed to the sideboard at the back of the dining room.

Having no idea what a "food replicator" was but not wanting to give Nodin the satisfaction of explaining yet another thing to me, I said, "Eggs and toast are fine."

After settling down at the dining table with a plate of food and a steaming cup of tea, I looked at Nodin inquisitively as I took my first bite. "Sooo...what's the story?"

"Well...let's see...how do I say this." Nodin smirked. "I'm...um...sure you've noticed the chemistry between us." His grin widened as he saw my eyes grow large and redness creep up my cheeks. "You know...the electricity that fills the air when we get close." He winked at me. Oh, he really was the most annoying— "There's a reason for it...and it's probably not what you think."

"Oh, I don't think about it," I said in a rush, almost swallowing my words. Nodin raised an eyebrow. "I mean, I've felt it before, so it's not that unusual...although it hasn't happened since—well, in a while."

"Before your awakening?" Nodin offered.

Startled by his comment, I looked up at him with my egg-laden fork still balanced in the air. "Yes. But how could you possibly know—"

"It's what I've been wanting to talk to you about. We're the same, you and I." Leaning across the table, Nodin touched my arm. A strong current seared its way up my arm, making my entire body buzz. "We're both Dormants."

The egg fell off my fork. Nodin let go of my arm and sat back down. I could have sworn that my heart stopped beating for a full minute as I sat in stunned silence. What were the chances?

Dormants were supposed to be rare—I mean, really rare. Not like someone-you-bump-into-at-the-train-station-who-then-rescues-you-from-an-angry-mob kind of rare.

"How's that possible? Aren't Dormants...an anomaly?"

"Worried you're not unique anymore?" Nodin laughed, clearly teasing me.

"No, actually—I'm relieved," I said, leaning back in my chair and placing the empty fork on my plate. A weight that I hadn't realized was there seemed to have lifted itself from my chest. I wasn't alone.

Nodin's grin subsided, and he leaned forward in his chair. "We're still small in number, but there's a few of us...at least in the Vestri Clan. My Clan's ancestors weren't as shy about mingling with normal humans as the Nordri, and they kept better records of those who did."

"So you've known your whole life you were a Dormant?"

"Not for sure until I was tested. The Clan gene can skip a few generations. It's not a dominant trait but a recessive one, so you'd have to get both pairs of alleles for the trait to exist in your person." When I looked a bit confused, Nodin added, "It's sorta like the genetics behind who gets blue eyes."

"Oh...okay." Passages from my biology book flashed in my head but the details were a bit murky. Recalling what Sigrid had hinted about our meeting not being accidental, I asked, "So our meeting wasn't an accident then?"

Nodin looked a little sheepish. "Well...your *Ljós* was a little hard to ignore in Litenhavn. Besides, I was on my way to Sigrid's anyway."

"*Ljós*...what's that? And why were you coming to Sigrid's?"

"*Wow*...so you really don't know anything about being a Dormant?"

I eyed Nodin to see if he was teasing me again, but the look on his face told me he was sincere in his question.

"Nothing. Nobody knew much about Dormants where I was discovered—the Clan members around me, that is—and certainly not my family. Really, my awakening was kinda an accident."

"I see. Well, you certainly came to the right place, then. Between Sigrid and myself, we'll be able to fill in some of the basics. To start, *Ljós* is the electric light that each Dormant has. Think of it as a companion to *megin*. It's what makes us different from the regular Clan members. But *Ljós* also connects Dormants together, which is why we can sense each other when we're near."

A million questions buzzed in my head but one was louder than the others. "But why did I feel the goosebumps with other Clan members before my awakening?" I couldn't help but think of Aedan's and my first touch. And there was Tristan—I'd felt it with him too.

"That was a reaction between your sleeping Clan gene and the *megin* in other Clan members." When I looked confused, he continued, "It's basically like two magnets pulling on each other and creating a magnetic field between them. When one is removed—in this case, you awakened your gene—the field goes away. That sensation is how Dormants get discovered. I experienced the same thing before my awakening."

"Huh. Okay." Something else was nagging me about what Nodin had said. "Wait a minute—why can Sigrid help? Did I miss something, or are you saying she's a Dormant as well?"

Nodin grimaced. "Oops...you didn't know? I thought that's why you are here. I mean, she is the only Dormant Forger that I know of."

"And why's that important?"

"Because only a Dormant Forger can forge medals for other Dormants," Sigrid said as she walked into the room. She wore a heavy, dark blacksmith's apron over a shimmering green robe that had green ivy with tiny white flowers embroidered on the high collar, cuff, and hem. It was an odd mix of work and formal attire. "Glad to see you're up, Elli. I hope you rested well. I see you've wasted no time in getting some answers to your questions."

"I slept well, thanks. And just a few." I was still trying to sort everything out in my head. In the span of a breakfast, I'd learned that I knew two other Dormants, which was really mind-blowing in itself—and that this new world was a lot more intricate than I'd ever imagined. I'd barely scraped the surface of the Clans' existence and now there was a whole other layer of complexities to understand.

"Yes, well, being a Dormant and a Forger isn't something we like to advertise...especially now with the Chairman's antics."

"What don't you like to advertise?" Mia asked as she and Joel entered the room from the terrace.

Both Nodin and I stayed silent, not sure how to answer Mia's question given what Sigrid had just stated. Sigrid brushed a hand over her face and tucked a loose strand of hair behind her ear. She scrutinized Mia and Joel. "Hmmm. I suppose the two of you will insist on being at Elli's ceremony, in which case you'd come to know anyway. Only a Dormant Forger can forge a medal for another Dormant."

"Well, that's bad! I mean, doesn't Elli need a medal? Where are we going to find a *Dormant* Forger—" Before Joel could finish his sentence, Mia gave him a gentle elbow in the ribs and cocked her head toward Sigrid, who had a patient smile on her lips. "Oh...*oh*...I see."

"Yes, well...now that we are all on the same page, I ask that you keep that information to yourselves. Brigitta and I have worked hard over the years to keep that knowledge confined to a handful of people that we trust implicitly. As you probably know, the

Chairman desperately seeks Dormants—but what you might not know is—that he is also trying to uncover the Dormants' secrets, in particular how our medals are forged." Sigrid's expression grew grave. "We *cannot* let him gain that knowledge. We may not know Chairman Arild's exact intentions, but one thing is certain—whatever they are, they aren't good. Thus, we must keep the secret safe...and the smaller the sphere of people, the better. As I recall, we didn't even share that information with the Gradys. And they are some of the most trustworthy people I know. Most refugees who come through Skogly, know me just as a Forger—not of Dormant medals—but of replacement ones. And you can't imagine the number of those I've crafted over the years. So many members who need and want a fresh start." Sigrid's gaze became unfocused for a moment as she was lost in thought.

Then, she added sharply, "And if all that isn't motivating enough, then perhaps knowing that if my status was to get out, it would endanger Elli and a multitude of others will help you forget that you ever learned it." Both Mia and Joel nodded. "Excellent. Now, Elli...Brigitta needs you in the herbarium. If you're both done with your breakfast, perhaps Nodin can show you the way?"

"Sure, I can take her." Nodin stood up, grabbing his coffee cup. "Elli, are you finished with those?" He pointed to my empty plate and teacup.

"Yeah, but I can clear them."

"I got it...going to the kitchen anyway." Nodin took the dishes from my hand and disappeared through the swinging door into the kitchen.

Sigrid came closer to me and put a hand on my shoulder. "After you're done at the herbarium, come back to the house and we'll go through the remaining steps for the ceremony. Mia and Joel can join you—it's a communal event." She smiled and gave my shoulder a small squeeze.

I glanced at Mia's and Joel's eager faces. By the looks of it, they were excited to participate. "Okay, sure. We'll be there."

"Great. I've got to go finish the preparation for the medal, but I'll see you soon." With that, she swept out of the room.

In the same instance, Nodin reappeared from the kitchen. "Ready?"

"As I'll ever be." I gave a small wave to Mia and Joel as I followed Nodin out through the front door.

The herbarium was a single-room log house with a greenhouse attached to the back. Bundles of fresh and dried herbs hung from the rafters. The scents of lavender, mint, basil, and thyme mingled in the air. Different-sized jars with small labels affixed to the fronts lined the wooden shelves attached to the walls. When Nodin and I entered, Brigitta was arranging small bundles of herbs on square pieces of burlap on the large central table.

"Hello there. So glad you're both here." She greeted us with a smile. "It's time we found your blend, Elli. For the Forging ceremony, we need to find the right combination of herbs in order for your symbol and runes to appear during the ritual. I took a few guesses at what I thought might work, but only your *Ljós* will tell you which is right."

She looked expectantly at me. I glanced at Nodin and then at Brigitta. "*Oookaay*...I give up. How will it tell me?"

"Brigitta, Elli is completely new to...well...Dormants," Nodin said.

"I see. So she—oh, excuse me, Elli—you haven't been taught anything at all? I hate it when people talk about me like I'm not in the room, don't you?" Brigitta gave me an empathetic look.

"Nope, nobody has taught me a thing about being a Dormant... mainly because they didn't know anything."

"Hmmm. That does present a challenge. Perhaps we need Sigrid after all."

"Let me try something first." Nodin approached me, holding out his hand. "Elli, take my hand and close your eyes."

I did as he asked. Electricity immediately sizzled between our fingers and palms, running up my arm into the rest of my body. It felt like I was vibrating. All my senses were on high alert. The smells in the room became alive. Even with my eyes closed, I could pick out dozens of more scents than when I first walked in—marjoram, rosemary, the remnants of soap on Brigitta's skin, Nodin's sweat—the list could've gone on for miles. I could hear the birds outside and tell how near or far each was to the log house. The lapping lake water seemed next door instead of a few blocks away. I could feel Nodin's steady heartbeat and pulse through his fingers. His hand felt rough and smooth in different spots, each of which I could distinctly identify.

"Elli, you've got to slow it down. You'll drain us both," Nodin said. I could feel his heart starting to beat faster.

"I don't know how!"

"Center yourself."

"*What?*" I was starting to panic. The electricity seemed to be seeping out of me into the room. I could make out the jar shapes on the shelves and the herbs hanging from the ceiling—and my eyes were still closed. Then Brigitta's voice cut in. "Elli, just think of a place where you're the most relaxed, focus on it, and draw some big deep breaths."

Place where I was most relaxed. Nothing was coming to mind. Aedan's medal felt like it was on fire on my wrist. I heard something crack like ceramic when placed under high heat. Then something crashed onto the floor, splintering into dozens of pieces. The smell of mushrooms grew strong.

"*Nodin!* We might need to rethink this." Brigitta's voice held an edge.

"She can do this...Elli, just concentrate." Nodin sounded

strained. "There's got to be a place, a safe place—somewhere you go to get away, to think."

The back porch, my home's porch on Auor...the army of pillows that my mom piled on the porch swing...the way the light shone through the windows during summer evenings...the collection of jars on the windowsills filled with seashells my sister and I had picked the previous summer. I felt my breath naturally deepen and my muscles relax as I thought of my favorite spot at home.

"Good, Elli. Keep thinking about it." Nodin's heart rate was returning to a steady beat. The energy that had seemed to pour out of me moments ago was slowly returning. "Now just breathe deeply and let me guide you."

I wasn't sure what Nodin meant by guiding me until I felt the tug on the electricity. I could feel the energy now flowing toward Nodin through our hands.

"Elli, we're going to take a few steps towards the table. Just keep breathing and staying in your relaxed space. And when I tell you to open your eyes, do so, okay?"

"Alright."

I felt Brigitta come closer. She placed one of her hands on my back and with the other took hold of my free hand. She guided me through the narrow space between the wooden shelves and table edge.

I heard Nodin's voice. "Okay, Elli. Open your eyes and tell me what you see."

My eyes fluttered open. Everything around me seemed to pulsate with lights of varying colors and strength. "Everything is glowing like they have little halos around them. It's so...so beautiful." I couldn't help but giggle. The sight was so surreal and bewitching. It felt like an alternate reality.

"Good. Now look at my hand over the herb bundles and tell me what you see."

I looked down at the table. Nodin's hand hovered above one of the burlap pieces. The herbs lying on the cloth had a nice green glow. Little green sparks seemed to randomly shoot towards Nodin's palm. I shared what I saw.

"Okay, how about this one? Any different?"

"No, it's the same."

It wasn't until we reached the sixth bundle that something different appeared. "Nodin, that one's different." Excitement filled my voice, but at the same time, a little waver occurred in the electricity between him and me.

"That's great, Elli, but keep calm. Take a nice deep breath." I did as he asked and the energy flow stabilized. "Good. Now, do any of the herbs in the bundle look different from the others?"

"They look like little white sparklers...oh, except for that one." I pointed with my free hand to the green-lit herb.

"Angelica...I should have guessed," Brigitta muttered as she picked up the herb.

Little green streaks of light created a wake in the herb's path as Brigitta placed it on a nearby table. My eyes couldn't help but follow the pretty waves. It reminded me of the aurora borealis we'd seen the previous day.

"Well, three out of four isn't bad," Nodin said.

"Yes, but how do we find the fourth...and quickly? Sigrid wants to do the ceremony today," Brigitta replied.

"Uh...I think...I may be able to help with that." My eyes were glued to the erupting fireworks coming out of a jar placed above where Brigitta had lain the discarded herb. "That one—it's having a field day."

Brigitta took the jar I indicated down from the shelf and read the label. "Feverfew...how interesting." She pulled out a stem with a dried white-and-yellow flower. It sparkled like a firecracker, sending multicolored sparks towards Nodin's palm. "We use it to treat fevers and headaches."

She placed it on the burlap cloth with the rest of the herbs. A strong, steady stream of white sparks erupted towards Nodin's hand, which still hovered above them.

"*Wow*...so cool," I whispered.

Nodin laughed. "I think we found our bundle."

He let go of my hand, and the energy flow broke. All of the auras extinguished themselves around me. The world looked plain once again.

I looked at Nodin. "How did you do that?"

"It's all about controlling energy. It takes practice and learning how to use your *megin* to direct your *Ljós*—probably something that we need to teach you sooner rather than later, because right now, how those herbs sparkled is how you look to another Dormant. They'd be able to pick you out of a crowd like the morning star in a black sky."

"Is that why you followed me from Litenhavn? Because you saw my...my glow," I asked.

"Well, like I said earlier, I was already coming this way...but yes, it made me take an interest in you." Nodin's hazel eyes examined my amber ones. "I knew there was something...um... different...about you. No trained Dormant would let their *Ljós* shine in such an uninhibited way."

"But what about the goosebumps? Does my *Ljós* cause those?"

"Yes and no. They result from the interaction of our *Ljós*. Think of static electricity—it's the result of a negative and positive ion imbalance on two surfaces. You need both ions for the reaction to occur. It's the same for us when our *Ljós* comes into contact. But when we're trained, we can control the distance and size of the reaction."

"Oh...*soooo*...is that why I only feel a tingle with Sigrid and not all the time?"

"Yes. She's got quite a bit more experience than either one of us—a master at the art of *Ljós* control."

"Ha! She had to be, or she wouldn't have survived under the Chairman's rule," Brigitta interjected. "But enough about that. You two need to get back to the house for the remaining preparations."

Nodin's now-familiar grin appeared on his face. "Yes, we certainly *don't* want to miss that."

Exiting Brigitta's herbarium, I got the sense that I wasn't going to be thrilled with whatever the next item on the prep list was. I tried to pry it out of Nodin as we walked down the grass-covered path towards Sigrid's house—but to no avail. He was like a vault.

As we came closer to the water, a strange white haze began to shroud everything. Then from the corner of my eye, I saw a bright light creep in, replacing the fog. *No, no, no, no.* Why was this happening now? I couldn't have a vision right *now*. I glanced at my right wrist with Aedan's cuff. There was no blue light under the medal. In fact, there was no round medal at all—just two shards. A large crack had split Aedan's medal.

WHAT HAD I DONE?

I reached for Nodin's arm as my world went spinning into white.

NINETEEN

The Orbpods

AEDAN

T he room was a square box—no windows, no furniture, and no carpet—just an empty cement box. Thyra's hasty explanation that the space was a Leikr training room had done nothing to illuminate its purpose. The only thing I was grateful for was the removal of the *Hepta Baugr* once the *Stór-menni* guards had shoved me through the doorway.

I rubbed my wrist, trying to soothe the chafed skin. It was the first time since my arrival in Clan territory that the dampener cuff didn't weigh down my arm. I could feel my *megin* pulsating in my body with its pent-up energy.

But I was determined to ignore it. Whatever the stated purpose of this room was, I was fairly positive that I was the real specimen to be examined. Tiny little cameras in the ceiling's corners betrayed their presence with red recording lights.

I sat down cross-legged on the floor. Even if whoever was watching me wanted me to perform with my abilities, there wasn't much I could do. I didn't have my medal to assist me, an apparent oversight by a man in a mint-green tunic and white lab coat who'd been thoroughly chastised by Thyra in the corridor outside the room. Muttering apologies and laying blame elsewhere, he'd scurried off with a promise to return with the required item.

A surprising vow since it wasn't clear to me how they were going to discern my runes without my help, but I'd decided not to concern myself with their problems. At any rate, I had no intention of using my ability, so the whole thing seemed pointless.

On the Autonomous Hover Vehicle ride over to wherever we now were, Thyra had tried to explain the basics of Leikr. She'd wanted to give an overview of the games before we began training. She'd said that they were a series of matches in which sixteen teams dwindled to an eventual two that played in the final round. The matches were scored by points earned for speed and the number of team players that successfully completed each course. The first rounds were played individually, but in the last matches, the remaining teams were pitted against each other in some sort of obstacle course involving tunnels and paired team members. The details were still a bit murky given the brevity of Thyra's description.

She'd also highlighted two complicating factors. One was the unknown element of what the Clan Creators and Engineers had fashioned as challenges. With a frown, Thyra said that it changed every year. The obstacles could be either a landscape or an opponent. As examples, she'd cited a lava field and a Draugr, whatever that was.

According to Thyra, the second complication would affect our team the most. During the games, all Leikr teams were allowed to use any means to slow the other teams down—with the noted exception of directly killing the other team members. And if you had a target on your back, as the Chairman's team always did, it meant that you took a lot of incoming fire. Apparently, beating the Chairman's team was considered a great *Sigra* as his team was always composed of the best players. And being crowned the Leikr victors, especially if the Chairman's team had played, brought many adulations and perks in Clan society.

I adjusted my legs on the cold floor. Well, the Chairman's team would be down a player in these games—so best of luck to the other teams. I couldn't think of anything I'd be less willing to do than earn or defend victory for the Chairman. I hadn't given him anything yet. And I wasn't about to start just because he'd moved me to a comfortable room and required that I participate in the Clan's pastime.

Besides, I now had my own mission, given my location change. Reo's stories of the Chairman's wife and the questions about his ultimate goal were still bouncing around in my head. I felt certain that there was a link between them. And knowing what it was would surely give the Resistance and other Clans an advantage.

Then there was the peculiarity of my family's missing DNA and surname. Why hadn't my parents told me or my siblings about any of it? Or maybe Claire and Edvin knew, and I was the only one left out. Or perhaps the Chairman was just lying—which was the most likely case. Whatever the answers were, I was determined to get to the bottom of them all—and this was my chance.

While shuttling me out of the building where I was housed this morning, the *Stór-menni* guards had inadvertently exposed some valuable information. Near the exit to the AHV landing pad was a placard on the wall with the names of each floor. And when passing it earlier, I'd noticed that the Chairman's office was listed on the 26th floor of the *same* building.

It was the perfect opportunity. For what better place to search for answers, not only to the Chairman's secrets but those of my family, than his office? He'd certainly have access to all the information, so it was just a matter of putting the pieces together— and finding the right moment and way to enter his enclave.

It felt good to have a purpose again. For the past several weeks, I'd sat in the Ginnungagap cell staring at whitewashed walls wondering if and when my family would come, whether Elin would be with them, and how I could help Reo and everyone else trapped in the awful place. And there had been nothing, nothing I could do. But now it was different. Being in the same building as the Chairman's office was only a tiny opportunistic window but one I intended to crawl through.

I wondered what Elin would have thought of my scheme. The last time I'd made covert plans was with her. Our mission had been to gain access to the book of awakening. And that had been successful...well, until Tristan and his aunt had entered. But at least Elin had learned what she needed, or so I assumed. We hadn't exactly had a moment to talk it over afterward. I wondered if she had been able to awaken herself with the information she'd gained.

Suddenly, my head seemed to be filled with her loud voice. I covered my ears. But it didn't help.

"AEDAN! Aedan...can you hear me?" Elin's voice asked.

My eyes flew open but she wasn't in the room. Her voice kept saying my name.

I must have been having one of those hallucinations Reo talked about. The windowless room, which reminded me of the Ginnungagap cell, had probably triggered it. I took a deep breath, trying to calm myself—but the voice was insistent.

Perfect...just perfect! I was losing my mind while a bunch of *Stór-menni* cameras recorded it. I took another deep breath, trying to block out the sound, but it persisted. Then I remembered Reo saying that sometimes it helped to talk to the hallucinations. The conversation was really with yourself, so it calmed the anxiety.

"Yes, I can hear you...and I'd appreciate it if you didn't yell," I whispered, trying to keep the *Stór-menni's* prying ears from hearing what I said. For good measure, I rested my head on my knees and closed my eyes, trying to hide my odd behavior.

"You can?" Elin's voice seemed surprised but at least was now at a more comfortable level.

"Yup, I definitely can." This felt insane. Of course, I could hear myself.

"Finally! I've tried so many times, but you never could hear me. Where are you? Are you okay?"

"Um...somewhere in Falinvik." It seemed strange, telling myself what I already knew.

"WHAT? Are you sure?" Elin's voice was panicked.

"Yeah, pretty sure," I scoffed. It was rather comical that I didn't believe myself.

"You can't be...you just can't. Your parents, sister, and brother are on their way to Ginnungagap to get you!"

This wasn't funny anymore. How could my own mind possibly know such a thing? Was this a Chairman's trick? Was *he* in my mind? Only one way to be sure.

"Elin, what happened between us in Ash Park after we escaped?" The only other person who could answer that was Elin.

"*Seriously?* You want to talk about our kiss *now*, when I've just told you that your family is trying to rescue you from the *wrong place?*"

"*Elin?* Is it really you? How is this *possible*? Why can I hear you in my head?"

"Yes, it's me! Who'd you think it was? Oh, Aedan...I have so much to tell you! After we left each other in Ash Park—Oh, no! He's coming...Aedan, he's coming...I can feel his eyes...I have to go. I'm so sorry—I just can't risk it."

"Who's coming? *Elin*, who's coming? What can't you risk?" But she was gone—her voice inside my head was gone.

I didn't understand any of it. How was she in my head? Maybe she *had* woken her *megin*—but a Telepath's or a Mind Interventionist's ability couldn't travel great distances. It would take an enormous amount of *megin* that no Clan member could possibly possess.

It seemed impossible, yet I was certain that I'd just talked with Elin. My mind was working a mile a minute to parse everything she'd told me—especially about my family.

The screech of the room's door interrupted my thoughts.

I lifted my head to see the Chairman stride in, his gray robes billowing in his wake. He had a medallion wrapped around his hand. Stopping by my side, he towered over me as I sat on the floor. His cold gray eyes pierced mine.

"Hello, Aedan. I heard that you were missing a medal, that one wasn't found on you when you arrived. Well, we certainly can't have that, especially during the Leikr ." He smiled in a self-satisfied manner. "My chief Forger examined your RDS report, and based on the detection scans' results, was able to engrave your runes. Of course, I took the liberty to offer instruction on the emblem since you are my...my guest. Here is your new—and I hope very much improved—medallion."

He let the silver chain slip between his fingers until the medal dangled in front of my face. I couldn't quite make out the runes as it swayed, but what was clear was the three interlocking triangles embossed in the middle. The Chairman had given me his emblem —the Valknut.

"I strongly suggest taking the medallion," The Chairman said, witnessing my reluctance. Through the still-open door, I heard the clatter of metal against the cement floor. Something was coming. "I'm certain that you will fare much better against these two pets with it...than without it."

The Chairman dropped the medallion in my lap as he turned with a whisk of his gray robes. Behind him, I could now see two giant gunmetal balls entering the room. Each had eight clickety-clacking metallic legs that protruded from its undercarriage in a slight V-form. They also had three cylindrical tubes with lenses on the side that faced me. The lenses zoomed in and out, adjusting to the Chairman's movement and my own as I quickly stood up, medallion in hand. Underneath what I could only refer to as their eyes was a wide rectangular opening that was currently shut.

With a clatter, the metal balls scattered to the side as the Chairman walked between them. Their movement reminded me of spiders. He stopped at the door, turning to face me.

"These Orbpods have been instructed to capture you by any means necessary...including bodily injury. I suggest defeating them instead. Oh, and if you're considering surrender...I wouldn't. They can be quite...um...enamored with their captives...and not in a good way." With that, the Chairman stepped outside the door but turned for a last look. "Happy Leikr training, Aedan. I'm sure it will be very eye-opening for you." The door slammed shut behind him.

The Orbpods immediately began to circle me. One moved left while the other went right. The clicking of their feet against the floor was the only sound. I backed away from them, trying to give myself some time to think.

Using my *megin* was now starting to feel like a certainty rather than a choice. The Chairman must have read my mind, since I actually had been thinking about surrendering to the Orbpods to avoid revealing my ability. That was until he'd said how they interacted with their captives. If he implied that it was unpleasant, I could only guess at the true horror. And given my newfound purpose, being incapacitated would definitely not be helpful... especially if my family was now in Clan territory.

I hadn't really fully processed everything that Elin had told me. But knowing that my family had come for me had made a tiny sliver of hope blossom in my heart. I sent a silent prayer into the universe that my family would figure out in time that I wasn't at Ginnungagap. There was nothing more I could do at the moment —other than trying to stay alive and unharmed.

The rhythmic metallic clicking against the cement floor brought me out of my thoughts. The Orbpods were advancing on me. Pincers had emerged from the right one's rectangular opening. They snapped together in a menacing way. The other still had its mouth closed, leaving me to guess at its purpose.

I glanced at the medallion in my hand. I had no choice. My *megin* would be unstable without it. Never mind the fact that I wouldn't be able to use my abilities while holding it. Grimacing with disgust, I slipped the necklace over my head. Immediately, I felt my *megin's* beat become steadier, even though I hated giving the Chairman any satisfaction no matter how small.

My mind worked furiously to find a way to disable the pods. There was nothing in the room that I could pick up with my ability and throw at the orbs. With eight legs, dislodging one would still leave seven more to contend with. Plus, I wouldn't be able to simultaneously knock out legs on both Orbpods. My only choice at the moment was to run to the room's other corner to buy some time.

I glanced at the ball on the right with its clicking pincers. Then I turned to locate the other. They were still at a distance apart where I could easily run between them with my *megin* speed. With a deep breath, I launched into action.

I ran as fast as I could between the pods. Out of the corner of my eye, I saw the balls' side with the lenses quickly swiveling to follow my path. Their legs changed direction without the orbs having to turn the rest of their bodies. Once again, the orbs advanced on my position. I'd bought a little time but not much.

I was able to elude the Orbpods a few more times using the

same technique. But they were learning quickly. With each of my successes, they closed the distance between themselves, narrowing the opening for my escape.

Now as the orbs approached me, I'd have to choose a side instead of going between them. I decided to go right. As I started to run, I saw the closer pod tuck its legs inside itself and withdraw its lenses. Then it rolled toward me at great speed. *It was going to pin me against the wall!*

In an instant, it was nearly upon me. I leaped to the side. With the aid of my *megin,* I landed a few paces from the Orbpod. I heard the pod crash into the wall behind me. A cloud of gray dust and debris filled the air. I felt a small singe on my cheek as a flying cement shard drew blood. I looked back. The orb was undamaged. However, the cement wall now had a giant gash with rubble falling into the room.

I smiled. Even though it was clear that the cement pieces weren't going to affect the Orbpods' outer shell, they would make the floor unstable and perhaps provide a distraction. As much as I hated revealing my unique ability, it was time. Raising my right hand, I pointed it toward the rubble and swept it across the room. The debris slid across the surface, looking like the crumbles on top of my mother's berry pie.

The Orbpod behind me extended its lenses, surveying the situation. Then with smooth efficiency, it sucked the lenses back in and started to roll towards me, crushing the cement fragments underneath its bulk. I frowned. My unstable surface was proving less helpful than I thought. But the Orbpod had revealed something useful. The fact that it had paused its rolling to use its lenses made me suspect that perhaps it couldn't see in its balled-up position.

I glanced at the other pod. It was trying to pick its way through the rubble towards me. Its eight legs were having trouble coordinating their steps given the debris-littered floor. Well, at least my trick had worked on one of them.

The rolling orb was getting closer. I decided to test my theory. I waited until the orb was a few feet away. Then I took a few big steps toward the left.

The orb continued speeding in its original path without changing course. It flew past me. A few seconds later, it crashed into the facing wall, sending more debris and dust flying into the room.

Meanwhile, the other Orbpod had grown frustrated with its lack of progress. It crouched at an odd angle, aiming its lenses towards me. Its rectangular mouth opened. With a *whoosh*, something black launched itself across the room right towards me.

Immediately, I raised my hand. Using my *megin*, I captured the item in mid-flight and held it suspended in the air. It looked like some kind of netting. I brought my other hand up and quickly worked to unfold the item. I was right. It was a black weighted net of strong material.

I looked back at the rolling orb. It was momentarily caught between two large pieces of the broken cement wall. I turned my head towards the other pod. It had risen from its low angle.

Pulling back my arms and hands as far as they could go while gathering the force of my *megin*, I threw the suspended net towards the standing Orbpod. Guided by tendrils of my ability, the net sailed through the air unhindered. It landed on the pod with a *clink*. Quickly, I moved my hands in a circular motion, tying the net's weighted ends around the orb's legs. I pulled tight. With a loud metallic *thud*, the orb collapsed on its side. The lower half of its legs flailed in the air. They tried to retract into the pod's body but were prevented by the net's thick lines and weights.

The sound of crushing gravel intruded on my victorious moment. I turned around just in time to see the other pod rolling towards me. It was inches away. I immediately somersaulted backward through the air. I landed on my feet near the broken cement wall.

Without a second thought, I ripped a leg from the disabled pod in the net. Across the room, the rolling orb crashed into the third wall. Aiming for the middle of its body, I threw the straightened leg like a spear. It easily pierced the orb's shell. The Orbpod shuddered in a few spasms and then became still.

I wiped the sweat, blood, and cement dust from my face and ran my hands through my hair. I took a deep breath to calm my panting. I had defeated the machines, but I couldn't help wondering what the cost of revealing my unique ability would be.

The room's door flew open. Thyra entered. Behind her, an army of little sweeper robots followed. They began to clean the rubble from the floor. Two armed guards appeared in the doorway, perching on either side.

Thyra approached me with a *Hepta Baugr* in hand. "Well done, Aedan! That was quite a show. I'm so pleased to have a Telekinetic on our Leikr team."

TWENTY

A Trap

TRISTAN

This was going to work. We had planned for every contingency. I was positive the intruders would be lured into our trap. And I would finally get everything I had been working toward and deserved.

There was no question in my mind that the invaders knew where the Unregistered's former cell was. They would not have come without knowing the crucial detail. After all, they were here to rescue him. And I was sure that they would waste no time in making their way to where they thought he was.

Given that there was no intelligence about how the intruders were going to enter and which path they would take to the cell, I had devised a trap at the destination rather than preventing their entry. The small army of Ginnungagap guards had been instructed to let the uninvited guests pass unhindered into the bowels of the gray fortress.

When the time came and our assault began, the maze of corridors that encompassed the lower section of the fortress would help entrap the Unregistered's rescuers. The chaos would scatter them into the labyrinth, where we could easily pick them off as they became lost. This would minimize any *Stór-menni* losses and keep the operation tidy.

I smiled in satisfaction. I had only had a day and a half to come up with the scheme. Then the additional outer perimeter monitors I had requested, picked up six infiltrators in a nearby forest. The short time frame had been a challenge, but I was confident about my plan. There would be no escape for them.

I paced the floor behind the seated Surveillance Unit sentries. Screens displaying every inch of the passages leading to the Unregistered's cell lined the wall in front of me. I could see the fortress's uniformed guards stationed in strategic sections of the corridors. Their concealed nearby presence would make for a swift intruder capture when the time came.

"Sir, we have activity on entry 32," one of the Surveillance team members announced.

I quickly moved to peer over the sentry's shoulder. On the screen in front of her was an open outer door leading to a small room with benches lined up against the walls. It was the access room to the Chairman's private landing pad. How had they managed to open it? I supposed it did not matter considering they were steps closer to being ensnared.

But where were the intruders? The room was empty. The screen fluttered for a few seconds and then displayed the same room but with the door closed.

"The secondary heat-signature cameras...NOW!" The sentry jumped in surprise at my urgent command. She quickly pressed a few buttons on the lower panel. A new display flickered onto the larger screens lining the wall. "Focus on the passages from that room leading to the cell."

She tapped a few more buttons. The screens showed three

separate corridors. In two of the passages, there were three heat signals indicating the presence of people.

"Do a comparison of the regular cameras side by side with the heat-signature ones." The sentry did as I demanded. The regular cameras showed no people in the hallways, whereas the heat-signature ones clearly indicated three in each. "How are they doing that?"

"I'm not sure, Sir. Perhaps an Illusionist...although there would have to be at least two—one with each group—or some other trick."

I ran my hand over my face. If they had Illusionists among them, it would complicate matters—but not insurmountably.

"Inform the corridor guards. They'll need to wear their heat-signature eyepieces."

"Yes, Sir." The guard was about to tap the Communicator on her wrist.

"And I want reports of the intruders' movements directly from the guards as well."

"Understood, Sir."

Leaving the sentry to pass on my commands, I walked back to my earlier position in the Surveillance room, where I could better see all the screens on the wall.

I wondered which one of the heat signatures was Elin. Knowing her impatient nature, she would be sure to be in the rescue party.

What, if anything, the Unregistered meant to her was not clear to me, but she had chosen him over me when gaining access to the book of awakening. And he had been caught in the process. So, with her sense of obligation, she was sure to feel guilty. Yes, she would want to be here. I scrutinized the generic-looking heat indicators to find any hint as to which one she was.

The interlopers were making steady progress through the

corridors. Another eight to ten minutes, if they didn't get lost, and they would be at the cell's door. Imagine their surprise when they found the cell empty. I chuckled.

A few minutes later, reports filtered in through the guards that the uninvited guests were now in the target cell block. The heat-signature cameras confirmed the statements. I strapped on my Communicator. I tapped once.

"Let them approach and inspect. We do not take them until they make a move to re-enter the corridors, understood?"

"Affirmative, Sir," the voice of the guard captain responded.

I watched on the wall screens as the intruders approached the cell door and peered in through the window. Their body movements betrayed their bafflement as they each took turns looking through the porthole. I smiled.

Then something unexpected happened. One of the intruders walked to the hall's other cell door and looked through the window. He or she seemed to call the others over to it.

The face of the cell's occupant appeared in the door's porthole. The heat-signature cameras could not display the facial expressions of the intruders, but judging by the captive's smile on the regular cameras, it was clear they knew each other.

Suddenly, the cell door popped open, allowing the occupant to walk out and embrace the intruders. Moments later, his image disappeared from the regular cameras.

"HOW DID THEY DO THAT? AND WHO IS THE CELL'S OCCUPANT? I want to know NOW. And bring up the tracker on his *Hepta Baugr* immediately!"

"Sir. Yes, Sir," a nearby Surveillance sentry responded. "Sir, at this time we do not know how they opened the door or how he vanished, but the cell's occupant is Reo Itō and a new heat signature has popped up...presumably his." He finished tapping a few more buttons on his console. "Putting up the *Hepta Baugr* tracking map now, Sir. Also, according to his file, Sir, Reo Itō is a long-time reformee at Ginnungagap...but the details are classified, Sir."

A map showing the fortress's layout appeared on a portion of the wall screens. A small red dot indicating the prisoner's presence flashed in the hall of the target cell block.

It had not been displaying for more than a minute when the screens suddenly enlarged beyond comprehension. Then, everything faded to black.

"ODIN'S BEARD! WHAT IS HAPPENING?" I yelled. This was no time for a camera glitch.

None of the sentries answered me. They were furiously typing on their panels and leaning over to talk to each other. The room was in chaos. Then a wagging finger appeared on the black screen as if to say "No".

"SOMEBODY ANSWER ME!"

"Sir...sorry, Sir...we aren't quite sure what's happening. Our best guess is...that is to say...it appears to be some kind of an unknown malfunction," the same nearby sentry answered. "It's as if the cameras started listening to someone else, and we can't get them to respond."

"Well, fix it! Get an Engineer on it." These sentries were useless. They had only passive abilities, which qualified them as glorified watchdogs but not much more.

The sentry shifted uncomfortably. "We are working on it, Sir...but..."

"But, WHAT? There are no 'BUTs' in this operation...get someone here immediately."

Suddenly, everything in the room went dark. Screens were black and lights were gone. Somebody quickly tossed a few emergency hovering lanterns into the air.

In the glow of the orange-yellow lights, I looked at the sentry. "Don't tell me...another technical glitch?"

"Um...Sir...I'm afraid it's worse, Sir." He cowered behind his chair. "The entire system has been shut down."

"WHAT!" I sat down on a nearby chair. This was going to ruin me.

"This has never happened before, Sir. This system should be impenetrable."

"Clearly, it isn't!"

My Communicator crackled. "Sir, we are getting reports of cell doors opening in the lower corridors and occupants emerging," the Captain's voice reported.

I couldn't afford to lose the Unregistered's rescuers. Capturing them was my last salvation from this nightmare. I tapped my Communicator. "Captain, I'm ordering you to take the intruders now! Ignore the other occupants. They have *Hepta Baugrs*...we can recapture them later."

"Understood, Sir."

"Um...Sir?" The sentry cautiously approached me.

"Yes, what is it?"

"Well, Sir...excuse me, Sir...but I overheard you with the Captain. The things is, the central system manages the *Hepta Baugrs* in the fortress...and with all controls shut down, the cuffs would become inert."

"ARE YOU SERIOUS!" The sentry nodded, unable to utter further words. Nausea ripped through my stomach. Fighting the urge to vomit, I stood up. "I want all the SASUs in the fortress deployed right now. And close all the fortress entries, even if it has to be done manually. *WHERE* is that Engineer?"

"Understood, Sir. Closing all doors and deploying the SASUs right now. They operate on isolated mobile units, so they should still be functional...but we won't have visibility. Also, as I was trying to explain earlier, Sir, Ginnungagap doesn't have an Engineer with the right ability to handle...this type of malfunction. The ability to communicate directly with machines is very rare. There are only a few of Technopath Engineers, and they're all at the Chairman's disposal in Falinvik."

I ran my fingers through my hair, bringing it to a disheveled state. "So, what are our options?"

"We are trying to reboot the entire system core now, but that will take at least..." he glanced at his Communicator. "At least seven more minutes, Sir, after which we should know whether it has become operational again."

"Sir." The Captain's voice crackled in my ear again.

"Go ahead, Captain."

"We are meeting heavy resistance in the corridors." As if to emphasize his point, loud bangs and screams could be heard in the background. "It seems that some of the inmates have been able to remove their *Hepta Baugrs* and are fighting us. There are several with Warrior abilities—QUICK, GET TO THE SIDE... WATCH OUT FOR—"

An explosion rocked the Surveillance room. A panicked voice, not the Captain's, came through the Communicator. "BREACH! EXIT BREACH, I REPEAT EXIT BREACH...CAPTIVES ESCAPING!"

My stomach heaved. I sat down in the chair, willing myself not to throw up. I could not recall any successful prison break from Ginnungagap in Clan history.

I had just overseen the first one.

There was only one last hope to minimize the damage. All my previous energy had evaporated. It seemed a nearly impossible task to tap once on my Communicator.

In a quiet, heavy voice, I said, "Someone, give me a status on the intruders."

For a few moments, all I heard was the rapid beating of my heart. Then, the Captain's voice came through surrounded by loud booms, crashes, and other strange strangled noises. "No sight of them, Sir...WATCH OUT FOR THAT ONE...we are unable to get through...USE YOUR ABILITY, SOLDIER...too many captives are loose. Once the SASUs get...INCOMING, DUCK... more control over the situation...ON YOUR RIGHT...we'll have a better idea, Sir."

"Understood, Captain." I dropped my head into my hands.

The whole situation was so much worse than anything I could ever have imagined—and there were *five* more minutes until the system came back online.

TWENTY-ONE

Double Vision

ELIN

I was trapped. There was nothing but whiteness. I'd hastily pulled the ripcord after my visit with Aedan, but it hadn't brought me out of my vision like it normally did. Instead, I was floating in a sea of white, trying to think of the most mundane things I could.

Something must have gone wrong in the exit process. In the beginning, I was so excited to see Aedan and for him to actually hear me. But then I sensed the approach of the piercing cold gray eyes. They were like searchlights in dense fog. Their beacons clawed through anything that came in their path. And I could tell they were looking for me. Just the thought of them made my skin crawl.

With their advance, I knew I couldn't stay. It would be risking another encounter with the Chairman. And he would've been sure to ensnare me with his mind, especially since I had no medal to protect mine. So I'd hurriedly pulled the ripcord.

I grimaced at the thought of Aedan's baffled face. There just hadn't been enough time to explain everything to him. My only solace was that at least he now knew that we hadn't forgotten or abandoned him. His rescue was underway—even if it was in the wrong place.

I tried again. Stone. Mud. Pavement. No banal thought was working—I was still swimming in whiteness. I needed to get back to my normal state so I could tell the others.

Recalling Mr. Grady's theory about Mind Interventionists' ability to interact with temporal visions, I was fairly certain that the vision had been set in present time since I had sensed the Chairman's mind. Which meant the Gradys had to be warned— Aedan wasn't at Ginnungagap.

Suddenly, the white fog started to swirl around me. What was happening? This wasn't how a normal exit felt. It grew faster and stronger, turning into a funnel. I closed my eyes to avoid the motion sickness that threatened to engulf me. Then I felt myself being sucked through the tip. Where was my mind taking me?

I opened one eye to peek at my surroundings. I was hovering amongst the clouds, and it was sleeting. I looked down. I immediately recognized the gray fortress from my previous vision. Ginnungagap. Suddenly, a strong gust pushed me down toward the stronghold's snow-covered roofs.

Once again I fell through the building, but I was faster this time. Everything was a complete blur. Then without ceremony, my plummet stopped. I'd materialized in some sort of hall.

There were three corridors that left the room. The two doors facing the passages had porthole windows. The hall's walls were made of large ancient stones that had been whitewashed some time ago.

Without warning, three figures entered the hall from one of the passageways. They wore black cloaks with an iridescent quality. The pulled-up hoods concealed their faces as I hovered above them.

They hadn't been in the room more than a minute when out of the third corridor emerged three additional people similarly garbed. They greeted each other with quick nods and immediately proceeded to the door on the left. Each peered into the room through the window.

"Where is he?" The whispering voice was all too familiar to me. Mrs. Grady.

I glanced around in desperation. Was this a future, present, or past vision? There was nothing in the room to tell me. No clocks, calendars, watches...not anything.

If it was the present or past—then I was too late. The Gradys were or already had been in Ginnungagap. I gathered all my focus like I had during my vision with Aedan and yelled, "HE ISN'T HERE. AEDAN ISN'T IN GINNUNGAGAP!"

But they all ignored me. I tried again, and again. But they couldn't hear me. There was nothing I could do. Why had Aedan heard me and they couldn't?

"All the Resistance's information said he would be in this cell. And their intelligence is rarely wrong. Plus, what Dara conveyed about Elin's vision confirmed it," a voice with a slight French accent said. Monsieur Tibadeau.

One of the taller figures approached the other cell door in the hall. He or she peeked through the porthole.

"*By Freya!* I know this man." I recognized the voice of Mr. Grady. The others quickly gathered around him at the door. "Dara, do you recognize him? It's Reo Itō. We must release him!"

An older Asian man's face appeared on the other side of the door's window. He wore a large smile as he took in the people on the hall side.

"Quickly, Gabriel. He's a good friend...and he might know where Aedan is," Mrs. Grady said.

Another cloaked figure pulled out a tablet from a Clan

backpack. I could only assume it was Gabriel as he placed his hand on the device. Oddly, he didn't type or tap any buttons, but underneath his fingers, the tablet started to glow with a blue light.

A few moments later, there was an audible click as the cell door's lock slid open. The man inside came out, and Mr. and Mrs. Grady warmly embraced him.

"Reo...how good to see you, my friend," Mr. Grady said. "Here, put this on—an ingenious invention by our young companion Gabriel. It keeps us out of sight from prying eyes."

From his Clan backpack, Mr. Grady pulled a black cloak similar to his. Reo accepted the article and slipped it over his shoulders.

"Thank you, Liam-san. It is good to see you as well. Many years have passed since we last laid eyes on each other," Reo answered in a Japanese accent.

Mr. Grady placed an affectionate hand on Reo's shoulder. "Indeed, Reo...too long. I'm sorry to find you in this place. Tell me, how long have you been in this cell?"

"Oooh, difficult to say exactly, but at least ten years. I was captured the night of the Great Carnage...but the first decade was spent with the interrogators."

Mrs. Grady lifted her hand to her mouth. Her eyes were wide with empathy. "You mean to say you've been imprisoned for *twenty* years?"

"Yes, Dara-san. But now, I'm so grateful to be freed." Reo bowed deeply. "How did you find me?"

"I'm sorry to say that we didn't know of your plight, Reo...we came looking for our son. He was supposed to be in the cell next to yours," Mr. Grady said, motioning to the other cell door.

"You mean to say that Aedan-kun is your son?" Reo's eyebrows rose in true surprise.

"You know him? You know Aedan? Have you any idea what happened to him? Or where he is?" Mrs. Grady peppered him.

"Yes...yes, Aedan and I have communicated for the last several weeks, but I never imagined that his family was you. I'm sorry to say they removed him three or so nights ago—hard to know exactly. It was the Chairman's personal guards who came, so I can only assume they have taken him to Falinvik." Reo stroked his chin. "Hmmm. I have never been one to believe in coincidence, which leads me to assume that the *Stór-menni* knew you were coming... and are most likely watching us this very moment."

"But they can't see us—we have the Concealment Cloaks," Edvin's voice piped up from one of the other hooded figures in the room.

"Aah...then you are not aware of the heat-signature cameras the *Stór-menni* recently deployed—yet another confirmation of our dilemma. I witnessed the upgrade from my cell a few days ago." Reo pointed to a small, flat item on the room's ceiling.

"Gabriel?" Monsieur Tibadeau asked, looking toward his nephew.

Gabriel placed his hand back on the tablet. The same blue light appeared but stronger in color. "*Oui, oui.* I see them now, Uncle. They were hidden deeper in the system and only exposed if specifically called for. Shutting them down now." Gabriel's French accent matched his uncle's.

"A Technopath...how very lucky we are." Reo seemed to brighten as he witnessed Gabriel's ability.

Gabriel lifted his hand off the device. "Uh... sorry, but I must break some more bad news...before I instructed them to take a little nap, the cameras conveyed that there are guards in *all* the corridors that exit this hall."

"Hmmm. Gabriel, I'm afraid we are going to have to go even further, then," Mr. Grady said, rubbing his neck. "It seems we cannot exit this place without a little help from the local residents. Can you open the cell doors in the lower section?"

"Sure, *fastoche*—or as you say, easy-peasy."

"Wait!" Reo exclaimed. "It won't be enough...we still have the *Hepta Baugr* problem." He raised his wrist, showing a black bracelet with a blinking red light. "None of the captives will be able to fight or be willing to exit their cells while this infernal device is active. The *megin* dampener is also a tracker, and only the gods know what else. We have to disable them."

Gabriel's fingers glowed blue on the tablet again. "The *Hepta Baugrs* can only be disabled when the entire system is shut down. That means *tout*—everything in Ginnungagap will be turned off."

Mr. Grady wiped his face with his hand. "Then...I guess we'll have to fully shut down the entire core system. You up for it, Gabriel? I know it's a lot to ask."

"*Oui*, I can do it, Mr. Grady." Gabriel gave a single, serious nod.

"Dad, are you sure? We are in the old bowels of the fortress. I'm sure in recent years the people incarcerated here were imprisoned without reason, but from what I've read...before that, they only housed the worst of the worst in the lower cells. We'd have no control over who got out with the entire system down," Claire's voice said from the remaining unknown figure in the room.

Mr. Grady turned to look at her. "Claire, we don't have a choice. These corridors are a maze. It would take too long to shut down individual ones, and it would also potentially give the guards a clear path to us. Plus, we've got to inactivate the *Hepta Baugrs*. No, we have to do the whole system. Gabriel, are you ready?"

"*Oui*...starting now."

Monsieur Tibadeau leaned closer to Mr. Grady. "Liam, once

we get out...our escape path takes us to the rendezvous point, not Falinvik."

"I'm not leaving my son."

"We don't have a lot of options."

"We'll improvise."

"You're risking all our lives—without a plan."

"Then we'll make one once we're clear. I'm not leaving my son." Mr. Grady turned pointedly to Monsieur Tibadeau.

Monsieur Tibadeau nodded. "Okay. But first, we have to get out of here."

Without warning, the lights in the room were extinguished. A few moments later, loud booms and screams could be heard from the three corridors.

"It's time. Stick together and keep your cloaks on—they may provide some protection yet," Mr. Grady instructed.

The room began to blur. A white cloud started to fill the corners. *No, no, no!* Why was the timing always so wrong with my visions?

I had to know whether the Gradys escaped. They were Aedan's rescuers. If they didn't get out, then who would rescue him...let alone, them!

The Ceremony

ELIN

T he first sign that I was finally free from my vision was the feeling of a comfortable bed supporting my weight. If I weighed something, then I must no longer be a wisp of smoke floating in the rafters.

As my other senses returned to my body, I could hear hushed voices around me. I couldn't quite make out what they were saying, but I recognized my name a few times.

My eyes fluttered open to find five familiar, worried faces stealing glances at me as they huddled around my bedside. Mia was seated on her bed whispering with Joel, who sat next to her. Brigitta was ensconced on my left, leaving Sigrid and Nodin to hover at the foot of the bed.

"*Oh, Freya have mercy!* She's awake." Brigitta clapped her hands together in a prayer position.

"Elli...Elli, are you okay?" Mia leaned closer to inspect my face.

"Um...uh huh...sorta...I think so." I rubbed my hand over my eyes and face, trying to push back the cobwebs that seemed to cloud my mind. "I have so much to tell you—all of you. It was so weird. I had two back-to-back—"

"Stop!" Sigrid interrupted. "It's imperative that we get you your medal immediately! We can't risk another episode—every medal-lacking moment is tempting fate with the Chairman."

"But I need to tell you what I saw—it's urgent!" I insisted, feeling a bit desperate. "The Gradys are in trouble! Aedan isn't at Ginnungagap—he is in Falinvik!"

Brigitta, Joel, and Mia gasped in unison.

Sigrid wiped her hand over her face, looking deeply pensive. "I see. That is *indeed* distressing news." Then determinedly, she clasped the bedpost. "But nothing right now is more urgent than getting you a medal...and some control! Everything else must wait. If the Chairman takes your mind, then everything is lost. All of the Dormants' secrets will be laid bare—and *everyone* will be in jeopardy. And we cannot have that under any circumstances! As my dear mama used to say, we must see to the blaze in front of us before we can tend to the rest of the fire." She began to bark orders at the others, silencing any further arguments.

Mia was assigned to help me out of bed and into the appropriate ceremonial garment while Joel and Nodin were sent to prepare the fire at the Forge. Before Brigitta bustled out of the room on an unvoiced mission, she gave a gentle pat to my arm, a quick empathetic smile, and then a nod to Sigrid.

When everyone besides Mia had left the room, Sigrid turned to us with a stern look. "Now, no dillydallying, girls. There is no time for sharing secrets. You must understand the seriousness of the situation. Every uncontrolled vision Elli has is an invitation for the Chairman to invade her mind." Under her piercing stare, we dared to do nothing but nod obediently. "I will see you at the Forge in five minutes."

Sigrid swept out of the room, her green robes fluttering in her wake. Once the door closed, Mia turned to look at me.

"You really okay?" She pulled back the comforter covers so I could swing my legs out unimpeded.

"Yeah, getting there. I've never experienced anything like it. I was stuck in my vision...and nothing worked to get me out!" I sat up in the bed and the world spun a little for a moment. I gripped the bedcovers and took a deep breath to steady myself.

"Then Sigrid is right—you need a medal right away. It was really scary, seeing Nodin carry you into the house looking like you were half dead. And then you were passed out for such a long time!" Worry furrowed Mia's brow. I reached out to hug her.

"I'm back now." It was the only comforting thing I could think of to say as I squeezed her. The truth was that I was equally freaked out by what had occurred. Having your mind listlessly float around in a giant cloud with no way out wasn't exactly a calming experience. But I didn't want to concern Mia any more than she already was.

Trying to distract us both, I asked, "So what's up with you and Joel? You guys seem to be getting close."

Color flooded Mia's cheeks. She reached for a folded white gown that had been resting on a nearby chair. "Um, I'm not sure. Sorta, I guess. Everything that's happened has just kinda thrown us together a lot, you know."

I grinned. "Do you like him?" A little smile appeared on her lips. "Oh, you do, don't you?"

"I guess. *Oh*, I don't know, Elli—he is the most annoying, irritating boy I know...but also super sweet and thoughtful. But it's not exactly the best time to be starting something—I mean, we're in the middle of a supernatural crisis and who knows what's going to happen."

"Mia, he's a great guy. Sure, he can be goofy, but nobody could ask for somebody more loyal and caring. And there's never a perfect time to start something—it just happens." I squeezed her hand.

"We'll see, I guess. I'm not even sure how he feels, anyway." Mia shrugged. "But we better get you dressed. We can have a good chat about everything later—Sigrid didn't look like she was in the mood to tolerate tardiness."

Mia shook the dress open, revealing a long, white, shimmering gown with a scooped neckline. Golden Ash tree leaves were embroidered on the hemline and sleeves. I caught the fabric between my fingers and twisted it in the sunlight from the window. Rainbows erupted on the surface.

"*Wow*...that's pretty. Where did it come from?"

"I know, right? Brigitta said there's a Clan Seamstress in the village," Mia said, eyeing the dress with a wistful smile. "I guess Brigitta put in an order with her this morning. Poof...gorgeous dress! Wish we *had* a Clan Seamstress on Auor. You're gonna look stunning!"

"Don't know about that. The dress is amazing, but I'm sure I look a mess." My visions usually had my body twisting and turning, which left my auburn hair looking like I'd been attacked by a flock of birds trying to roost. The unenviable bedhead was not something that could be cured in the five minutes Sigrid had given us. Touching my hair to assess how bad it was, I asked, "Mia, how long was I out?"

The longest time I'd ever been inside a vision before was around fifteen minutes. Given that there had been two in a row, I guessed that maybe thirty minutes had passed.

"Well, Nodin brought you back...*knocked out,*" Mia emphasized, mimicking her mother's horrified voice. "After your visit to the herbarium, which was probably around 11am. It's now 3pm...so four hours."

"*Four hours!*" I gasped.

The gown slipped from my fingers. No wonder everyone was out of sorts. Mia scooped the dress from the floor. Sigrid's urgency about my medal was starting to make a whole lot more sense. If I got dragged back into another vision, who knows how long I might be trapped again.

"Yeah…it was crazy. We were starting to worry whether you'd come out of it at all." Concern practically poured out of Mia's brown eyes. Then, as if to distract herself from the memory, she grabbed my brush off the bureau and began to tackle the rat's nest on my head.

"Oh, ouch! I guess we'd better get me that medal…*tout suite.*" I smiled, hoping my attempt at a little French would lighten the mood while I tried to endure Mia's brush strokes.

WHEN WE GOT TO THE FORGE, BRIGHT ORANGE AND YELLOW flames were dancing feverishly in a circular stone fireplace outside the metal workshop. The boys had done an admirable job in building the fire.

The Forge itself looked like something caught between an ancient smithy and a modern wood cottage. There was a wide, covered porch that ran along the left side of the structure. An inviting red door and a small window were positioned midway on the wood-plank wall. A breeze fluttered the cream ruffled curtains in the slightly open window and the flowering potted plants that lined the porch. I assumed these were Brigitta's contributions as they were a far cry from Sigrid's no-nonsense style.

To the cottage's right was a wide opening to a blacksmithing area. In the darkness at the back, you could just make out a kiln and a forge amongst the various iron tools tidily hanging along the walls. Where the smithy shed ended, the green grass began sloping to the lake, where the water glistened aqua-blue in the artificial sunlight. On the building's other side, the swaying meadow continued up the hill until it met the evergreen forest. It was a beautiful, peaceful spot, but clearly the Forge had been distinctly set apart from the rest of the village. And I couldn't help but wonder why.

A few feet from the fireplace, a ring of tall stone columns reminiscent of Stonehenge had been erected, defining a border for the space. Torches had been placed on top of them, and a small, silent drone flew from one taper to another, lighting each while battling the breeze that threatened to extinguish the newly lit wicks.

Upon seeing us, Nodin and Joel rose from their comfortable seats on a wooden bench in the shade of the cottage's porch. They were both dressed in tunics of white wool, belted by a silver cord, with three asymmetrical silver buttons dropping from the neckline. Underneath, they wore matching pants. As they walked toward the circle, Nodin flashed us a knee-melting smile while Joel fidgeted with his collar and long sleeves.

A few seconds later, Brigitta and Sigrid emerged from the wide doorway that led into the smithy. Sigrid was still in the green dress and blacksmith's apron she'd worn earlier, but Brigitta had changed into a simple white gown that reached the tips of her slender brown shoes. The dress matched the one Mia had slipped on before we left our room.

In her hands, Sigrid carried long iron thongs and a small iron pot with a pouring spout. Brigitta held several medium-sized burlap sacks that I assumed included the four chosen herbs from my visit to the herbarium.

"At last! Welcome, Elli and Mia. You look great," Sigrid greeted us. I patted my hair self-consciously. Mia had finally given up on it and pinned it up into some sort of French twist. "I'm sorry for the hasty ceremony, Elli. Between your late arrival yesterday and today's incident, we've lost precious time to walk you through everything. But I'm sure we'll manage. I'll guide you as we go along. Just trust the process, and everything will be fine." She gave me a confident look and a nod.

I swallowed hard. Maybe it was better this way—not knowing everything beforehand. I couldn't get nervous about steps if I didn't know what they were, right? A murder of crows took flight in my stomach, disagreeing with my rationale.

Really, how hard could this be? It's not like I would be hammering steel or doing some sort of high-wire act. I took a deep breath, holding on to the thought.

Sigrid continued, "Now, everyone, quickly gather around." She swept her hand towards the fireplace. "Make a circle...no, Elli, you need to be on this side next to me." She indicated to a spot facing the lake.

My expression must have betrayed some of my apprehension, since Nodin smiled and winked at me encouragingly while striding to the other side of the circle. And Mia, walking to the spot on my right, squeezed my hand and whispered, "You're gonna do great." Even Joel gave me an empathetic smile as he stationed himself next to her.

Meanwhile, Sigrid stood placid-faced to my left as she waited for everyone to congregate. Next to her, Brigitta stepped into the last spot, closing the circle. Placing the kettle on the fireplace's stone ledge, Sigrid reached into her robe's pocket and pulled out a sparkling silver ribbon roll.

"Here, Elli grab the end." I did as she directed. Holding onto a section, Sigrid passed the rest of the roll to Brigitta, who did similarly. Eventually, the other end of the ribbon made its way to me with each person around the circle clutching a portion. "Okay,

Elli. Touch the two pieces together and retain one end in each hand."

The moment the two ends met in my hand, the ribbon stiffened, becoming a circular bar. A flood of emotions seemed to flow from each end up my arms and into my body. There was excitement, apprehension, bafflement, confidence, nervousness—it went on and on.

"What is this?" I asked, trying to absorb each sensation before another crashed over me.

"It's an Energy Ribbon. The initial effect should wear off shortly. It'll provide you with additional 'resources' for the Forging, since you'll need the support of each person's essence to complete the cycle," Sigrid replied, glancing around the circle. "Okay, then...everything is set." She turned to look at me. "Elli, the first part of the ceremony is quite simple. Brigitta will toss your chosen herbs one by one into the fire to reveal your runes. But before that, she will ready the flame and create a smoke shield so you can see the runes. Ready, Elli?" I swallowed hard but nodded. "We'll now begin the process. Brigitta, if you will."

Brigitta let go of the bar to pick up one of the burlap sacks she'd dropped at her feet. I instantly felt a drop in the energy flow. She tossed the sack into the fire. Immediately, the flames turned blue-green and revealed a gold cylindrical cup hovering in their center.

"Elli, once Brigitta creates the shield, you need to focus on the flames. Things will get a little smoky and the cloud might hide the rest of us, but keep holding the bar and you will feel us. Also, it might get a wee bit toasty...but in the flames, your runes will reveal themselves one by one. There are four of them, and we need *all* four to be successful, so it's essential that you look—and that you look carefully. Lastly, you must speak them as they come."

Speak them...what did she mean, 'speak them'? I didn't know a lick of Old Norse. "Um...Sigrid, how will I know how to say their names?"

"Just trust the process, Elli. The fire will tell you. All will be well." Sigrid gave me a confident nod. "Brigitta?"

Brigitta reached for two more bags at her feet. She tossed one into the flames. The air around me filled with thick smoke. The last thing I saw through the haze was Brigitta getting ready to throw the next sack into the fire.

'A *little* smoky'...seriously? Sigrid really had a way of understating things. Oddly, the smoke didn't make me cough. It just hung in the air like a curtain, shielding me from everything besides the blue-green flames that danced in front of me. And sure, why not. Everything else about this was *really* normal. I mean I was standing in the middle of a smoky Stonehenge with a peculiar blue-green fire, holding onto a silver ribbon that wasn't a ribbon, and waiting for some runes to magically appear.

Okay, so maybe this wasn't the weirdest thing that had happened to me in the last few months. I mean, there had been the whole Ash tree thing and herbarium. But it was up there.

Wait, what was I supposed to do again? Oh, right! The flames. Focus on the flames. Grip the bar. Sigrid had instructed. Okay, then.

I wrapped my hands around the cool metal a little more tightly. Thankfully, the flood of emotions had receded and now I just felt a steady drumbeat of energy from the ends. I stared intently into the flame.

Nothing happened. No runes were materializing. Maybe something had gone wrong—or maybe I'd done something. I mean, I had no idea what I was doing—which seemed like the story of my life since being introduced to the Clan world. And well...maybe even before that, if I was being honest.

Without warning, something bright flashed in the flames,

disrupting their dance. I peered more closely. It felt like my eyeballs were being roasted. A wee bit toasty, indeed.

Blinking a few times for the moisture, I made out the remnants of a burlap sack and the bluebell flowers of the Comfrey plant being gobbled by the heat. From the spot where they had perished, a distinctive golden wisp rose.

Suddenly, I felt a strong force sucking strength from me. A cold weariness seemed to caress my heart. The gold thread started to grow more distinct, forming a figure that reminded me of the letter R but was more jagged. A slight breeze tickled my ear and an ethereal whisper repeated the word *För*.

I was so caught up in the strange, surreal moment that I nearly forgot to recite the word out loud as Sigrid had directed. I stuttered but finally managed to say it—just in time as another burlap bag burst into the blue-green fire.

This time the flames feverishly devoured the yellow Dandelion flower from the burlap. I strained to see the golden thread as it rose from the remains. It drew more of my essence than before and was taking longer to find its shape.

I could feel beads of sweat rolling down my face and over my cold body. It was an odd sensation as I was caught somewhere between sweating from the flames' heat and the cold from the energy draining.

I gripped the silver bar tighter, siphoning more strength from it. I could feel my blood pulsating throughout my body. I remembered Aedan once describing what his *megin* felt like. He'd said it was like a steady drumbeat in his veins. It sounded similar... maybe that was what I was feeling. Since I was never aware of my body during my visions, the sensation of my *megin* had remained a mystery to me.

Finally, the wisp revealed its runic nature. The figure looked like an upside-down bent letter L. Like clockwork, a strange voice whispered the word *Dreyma*. I quickly repeated it.

As I waited for the next rune, my breath became labored, and a hammering was starting in my ears. I adjusted my hands on the ends of the silver bar, hoping it might help. Like cool water, new energy streamed into my hot veins. I took a calming breath to quiet my panting and the pounding in my ears.

A loud spark and a sizzle announced the arrival of the next bag. The yellow-and-white flower of the Feverfew plant took only a second to be consumed by the blue-green flames. By now, my eyes felt like sandpaper, but I continued to focus on the golden wisp. The thread drank thirstily from my essence as it snaked into a wide sideways-looking V. *Opinberun*, the whisper came. I managed to squeeze out the word even though weariness threatened to engulf me.

The three runes had been very greedy in their thirst. And I could feel icy claws spreading out from my heart toward my limbs. How was I ever going to make it through the last rune? All I wanted to do was lie down, close my eyes, and be done. I was certain that at this point the only thing holding me up was my bones.

I adjusted my hands on the silver bar again, but this time, all that came was a trickle. My breath was coming out in gasps like I'd sprinted for miles. The thumping in my ears was deafening now. Would I be able to even hear the last rune? I had no idea.

The flames sputtered, declaring that the last sack had been thrown. Involuntary tears flowed down my face as I searched the hot blue-greenness for the wisp. As the last pieces of the Sage plant fizzled, a small gold cloud formed and hung loosely above the spot.

I could feel it trying to pull strength from me. But nothing was forthcoming. I dug deep, all the way to my toes, trying to find something to give it. A few tendrils seemed to flutter upward from the cloud. I closed my palms around the bar ends more tightly. I let them cut into my skin, hoping to pull out what remained there. The cluster of threads climbed a little higher but did not form anything.

I had to get the last rune. It was imperative. I searched my entire body for any last little bit of energy I could feed the wisp. Nothing seemed to respond. If I didn't help the rune form, everything would be wasted. The medal wouldn't be complete with just three—and it would be useless to me.

I desperately needed the fourth. Otherwise, I would be a liability for everyone...an appetizer for the Chairman...and who would help Aedan and his family then? Aedan, who was stuck in some cement room in Falinvik, and me, the one person who could quickly find his exact location—but only if we successfully forged my medal.

He'd looked thinner and paler. His sea-blue eyes had carried a weariness in their depths. I thought about the first time I'd met him. He'd had an easy stride and a mysterious smile, which I now knew weren't the sole reasons for my goosebumps but had certainly contributed. I wanted to see that carefree grace again—I wanted to see him again.

He'd helped me through so much over the past few months. Everything from Tristan to Clan history to the book of awakening and even Candice's 'mean girl' onslaughts. He'd protected me, made me laugh, and consoled me when I needed it. I'd never really gotten a chance to tell him how much it had meant to me. Now I'd probably never see him again. And I had only myself to thank for that.

The coldness around my heart reached my fingertips and toes. I'd tapped out the last reserves for the wisp. And it hadn't formed.

The fourth rune was lost. Everything was lost. I had failed.

Slowly, I let go of whatever was still struggling in me. There was no longer any point in holding it back. I could sink to the ground and be done.

Then, to my astonishment, the more I let go, the more I felt something glimmering inside me. *What was that?*

I closed my eyes and followed the ray. The weariness in my body was so extreme I didn't even stop to think that it was really weird that I could see light within myself. It sparked and crackled like a firecracker as it guided me deeper.

When it finally came to a stop, the electric light attracted similar ones, growing stronger and more willful until the bright mass encompassed everything. I let go of any remaining control that I'd held on to. I felt the light burst straight out of my body toward the fire and down my arms into the silver bar. There was no containing it. Joy and warmth crept back into me as the glow filled every nook and cranny.

I opened my eyes in time to see the wisp in the fire rapidly grow into a strong rope. The streaming light from inside me fed its insatiable hunger. It developed into the letter X with a line across the left and right sides. No longer a whisper, the ethereal voice sang, *Vekja.* I quickly said the word.

I'd done it! I had no idea how but I had the fourth symbol! I drew in a deep, stuttering breath and then slowly let it out. The peculiar light pouring from me vanished.

I let go of the silver bar and sank to the ground, grateful that it held me. I gasped for breath and allowed the cool earth to soothe my pounding head.

Was this how all of the Clan members experienced their ceremony? If it was, there should definitely be a warning label attached. "Warning: may cause extreme energy loss and possible death."

Out of the corner of my eye, I saw the fire spark upward as

something else was thrown into it. Immediately, the smoke was sucked from the space, revealing the other participants in various positions.

Nodin and Joel leaned against the stone columns. Mia sat on the ground panting. And Brigitta was helping Sigrid sit down on the porch steps. They looked as exhausted as I did. Nobody said a word.

After letting everyone rest for a bit, Sigrid rose to her feet. Brigitta was instantly by her side, helicoptering in case she needed assistance.

Sigrid squeezed her hand reassuringly. "I'm fine, Brigitta. Just needed to catch my breath, that's all."

Brigitta reached for a basket that had been hidden behind one of the porch posts. From underneath a towel, she pulled out a large cookie and handed it to Sigrid. After making sure Sigrid took a bite, she walked to each of us and gave us one.

"Here, Elli. It'll make you feel better," she said, placing a cookie in my hand.

Amazed that Brigitta still had the energy to stand and walk, I said, "Thanks. What is it? A miraculous cure? Is that why you're fine while the rest of us are barely able to stand?"

She smiled. "It's a gingersnap...my own special recipe. And I wasn't holding onto the silver ribbon for as long as everyone else. I had the burlap sacks to contend with. But don't worry, the sugar and ginger will help restore some of the energy you lost."

While Brigitta and I spoke, Sigrid slowly walked over to us. "How are you, Elli?"

"Never been so exhausted in my life...but I'm still here." It was the best assessment I could make under the circumstances.

My whole being felt dragged down and my legs were wobbly. But thankfully, the pounding in my head was now more of a knocking and the coldness around my heart had receded.

I bit into the gingersnap. The blend of butter, spice, heat, and sugar melted in my mouth in an utterly satisfying way. "Was that a normal ceremony experience?"

"Hmmm. Each one is different, but your runes certainly took the most energy I've seen in...quite some time." She had a thoughtful expression as she paused for a moment. "Also...I'm sorry to say that we aren't done yet. We have one more step to complete: the central symbol and the actual medal-forging."

At the distressed look on my face, she added, "Don't worry... this one will be much easier. I will be there to help you—it's the *Ljós* energy we'll need this time." She tilted her head, inspecting me for a moment. "Hmmm. Elli, your *Ljós* isn't as bright as usual."

I grimaced. I now understood where the electric light for the last rune had come from. "Um...I...uh...well, you see...with the last rune."

"Don't tell me. You used your *Ljós*." Sigrid frowned.

"Well, to be fair, I didn't know what it was at the time...and second, everything else was tapped out. It was that, or walk away without the fourth rune." I couldn't help sounding a little defensive. "Plus, I had no idea I'd need all of my *Ljós* later." If they weren't going to tell you all the steps involved, then they could hardly blame you afterward.

"I see. Hmmm, not ideal...but we can make do. Thankfully Nodin is here, which gives us an advantage. Very rare to have three Dormants present for a medal-forging." She beckoned Nodin over with a crook of her finger. His usual stride was a bit more tentative than normal, but it was still a lot more than I was capable of at the moment. "Finish your cookie so we can begin before we lose all the sunlight."

TWENTY-THREE

The Screens

TRISTAN

I needed a quiet place to think. The surveillance center was in complete chaos while the system mainframe rebooted. Sentries were nearly climbing over each other, trying to re-establish control with the limited methods at their disposal. None of them had ever faced a similar situation.

I let the door bang behind me as I walked out. A sentry quickly followed and called out in a panicked voice, "SIR...Sir, where are you going?"

"I WILL BE BACK! Continue the search for the intruders!" I held little hope that we would find them, but there was no reason to pull back the search yet. I continued down the corridor, not pausing to acknowledge the sentry further.

I walked up and down hallways, not having a clear direction. Suddenly, I heard hurried steps behind me. I spun around to see two frightened inmates skidding to a halt a few paces from me.

Instinctively, I tapped into my *megin*. A fire began to grow from my palm.

The inmates' eyes grew large. They turned on their heels and began to scurry in the opposite direction. The little rats were everywhere it seemed.

Without bothering to aim properly, I threw the blazing fireball in the direction they had rushed. There was no point in pursuing them. No cell would hold them until the system was online once more—and I knew better than trying to corner two desperate escapees. I continued in my original direction.

After a short while, I found myself standing in front of two large Caelum metal doors at the end of a corridor. The Chairman's Ginnungagap office.

With the system down, I knew the doors would be unlocked. It would be quiet in there. Empty. No one would dare enter the chamber.

Before I could fully grasp what I was doing, I pulled on the handle opening the right door. I was fairly certain that my cell at Ginnungagap was already reserved after today's debacle—so another infraction would hardly be noticed.

Anyway, it was too late to back out, I thought. My imprint had been logged by the Caelum door handle for future scans to detect.

I strode into the office. It was a sparse room that reminded me of the Chairman's office in Falinvik. On the facing wall, a large fireplace took up most of the space. It was built from ancient stone, and carved dragon heads acted like cornices to the mantel. On my left was a huge, heavily reinforced window looking out on the snowy mountain landscape. And to my right was the Chairman's desk and floating chair, exact copies of the ones in Falinvik.

Without a second thought, I walked over to the chair and plopped into its cushioned comfort. I was momentarily disconcerted as the inside molded to support my body perfectly. But then I leaned back and closed my eyes. It was quiet. I might get a few extra years at Ginnungagap for this—but it would be worth it.

Then something *pinged*.

My eyes snapped open. There in front of me, the Chairman's screens sputtered to life. The system must have rebooted itself.

As the displays slowed their fluttering, I could see the various reports that the Chairman had viewed since his last visit. I was amazed at how readable the reports were despite the screens' translucent nature.

While I was thinking about what a massive security failure it was that a system reboot allowed access to the Chairman's information—something caught my eye on the right screen.

A personnel file was open. The file was old and from an obsolete database that the *Stór-menni* had not used in fifteen years. At the top corner of the file was a black and white image of a man wearing a uniform reserved for the Chairman's top commanders.

None of this would have been that unusual—except there was a black bar running across the man's eyes, the word CLASSIFIED was emblazoned on the file, and a red alert blinked at the bottom of the page: DNA UPLOAD CONFIRMED. MATCH DETECTED.

DNA match for *who*? Who was this man, and why was the Chairman interested in him? All *Stór-menni* personnel files, including their DNA profiles, had been updated into the new system. So why hadn't his been entered?

The text in the file was encrypted and could not be read without entering the correct key. I doubted that my Hunter key had enough clearance levels to open the file. Calming my twitching finger that longed to hit the decrypt button, I leaned in to scrutinize the man's picture.

He looked like he was in his mid-to-late twenties in the photo. What could be seen of his features beyond the black bar was well-proportioned. His hair was thick, black, and wavy, neatly curling across his forehead.

Something nagged at the back of my mind. The picture reminded me of someone. I leaned back in the chair, trying to recall who.

In my memory, I could see the black wavy hair dancing in the cold breeze as snow swirled around us—*the Unregistered!* I was positive. The hair was the same, and re-examining the image, even the features bore an uncanny resemblance to the Unregistered's. There was no doubt in my mind that the two were related.

Apparently, I had caught a much larger fish than anyone but the Chairman—and now I—knew.

Yet a few crucial pieces of the puzzle were still missing. Who was the man in the photo? What was his role in the *Stór-menni?* And where was he now?

My finger hovered towards the decrypt button on the screen. What could be the harm now? I was already Ginnungagap bound.

But before my finger could reach the button, the screens fluttered twice, and the light from the slits on the desk disappeared. I sighed with annoyance. Of course, they would go out *now!*

The tidbits I had garnered from the file would not be enough to bargain with the Chairman. Without at least a name, I was out of luck.

It would have been a long shot anyway, I thought. Overseeing a historic prison break vs. capturing one Unregistered—no matter who his family was—would have been a tough sell for a pardon. I just had to accept my fate...I was going to be imprisoned at Ginnungagap—where I currently sat in the Chairman's chair.

The irony of the situation did not escape me.

TWENTY-FOUR

The Forging

ELIN

The artificial sun had dipped lower in the sky, burning more orange than yellow. Everything it touched was highlighted with gold, reminding me of spring evenings on Auor. Sigrid was right. Twilight wouldn't be long now. I hurriedly stuffed the cookie's remainder into my mouth and silently prayed my legs would be up for standing.

As I struggled to rise, Nodin placed a strong hand underneath my arm and pulled me upright. I didn't feel the normal overwhelming electricity that his presence or touch usually solicited. Hmmm, I guessed my *Ljós* was a little tapped out.

He continued to hold me as I took hesitant steps to where Sigrid stood at the edge of the fireplace. I wobbled a few times and he adjusted his position to slide his arm around my waist, bringing me closer to his sturdy frame. In any other circumstance, my cheeks would've been blazing red at his closeness...but in that moment, the only emotion surging was gratefulness.

Once we made it to Sigrid's side, she turned to us. "Normally, this is a two-party affair for the Forger and Dormant. However, given our current circumstance…we'll need your *Ljós* as well, Nodin. Are you up for it?" He nodded. "Great, thank you. You'll need to pour your *Ljós* into Elli, who will then direct it to the golden cylinder. It's the light from your body, Elli, that will choose the emblem. My *Ljós* will then forge the medal."

"What about the runes? How will you know what they are?" I asked.

"You already told the fire what they were…you *did* say them out loud, right?" I nodded. "Good…then the blue-green flames will remember." Sigrid patted my arm reassuringly.

"What about directing my *Ljós*? How do I do that? It was… sorta…accidental before." I looked up at Sigrid.

"Luckily, this isn't a delicate operation. Once you feel the borrowed *Ljós* from Nodin reaching a peak, just let go…and I mean, of everything. The light and flames will know what to do— they are like two differently charged ions attracting each other." She glanced at both Nodin and me. "Ready?"

The words I really wanted to utter were, "Heck, no!" I was so tired—more than I think I'd ever been in my life. Brigitta's gingersnap had helped a little, but I needed a whole vat to feel anything like myself.

But necessity is an unrelenting master. So I straightened in Nodin's grasp, hoping it would give at least the appearance that I was up for the task, and answered, "Ready."

"Good to go," Nodin replied, managing to take my hand with his free one. I felt an immediate surge of his *Ljós* pouring into my palm, up my arm, and into the rest of me. The tingling warmth of the electricity felt heavenly. It enlivened every cell, driving out the remaining coldness.

I closed my eyes, focusing on the pooling light inside me. That was one consolation of the fourth rune experience—I now knew what my *Ljós* looked and felt like.

When the growing mass had attracted enough of the tiny electric orbs where everything in the space was absorbed by their presence, I did as Sigrid had said. I let go. Immediately, I felt the *Ljós's* attraction to the flames.

I opened my eyes to witness the light shoot out of my sternum again. The glimmering stream was much bigger this time, and I could see it had definition. It was a bundle of lightning bolts shooting in steady spurts toward the fire. I assumed its larger size was thanks to Nodin.

On my right, Mia's and Joel's eyes were wide and their mouths hung slightly open. Next to me and with the iron thongs, Sigrid reached for the black kettle that was still balanced on top of the fireplace's stone rim. She guided it into the fire with the spout above the central golden cylinder. She tipped her arms and out poured a silver liquid into the cup. It sizzled and splattered as it met the hot surface. After the kettle emptied, she brought both out of the fire and laid them on the ground next to her.

Then she began to whirl her arms around as if she was gathering something from the air. Finally, she stopped and pointed her hands toward the flames. Out burst a similar sparkling but more controlled ray. It hit the golden cup and pulled my *Ljós* down to meet it. She twisted her hands this way and that. Small beads of sweat were starting to gather at her brow.

Suddenly, the fire started to hiss the words I had heard with each rune: *För...Dreyma... Opinberun...Vekja.* It whispered them over and over again as Sigrid battled an invisible force to contain them to the golden cylinder. Then, not quite sure who was winning as the flames grew higher and higher with half of my *Ljós* wrapping around it, I heard a loud pop and crack, and the flames rang out with the word *Askr.*

Immediately, everything was extinguished. The fire, the torches on the stone columns... even the artificial sun set.

Everything—except my *Ljós*. It continued to wildly pour out of me, shooting in every direction as it had in the herbarium. The stone columns shook as the lightning bolts reached them. The workshop seemed to heave as one struck it. Even the Bubble Shield Wall in the sky crackled as a few reached it.

I heard Sigrid yell, "Everyone down!" I witnessed Joel, Mia, and Brigitta drop to the ground. Then Sigrid spoke again—this time to me, in a very calm voice. "Elli, you have to let go of Nodin's hand now."

I tried to loosen my fingers around his hand but our palms seemed glued together. "It won't let go. It won't let me!"

Beside me, Nodin had dropped to his knees. His face was twisted like he was in pain.

"Elli, you have to do this...you are draining him." I was starting to panic. How was I supposed to let go if the *Ljós* didn't want to? "Listen to me, Elli. Close your eyes and find the same spot within yourself where the light gathered." I did as she directed. It was bright white-hot in there. I heard a crack and a boom somewhere close by. I flinched. "Just ignore that, Elli...did you find the spot?" I nodded. "Okay, good...now start squeezing the light from the sides like you were going to fluff a pillow. Be gentle but firm."

With my imaginary hands, I started to pat the sides of the bright mass inside me. Slowly, it started to sink inward, becoming smaller.

"Good, Elli...keep going." After a few more seconds, she added, "Try letting go of Nodin's hand again." I opened my fingers again and this time our palms disconnected easily. "Excellent. Keep fluffing that pillow until the light is just one little orb again... and remember to breathe, okay?"

Instinctively, I took a breath. Otherwise, "Uh huh" was all I managed to say as I focused on the *Ljós*.

After a few more minutes, my Ljós became a bouncing, tiny

electric ray again. Feeling more in control and since there were no longer any loud cracks or booms, I opened my eyes.

I was still by the fireplace. Without the flames, I could see to the other side where the lake was. Something caught my eye beyond the lake. There was a flurry of activity with several drones dancing around the air, hosing water at smoldering trees.

I grimaced. "Did I do that?"

I turned my head towards the workshop, where everyone had gathered on the porch. Brigitta was sitting by Nodin on the bench nearly force feeding him her gingersnaps. Joel and Mia were busy helping Sigrid brace one of the porch posts that had come loose. "And that?"

"Yes...but it could've been worse. It's why the Forge is way out here. Sometimes the forging ceremonies are a....a bit unpredictable. But not to worry, no permanent damage was done," Sigrid said as she finished kicking the post back into place.

"And Nodin...I don't even know what to say, besides that I am so very sorry. It wouldn't let me let go. It was...was...um...I really hope you're okay?" I walked closer to the porch.

"I get it...I'm just that irresistible." Nodin gave me a weak grin. "I'll be fine, especially at the rate Brigitta is shoving these gingersnaps into my mouth."

While we spoke, Sigrid had gone back to the stone fireplace and retrieved something from the gold cylinder. She now approached me with it. Out of her pocket, she pulled a delicate silver chain and looped it through the object. "Here, Elli...this is for you. I suggest putting it on immediately and laying it next to your skin."

She placed the item in my hand. I looked down. It was my medallion. Carved on the four cardinal points were the runes I'd seen in the fire. In a decorative manner between them were branches of an ash tree. And in the middle...well, in the middle was a symbol I'd never seen. It was a diamond shape with strange rectangular lines flowing from a central one. On the top of the pattern was an ancient-looking bird, which bore a remarkable resemblance to the Nordic bird charm Anders had given me on my birthday.

"Thank you, Sigrid. Thank you *everybody*! It means so much—and saying 'thank you' doesn't even seem to cover it. I know it was...a lot," I said, looking at each worn-out face in front of me. I looped the necklace around my neck. Sigrid nodded and patted my arm.

Mia came over for a closer look. "What do they mean—the runes and emblem?"

"Well...with your permission, Elli—medals are usually a private thing." Sigrid looked at me.

"That's fine...I'd like to know as well."

"Okay, then. This one"—she indicated the X with the closed sides—"means 'awakening.' And this"—she pointed to the wide V—" is 'revelation.' And the bottom is 'dreams'...and the last one that looks like an R is 'journey.'"

"And as for the emblem...well, that *is* interesting. It's one of the Forgotten Symbols of the Dormants. It is the Old Norse symbol for the Ash tree." She cocked a knowing eyebrow in my direction but didn't say anything else.

"Forgotten Symbols? What are they?" Mia asked. Her eyes gleamed with curiosity as she readied herself to dive into another myth or secret.

"Hmmm...they are a story for another time," Sigrid replied. "I'm now much more interested in seeing Elli take her new medal for a spin." Her eyes shifted to me. "I know you're beyond tired, but would you be up for a small test?"

I look at the groups' eager faces. Even though Nodin's *Ljós* had driven most of the weariness out of me and I felt I owed something to everyone for the ceremony—not to mention almost killing them —I hesitated. The destruction around me wasn't exactly confidence-boosting.

As if reading my mind, Sigrid added, "It will be quick and simple...just to let us know everything is as it should be. I will guide you through it."

I supposed I would have to try it at some point. And better under Sigrid's supervision than by myself. "Alright. What do I do?"

"Excellent. In a few seconds, I will perform an action...and I want you to stop me."

"*What*? I don't understand." I was baffled. Stop her? How? I'd never had a vision that was a few seconds in the future—let alone aimed for a specific person.

"Just close your eyes, Elli. Clear your mind. Tap into your megin. I'm sure you can feel it flowing inside you now." She was right. I could now feel my *megin* gently pulsing against the medallion on my chest. "And then focus on me. Let the vision come—but only for a few seconds. Just see my intent—then snap out of it."

"Okay," I replied, closing my eyes. I cleared my mind like Mrs. Grady had taught me, gently taking deep breaths.

"Good, Elli. Now reach toward your megin. Feel its ebb and flow. Then take hold of it—and tell it what to do." Sigrid's voice was serene like the caress of the breeze. It made the whole thing sound simple and clear.

I used its calm melody to gently tap into my *megin*. I had never consciously done it. It was my first time—and I finally understood just how uncontrolled my visions had been.

I told my *megin* to show me Sigrid's intent. And it was effortless. There was no pain or blinding white light. Just a slight shudder of air. Then I saw Sigrid clear as day below me.

She said something to the others that I couldn't quite make out. Suddenly, she lunged toward Mia and grabbed her arm. Quickly, I summoned the ripcord and was out of the vision.

I shook my head to clear the cobwebs in my mind. Then, before Sigrid could fully raise her arm or take a step forward, I was beside Mia pulling her out of Sigrid's reach.

"Excellent, excellent," Sigrid laughed. "I always did admire Temporal Visionaries."

Everyone else clapped and smiled. I was amazed. Never had summoning a vision been so seamless.

"How did I—I mean, it was so easy this time. Is that how it's going to be from now on?" I asked, excited.

Sigrid smiled. "Elli, it was a great start. Wonderful in fact. Your time with Mrs. Grady seems to have been well spent"—her face drew into a sympathetic expression—"but no, it won't be that simple, unfortunately. My understanding, thanks to an encounter with another rare Temporal Visionary many moons ago, is that a vision's difficulty is determined by your distance from the subject plus the time—forward or backward—from the present moment. In this case, I was standing at a very close proximity to you and the vision was only a few seconds in the future...thus, it should—and was—a very simple vision for you to call."

"Hmmm. I see." I couldn't help the tinge of disappointment that pinged inside me.

"But like I said, an excellent start, Elli. You should be very proud of yourself." Sigrid patted my arm.

"How quickly can Elli fire up these short simple visions?"

Nodin asked, trying to decline another gingersnap from Brigitta. "It could come in very handy."

"Yes, I see what you mean, Nodin. Elli could potentially outmaneuver an opponent not by strength or skill but by simply knowing what they would do next." Sigrid tucked the loose tendrils of her hair behind her ear as she thought. "I think that it mostly depends on her—you, Elli."

She eyed me for a moment. Then she straightened and said, "But that's a topic for another day—we should now turn to the other fire in our midst and hear the details about Elli's earlier double visions."

"And you can do that over supper," Brigitta commanded as she stepped down the porch steps holding on to Nodin and ushering us back towards the house.

TWENTY-FIVE

New Plans

ELIN

Everyone was unhappy. Sigrid was unhappy that I was insisting on going. Brigitta was unhappy that any one of us was going. Mia and Joel were very unhappy that they *weren't* going. And Nodin...well, I wasn't entirely clear on why he was unhappy, but his sour face left no doubt about his feelings. Lastly, I was unhappy that everyone else was unhappy and that they didn't seem to understand why I had to go to Falinvik.

It wasn't quite the reaction I'd hoped for after I finished sharing my visions, but at least everyone agreed that something had to be done. Given our foul moods and empty supper plates, it was decided that the best course of action was a good night's sleep. The long day had been long enough. So, grumbling to ourselves, we all headed to bed.

Early the next morning, a renewed discussion took up most of breakfast, but by the end, logic prevailed. It really was simple. I was the only one with Temporal Vision, which might be the sole way of finding Aedan and the Gradys. Besides Brigitta, Sigrid was the only one in our group who could find the Resistance in

Falinvik, and she was also the only person who could teach me how to control my *Ljós*. Thus, the two of us were an essential unit.

Mia and Joel couldn't come because no one without *megin* could enter through the *Stór-menni* Shield Wall, no matter how concealed they were. Brigitta insisted that Sigrid and I shouldn't go by ourselves, but she couldn't leave Skogly since either she or Sigrid had to stay with Mia and Joel. Apparently, it was a village rule. Guests were one thing but strangers without their host were quite another.

So, Nodin was the remaining option. Before he was even asked, Nodin volunteered with a sly smile—which left me wondering whether there was more to his eagerness than just accompanying us. He never *had* revealed why he'd come to the Nordri Clan territory. But my silent ponderings were pushed to the corners of my mind as the whirlwind to organize the trip began.

We all agreed that time was of the essence and that the three of us should leave as soon as possible. Without too much ceremony, we rose from the table and agreed to meet in the living room in an hour, ready to depart.

Mia and Joel said they didn't mind clearing breakfast given everything the rest of us had to do. Not that the cleaning was much of a chore considering that it mainly consisted of piling everything into a dumbwaiter-looking device, pressing a button, and watching the mess disappear to God knows where. But the offer was still a nice gesture, especially since their glum faces expressed their disappointment at being left behind.

With a "thank you" and a wave of her hand, Brigitta bustled off to her herbarium, muttering something about making a tea to dim my *Ljós*. Sigrid had a distant look on her face as she began hurrying like a gazelle between her upstairs bedroom and downstairs study while making little sounds like "oh, that's where it is" and "can't forget that."

As Nodin and I, going to our rooms to pack, passed Sigrid on the stairs, she paused for a moment. "Don't forget to change into your Clan cloaks and clothes. We need to blend in...and obviously, it's still winter out there."

"Okay, Sigrid," I said.

"Sure," Nodin called after her as she disappeared around the corner. He looked at me with a grin. "You wanna race?"

Without answering, I sprang up the remaining steps. I could feel my medallion thump against my chest as I took them two at a time. Triumphantly, I turned to Nodin. "Ha! I win!"

"Cheater!" Nodin sent a small gust of wind up the stairs, which blew my hair into my face. I laughed and hurried into my room, feeling like our trip would be infinitely more fun with Nodin along.

I plopped onto my bed to think for a moment, absentmindedly twirling my phone in my hand. Everything was happening so fast. It hadn't even been two full days since we'd arrived in Skogly. And now I was leaving.

Anders would not be happy about the developments. I wasn't even sure what to text him. He wouldn't want me to go. But I didn't really see a choice in the matter. I couldn't just leave Aedan and the Gradys in trouble while I kicked back in the safety of this haven. Not when I was in the unique position to help find them. Plus, I had done what we'd originally agreed. I'd come to Sigrid's and gotten my medal. Technically, I'd never promised that I would stay.

I fingered the medallion around my neck. I wasn't quite used to its presence against my skin. It had a strange calming and focusing effect on me, which I didn't mind.

I thought about what Sigrid had said about the difficulty of a vision equaling distance and time from the present. We were fairly close to Falinvik—where Aedan was. And if I kept the vision to the present time and short, what could be the harm? It would be good to check that he was still there and okay, at least that's what I told myself before closing my eyes.

I took a deep breath in and focused on my *megin's* steady beat as it thumped against my medallion. Then I told my *megin* to show me Aedan and right now, crossing my fingers that it would work.

It took a bit longer to formulate than with Sigrid. The familiar white, thankfully painless, cloud flooded my mind for a few seconds before dispersing. Then I was hovering above Aedan, who was stretched out on a comfortable-looking bed in a modern room. He was sleeping soundly, his chest rising and falling in a steady rhythm. His black wavy hair had endearingly tumbled across his face, but it couldn't hide the small fresh scar on his cheek. A resentful flame ignited in my chest. What were they *doing* to him?

As I was about to call out to Aedan, I sensed the cold, piercing eyes. They were close. Too close.

My heart started to hammer.

The grey beacons had me in their sights. I could feel the Chairman's mind bumping against my own.

Oh, crap! He was trying to claw in.

This couldn't be happening—it *can't* happen! His grey eyes were nearly inside me.

Mud. Mud. Mud. Mud. I stammered.

Instantly, I was back in my room at Sigrid's, panting and clutching the blanket on the bed. He had nearly had me.

I tried to calm my breathing. I was positive the only thing that had saved me was my medallion. It had slowed his intrusion, and my vision had immediately obeyed my ripcord.

I had escaped but only by the skin of my teeth—and it was

definitely *not* an experience I wanted to repeat.

The odd thing was that I could swear the Chairman had been waiting for me. He had been on me like a flea on a monkey's back even though he hadn't been in the same room as Aedan. The only explanation I could think of was that he must have felt my presence when I visited Aedan last time—and was now keeping an eye out for me.

Fudge nuggets! As Anders would say in the presence of children. This was going to complicate things.

I'd hoped that with my new medallion, I could visit Aedan whenever I liked and perhaps even talk with him. But the Chairman had now crushed those hopes.

I fell backward onto the bed and brushed the loose hair out of my eyes. How and when was I going to tell the others? Certainly, not before Falinvik. I didn't want them to think my usefulness to the mission had changed. And it wasn't like I would compromise anything—I now had my medal and much more control over my visions. I just had to avoid visions of Aedan in the present time, and everything would be fine.

Besides, not only were the Gradys and Aedan in danger, but eventually, if nothing was done, then it would also cascade to encompass my family and friends back on Auor. There was no question in my mind that I had to go.

Feeling good about my decision, I sat back up. Things weren't anywhere near how I'd thought they would turn out when we'd left for Skogly. Yet in an odd way, I was getting what I'd been hoping for all along—I was finally going to rescue Aedan...and in so doing would help save my family and friends as well.

Taking a deep breath in and out for courage, I picked up my phone and opened its messaging app and started to type.

ME: Hi Andee - a small change in plans...

TWENTY-SIX

Baldur Street

AEDAN

Thyra's obsession with shopping was starting to border on my sister Claire's. Although Thyra wasn't shopping for clothes.

This was our third excursion to Falinvik's markets in as many days. So far we'd stuck to the exclusive selection around central Falinvik, but today's trek had taken us to the shops on Baldur Street.

Thyra was determined to find the best spears, shields, armor, and swords that Falinvik had to offer. Only those would do for her Leikr team. And apparently, the rather dodgy collection of stores on Baldur Street was the place to find them.

I was being dragged along because Thyra saw it as a way to kill two birds with one stone. I would see another Clan neighborhood and could soak up the culture while she gathered what we needed for the games. She also probably didn't mind the extra pair of hands to help carry her various purchases.

The shopping trips would've been torture if it hadn't been for two things. First, Thyra pretty much gave me free rein to explore and wander around the markets without her. She knew the *Hepta*

Baugr wouldn't let me stray more than fifty feet from her, and she could always locate me with its tracker. Plus, given the Chairman's emblem boldly woven into the chest of every piece of clothing I wore, none of the local people dared to meet my eye or address me. Those who did speak did so only after I initiated the conversation. Then their answers were polite but brief. Despite these drawbacks, it was the first bit of freedom I'd had for months.

Second, I quickly learned that my perception of what spears, armor, shields, swords, and the like constituted was vastly out of date. Take, for example, the Clan shield. It was not a heavy piece of metal with a handhold on the inside, but rather a tiny electronic thumb loop that, with a slight upward movement, produced a nearly invisible and incredibly strong barrier. The modern shield's size was still equivalent to the Viking's and it had the same purpose, but that was where the similarities ended. Begrudgingly, I was fascinated to see the Clan tech and even try it when Thyra requested.

My thoughts on Thyra herself were still forming. Except for one afternoon, we'd spent nearly every day together since she picked me up from Ginnungagap. Yet she was an enigma to me. She was casual and even funny at times but could flip a switch to a commanding "don't mess with me" presence on a dime. Her confident air never faltered, and it drew instant respect from those around her. And from what I'd seen during our training sessions, she was a fierce and skilled fighter...to the point that if Thyra was, hypothetically speaking, having a bad day, I would've crossed to the other side of the street to avoid her. And I hadn't even seen her unique ability yet.

She never spoke about herself or her feelings about Clan society. Everything was focused on me and getting ready for the Leikr. She didn't press or ask me about my family or Elin either. It was like she'd decided it wasn't her problem so she avoided the whole issue. I wasn't sure if it made me like her more or less—which I guess meant that some part of me liked her at least a little bit. I probably would've liked her a lot more if she wasn't my guard, a *Stór-menni*, and the Chairman's niece. One was bad enough; all three made it an impossible thought.

Given the intense preparations for the Leikr, I'd made zero progress in my efforts to find a way into the Chairman's office. Plus, I was plagued by worry about my family's safety and whether they'd learned about my removal from the gray fortress in time. It was all I could think about in the lone quiet hours of the night when I otherwise might've been formulating a plan. The one thing that gave me an ounce of comfort was the realization that no one around me had said a word about their capture. If that had happened, I was positive that the Chairman would've been crowing victoriously.

Also, much to my puzzlement, I hadn't "heard" from Elin since the incident in the training room. I was hoping she might "visit" again to let me know what had happened. Her voice in my head had been strange yet at the same time really good to hear, even if it had been for just a few seconds.

Thinking about the interaction, I was convinced that Elin had awakened her abilities. She must have the gift of Telepathy. And perhaps her being a Dormant extended the distance she could use her ability. It was the only reasonable explanation. How else would she have been able to "speak" with me from Auor?

Knowing my parents, I doubted that they would've let her come along to rescue me, so that's where she was bound to be. Plus, she'd said that *my family* was on their way to Ginnungagap, which meant that she wasn't with them. Both a sense of relief and disappointment swept through my body. At least she was safe.

A jingling sound brought me out of my thoughts. It was the little bell attached to the shop's front door, which Thyra had just pulled open. The store was the same one that Thyra had visited earlier that morning when inspecting spears. She hadn't made the purchase then but now seemed convinced that they were in fact perfect.

Despite the freezing temperature outside, I'd decided to skip the haggling over how many government IOU tokens they were worth. The conversations were often unpredictable and could take minutes or hours depending on the participants. Having had a good look at the staunch-faced shop owner a few hours ago, I was guessing the latter in this instance. So, I'd remained on the street to enjoy a few moments of freedom and perhaps walk around a bit poking in the open-air market stalls that lined the middle of the street.

Falinvik's architecture boggled the mind. Shiny art deco skyscrapers made up the city center where the Chairman's office and my current residence were. But here, the buildings were an ode to Viking style with their dark lumber facades and crazy number of eaves. The tops of the eaves were decorated with carved snakes or dragons that unpredictably stretched into the air, creating havoc for the Automated Hover Vehicles that whizzed overhead.

The Baldur Street shops were placed so closely together in a perfect row that one flowed into the next without delineation. Their doorways were set back in alcoves and united by a slanted overhang that ran the length of the street. I wasn't sure if it was purposeful, but the tilted structure naturally hid the comings and goings of the stores' visitors.

The people on the street had a gruff appearance. Most were traditionally garbed with their clothing color in dark hues. Many had their hoods pulled up, disguising their faces, while an occasional swish of a cloak revealed a seax neatly hanging from a belted waist. The shop patrons hurried in and out of stores, keeping to themselves and concealing their purchases. I got the feeling that Baldur Street wasn't a place where you'd want to linger during the wee hours.

Pretending to be interested in the wares of a nearby market stall, I warmed myself under the hovering heat drone. Each stall was assigned at least one. The small, silent helicoptering devices put out enough heat to melt the snow in a circle around the stalls.

The hawker, puffing on his pipe, eyed me warily as he straightened his strange toaster-oven devices for better viewing. Getting the sense that my allotted warming time was running short without a purchase, I stepped back, giving a slight smile and a nod to the disappointed vendor.

As I looked down the street for another stall to inspect, a figure in a light-gray cloak standing directly in my line of sight about fifteen feet away caught my eye. She pulled her hood back for just a second before quickly stepping underneath the slanted overhang of a nearby shop, but there was no mistaking the auburn hair and amber eyes. My heart jumped, making a dive into my stomach.

It was Elin.

What was she doing here? *How* was she even here?

I glanced down at my *Hepta Baugr*. It was still blinking steadily. I quickly estimated that I'd walked about twenty feet down the street from Thyra's location and maybe another ten when I crossed the street. It was going to be cutting it close to the fifty-foot margin, but I swiftly moved to where I had seen Elin disappear.

She stood tucked into the corner of an abandoned store's doorway. The hood of her cloak was still up, but her pretty amber eyes were brimming with excitement. She had a large smile on her face. When I got close enough, she pulled me into a tight hug. I squeezed her back. I'd forgotten how good she smelled.

"Aedan, how are you? Are you okay? What are you doing

here?" Questions poured out of her as she let go of our embrace. A little color had risen into her cheeks.

I couldn't help smiling in response. "What am I doing here? What are *you* doing here, Elin?" I glanced around us, looking for anyone staring at us a bit too long. "My guard isn't too far away. And anybody could be watching us. Don't you know how dangerous this is? Don't get me wrong, it's amazing to see you...but this is super risky."

"I know, I know, but I saw you at the stall...and we were here for something else entirely...and it just felt like...like kismet. I mean, it's got to be the biggest coincidence ever that we're in Falinvik to rescue you, and there you are...on the street...on our first day. I never imagined finding you would be as easy as bumping into you on the street."

A figure slid from around the corner in a navy-colored cloak. Before I even had a chance to take a fighting position, he addressed Elin. "We should go. It's not safe to stand here. You can have your mini-reunion later. Come on!"

Seeing the surprise on my face, Elin said, "Aedan, this is Nodin. Nodin, Aedan." The man pushed back his hood a little to reveal a face with light-brown skin and deep-brown eyes. There was no question that he was handsome, and for some reason, I found that irksome.

Given that Elin stood between us, he just nodded in my direction. "Nice to meet you. But we should go. Sigrid's bound to come out any minute...and you know she said it might be a hasty departure. So, come on...get your friend and let's move." He placed a hand on her shoulder. A knot in my stomach tightened.

"Okay, okay...Aedan, you re—" Elin started to ask.

"Wait, Sigrid's here?"

"Yeah. I'll tell you all about it—but Nodin is right. We should go." She started to turn to follow him.

"Elin, I can't go."

"What do you mean, you *can't* go? We're here...we have a plan to get you out...it's gonna—"

I raised my wrist with the *Hepta Baugr*. Before I could even say it, I saw the light in Elin's eyes dim.

"You have a *Hepta Baugr*." Her voice was full of disappointment. She obviously knew what it meant. "You didn't have one the last time I saw you."

"Well, you didn't think they would just let me wander around the streets free, did you?" I gave her a weak smile. "And if by last time, you mean in the Leikr training room—then yeah, training is the only time they remove it."

Elin frowned. "I was kinda hoping it was an oversight. Shoulda guessed it was too easy." She paused for a moment, looking puzzled. "What do they have you training for?"

Just then, given that my wrist was still in the air, I noticed that the *Hepta Baugr's* red light was blinking more rapidly. The tracker had been initiated. Thyra must have finished at the shop.

"It's a long story. The short version is that the Chairman is making me participate in the Clan games—the Leikr. Come visit me, and I'll tell you more." I grinned at Elin. It was a dare and a wish in one.

Since my eyes kept shifting to her lips, remembering our kiss, I noticed that their corners turned down.

"Oh, Aedan! I *wish* I could. But he's always watching—and I can't take the risk. If he catches me—" Elin wasn't making any sense.

"Elin, *who's* always watching? Who's he?"

"The Chairman. He can see me when I try to visit you."

"*What?*" I was stunned. How could the Chairman see her? It didn't make any sense. But it did help to explain why she hadn't visited me again—and it wasn't because of her new friend in the shadows.

Just then, an intermittent beep began to sound from the *Hepta Baugr*. Thyra must have walked the wrong way and triggered the fifty feet boundary alarm.

"I have to go—they're tracking me. One more thing...is my family, are they okay?" I didn't move. I needed to know that my family was okay. And I was reluctant to leave Elin's side.

She hesitated. "Honestly, I don't know. But don't worry. We're working on finding them. And we'll figure it out—both you and them." Elin smiled encouragingly at me.

I couldn't help myself. I swooped her back into my arms for another hug.

"They have me in the Chairman's tower...if you figure out how to remove a *Hepta Baugr*," I whispered in Elin's ear.

Her soft cheek brushed mine as she pulled back and determinedly looked me in the eye. "Not if—but when."

Nodin cleared his throat. "*Ahem*...hate to break this up, but I can see a determined-looking *Stór-menni* woman marching up the street. We need to go...now, Elli!"

He grabbed her hand and pulled her. I let go. With a last look, I turned and hurried back out on the street to head off Thyra's approach.

Elin called after me. "We'll be back for you...just be ready."

As I walked down the cobblestone street pretending to casually look at the market stalls, a deep longing ached inside me. It was so hard to walk away from Elin—and the attempted rescue, of course. But leaving with them hadn't been an option. We would've been caught in a matter of minutes with the *Hepta Baugr* still active. And being captured was not something I was willing to inflict on Elin—especially when I hadn't a clue to what the Chairman was up to.

Knowing that Elin was in Falinvik and a potential rescue was now imminent, I was more determined than ever to find a way into the Chairman's office to discover his secrets as well as my family's —before time ran out.

A tap on my shoulder interrupted my thoughts. Faking my surprise, I turned. "Oh...hi, Thyra. Done already?"

Thyra clutched a bag with six foot-long metal sticks jumbled inside. "Yeah, although I'll have to remember to write up a report on that shopkeeper—his bargaining is highway robbery." She inspected me for a moment. "Everything okay? You look a little flushed. You're not sick, are you? We can't afford that—the start of the Leikr is only a few days away."

"I'm fine. It's just the cold...freezing today, if you haven't noticed," I replied.

"You sure? We should get you inside. Maybe we should have the medic check you out just in case. There isn't any room in the games for illness—everyone has to be in top shape so we can actually survive unscathed. Or at least, mostly so."

I reassured Thyra again that I was fine as we started to walk back to the AHV. She continued to talk about what provisions we still needed, but I was lost back in my thoughts.

Seeing Elin had made me almost forget the reason we were at the market—the Leikr. So there were actually *two* things I needed to do before time ran out—unravel the aforementioned secrets... and survive the Leikr. And I wasn't quite sure how I was going to do either...yet.

Epilogue

TRISTAN

Thyra delivered the news when I reached Falinvik. Chairman Arild had refused to even see me. And I could hardly blame him. My failure at Ginnungagap had been absolute.

When I received her summons, the desperate search for the intruders had still been ongoing. I had insisted on it, especially after what I had learned from the Chairman's screens, even though there was little hope of finding the intruders in the gray fortress. After all, it had been twenty-four hours since the incident.

Thyra was waiting for me at the transport landing pad in Falinvik that afternoon. Her face was unusually grim. She gave me the courtesy of waiting until the other passengers had cleared the tarmac. Then she spoke.

"Tristan...the Chairman and I have read your report. I cannot begin to express how disappointed both he and I are. A jailbreak at Ginnungagap, especially of this magnitude, has never occurred in Clan history." She paused for a moment, letting the words' weight settle. "I, however, can understand that unforeseen circumstances do occur in the field. And a Technopath with the intruders would certainly account for one. Thus, I was able to limit the consequences...to a degree." My eyes flew to her face to see if she was joking. What did she mean, "limit"? How could anyone limit what waited for me? I had prepared myself to be summarily dispatched right back to a Ginnungagap cell. But not even a glimmer of amusement was hidden in her eyes.

"There is no easy way to say this...but Tristan." Thyra straightened herself to a stance of attention. I followed suit. "You are hereby with a *Láta* Order stripped of the rank of Lieutenant and Clan Hunter, removed from my Hunter Squad, and relegated to Clan Internal Affairs."

Her eyes wavered to my face to see my response. But I remained stoic. I had promised myself that whatever the consequences, I would take them like a true Clan Hunter.

Thyra continued, "There you will focus *solely* on investigating incidents in Falinvik and bringing any non-productive members to justice. You will no longer be allowed in or acknowledged by Protective Services as a member. You will need to find new accommodations, your medallion will be replaced, and your old Hunter one confiscated. This is effective immediately. Is that understood?"

I gave a sharp nod in response and discreetly let out my breath. Given that a few moments ago I had been certain my life was over, this was an excellent turn of events—despite the fact that Clan Internal Affairs, which handled minor non-productivity infractions and the rare crime that occurred in Falinvik, was considered the wastebasket of *Stór-menni* divisions and working there would be seen as a cosmic demotion for a Clan Hunter.

"You okay, Tristan?" Thyra asked, her stance more relaxed again.

I looked at her. She probably had a lot to do with saving my skin. And I hated it. Having to be beholden to her was unbearable, but it was a fact of life now. "Thank you, Thyra. I am not sure how you did it—kept me out of Ginnungagap—but I am grateful."

"Yes, well...a story for another day. Unless there is anything else? I'm short on time and must get back to...um...my other assignment." She paused, for only a second, out of politeness. "Be well, Tristan...I'm sure our paths will cross again." With that, she turned and walked away.

In total, my punishment would be seen as a minor step up from the humiliation of being sent to Ginnungagap, but to me, it meant everything. Thyra's announcement had returned the minor glimmer of hope that had been so thoroughly extinguished a few days earlier at the gray fortress. I now had another opportunity to set everything right.

Elin and the Unregistered's family had not been caught. And the Unregistered was now somewhere in Falinvik. Which meant only one thing—Elin and his family would be making their way here. I was certain of that. And I had just been assigned the task of investigating and pursuing criminal elements in Falinvik. I smiled to myself as I walked off the tarmac.

Extras

Translation Dictionary

Old Norse Words

Austri: one in the East

Hvíla: sleep, rest, lie

Láta: declare, command

Leynask: hide oneself, be concealed

Mannlegur: human

Megin: ability, might, power; strength; supernatural strength

Nordri (also Norðri): one in the North

Smá-menn: insignificant men, men of little power

Stór-menni: big men, men of rank

Sudri (also Suðri): one in the South

Vestri: one in the West

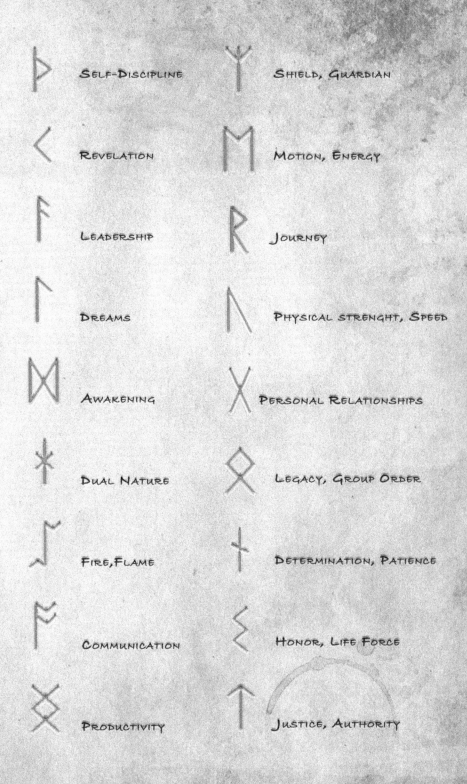

ᚦ	Self-Discipline	ᛉ	Shield, Guardian
ᚲ	Revelation	ᛗ	Motion, Energy
ᚨ	Leadership	ᚱ	Journey
ᛚ	Dreams	ᚢ	Physical strenght, Speed
ᛞ	Awakening	ᚷ	Personal Relationships
ᛏ	Dual Nature	ᛜ	Legacy, Group Order
ᛋ	Fire, Flame	ᛐ	Determination, Patience
ᚠ	Communication	ᛎ	Honor, Life Force
ᛥ	Productivity	ᛏ	Justice, Authority

Thanks for reading!

I hope you enjoyed *The Gray Fortress*! If you'd like to support the continuation of the Nordri Series, the best way is to help other readers discover the book.

Share your enjoyment of the book with your friends and family, and please leave a review on **Amazon, Goodreads, and Bookbub**.

To hear news and updates on my books, please sign up for my author newsletter at: www.jovisuri.com/newsletter

Or follow me on:
Twitter @auorauthor | Facebook auorauthor

NORDRI SERIES
BOOK #3

COMING SOON

Sign up for Jo's newsletter to be the
first to hear when **BOOK 3** is available.

Also, get exclusive deals and sneak
previews before anyone else!

www.jovisuri.com/signup

CATCH UP ON THE NORDRI SERIES

Book #2

Continue the extraordinary journey in the frozen fjord!

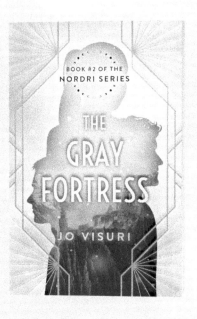

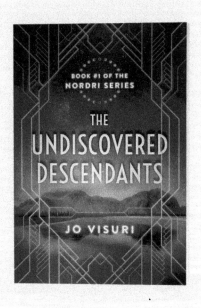

Book #1

Start the adventure on mystical Auor Island!

Learn more at www.jovisuri.com

Acknowledgments

Writing *The Gray Fortress* has been a labor and a joy, but one I could not have done without the support of my family, friends, collaborators, and supporters.

As always, I would first like to thank my family and friends for their continued support and patience. I know I've spent many hours, including weekends and evenings, toiling away on the book rather than in your pleasurable company. Despite this, you have remained steadfast in your enthusiasm and support for my work—and I am so grateful!

A big thank you to my other set of eyes, my fabulous editor Susan Grossman. Your corrections and suggestions take my books from good enough to great.

And to my Beta Readers, your comments and insights provide much-appreciated guidance, and your eagerness to read my work gives me that boost to keep going.

Lastly, a great big thank you to everyone who has supported the birth of the Nordri Series through your purchase and reviews! It would not have been possible without you.

About the Author

Jo Visuri was born and raised on an island in Finland's famous archipelago, where she found her one and only Viking coin at the age of six. After spending a few formative years living by a Norwegian fjord, Jo's family uprooted to the sunny beaches of Los Angeles, CA.

A graduate of Brown University, Jo has been privately writing stories since she could read one. She concocts myth-inspired fantasy tales appropriate for all ages that take the reader on adventures in the real world with magic, hidden worlds, secret societies, and tales of family and friendships.

She now lives and writes in San Diego, CA, when she isn't distracted by her cuddly and demanding senior dog.

Subscribe to Jo's Newsletter for exclusive content and to be automatically notified when she releases her next book: https://www.jovisuri.com/newsletter

 facebook.com/auorauthor
twitter.com/auorauthor
 instagram.com/auorauthor
bookbub.com/authors/jo-visuri

Lightning Source UK Ltd.
Milton Keynes UK
UKHW021834041122
411674UK00011B/231/J